THE FIVE PRINCES

DEIDREA DEWITT

Book design by ebooklaunch.com

ISBN 978-1-7342866-0-1

deidreadewitt.com

THE FIVE PRINCES

BY DEIDREA DEWITT

"Man is not truly one, but truly two."
The Strange Case of Dr. Jekyll and Mr. Hyde

*Dedicated to Lloyd Alexander
Your stories inspired me the most.
Thank you for sharing your magic with the world.*

1

WELCOME, YOUR HIGHNESS

"And this is the ball-gown of the late Queen Cerene of Aujina, who was said to be the most beautiful of all queens in our country's history."

I bet they said that to all the queens.

I wrinkled my nose at the puffy layers of red and gold lace on the ball-gown locked away behind a massive glass case. The headless mannequin was constructed to be the same size and shape as the royal queen, and if I stood in front of the glass just right, it looked like I was wearing the dress instead of the mannequin. I shook my head at my reflection. Not my style.

I stood back as everyone in the tour group cooed, snapping pictures and taking selfies.

One of the other tourists leaned in towards me. "You know," he said, "I heard an interesting rumor about the late queen …"

"Marina!" the tour guide called over the crowd, walking towards me with her permanent smile. "What do you think of the dress? Wouldn't you like to wear a dress as lovely as this one?"

I cocked my head to the side, considering it.

That was a lot of lace.

"Nah," I replied. "I don't wear anything I can't roundhouse kick someone in."

The tour guide's smile widened, but it didn't go up to her eyes. "Well then!" she said, spinning around to the other tourists. "Let's continue!"

We continued to wander around the castle. It was stunning, to say the least. Twisted wood columns held up grand Greek arches reaching three or four stories high, while gold-and-diamond chandeliers hung from the ceiling. Each room was decorated with traditional gold and teal flower patterns, splashed with modern pieces of cherry furniture and white linens. My footsteps echoed against the marble floor as we walked deeper into the Grand Hall.

"If you look towards the ceiling, you'll see the great history of our dear country of Aujina," the tour guide said. "Starting with the first sunrise to the building of the Cyrus Tower, now the tallest building in the world. It brings in lovely tourists, such as yourselves."

"I came here for the food," another tourist said, squeezing the tips of her fingers together and raising them to her mouth. "This country is known for its famous fisheye soup. We're actually going to eat it tonight in this very castle with a special guest! I wonder who it is? Can you believe it?"

"Fisheye soup, huh?" I replied, trying not to outwardly cringe.

"Did you see the tower?" one of the other tourists asked us both.

I nodded. "My dad planned the entire trip. A train to the countryside, cultural museums, landmarks, the Cyrus Tower, and then the castle itself."

"Sounds wonderful!"

I rubbed the side of my face, nodding unenthusiastically. It was a wonderful trip, but it felt more like a field trip than a graduation present. My parents had arranged the entire thing, but Dad had business in Hong Kong and Mom had a fashion show in Milan, so neither of them had come with me. And God forbid I was left alone for more than twenty minutes. Dad hired tour guides, escorts, and even police officers to watch me for the entire two-week trip. How do you even hire a police officer?

I guess the CEO of a massive international trade company can do anything he wants.

As the tourists began to talk about fisheye soup again, I looked up at the intricate designs in the ceiling. There was a lot of history here, so different from the simple Californian mountains. Here there were turquoise temples, myths of ancient heroes and magical dragons, people who shape-shift from human beings to animals. The ceiling showed the battles of the past and the technology of the present. There was a long string of kings and queens painted around the border of the giant ceiling mural. One of the queens was painted holding a wine glass overflowing with deep crimson wine. The painter had done a shoddy job, though. It looked more like blood than wine.

My eyes fell from the giant painting to the mezzanine, meeting the gaze of a man with dark hair and a white suit.

He was looking straight at me.

He cocked his head to the side as he continued to look down at me from the indoor balcony. No one else seemed to notice him. By the clean cut of his suit and hair, I assumed he wasn't a worker. If he was, he was a well-paid one.

He kept staring at me and, not knowing what else to do, I waved. He gave a small nod and bow, then turned on his heel. After a few steps, he tripped, knocking into one of the statues by the entrance. The clattering got a few people's attention, but he didn't turn around. He grabbed the statue before it fell, set it upright, then walked briskly out of the room.

Did I know him?

"Next, let me show you to the gardens," the tour guide said.

We stepped out into Aujina's version of a June day, humid and sticky compared to the mountains back home. The air was thick here, but it wasn't unpleasant. The musk of the castle gardens hung in the air as we walked through them.

Finally. Nature.

There were fields and rows of roses, gardenias, lilies, and a hundred other flowers that I didn't know the names of but wanted to learn. The tour guide yammered on as we walked through the vineyards, looking at the thousands of grape clusters beginning to ripen.

I looked over my shoulder, back at the castle. How many years of history were wrapped up in this place? It wasn't the most popular country on the map, but it had its own charm. Dad talked about it often, as if it was the best place in the world. He often talked about his business trips here, showing me pictures of the great lakes, snow-covered mountains, and gentle countryside.

He always said we'd visit together. Instead, I got the hired help. It was always the hired help.

When we got to the gardens, the tour guide showed us around, pointing to various fruits and plants I had never seen before.

"And here we have the sweet and sour rambutan, King Cyrus's favorite fruit."

King Cyrus. He must have been hiding around here somewhere. It would have been interesting to meet the royal family. I didn't know a lot about them. My dad always went on about them, but I never paid any attention, to be honest. I knew the king and queen had died, and their oldest son, Cyrus, had taken the throne as king. He had a brother or two, I think, but I couldn't remember much else. Except that Cyrus was a twenty-five-year-old king, ruling alone. I was only a couple of years younger. I couldn't imagine not having either of my parents. How lonely must he have been?

I raised my hand to my neck, my fingers searching for the jade necklace my father had bought me.

It wasn't there.

Damn. The chain must have broken again.

I knew it was around here somewhere. I had been fiddling with it just before we reached the gardens. I wasn't about to interrupt the grand ramblings of Ms. Plastic Smile, so I turned back to look for it without saying anything.

It wasn't expensive, but it was meaningful. Dad had bought it for me on my sixteenth birthday when we were together in a pop-up shop in Chicago. There were only a few times we took family vacations together. That was one of them.

Retracing my steps, I found it beside a bed of yellow roses. I inspected the broken chain and bent the clasp back into place.

That would have to do for now. Again.

Now to find the tour group. Not that I was interested in hanging out with Ms. Plastic Smile all day, but dinner was happening soon, and I had been starving for the last hour. If I lost the tour group, I lost dinner, and I wasn't willing to lose dinner.

I walked back through the gardens, following the path into the vineyards. There was a path that veered off to the side, leading to a maze of vineyards, vines stacking high above my head and creating an arched ceiling. There were pockets of sitting areas with benches. All of them were empty.

Except for one.

On one of the cherry-wood benches was a man in a navy-blue button-up shirt and white pants, reading a book. His black hair was pulled back in a man-bun, which made most men in California look like hipsters, but made this guy look like an ancient warrior.

He didn't notice me.

"Um, excuse me," I said, "have you seen the tour group?"

He raised an eyebrow before he raised his head to look at me. His eyes were deep set and a dark brown that brought a richness to his dark hair and wild eyebrows. He gave me a once-over, then looked back at his book. He turned the page.

"I have not," he said. "I told them specifically not to come this way."

"Ah, I see. Do you work here?"

"Does it look like I'm working?"

"You could be on your lunch break. I don't know."

He shut his eyes for a moment and sighed. "You keep talking. It bothers me."

"You don't answer my questions," I returned, annoyed at his attitude. "That bothers me."

He looked up from his page and opened his mouth to say something else. Instead, his eyebrows matted. Suddenly, he shut his book and leaned forward.

"You," he said, narrowing his eyes. "Have we met before?"

"No," I replied. I would've remembered that scowl if we had.

He tapped his fingers against his book in thought. His eyes widened for a moment, then he pulled out his cell phone. He swiped a few times and got up from his seat, shoving the phone in my face.

"This. Is this you?"

I looked at the picture. It was me with Mom and Dad on a trip to Italy last year.

"Yeah, that's me and my parents. But how did you?"

He dropped his arm, frowning. "It's you, then?" He looked me up and down, pursing his thin lips.

"What are you talking about? How do you have that picture?"

He stepped in closer, leaning down to look me directly in the eyes.

"You …" he said. "You don't belong here."

He walked away, leaving his book on the bench. I leaned over and picked it up, running after him.

"Wait!" I called. "Who are you? Why don't I belong here?"

But he was already gone. The vineyard was too much of a maze to search for him forever, and after a few minutes I gave up. Dinner was more important. I could just hand the book off to someone else in the castle. It would have been easier to return the jerk's book to him if I had gotten his name, though.

I looked down at the book.

The Strange Case of Dr. Jekyll and Mr. Hyde

Huh. Maybe he was looking for the other half of his personality. The nice part that was destroyed by scowling and half-assed sentences.

I flipped open the book, hoping to see a name, but there wasn't one. Shrugging, I put it in my bag.

"Marina! We lost you for a moment!"

I jumped as the tour guide's smile came into view.

"Sorry about that," I said.

"Please, come with me," she said. "We're late."

The tour guide took me back through the castle and up the staircase.

"Is the dining room upstairs?" I asked. "Aren't we going to dinner?"

"Oh, dinner will be a bit later!" she said happily, as if it wasn't the most disappointing thing she'd said all day. "We have another stop before that. This way, please."

I kept following, down the wide hallways lined with crimson carpet and white tapestries with gold patterns. With how large this castle was, my feet were starting to hurt.

The tour guide stopped at the last door in the hall and knocked.

"Enter," a strong male voice said on the other side.

The tour guide turned to me. "Best smile, my dear."

She reached up and, taking me by surprise, pinched my face into a smile. Did she think I was six? I complied but dropped the fake smile as soon as she turned away.

The door opened to a grand parlor, with large leather couches and a bar at the back. I expected to see the rest of the tour group assembled, but there was just one person: a man in a white suit reorganizing the pieces on a chess board in the middle of the room.

The same man who had been watching me from the mezzanine.

He jumped up when he saw us, knocking over the chess board and pieces.

"How many times …" he grumbled, looking at the mess he had caused.

He left the pieces where they were and stepped over to us, giving me a bright smile with his pale lips and dark eyes. He couldn't have been much older than I was, but the way he stood up straight, pulling his broad shoulders back, showed the maturity of someone twice my age. Clumsy perhaps, but mature.

He lifted his wrist, looking down at his watch. "You're seven minutes late, Catie."

She bowed deeply. "My apologies, Your—"

"You realize my schedule can't be rearranged," he said, tapping on his watch. "I have a meeting at 5:35. If that meeting is pushed back any further, it will cut into my video conference with New York. And if New York goes over its allotted time, that will push back my other tasks, and I'll lose possibly 30 minutes of sleep. That will disrupt my REM, and the entire balance of my sleep cycle for tomorrow's activities."

He kept tapping on his watch, frowning. Wow, this guy was worse than my dad. Why was I here to meet him?

He looked up from his watch, an eyebrow raised as if he'd heard what I was thinking. "You must be Marina?"

I raised an eyebrow back at him. "Yeah, that's me."

The tour guide nudged me. "Try to be a bit more formal, dear."

I frowned. "Uh … Yes … that is I?"

The tour guide grimaced. The man chuckled.

"Formalities are not your specialty," he said, tapping on his watch again. "I'll have to note that while scheduling."

"Scheduling what?"

"We'll talk about that in a moment. First, I must introduce myself."

He stepped forward, holding out a hand decorated in gold rings. I took it for a handshake, but he brought it up to his lips instead. He gently kissed the back of my hand, then put his other hand on top of mine. I'd never had a stranger kiss my hand before. Well, except for the guys I had punched in the mouth. That probably wasn't the same thing, though.

"Catie, please wait outside for a moment," he said.

The tour guide looked between us, then bowed and left.

"Allow me to officially welcome you to my home," the man said, still holding my hand. "I'm King Cyrus."

I drew my hand back. "King?"

He smiled ear to ear. "Yes. And it's an honor to finally meet you … Your Highness."

2

THE DINNER GUEST

I turned to see if there was someone else behind me. There wasn't.

"I know it's strange," he said. "Your father told me that you had no idea of your royal heritage. Honestly, I'm not sure of the best way to tell you all this."

"Royal heritage?"

He nodded. "Yes. You come from a long line of royals, Marina."

Well … that wasn't in my DNA test.

"How do you figure?" I asked. "Are we related?"

The king snorted and covered his mouth with his hand. "No, you and I are not related. Your parents are royalty. You are a princess, my dear."

I wasn't sure whether to laugh at him for saying I was a princess or for calling me *dear*.

"My father and your father were close friends," he continued. "I believe your father expects the same of us. That's why he sent you here to be trained up as a princess. By me."

His smile was warm and sincere, but a little too much like my dad's smile when he was in the middle of a prank.

"Nice try," I replied. "My father organized this trip as a graduation present."

"Yes, he wanted you to finish college first. Business major, wasn't it?"

"Uh … well …"

"But he tried to get you to major in political science, right?"

How did he—

"And when you refused," the king continued, "he tried to convince you to study economy, trade, and even technology. But he couldn't win. Right?"

I didn't answer. There's no way this guy could know all that. I didn't fill that in on any visa forms, right?

He scratched his sharp chin. "Business is a good subject for any member of royalty, I think. After all, business affects economy and trade, right? When I mentioned this to King Tylier, he saw the appeal of it among royal studies." He paused, opening his hands. "You're welcome."

King Tylier? I cringed. What a weird thing to call my dad.

"Not to be rude, Your Majesty, but I think you're confused," I said.

The king pressed his lips together. "I don't think I've been accused of confusion before."

"My dad can't be a king," I replied. "We live in California …"

"Most of his business is handled over video conferencing. Over the last five years, he's traveled here for negotiations."

Dad did go out of town once a month. But wait, no …

"He hates politics."

"Because he has to deal with them all day, I'm sure. I hate them myself."

"He also can't take anything seriously."

He puffed out his cheeks. "Yes, well you said it, not me."

I shook my head. "You're crazy. You really expect me to be—"

My stomach growled, throwing off my train of thought. It was enough to get His Majesty's attention too.

"I apologize. I was inconsiderate to give you such big news right before dinner," he said. "Also, I've run out of time to tell you anything more. We're cutting into my scheduled bathroom break."

I raised an eyebrow at him.

He called the tour guide back into the room. She looked me over suspiciously.

King Cyrus waved her over. "Catie, take Marina to the dining room. I'm sure she's starving by now."

The tour guide smiled and bowed. Though my stomach was yelling at me, I had too many questions to be bothered to feed it.

The king put a soft hand on my shoulder. "Don't worry. I'll do my best to take care of you. I told your father I'd look out for you, after all."

I looked at his hand on my shoulder. He plucked it off, rubbing his neck.

"We'll speak more after you've had dinner," he said. "Please enjoy it with your tour group."

I was about to say that I'd rather talk now, but the tour guide interrupted me.

"You mean, you won't be joining us, Your Majesty? I thought you'd be our guest for the evening?"

"Afraid not. Nikos will be joining you." He wrinkled his nose. "Good luck with that."

Nikos. Nikos … I knew that name …

Before I could ask any other questions, he gestured for the tour guide to escort me out. She bowed and motioned to the door.

I looked back at him before leaving. He only smiled.

This wasn't real … right?

§

I sat at the dining table, head spinning.

Princess? I couldn't be a princess. That didn't make any sense. Dad was a businessman. Mom was a fashion designer. They weren't royal people.

"And now I'd like to introduce you all to a special guest," the tour guide said. "Someone I'm sure you'll all be thrilled to meet in person."

I looked up. She wasn't talking about me, right? This was all a prank. I looked for cameras in the ceiling.

"May I introduce to you His Highness, Prince Nikos!"

The girls in the tour group gasped as a tall figure entered the room. One even screamed. Some stood to their feet, while others froze to their chairs. The men were just as excitable, pulling out their phones to take pictures.

That's why I knew that name. Prince Nikos — also known as the World's Prince.

The World's Prince was famous for his humanitarian projects, his elegant style, and his humble personality. The media used his nickname more than his real name, referring to him as every woman's dream prince.

He stood at the edge of the table, giving the bright smile that I had seen from time to time on TV. It was strange to see it in person. His dark hair was pulled to the side in a wave exactly like all his media appearances, as if it was glued that way. But he was much thinner than I imagined he would be, with narrower shoulders and waist. The fantasy of the World's Prince and the reality of the skinny teenager in front of me jarred.

"Hello, everyone!" he said, his voice as bright as his face. "It's a pleasure to meet you all. I'll be your host this evening. I hope you don't mind."

"Of course we don't mind!"

"I love you, Prince Nikos!"

"I named my labradoodle after you!"

He smiled at the comments, his face glowing. "Would anyone like to take some pictures?"

A bunch of girls screamed and ran up to him, handing their phones to the tour guide. I knew he was a few years younger than I was, but his face was even more youthful than I remembered from the news. On the flip side, there was a sharpness in his eyes and his smile that reminded me of the criminal mugshots I saw in the segments right after.

His sharp lips curled up as he bowed to me. The other guests turned to look at me, as confused as I was.

One of the guests hopped over to me and tapped my arm. "Don't you want a picture?"

Before I could respond, the tourist pulled me out of my seat and brought me over to the prince.

He looked down at me, cocking an eyebrow. "You want a picture too?"

I looked up at him, trying to figure out the right words to say. I never had this problem when meeting celebrities at concerts when Dad got me backstage passes.

I never *did* ask how he got those.

"Sure," was all I could come up with.

He snorted, taking the phone out of my hand and giving it to the tour guide.

"You're shorter than I imagined," he said.

"What?"

He leaned down, draping his arm around my shoulder and leaning his head against mine. The rest of the girls squealed at the gesture, but I leaned my head to the other side.

"Personal space," I muttered.

"Look at the camera, Princess," he replied.

My stomach dropped. He grinned. I frowned.

And that's how the picture came out.

I sat as far away from him as possible. That gave plenty of space for the girls at the table to fawn over him. He glanced at me from time to time, staring for a moment and then narrowing his eyes.

Princess. He called me Princess.

It was a pet name, right? Not my actual title. Had to be.

"I hope you all enjoy the soup tonight," he announced at the table. "It's our country's signature dish. It may not be the most visually appealing, but if you live here, it's something you have to adjust to."

His eyes fell on me when he said it. He rubbed his tongue between his teeth.

First were the appetizers. A half dozen men in white shirts and black-waisted aprons brought out platters of local fruits and vegetables, and tiny slices of bread with jam. I nibbled on some pumpernickel, playing over King Cyrus's words in my head.

"Your father told me that you had no idea of your royal heritage."

Trips around the world. Backstage concert tickets. Private schooling. All of those were because Mom and Dad worked hard, right? It wasn't because of royal inheritance. How could it be? Our house was small — only two bedrooms and an office. We celebrated Christmas with my Uncle Lloyd and Aunt Tina every year. They weren't royalty. They owned a karate dojo. I had to clean the floors of the dojo every night in exchange for karate lessons.

That's not something a princess would do. Right?

"Let's play a game, shall we?" the prince asked, bringing me out of my thoughts. "I'm going to ask each of you a question. For each answer, you can ask me any question you want."

Some straightened in their seats, smiling.

He started with the first woman on his left. "What is your favorite part of the castle?"

Her shoulders went up to her ears as she smiled. "You are."

He chuckled along with the rest of the table. "A fantastic answer! Now, since you gave me an answer, you can ask any question you like."

"Do you have a girlfriend?"

He laughed harder. "I've loved every woman I've ever met. It's so difficult to give your heart to one woman when you've given over your heart to so many."

The table awed. I tried not to barf all over my dinner plate. He'd basically admitted to being a player, yet these girls were practically handing over their souls for his attention.

This went on for the entire first course. He asked questions about favorite places in the country, worst experiences on the trip, and even if people liked his left profile or right profile more.

"Your turn," he said to me, smirking.

I sat up, waiting for my question.

"How would you address skyrocketing unemployment in a recession?"

Everyone looked at each other.

"What?" I asked. "Come again?"

He picked up his fork and waved it around, then stabbed a grape and put it in his mouth. "I'm just curious about your insight."

His cheeks puffed up as he chewed the grape.

Before I could respond, the waiters came out with the second course.

"Ah, yes, the kingdom specialty!" he said as they walked out. "Please enjoy it."

He continued to stare at me, chewing grapes. I was going to sock him in the mouth if he kept chewing with his mouth open like that.

I excused myself and went to the bathroom instead.

Freezing water from the faucet told me that this wasn't a dream. Two royal members had acknowledged me. The problem was, I didn't know what anyone was talking about.

Was I really a princess?

That could be a good thing. Lots of free travel and an endless supply of hot wings, maybe. But I was going to take over Uncle Lloyd's dojo next year. I had trained in karate since I was seven years old. I had tournament trophies. I'd majored in business. I'd studied for this my entire life.

I wasn't giving that up. Not for anyone or anything.

Prank or not, my path was set.

I stepped out of the bathroom, wiping excess water on my pants. Mom hated it when I did that. Was it because she was a fashion designer? Or because she was a queen?

I shook my head. I wasn't thinking about this now. And I wasn't going back to that stupid dinner table so the World's Prince could ask me more economics questions.

Instead, I wandered further into the castle. What would it be like to grow up in a place like this? Servants and riches? Expensive collectibles? Designer clothes?

I couldn't imagine growing up with those kinds of things. I was fine with weekdays at my uncle's dojo, and a collection of weekends camping or hiking deep in the mountains.

"Stop being so reckless, Evann."

I turned around. The voice echoed down the hall, but I couldn't see any faces.

"Don't you understand your duties?" the voice continued.

"I do," a second voice said firmly.

I followed the voices.

"Your father was the same way, God rest his soul. That's why he died so young."

The doorway opened to a teal-and-gold room, filled with lavish benches and tall vases. Two men stood at the far end. One was large, with broad shoulders, wearing a full military uniform. The other was about half his size, with reddish-black hair and long shoulders that he held squarely.

"I have no intention to die early," the smaller one said. "It was a simple application."

"An application to the afterlife," the larger man said. "If the king hadn't denied your application, you'd be in a world of hurt right now. Stop going behind my back for these things."

The redhead bowed his head, not in agreement but in acknowledgment. I had done that myself when my uncle scolded me during training.

"You're dismissed for the evening," the larger man said, beginning to walk away. "Expect hard training tomorrow. You've earned it."

The redhead bowed again as the larger man stepped away. When the man had left the room, the redhead took three steps backwards, collapsing on one of the lavish orange cushions.

"Damn you, Cyrus," he muttered to himself.

I bumped the door, making it creak. The redhead looked over at me.

"Reveal yourself," he commanded.

I froze. He stood.

"I said reveal yourself," he said again.

I stepped backward, only to trip on my own feet and land on my butt. The door swung open and sprung back to hit me in the side. When I went forward, I slammed my head in the second door.

"This is the most annoying day ever," I muttered to myself, holding my face.

There were footsteps before there were feet. The redhead was now in close range, and through the one eye I wasn't holding in pain, I saw two of the purest black eyes I had seen in my entire life.

He cocked his head to the side. "Well. Aren't you interesting?"

I grimaced. "You don't know the half of it."

I brought myself to my feet, trying to open my throbbing eye. Standing at squinting-eye level, the redhead was a little more rugged than I'd first thought. Compared to the man he was speaking with earlier, he was thin, but compared to me he was pure muscle. He had a thin goatee, something I wasn't accustomed to seeing on most Aujinians, which was a shame because black stubble on cinnamon-brown skin was a seriously underrated type of sexy. His goatee matched his reddish-brown hair, which made it even more exotic.

His eyes widened. In a moment, he bowed at the waist. "Forgive me, Your Highness. I did not recognize you."

"Oh God, not you too," I said. "Why does everyone here keep calling me that?"

"Because you're a princess. And a rude one at that."

Prince Nikos walked in through the side door, raising an eyebrow at the redhead. The redhead bowed at the neck.

"You know who this is?" Nikos asked him, pointing at me.

"I've only just realized."

"You ditched me at dinner," Prince Nikos said to me, scowling. "That's not very good manners, *Your Highness.*"

He hissed out the last part of *highness* like a swear word.

"Why are you here, Ev?" Prince Nikos said, turning to the redhead. "I thought you'd be in the guards' quarters?"

"I have night shift for the west side of the castle until two in the morning," the redhead replied.

"Midnight shift? You quit being my assistant for this nonsense?"

"Being your assistant was nonsense."

"It wasn't that terrible."

"I still have burn marks."

"I told you already! I didn't know hairspray was *that* flammable."

I took a step back.

"Don't go anywhere," Nikos said, pointing at me. "I don't appreciate your wandering off from dinner. Cyrus will have my head if we lose you again."

"You're all confused," I said. "You have to be."

"We're not the ones who are confused," Nikos said. He put his hands behind his back, repeating one word at a time. "I am Nikos. I am a prince. You are Marina. You are a princess. This is Evann. He is a loser."

Evann knocked his elbow into him. Nikos scowled.

"See if you ever get promoted," Nikos returned.

Evann responded with a poker face.

I fumbled for my phone. "Give me your Wi-Fi password. We'll call my dad and he'll straighten this whole thing out—"

"That's not a bad idea, actually," Evann said, nodding. "If we can get ahold of King Tylier—"

Nikos groaned. "Get my brother to break his precious schedule? Do you want to hear his endless nagging?"

"He won't do it for me," Evann replied. "He would only do it if one of his *dear little* brothers asked him for a favor."

"Give me one good reason to do it."

"Because, as a prince, you are eager to help your fellow men and women in their time of need."

Nikos raised an eyebrow. "I'm sorry. Have you met me?"

"And if you don't," Evann continued, "I'm sure the princess will find herself in your *constant* care until Cyrus agrees to meet with us."

Nikos spun towards the door. "Alright, let's go."

Evann bowed to me. "Please, come with us, Princess."

Prince Nikos ordered Evann to take me to the meeting room as he split off to go find King Cyrus. Evann led me to the second floor, to a room with a long table, a dozen leather chairs, and a large screen at the front. Evann gestured to one of the seats.

"Wait here, please. It may be a few minutes. Are you hungry?"

"I'm fine."

My stomach growled in betrayal. Evann's lips pressed together.

"I'll bring you some fruit, just in case," he said.

He turned and nodded to one of the guards as he walked out.

I looked at my phone. All we had to do was call Dad. He would say something like, "Gotcha again!" and do his annoying finger-gun gesture and then I could go home, punch him, and we could laugh about it.

That's what would happen.

None of this was real.

3

THE TALK I

After a thousand failed attempts at guessing the Wi-Fi password myself, King Cyrus arrived. The guards bowed to him automatically, but he ignored them, smiling at me.

"Nikos told me you'd like to contact your father?" he asked.

I stood from the chair. "Look, it's not that I don't appreciate the idea, but I don't want you going around calling me *princess* and *your highness* when I'm—"

Before I finished, Prince Nikos entered the room. "Good, you're still here. Thought we'd have to chase you all over the house."

Cyrus's eyes softened as he stared at me. "I don't mind it."

I cleared my throat and dropped my chin.

Nikos sat in one of the chairs, throwing his legs over the side. "What kind of king doesn't tell his daughter she's a princess, then makes someone else clean up the mess?"

"Hush," Cyrus reprimanded, his voice dropping an octave. He turned back to me. "Don't stress, my dear. As soon as Julian arrives, we'll call your father."

"Julian?"

"My younger brother," Cyrus explained. "You've already met Nikos, the youngest."

Nikos threw up a peace sign while looking at his cell phone.

"Charmed, I'm sure," I muttered.

"Evann," Cyrus said, "Prepare the video conference call. Has King Tylier confirmed his availability?"

Evann nodded. "He has. Unfortunately, Queen Leona won't be able to join us since she has a fashion show in Milan."

I sank back down into my chair. They knew about Mom, too.

"Ah! Julian! There you are."

I looked up to a man wearing glasses, a man bun, and a scowl.

"You!" I said, pointing at him.

He sighed. "Again?"

"You've met?" Cyrus asked.

"She interrupted me while reading."

Nikos chuckled. "Bad move, Princess."

"Why am I needed for this phone call?" Julian asked, monotone.

Cyrus patted his brother's shoulder. "Because I want us all to be on the same page regarding our new royal guest. Now sit down."

Julian sat next to Nikos, nudging him. Nikos sat up but didn't take his eyes off his cell phone.

Cyrus nodded to Evann. "Call him."

The computer buzzed and my dad's face appeared on the screen.

"Hey, princess!" he said, grinning.

I stood from my chair. "Stop calling me that!"

Everyone looked at me. I wrinkled my nose and sat back down.

"But you're my princess, princess," he said, laughing. "And as you've figured out by now, you're everyone's princess."

"Stop joking around, Dad."

He shrugged. "I wish I could say I was, but the fact of the matter is, you're a princess. You're royalty."

I looked around the room. "There are hidden cameras around here, right? You're playing me."

"Nope," he said. "No hidden cameras. No playing. Just good old-fashioned, life-long secrecy."

"So, let me get this straight — you're telling me that you bought me a first-class ticket to a foreign country so I could meet the royal family and have them break the news to me?" I paused. "Is this why you bought me new clothes?"

"I thought you'd hate me less."

He was smirking, but it wasn't his prank smirk. My stomach sank.

"I thought it was a graduation present!" I said. "Not a hey-your-life-is-about-to-change-forever present."

"I mean, they have the same general theme, right?"

"Perhaps it might be best to tell her your idea for accepting the crown," Cyrus interjected. "It might make the whole process easier to swallow."

"Wise idea, as always, Cyrus."

Cyrus. Not King Cyrus or Your Majesty. Just Cyrus.

"Princess," Dad continued, "You'll be staying with Cyrus, Nikos, and Julian for the summer. They'll train you on your royal obligations. At the end of the summer, you can decide if you want to take the job."

"So I have a choice?" I asked.

"There are a few conditions. At the end of the summer, Cyrus will give me a report on how you did. He will give me his honest professional opinion on whether you are qualified to be a ruler."

I opened my mouth to say something, but Dad cut me off.

"If Cyrus says you are qualified, then you may choose. You can be a princess, or you can go back to the life you had before. I won't stop you. I'll be crushed inside and won't be able to show my face in my kingdom ever again, but I won't stop you."

I sighed, half-growling.

"Of course, if you decide to be stubborn and not listen, I have to take away certain opportunities," he continued. "If Cyrus disapproves of you as a princess, you'll be sent to a royal university in Europe."

"More school?" I exclaimed. "You can't be serious!"

"Very much so,"

"Wait," I said. "If I do that, then I can't get my certification at the end of the year."

He couldn't be serious. He wouldn't take away my opportunity to become a karate instructor.

Why would he do that?

"If Cyrus says that you've met his expectations," Dad cut in, "then there is no need to send you to an academy or take away your chance at getting your certification. I've already spoken with your uncle, and he's agreed to my conditions."

He already talked to Uncle Lloyd? That meant I didn't have a choice in this, did I?

"If you still want to take over your uncle's studio," he said, "I will allow it, but only with Cyrus's approval."

I looked at King Cyrus. He clasped his hands behind his back, looking at the ground.

"Why would I need to have King Cyrus's approval? Why can't I go back to my regular life?"

"Because if anyone finds out who you are, I need to know that you can handle it. With or without me."

The words vibrated in my chest.

"Enjoy your time for now," Dad said. "We can talk more soon. I have a table of businessmen waiting for me, and they don't like to negotiate over cold soup."

"But, Dad—"

He interrupted me before I could finish my sentence.

"Listen to Cyrus and behave yourself," Dad said. "I don't want you elbowing anyone in the face or putting them in a headlock."

"I'm not making any promises," I threw back.

"Close enough," he said. "Love you, princess. Gotta go!"

He shot his finger gun and the screen went blank.

"But, wait!" I yelled at the screen.

No response. I slumped back. This couldn't be happening. I didn't want any of this.

I thought after graduating college my parents wouldn't be able to dictate what I did anymore. I thought I would be independent and self-sufficient, like everyone else my age. But even now, they could manipulate everything – from where I traveled to what I did with my future. I didn't even have any resources to go up against them. No money, no connections, and no escape from the hired help my father always seemed to have on hand.

Never had I felt more like a child, not even when I was a child.

"This is a lot to adjust to," Cyrus said, "but we're here to help.'

I shook my head thoughtlessly. He'd really done it. My dad had really left me here with total strangers for … wait, how long? Until fall? It was June.

I groaned.

"Well, this should be exhausting," Julian muttered.

"I'm not thrilled myself," I said.

"It's an odd and overwhelming set of circumstances, I agree," King Cyrus said, ever the diplomat. "Regardless, we will do our best to give you any information and advice you need. Since we will be giving our best, can I ask the same from you?"

His dark eyes went straight through me. I shifted in my seat. What was I supposed to say? What do you tell a king?

"Sure," I said.

He nodded, smiling.

At least one of us was satisfied.

§

Evann showed me around the castle grounds until sunset. He told me that there was more to be seen on the castle property, and I could explore on my own in my free time. It could be kind of fun to explore, I guessed.

"And finally, your room," Evann said, bringing me to a massive red door. "I think you'll like it. It has everything a princess could ever want."

"Hot wings and a mini-fridge?" I quipped.

He smiled, touching his nose with his index finger. "Always a possibility."

He motioned for me to open the door. I cracked it open and peeked inside. Through the crack, I saw a massive bed on top of a gray fur rug, draped in silver-and-rose bed sheets. There was a white vanity, a mirror that took up an entire wall, and a bookshelf next to a giant armchair.

"Wow …" I couldn't help but say even though it made me sound like a star-struck teenager.

I opened the door wide.

BWAAAAAAAAAAA!

I screamed as I turned toward the ear-piercing noise, automatically kicking out in front of me.

My foot put a deep dent in the wall.

I froze.

Evann pulled the door back, revealing an air horn duct-taped to the wall.

"Ah," he said. "Nikos was here."

I grabbed my pounding heart and bent over to breathe. "That scared me to death!"

"Remind me not to sneak up on you." He touched the dent in the wall.

"Oh God, I'm so sorry! I just reacted."

"Are you a UFC fighter? That's quite a kick."

"My uncle runs a karate dojo."

Evann burst into laughter. "That's right. I forgot about Prince Lloyd."

Prince Lloyd? That was even more bizarre than King Tylier.

"You're not at all what I expected, Princess," Evann added.

I dropped my head. "Sorry."

"It wasn't an insult." His eyes sparkled. "If anything else sneaks up on you, let me know," he said. "There's an intercom next to your bed."

"You guys don't have cell phones? Can't I call you?"

His face scrunched up. "Yes, about that … Your father asked that I confiscate your cell phone."

I stepped back. "He what?"

"He doesn't want you to be distracted, or to have any information leak about your whereabouts. Also, he said you'd probably use it to plan your escape."

I automatically reached for my back pocket. "I'm not giving it to you."

"I'm afraid you have to, Princess."

I jumped back. "I don't have to do anything."

He held his hand out, stepping forward. I shook my head and moved back, running to the corner of the room. He followed. I moved the armchair between us.

"You're making this difficult, Your Highness," he said.

"You say it like it's a bad thing."

I hopped on the bed and ran over to the other side, but in a second, Evann's arm wrapped around my waist and pulled me back to him. His body pressed hard against mine, his firm arms reaching behind me and plucking my phone out of my hand. He lingered for a moment, before releasing me and taking a step back.

My phone. My precious phone was in the hands of some stranger. My pictures, my books, my friends. Captive.

I jumped up to save them, but it was too late. Evann tucked the phone in his inside coat pocket.

"When do I get it back?" I asked.

"When it's safe for the public to know where you are."

"When will that be?"

"Probably when your father comes. I apologize. I wish I could give you more answers."

I slumped down on the bed, my emotions puddling to the floor.

"I'll leave you to unpack," he said, pointing to my suitcase on the side of the room. They must have asked the hotel for it. "Let me know if I can do anything else for you."

He bowed and left before I could ask for my phone and my freedom back.

I took my time unpacking, waiting for someone to come in and tell me it was just a joke. They didn't.

By the time I finished packing, I was ready to take a shower and go to sleep. I opened the bathroom door to a double sink, another gray rug, and a shower that could fit at least four people. At least I was going to take the most glamorous shower of my life.

"You're making this difficult, Your Highness."

Me? *I* was making this difficult? They had taken away my cell phone and my plans for the summer, without a decent explanation. They had taken away my freedom. They had taken away everything I had ever known.

How was I the one making things difficult?

I lay on the bed, putting my head on the pillow. My thoughts were too heavy to hold up.

How could this be real?

As my hands slid under my pillow, something crunched against it. I pulled out a little slip of paper and unfolded it.

Don't worry. You won't be a princess much longer.

4

Tasks and Assignments

"We can't go in," Evann said. "It's 7:57."

I blinked, looking at the oversized door in front of us, then at Evann. "We're supposed to meet Cyrus at 8 o'clock, right?"

"Yes. Three more minutes."

I laughed. "You're not serious, right?"

Evann looked at his watch again, not answering. I gave up, humming *We Don't Talk Anymore* passive-aggressively until he motioned for me to follow.

He opened the doors to the same parlor where I'd met King Cyrus yesterday. He was at the chair by the chessboard, Nikos lying on the couch across the room.

King Cyrus stood when I arrived. Prince Nikos slid further into the couch.

"Marina!" Cyrus greeted me. "You came on time. Excellent." He pressed some buttons on his watch. "Did you sleep well?"

I raised an eyebrow at him purposely. He raised a hand to the back of his neck.

"Yes, well, I suppose it might have been difficult," he muttered.

"She didn't even bother to put on makeup," Nikos added. "I can tell from here."

I felt my lip twitch.

Cyrus approached me, taking my hand in his and kissing the back as he had the first time. If anyone back home did that, I'd punch them immediately. But Cyrus had a strange warmth to him when he touched my hand and brought it to his lips, as if my hand was something he was supposed to hold delicately, so I couldn't be offended at the gesture. Also, it was his country and his culture.

"I took the liberty of making your schedule," Cyrus said, handing me a folder.

I opened it up and looked at the first page. "Diplomat meetings? Video conferences? A UN meeting? Wait, why are there bathroom breaks scheduled in here?"

Cyrus frowned. "My apologies. That's my schedule. Your schedule should be over here."

He took the front page from me and flipped to the third page of the folder. There was a list of subjects, followed by times and locations.

"My brothers will tutor you in these subjects," Cyrus explained. "I've already extracted the books you will need from our library."

He waved his hand over to the table beside us.

My jaw dropped.

"You have to be kidding me!" I said. "There's at least fifteen books in that pile!"

Cyrus's eyebrows mashed together. "Are you unable to speed-read?"

"She's probably been hit in the head too many times," Nikos muttered.

"You know, I'm pretty good at hitting people in the head as well," I replied.

Nikos's lip curled. I glared at him.

Cyrus turned back to the tower of books. "Is it really impossible? I thought I had curated a reasonable amount. Not a problem, I can go through them again, I suppose." He looked at his watch. "But when to schedule such a thing? How long would it take? An hour? Two?"

Between Nikos's comments and Cyrus's constant button pressing, I was about to lose it.

"I can do it," I lied. "I can read all of them."

"It's not a problem if you can't—" Cyrus began.

"I said I could, so I will."

Cyrus dropped his watch, pouting slightly. "Very well. If you insist. Evann, could you assist Marina in taking these textbooks back to her room?"

Evann stepped forward, but I waved my hand at them both. "I can take care of it. All of it. Don't you worry."

I walked over and shoved my hands under the books, wrapping my arms around them. I clenched my teeth.

"I'll see you gentlemen at breakfast," I said, walking out the door.

No one here was going to tell me what I couldn't do. Not now, not ever.

§

Breakfast was laid out by nine, and although I expected something lavish and ridiculous, it was actually ... touching.

It was an American breakfast.

There were pancakes, eggs, hash browns, and toast triangles. There was fruit. There was orange juice and pineapple juice, coffee and milk. And even some steaming hot water and oatmeal. Normally all I ate was half a bowl of cereal and a banana for breakfast, but suddenly I was hungrier than normal.

"Did you do all this?" I asked Cyrus in wonder.

Cyrus's ears went red. He pursed his lips and nodded. "I'm king, after all."

Not looking at me directly, he inched the plate of fruit and eggs my way. I took some, along with a bowl of oatmeal.

Julian and Nikos arrived shortly afterward, earning a frown from Cyrus.

"You're both late," he said, looking pointedly at his watch.

I leaned over to look at his watch: 9:04.

"There was duct tape on my bathroom faucet this morning," Julian replied flatly. "Because of this, I was forced to change my clothes and reprimand the culprit behind the duct tape."

Nikos smiled.

"It sounds like you're bored, Nikos," Cyrus said. "I'll have to find you something suitable to do with your time."

Nikos shifted in his seat, shooting Julian a glare. Julian didn't acknowledge it.

Evann stood behind us, watching. It felt weird to have him standing around me all the time, saying so little.

"When do you eat?" I asked him from the table.

His eyes widened for a moment before he responded, "I eat after the royal family."

"Aren't you starving?"

"My duties come first, but thank you for your concern, Princess."

His eyes wandered over to Cyrus. Cyrus palmed the butter knife in his hand.

"I've decided to throw a ball at the end of the summer in honor of your parents' arrival," King Cyrus said.

"A ball?" I asked, choking down my oatmeal. "Like, one of those royal balls that you see in the movies, with the orchestra and the puffy dresses?"

"The dress is only puffy if you'd like it to be," King Cyrus said. "You control the puffiness scale."

He smiled, waiting for my response, but it was too early to laugh. In fact, now I was ready to leave altogether. They wanted me to dance in front of people?

"It would be the best way to both welcome your father in the fall and announce your position publicly, if you choose to take it," Cyrus continued. "They're a lot of fun, too."

"Says you," Julian said, sighing.

Nikos didn't have a response at all. The only thing he had been doing all morning at the breakfast table was shooting me long glances with a flat face.

"Have you ever danced before?" Cyrus asked me.

"I mean … I did some school dances."

"A formal ball will require something more sophisticated than an awkward prom dance," Julian commented.

I glared at him. He returned the favor.

"What Julian means to say is that we do more traditional dancing here," Cyrus chimed in. "Do you have any experience with the waltz?"

Not even a little bit.

"Maybe," I replied.

"I see," Cyrus said, smirking. "Lucky for you, we have two experts right here."

Julian and Nikos looked up from the table.

"What?" they both protested at the same time.

Cyrus slid his knife through his cantaloupe. "You are both princes of this castle and, therefore, have the honor of fulfilling your duties — whether that be running the economy or humbly teaching the art of dance to someone less experienced than yourself."

They said nothing in return.

"Then it's settled," Cyrus said. "We'll have a ball at the end of the season. Julian, you'll give your first dance lesson tomorrow."

"It will be my pleasure," he said.

The edge on the last word made me think that it wouldn't be a pleasure for either one of us.

§

Three and a half seconds. That's how long it took to realize that Julian as my dance instructor was a mistake.

He frowned, looking down at my shoes.

"You're wearing dirty sneakers on my ballroom floor," he said. "Your mother works in fashion. You only have one pair of shoes?"

I shrugged. "No. I have three pairs, but I expected to come here for two weeks. Not two months."

He raised his hand, waving at Evann. "Make a note. Call in an order for proper dance shoes."

I raised my hands. "You don't have to do all that."

"I do, actually," he said. "I can't have you messing up my floor."

"If it means that much to you, then I'll take them off."

I kicked off my tennis shoes and stepped on the floor with my socks. It was slipperier than I expected. I fell straight on my butt in front of him. He sighed and looked to Evann. Evann just smiled and shrugged.

"Get her proper shoes for her next lesson," Julian said, looking around the room. "Have you seen Tai?"

"Not since yesterday when I caught him sleeping on the kitchen counter."

Julian adjusted his glasses. "Ugh. I do so much for him, and he … Call him."

"No need, Your Royal Sourness," a voice said from the other side of the room. "I'm here."

A man with sharp eyes strolled over to us, wearing ripped black jeans and a gray hoodie. He carried a bag lazily over his shoulder, the random binder rings on his bag somehow highlighting the silver diamonds in his ears. He glanced at me and winked, then threw his bag under the piano bench on the side of the room.

Damn, he was beautiful.

"Where have you been?" Julian asked.

"Raiding your refrigerator," the man replied. "You're out of cheese, by the way."

"Noted. Make sure you're early for the next dance lesson."

The pianist saluted.

Julian turned back to me. "The first thing we'll practice is the stance."

With that, he stepped forward and wrapped his hand around my waist. I kicked him in the leg.

He yelped, grabbing his leg. "What was that for!"

"You can't sneak up on her, Your Highness," Evann said. "She's stronger than she looks."

I didn't mean to kick him, actually. It was a reflex. I didn't regret it, though.

Julian winced, stepping back towards me. "Trust me, if it were up to me, I wouldn't do this at all."

He pulled me back into his arms. One hand rested on my waist, the other took my hand in his. For such a cold creature, he had incredibly warm hands.

He moved the hand I had on his arm up to his shoulder. "*This* is a proper stance. They probably didn't teach you this at the middle school spring dance."

"Prince Charming Academy didn't teach you any manners either, so I guess we're even."

He raised an eyebrow, then took my hand in his and held it up between us. I could feel his arm muscles through his shirt while his dark eyes glared into mine.

The pianist started to play a bouncy tune on the piano while Julian barked orders at me.

"Stand up straight. Don't look at your feet. Don't look that way either. Look directly at me. Wait for my lead. Why aren't you waiting for my lead?"

I stepped on his foot. He cussed, backing away.

"That was on purpose, wasn't it?"

I pursed my lips and shrugged.

"You've got a lot of nerve," he growled.

"So do you," I returned. "Regardless of your status, I can't learn how to dance with the horrible way you're teaching."

"She's right, you know," the pianist cut in. "You're too rough around the edges. It's messing up my fingers."

"I pay for those fingers to do their job under any condition."

The pianist snorted. "Easy, sailor. Buy a lady dinner first." He gave a smug grin, showing his soft pink gums.

Julian sighed and held his hands out to me. This time he stayed in one spot, allowing me to come to him. I didn't want to.

He waved his hands. "Here."

I took one step forward. He did the same.

"Are you this stubborn with everyone?" he asked. "Or am I the lucky victim of your rebellion? I can't imagine what suffering your parents endured during your preteen years."

"I can't imagine why your parents wanted you at all."

His fingers gripped mine as he took his stance. The air shifted, and the shadows of his eyes darkened.

"Be careful, Marina," he said, voice low. "I know your parents. You know *nothing* about mine."

His hands loosened, but the darkness in his eyes didn't. Something about his statement was a threat, I was sure. But how?

5

ESCAPE

"**A**re you always that awkward?" the pianist asked, the teasing note in his voice taking away the sting of his statement.

Julian and Evann were talking on the side of the room, out of earshot. From Julian's hand motions and scowl, I had a feeling they were talking about my many inadequacies.

I sighed. "As much as I would like to say no …"

"So why lessons with Julian? You both seem annoyed with the situation."

I wasn't sure who this guy was. Even though he was intoxicatingly gorgeous, it probably wasn't the best idea to give away any information.

"There's a ball at the end of the summer," I said. "It requires dancing. Julian is helping."

The pianist raised an eyebrow. "Julian? Helping?"

"Begrudgingly," I added.

"Julian has high standards, but he's not unfair." He shut his piano book and shoved it into his backpack. He looked at Julian, dropping his head from side to side to pop his neck. "He must see something in you if he's bothering at all."

The only reason Julian was doing this at all was because of Cyrus. He didn't see anything in me. That wasn't possible.

Maybe none of them ever would. And if Cyrus decided I wasn't good at anything, I had to give up everything.

"I want to leave," I whispered to myself.

"Do you?" the pianist asked, his eyebrows shooting up.

He looked over his shoulder at Julian and Evann, smirked, and then bit his lip.

"Then let's go."

"Go wh—"

He grabbed my hand, intertwining his fingers in mine. Before I could say anything, he pulled me out the back door and into the castle yard.

"Where are we going?" I asked when we got outside.

He put a finger to his lips, hushing me. Gripping my hand, he broke into a run, and I had no choice but to run with him to keep myself from being dragged. We ran until we got to the castle garden.

He let go of my hand. I stopped to catch my breath.

"Why did you bring me here?" I asked.

He put his hands on his head, panting. "It sounded like you needed break. My job is to serve." He laughed to himself. "Come on. Let's look around garden before they figure out we're gone."

I suddenly realized he didn't have the Aujinian English lilt. His English was a little broken in places, the pronunciation of his vowels slightly skewed.

"Who are you exactly?" I asked.

"I'm Tai. I'm a little this and a little that. Mostly, I'm musician."

"Are you famous?" I teased.

"Maybe. But not for reasons you think. I work mostly for Julian. Sometimes with Nikos, when he doesn't have a snake up his ass."

"I can't imagine working with either one of them is pleasant."

Tai shrugged. "Julian pays me well. Nikos is just angry kid. I was the same way at his age."

"And how old are you now?"

"Any age that suits me."

He winked before licking his bottom lip. I tried not to noticeably tremble.

He asked me to introduce myself, and I gave him my name and hometown. He asked me why I was visiting. I said that I was a friend of the family.

At least, I was supposed to be.

"Anyways," I continued, "I'm stuck here until the end of the summer."

"You don't seem the type to like walls."

I nodded. "You've already figured me out, eh?"

He stopped, turning around to face me. He cocked his head to the side. "I'd like to figure out more of you, if you give me permission."

All the blood in my trembling knees went straight to my face.

"Tai!" a voice yelled over the gardens.

We both turned towards the voice. Through the tall rose bushes, I could see Julian and Evann running through the gardens, frantically looking from side to side.

"Ha!" Tai said. "I'm already in trouble. Is it even noon yet?"

I grabbed Tai by the bottom of his shirt and dragged him with me as I bolted behind one of the rose bushes. Tai grunted as I made him sit but didn't make another sound as we pressed ourselves between the rose bushes and the vineyard fence. I leaned back, trying not to get any rose thorns in my eye.

They called out our names again. Tai turned towards me, his eyebrows bouncing in amusement. I couldn't help but smile with him.

After a few more calls, Julian growled and left. I could hear him muttering something like "Take care of it yourself" and "Not interested."

When they had left, Tai propped his arm on his knee and leaned back against the fence.

"That was fun," he said. "But why did we do it?"

I stood and stepped over him. "Because I don't like dance lessons."

I heard his footsteps crunch behind me as he leapt up to follow me.

"You intrigue me," he said, bouncing ahead. "Doesn't every girl dream of staying at a castle and dancing with princes?"

"Sure, but dreams and reality are different."

"You don't want your dreams to come true?"

"No. Yes. Well ..."

He abruptly stopped and turned back to me. I almost ran into his chest. Not that I would have minded.

"So, what next then?" he asked.

I looked around the gardens, then up to the castle again.

"I don't know," I replied honestly.

"Well … when you figure it out, let me know. I want to see if it'll be fun or not."

With the same wink he came in with, he walked out.

6

THE YOUNGEST

I refused to go back to the ballroom.

What was the point of stupid princess lessons if Dad knew my karate instructor certification was the most important thing to me? Why was I the one being punished for his lies?

I wasn't going to allow it. I was going to follow my own path.

And right now, that path was leading me around the castle vineyards.

Vineyards weren't something I saw often in my part of California. The good vineyards were all in Napa Valley, the place I always assumed rich people without kids went for vacation six times a year. I never would have put my family in the same category. Dad only bought wine once a year. Mom sold hideously expensive clothes, but she rarely bought them for herself.

But maybe there was a big castle somewhere in another country, storing massive amounts of alcohol and high heels.

Where was our kingdom, anyways? Did we even have one? What did it look like?

I shook it out of my brain. No way. No questions. I didn't care.

"That dress brings out your eyes. You have good taste, as always."

I looked around to find the voice I had just heard. It wasn't for me, right? No, I was wearing jeans.

On the other side of the rose bushes, Nikos smiled as he spoke with a girl wearing a short white and blue summer dress with a large straw hat. She smiled back at him, dropping her head demurely. He fumbled around in his coat pocket, then pulled out a small box.

"I saw these when I was in Taiwan," he continued, his voice low. "The man selling them, he said — well, he said a lot of things — but he said they were inspired by cherry blossoms. You like cherry blossoms, so ... um ..."

Did Nikos have a twin brother? Whoever this bumbling kid was, it wasn't the cocky and confident World's Prince.

He handed her the box. She opened it, and then dropped open her mouth at the sight of whatever was in it. She shut both the box and her mouth, then gave a pleasant pink smile.

"They're beautiful," she remarked. "But I'm sorry. I can't accept them."

Ouch.

His face fell a little, but it sprung back into a smile. His World's Prince smile.

"It's nothing, really," his voice normal again. "A friendly gift. You've worked really hard this year, and—"

She put her hand on his, tapping it lightly. "I don't see it as a friendly gift, Prince Nikos. So, I'm sorry, but I can't accept it."

He licked his lips and dropped his hands, looking down at the box.

"I have to go," she said, bowing. "Please let me know if I can assist you further, Your Highness."

"Please don't call me that. You don't call him that."

She nodded and walked away. He stared after her, palming the box in his hand. With a grunt, he shoved it back in his pocket, throwing his head back. As his head fell to the side, his eyes met mine.

"Why are you here?" he demanded.

I pursed my lips. "I could ask you the same question."

His long legs brought him over to me in only a few paces. He stared down at me.

"How long have you been there?"

"Long enough to watch you get rejected. Hard."

His eye twitched. "Did you enjoy the show?"

"I give it a four out of ten. I'm not into second-hand embarrassment."

"Just mind your own business. And don't go blabbing this around to anyone. Not that you have any friends here anyway."

He started to walk away, but I couldn't let him have the last word like that.

"Maybe in a few years you'll grow into your ears and learn how to talk to a woman."

He spun around, grabbing me by the wrist and pulling me against him. I thrust my palm into his chest, but it didn't faze him.

"I may be young," he growled, "but I'm not a child. Remember that."

He let go, glaring at me one last time before walking away.

Sensitive little punk. It wasn't my fault he got rejected.

I found a bench and slumped into it, hands in my pockets to take off the bite from the wind. The sun was setting, the warmth going down with it. There were more shadows than I liked, but I wasn't about to go back to that castle to grab a hoodie. I could freeze here. That would be fine.

There were footsteps again. Maybe Nikos was back to give me more attitude. Or Tai was still wandering around. I hoped it was the second.

It wasn't either.

At first I thought Evann was bowing, but then I realized he was holding his knees to get air.

"How … could you … run away … like that?" he huffed out. "Do you know … how much … Ugh, wait. Don't go anywhere. I need to yell at you, but I need a minute."

He held his side while he caught his breath. Clearly, he had been running around the yard for a while. Julian may have given up looking for me, but Evann, as the castle guard, didn't have that option. I sat on the bench and apologized through an elaborate scolding that put Dad to shame.

"If anything happens to you, they'll gut me alive in the public square!" he said. "Do you want that? Do you want to sit in the front row as they cut me open?"

"Wait, they do that here?"

"Not anymore! But they'll bring it back if you disappear on me again!"

"I'm sorry. I'm sorry! How many times do I have to say it?"

"What happened?"

"Nothing,"

He sat next to me. "You're a bad liar. I wish I could be mad at you for it."

He patted his chest and coughed, smiling through his hyperventilation. He leaned back and looked up, and I couldn't tell if he was waiting for me to say something to him, or if he was watching the sun set.

I don't know how long it was silent for, but it didn't seem to bother him. It bothered me.

"Evann …" I whispered. "I don't think I can do this."

He took a deep breath. "Why?"

"I … I shouldn't be a princess."

"Ahhh," he said. "It's hard to accept who you are, isn't it?"

"Of course it is!" I said, standing up. "A week ago I was a college graduate. This week I'm a princess? That's not normal. That's not even logical. Also, it's not fair."

"Things aren't always fair, that's true." He smiled, his bright eyes bursting with warm affection like a golden retriever. "But in all situations, fair or unfair, there is always a choice. I recommend that you do your best, so none of your options are taken from you."

"I don't want to do my best," I grumbled.

He took my hand in his and held it to his chest. He did it as if we were old friends, as if it was something we did all the time.

"In these situations," he said, "your best is all you can do."

I pulled my hand out of his and looked away.

"Let's go see His Majesty," he said. "It's almost time for your meeting."

I reached for my phone to check the time and remembered that I didn't have a phone anymore. I needed a watch for this place.

Evann patted me on the shoulder and stood to walk ahead. I supposed there was nothing I could do but follow. I stood, slipping my hands in my back pocket. My hand crunched against something.

I took out a folded piece of paper.

How long had that been there?

I opened it. There were heavy black scribbles across the page.

All good things come to an end. Right, Princess?

7

THE NEW SPY

There were more dance lessons. Etiquette lessons. History lessons. There was a stack of books I suffered through, some because the English was ancient and others because they were incredibly boring. I flipped between staying up late and taking notes, to almost taking all my books and throwing them out the window. But since Evann had taken my phone I had nothing but time anyways. My choices were between eating, sleeping, sitting on the balcony outside my room, or reading.

If this was what being a princess was like, I was over it.

There was a knock at my door.

I shut my textbook, happy at the interruption.

"Come in!"

The door swung open. "You're not even going to check who it is?"

I scrunched my nose. Nikos.

"You're right. Go back outside and shut the door. I'll ask this time."

"You'll lock the door."

"Damn. You weren't supposed to catch onto that."

He gave me a fake grin. "Is this how you treat someone who brings you presents?"

Before I could ask, a half-dozen workers came in, each with a full rack of clothes. Nikos directed them to my closet, which had only one-suitcase's worth of clothes, taking up one-sixteenth of the closet space I was gifted.

"Formal on the left," he commanded the workers. "Dresses in the front and pantsuits in the back. Then casual on the right … with the *other* things."

His nose curled at my clothes.

"Don't look at my clothes like that," I said. "They're solid pieces."

"Solid pieces from your middle school days, no doubt," he replied.

I pressed my tongue against my teeth.

"In your current position, you need to have a more mature look," he continued. "It makes the people feel more comfortable with you as a ruler. Wearing a rock-band t-shirt from ten years ago in a leadership position is quirky if done once. It's questionable if done regularly."

He grabbed my hand and pulled me in front of the mirror. He stood behind me, hands on my shoulders.

"We need to create a style for you," he said. "Something uniquely you, but a professional version."

I wriggled out from under his hands. "I don't want to change who I am."

"You're not changing who you are. You're improving who you are. Isn't that what you're supposed to do as an adult?" He snorted, walking away from the mirror. "And you think *I'm* the one who's childish."

I couldn't see anything that needed improvement. My body was healthy and my clothes fit. Alright, so they were a little baggy and unprofessional. That was the look I was going for anyways.

He went over to my dresser, playing with the makeup and perfume sitting on it. There wasn't much. "I've hired a stylist for you. She'll help you create a style of your own to present to the public."

"I'll continue to be myself, thank you."

He shook his head. "You still don't get it. You will be yourself. Just a different side of you. Or are you completely one-dimensional?"

I opened my mouth to chew him out, but before I could, a familiar figure walked into the room. She had a graceful, soft air about her, her hair pulled back in a loose bun and her lavender dress wrapping elegantly around her body.

Where had I seen her before?

"Juniper will handle your styling from now on," Nikos said. "She has a detailed eye for fashion and makeup and will teach you what you need to know about being presentable."

His eyes lingered on her for a moment.

That dress really brings out your eyes…

Wait — Nikos hired the girl that rejected him to give me style advice?

The girl named Juniper bowed and smiled. "It's an honor to be of assistance," she said.

I raised an eyebrow at Nikos. *Does she know who I am?*

He jerked his head to the side. I wasn't sure if he was answering my unspoken question or if he was telling me to say something.

"I appreciate the help," I replied.

We gave each other a brief introduction. Juniper had majored in fashion design and was interning at the castle because of her instructor. Nikos eyed her as we talked, his eyes and lips both softening.

I'd never seen him look so … sweet.

"Juniper," Nikos said, after our introductions were finished, "I'd like you to spend a couple of hours with Marina deciding on her basic look, then spend some time with her on a skin-care routine. Her skin is a bit ashy."

"Your soul is a bit ashy," I replied.

He stuck out his tongue at me when Juniper wasn't looking.

"There are a few supplies I'll need," Juniper said to Nikos. "If you give me a moment, Your Highness, I can go get them from my room and start right away."

He nodded. She bowed and left, and his eyes lingered on her as she walked out. I reached up and tapped his head.

"Obvious much?" I taunted.

He grunted, waving my hand away. "I wasn't trying to be discreet. Actually, I have a favor to ask."

"Why would I do anything for you?" I asked, crossing my arms.

"Because I may or may not know exactly where your precious phone is. If you'd like to have it back, I can help." He chuckled. "Look at that. That's the first time I've seen your face light up."

I adjusted my expression. "What do you want, exactly?"

"Girl talk."

"You want to talk shoes and nails?"

"No, I want you to talk about men. With Juniper."

I squinted, finally understanding what he was getting at.

"I want to know what she's interested in when it comes to men," he said. "Truly. If I ask, she'll manipulate the answer. If you ask — as a friend — she'll be honest."

"You want a wingman."

"No, I want a spy." He raised his eyebrows. "Don't you want your phone back? A connection to the outside world?"

More than anything. I was bored and lonely and talking to anyone about anything was better than the conversations I was having in my head.

"I'm getting by," I replied.

He laughed. "You're a bad liar. We'll have to work on that."

"Why would I want to be a good liar?"

"Because," he said, starting out the door, "that's the only way to survive this place."

§

The long day ended, but my thoughts didn't. So many things rattled around in my brain, robbing me of sleep.

I couldn't stand to be in my room anymore. Even though it was well past sundown, I got up and went out to the front of the castle yard. There were a thousand guards per square foot. A little night walk would be alright.

The night air was cool and a little humid, but it was peaceful. Cicadas hid around the yards, screaming at the moon, accompanying the rushing sound of the fountains. I walked down the main pathway, looking into the line of trees on either side. It wasn't a weekend walk in the forest, but it was close.

I went off the path and into the trees, the crisp ground crunching beneath me. It wasn't as pretty as the gardens, but it was quiet. Maybe if I shut my eyes, I could imagine myself home again.

It didn't work.

I walked further in, curious at how far it would go. It went farther than I thought. The trees were planted, not naturally grown like the forests back home, but there was still something charming about them.

It would do for now.

My footsteps stopped, but another set of footsteps continued.

I couldn't see anything around me except for the faint light of the walkway off in the distance. Had I really gone *that* far?

I heard the crunching sound again.

"Hello?" I called out.

No answer. Just silence.

I took a few steps forward, then stopped. Two footsteps crunched after mine.

"Who is it?" I asked, trying to sound commanding.

Still no answer.

"This isn't funny anymore," I said.

A deep voice echoed behind me. "I agree. It's not funny."

Darkness. There was nothing but trees and darkness.

"Not funny that a nobody becomes a princess in a day," the voice continued.

"Who are you?"

"A messenger."

"A messenger? From whom? Wh-What message?"

There was a pause. The next word came out in just a whisper.

"*Run.*"

8

RUNNING

I didn't have to be told twice.

I raced through the trees to reach the light at the end of them. Feet crunched behind mine.

It was too dark and there were too many trees to see him. I looked back once but scraped my arm against a tree as soon as I did.

I couldn't scream. Only run. Did he have a gun? A knife? If I had to face him, the wide-open space was the best place to do it.

But first, *run*.

I ran out of the trees, breaking free into the light. I didn't waste time looking back. I ran straight for the entrance of the castle, past the guards, hoping they would stop him.

I ran up the stairs at full speed, straight to my room. I shut the door behind me and tugged on the lock, then sank against the doorframe as my heart pounded in my temples.

Was it a prank? Was it for real? First the notes and now this.

I played his voice over and over in my head until it started to blur. I had never heard that voice before. A worker at the castle? A guard? Who would have it in for me?

Knock, knock, knock.

I screamed.

"Princess?" Evann said on the other side of the door. "Are you alright?"

I crawled to my feet, hands shaking, and opened the door. I tried to look calm.

He stepped inside, not waiting for an invitation. "I got a call. Is everything okay?"

My heart ripped apart my throat.

"Everything's fine," I said.

"You're out of breath."

"I went running. I'm an athlete, remember?"

I slapped his arm and gave a breathy laugh, getting dizzy instantly.

"You went running at eleven at night?" he asked, raising an eyebrow.

"Couldn't sleep."

He scratched the faint stubble on his chin. "Is that so? Well, I suppose if you were only exercising, I have nothing to be alarmed about?"

He stared at me for a moment, waiting for an answer. I could have told him the truth. I could have shown him the letters. But if it was a silly prank, I was going to look like an idiot. I couldn't risk looking like an idiot.

I nodded.

He nodded slowly. "In that case, goodnight, Princess."

He bowed, stepping out and shutting the door behind him. My heart continued pounding, my stomach beginning to flutter with nerves.

Was it a prank? Or was it for real?

§

"Did you hear what I said?"

I looked up at King Cyrus as he leaned over the chess table.

"No, I'm sorry," I said. "I spaced. What was that?"

He chuckled. "I said that if you ever start to feel overwhelmed, let me know. I'm here to help."

"Overwhelmed? It's just chess."

He moved his pawn. "I wasn't talking about the game, my dear."

I pressed my lips together and nodded politely.

For the last week I had spent every evening in the parlor with King Cyrus after dinner, playing a round of chess. I enjoyed the game but was getting tired of him beating me at it.

"How are you so good at this?" I asked.

"I've had many worthy opponents. Your father included."

"You've played my father at chess?"

He nodded. "When I was younger, my father invited him often."

Where was I during this? King Cyrus was only a couple of years older than me, even if he did speak to me like a wise old uncle.

"I don't know anything about your parents," I said. "What were they like?"

He raised an eyebrow. "Your father never mentioned them?"

"He didn't mention a lot of things."

"Ah. Right." He licked his lips and straightened the pieces on the board. "Father was soft-hearted and passionate. He passed away when I was ten. Our mother was strong and beautiful. She passed away a few years ago."

"It must have been hard for you."

"It's all right," he said. "Mother prepared me to run the country on my own. And your parents have given me quite a bit of assistance. I'm indebted to them."

I sighed, moving my pawn. "I always thought Dad was away on business trips. I didn't realize he was — you know — running a country. Why did he go so far out of his way to keep everything a secret? I don't feel prepared for anything."

I moved my knight. King Cyrus took it out with his rook.

"No one feels ready at the beginning," he said. "Sometimes the best learning experience is the one you're not prepared for."

We played a few more turns, focused silence between us.

"King Cyrus—"

"Cyrus," he corrected with a smile. "We're much the same station. Just call me by my name."

"But you're a king,' I pointed out. 'I'm a princess, right? I think you're higher."

He shook his head. "Strictly speaking, perhaps. But you're an only child. You're a crown princess. Didn't you realize how things were going to eventually progress?"

I picked up my pawn, but it was suddenly melded with my hand. Cyrus leaned forward and opened my palm, extracting the pawn and placing it back down on the board.

"Don't panic, my dear," he said. "There's not that large of a difference. Trust me. It's nicer, actually. Your title is shorter, so it's easier to fill out paperwork."

"Are you seriously joking right now?" I snapped.

He frowned. "I never joke about paperwork."

"Cyrus!"

He laughed. "That's the spirit. Very casual."

I bent under the table, hoping reality was hidden somewhere under it. Queen? No way. That wasn't real. Princess was bad enough.

Cyrus's face came into view, his fluffy black hair hanging down. "Panicking?"

I nodded. "Slightly,"

"That's completely normal."

He smiled and went back to the surface. The blood rushing to my head was making me dizzy, so I went up for air with him.

"I wouldn't panic about your promotion yet," he said, straightening some of the pieces. "One responsibility at a time. A human being can only handle so much future at once."

My thoughts were rushing through my head, but none of them were forming together into a complete sentence.

There was a tap on my shoulder. When I looked up, Cyrus was holding a small glass of dark amber liquid.

When did he get up and go get a drink?

He handed it to me, sitting back down.

"Forgive me," he said. "I was far too flippant. I was hoping to lighten the mood, but …"

He raised his hand to his neck in a nervous gesture that was becoming familiar to me. I sipped on the alcohol, watching his eyebrows scrunch.

"It's alright," I said through my burning throat. "None of this is your fault, anyways."

"I'm trying to make your stay as comfortable as possible, but I don't think I'm doing a great job of it. I wish I had more time to spend …" He paused to take a sip from his own glass. "Should we stop the game?"

I shook my head. "It's alright. I don't want to give up yet. I still want to beat you."

He smiled, putting down the glass. "A fine goal, indeed."

I sucked down more of the drink.

"Cyrus," I asked some time after emptying my glass. "Why don't you have a wife? Aren't kings supposed to have queens?"

He laughed. "In theory, but it's not always the case. The only option for me at this point, really, is an arranged marriage. I never liked the idea of those. I always figured if there was a queen I wanted …"

He moved his bishop diagonally right until it was one space away from my queen. He picked up my queen and wrapped his hand around it, looking me straight in the eye.

"… I would just take her for my own."

My stomach clenched. Maybe I had drunk too much alcohol.

"And that's checkmate," he said. His lips pulled to one side, and for a moment I saw a bit of cockiness. It disappeared in a flash, replaced by his usual cordial smile. "You didn't win against me this time, but I look forward to when you succeed. Same time tomorrow?"

$$9$$

BAD COMPANY

I wandered around the castle. The food at dinner was rich, and my sluggish self was getting tired of all these calories without any exercise.

I missed my uncle's dojo. I missed working out until I wanted to throw up. I missed pushing myself to my limits. I missed my students. Ian was going to have his black belt test at the end of July. He had a habit of dropping his left arm when he kicked, and he was weak in his sidekick. I'd promised I would help him with that. Karen had only been there a few months. She was shy and reserved, but she had become more powerful the more I worked with her. She was most comfortable training with me. What would happen if I wasn't there to train her? Not to mention Sarah. She was twice my age but could beat my ass in every way. Then, after class, she would take me to lunch and listen to me complain about everything from boys to bad kung fu movies.

I missed them. I missed them so much it hurt.

And now there was a possibility I'd never see them again.

"Why the big face?"

I turned around, Tai's beautiful, playful smile behind me.

"I think you mean *long* face," I corrected.

"Ah, is that the phrase? English idioms are so difficult. Either way, you look sad. What are you thinking about?"

"Home."

"You miss it?"

I nodded.

"Tell me what you miss. Maybe I can help."

He walked with me for a while, as I talked about my uncle's dojo, my classmates in business school, the small cafes and tourist shops in my hometown, the apple orchard festivals, and the long hikes through the mountains. I don't know how long I rattled on for, but he stayed quiet and attentive as I talked.

"Well, if you'd like to hit something, I know someplace," he said.

He took me to another part of the castle, a small bounce in his usually relaxed step. I followed, half out of curiosity, and half because I loved the musk of his cologne.

He brought me to two large, teal doors, then turned to put his index finger to his lips. I smiled. Everything was a secret to Tai.

The difference was, his secrets were fun.

He opened the doors, revealing a massive training room. It was four times the size of my uncle's dojo, with weights, gym equipment, and even a large padded area for sparring. Two men were in the center, fully geared, beating the hell out of one another.

I had never been more excited since I got here.

Tai motioned for me to follow him, and we tip-toed to the side of the room where there were a few chairs for spectators. We sat, watching the men duke it out in the most professional way possible.

"Bring your shoulders up more," one of them instructed, "and pull your heel up."

The second one did what he was told. He was bouncing a little too much, expending a lot of energy. Regardless, he was fast and calculated in his moves, and he had no problem getting in solid hits against his opponent.

"Better! Keep it going!" the first one said again.

The second fighter only doubled his speed, as if he had a secret reserve hidden in his back pocket. He shot out moves like a machine gun, each one as powerful as the one before. But it was only for a brilliant five seconds. After that, he stepped back, his heavy breathing louder than the first man's voice.

"Easy, Evann. Don't black out again."

I almost jumped from my chair. *That* was Evann?

He pulled off his headgear, putting his hands on top of his head while he sucked in air. Sweat had matted his hair, and it was dripping down his face like he had been out in the rain. The first man patted him on the shoulder.

"Get some water," he said.

Evann bowed, turning towards us. Tai waved.

"Your—" Evann stopped, looking between Tai and me. "You're here."

He swallowed, eyes slightly wide, as if avoiding my title was the hardest thing he had ever done.

"Still the best fighter in Aujina, I see," Tai said.

Evann huffed, guzzling down half his water bottle. "Best? If I'm the best, then our country is in trouble."

"You're pretty damn good," I said.

His eyes met mine for a moment before he looked at the ground and smiled. "Thank you, Your— you're too kind. But I still have a long way to go. What are you two doing here, anyway?"

"Marina was bored," Tai explained. "I thought she'd enjoy training center."

"Were you going to spar with her?" Evann asked, raising an eyebrow.

Tai threw his head back and laughed. "No chance. I'm musician, not fighter."

Evann eyed him for a moment but said nothing as he drank more water.

"Can you teach me?" I asked Evann.

His eyebrow bounced. "I could. If I wanted Cyrus to murder me."

Tai clicked his teeth. "Cyrus doesn't let you do anything fun, does he?"

Evann didn't answer.

"You would think he would be more lenient given how long you've been here," Tai continued. "I get away with everything."

Evann shrugged. "He has his reasons."

"You say that almost every time I see you. Do you even mean it anymore?"

Evann finished off his water and tossed the empty bottle to the side. "My break is over. I'll see you around."

With an automatic bow, he walked away.

Tai walked me back to my room after giving me his own personal tour. He showed me the best places for hide-and-go-seek, his favorite places to nap, and his favorite view — the kitchen refrigerator.

The last stop was his music room. It was like an elegant music classroom, with wood floors, scattered instruments, and music sheets haphazardly thrown around the room.

"Welcome to my home," he said. "If you want to take nap, I recommend red sofa, not brown one."

"Can you play all these instruments?" I asked.

He nodded. "I have to. The leader of the orchestra has to hear and understand everything."

"Wow. You're talented. What school did you go to?"

"Didn't go to school."

"Homeschooled?"

He raised an eyebrow. "What's that?"

"When you stay home and your parents teach you."

He shook his head, a strange glint in his eye. "I worked in my mother's restaurant. That was my education."

He picked up a strange guitar and started tuning it.

"How'd you get this job, then?"

"Julian found me playing in public square. He offered me the job. I took it. Sometimes you're that lucky."

He plucked the strings in a random melody.

"Julian did that?"

I couldn't believe the world's biggest skeptic could be so generous and so willing to take a chance.

He nodded. "Julian is quite the softie. He doesn't show it much. Only around the arts."

I snorted. "Unless it's dance lessons."

He chuckled in return. "Yes, he's particularly tough on you. It's amusing."

"I'm not amused. I feel so uncomfortable around him." I slumped down in one of the chairs.

"Why? Aren't you friend of theirs?"

I bit my lip. I couldn't say much more about who I was, right? Not that it mattered with Tai. He was chill and acted like my friends back home. Truth is, I didn't really understand who I was anymore, and I didn't care to explain it since I couldn't figure it out.

"I don't fit in," I said simply.

He pursed his lips and nodded. "Yes. I see that. Cyrus, Julian, Nikos, even Evann … they're very close. Quick as thieves. And I know my share of thieves."

"*Thick* as thieves," I corrected.

"My sentence makes more sense."

I rolled my eyes, but it didn't seem worth laboring the point.

"Maybe I'm not used to this kind of living," I said. "I'm used to building campfires, taking hikes in the mountains, cooking barbeque …"

"You can cook?" Tai interrupted, sitting up a little.

I nodded.

He leaned back again. "Careful, Marina. You're turning into my dream woman."

I scoffed. "Quit with your nonsense."

"It's not nonsense." He leaned forward, his face close to mine. "Unless … you're uncomfortable with me, too?"

My mouth went dry.

The door creaked open.

I didn't expect Cyrus to walk through.

Tai leaned back in his chair again. He nodded his head in a quick bow. "Your Majesty."

Cyrus's eyes floated between us. His jaw ticked. "Have you seen Nikos?"

Tai looked around the room. "Not here."

"We had a meeting at noon, but it seems he's … well … he's around here somewhere, I'm sure." Cyrus nodded to himself, his eyes drifting back to mine. "Marina … are you alright?"

I nodded, unsure of what he meant. He tapped his fingers against the doorframe.

"If you see Nikos, tell him he's late and that he needs to take his responsibilities more seriously."

Cyrus's voice was an octave lower than usual. He frequently lectured about time, but he never seemed angry about it.

He shut the door without looking back.

"How amusing," Tai said, scratching the side of his face and smiling.

"What?"

He smiled at me. "You can't tell? King Cyrus doesn't like me hanging around you."

§

After a couple of hours with Tai in the music room, I wandered back to my room alone, repeatedly playing over Cyrus's expression in my mind. His eyes had been so cold compared to their usual warmth. Why would my hanging out with Tai bother Cyrus?

I went into my room, took a shower, and got ready for bed. As I started for my bed, a white piece of paper pinned on the door caught my eye.

That wasn't there before.

I grabbed the note from the door, the same familiar handwriting on the page.

Not much longer, Princess. Enjoy this life while you can.

I growled, crumpling the paper in my hand. Someone in this castle had taken this prank far enough. I was done with this.

It was time to find out who was doing this and end this nonsense.

10

SNEAKING

The first person on my list of people who hated me was Julian. He seemed like the best place to start.

I had to find a piece of his handwriting. If it matched the handwriting on the notes, it was him. So far, I'd only met him in the ballroom for dance lessons. How could I match his handwriting to the notes?

There had to be something in his bedroom.

But how do you get into a prince's bedroom?

In the sort of movies that I liked to watch, the heroine would ninja chop the guards and sneak in undetected, but even I knew those movies were stupid. That would only get me killed or in serious trouble. It wouldn't get me inside.

There was only one thing I could think of.

"Tai," I said, tapping him on the shoulder.

He remained fast asleep on the piano bench. I tapped his shoulder again. He stirred, opening one eye.

"Is it lunchtime?" he asked.

"How do I get into Julian's bedroom?"

He opened both eyes, then crossed them. "Secret rendezvous?"

"Never. He … stole something from me. I'm just going to go get it."

He chuckled, sitting up and stretching his ribs. "Did he steal your panties, jailbird?"

I was about to punch him for the panties comment but stopped. "Jailbird?" I hope he didn't mean "jailbait".

He yawned. "Isn't that what they call people like you in your country? Someone who doesn't like being caged up?"

"No. A jailbird is someone who's in prison."

"Well, isn't that what you are — in prison?"

I didn't answer.

"Not that I believe Julian stole something from you," he said, "but if I help, what's in it for me?"

I tried to think of anything I would have that Tai would be interested in.

"How about a kiss?" he asked.

I froze. He smiled.

"You're too easy to torture. Hold on."

He pulled out his phone. "Hey, Barns, I'm in bit of mess, can you help me out? I loaned Prince Julian some sheet music and forgot to get it from him, but I'm already at venue and the prince is at a media conference. I'm sending someone to grab it for me. Do you mind letting her into his room?" He looked me over for a moment. "Yeah, she's wearing ripped jeans and hoodie. Real casual kind of gal. She's with me. Go ahead and let her in. I already talked to the prince about it. Thanks."

He hung up, smirking. "You're lucky I like you, jailbird."

"I really appreciate it, Tai."

I stood up to go, but Tai grabbed my hand before I got far.

"I wasn't joking about the kiss, you know."

He stood, stepping in closer to me. I thought about trying that chop to the neck, but I couldn't bring myself to move. He leaned in.

Then he stopped.

"Don't worry," he said, smiling. "I'll collect later."

§

Thanks to Tai, I was able to walk into Julian's bedroom without any problems.

I don't know what I was expecting, but I wasn't expecting the sexy study kind of vibe. The room was huge, a combination of bedroom and study, the furniture dark and elegant, but simple. The wood was complemented by red-and-gold fabrics on the bed, large reading chairs, and heavy curtains. Even though it looked like it was built to shut out the world, it was warm and inviting. Incredible considering how cold Julian was.

It was going to take some time to navigate through all this, but fortunately he was at a media conference, so I had time.

I started looking through his desk. He had to have a notepad or something around here. But no matter where I looked, there weren't any pens or pads around.

Maybe he wrote in his books? I went to the bookshelf, which was smaller than I thought it would be. I paged through his books, one by one. Political science, classical literature in multiple languages, and a few random history books. I giggled at the two romance books I found, including a copy of *Pride and Prejudice*. Ironic seeing how he judged everyone automatically.

There was one book lying on its side with a vase sitting on top of it. I carefully removed the vase and took out the book, flipping it open.

It was a journal. Jackpot.

I flipped to a random page in the middle, taking one of the notes out of my pockets. I held the handwriting side by side.

Not even close. My threat letters were a little blocky. Julian had a calligraphy style of handwriting.

I folded the note with one hand and put it in my pocket, ready to close the journal and get out of the place. Until one of the lines caught my eye.

Someday we'll be free from this torture. Someday I won't have to watch my brother suffer.

I stopped … then turned back a page and started from the beginning.

Cyrus was worse this morning. He was completely drained, unable to even speak. Whether it was from exhaustion or shock, I don't know. Maybe both. He never says his true feelings, not even to us. I think Evann is the only one who knows what's inside his head these days.

Evann? Why would Evann know?

I checked the date of the entry. It was written almost ten years ago. Evann had been here that long?

I read some more.

I don't know why Cyrus talks to Evann and not us. We want to help him, but he won't let us carry any of his burdens. Stubborn idiot. I'd beat him across the face if I didn't know any better. He's already done too much … I hate that all I can do is sit and watch as my older brother closes himself off from the world. Nikos is too young to understand. All he says is, "Cyrus is broken." He's not wrong. Nikos just doesn't realize that all of us are. Someday we'll be free from this torture. Someday I won't have to watch my brother suffer.

Cyrus … what was wrong with Cyrus?

"Again?" a voice said from the other side of the door. "How is that my problem?"

Shit. Julian. Wasn't he at a press conference?

I dove under the bed.

The door opened. Julian's shoes came into view. He sat on the bed, taking them off.

"She wanders constantly," he said. "I wouldn't make a big deal of it. It's something we'll have to accept, along with her poor attitude, bad dancing skills, and questionable grammar."

I squinted.

"She's probably bored, among other things. She doesn't need to be babysat. She's a little reckless, but she's otherwise harmless. I'm not worried about her. Just let her be."

I rested my head on my hands. The arrogant Julian was standing up for me?

I heard the person at the other end of the line mumble.

Julian chuckled. "I said she didn't need to be babysat. I didn't say she was an adult, despite her age. She's like a whiny teenager. It's like raising Nikos all over again."

I gripped onto the carpet.

He hung up the phone, muttering to myself.

"Always the troublemaker," he said, snorting.

I wanted to pop out from under the bed and give him a piece of my mind, but I wasn't about to get caught. Julian already hated me, so if he caught me here …

Zip.

Suddenly, pants pooled around Julian's ankles. I stared at his bare legs, frozen.

This wasn't good.

Black shorts followed right after.

No, not shorts. Boxers.

Holy crap. I could never come out now.

He leaned down to pick them up. If he looked under the bed, I was dead.

But his face never came into view. His bare ankles circled around the bed, then padded off towards the bathroom. He shut the door. The shower water turned on.

I had never been so close to death.

When I heard the shower door shut, I ran out as fast as I could. And I kept running. All the way back to my room.

Where Evann was waiting.

He stood outside my door, leaning against the wall. When I reached him, he cocked his head to the side.

"Another run?" he asked.

I swallowed, nodding.

"I was worried," he said. "You could at least let someone know before you wander about, Princess. If anything were to happen to you—"

"Do I have to let you know what I'm doing all the time?" I retorted, trying to catch my breath. "It's bad enough I can't leave. Can't I go for a run without someone trying to keep tags on me?"

He ran his tongue against his bottom lip, not looking at me. He then formally bowed, making my stomach sink. I hated it when he bowed to me like that.

"My mistake, Your Highness. Please, do as you wish."

He turned to walk away.

"Wait, Evann," I said. "I'm sorry. I didn't mean to snap at you. You're just doing your job."

He turned his head over his shoulder. His lip twitched to the side. "Right. My job."

"How long have you been at the castle?" I asked.

"As a guard?"

"As a person."

He chuckled. "I've been here since I was seven."

"Seven!" I replied.

He nodded. "I suppose it's been over — what? — twenty years now? Eesh, I've gotten old."

"Why so long?"

"My aunt was a castle nurse. Through a recommendation, she got my father a job as a guard. He fulfilled his duties until the day he died. Now, I continue his work."

"What about your mother?" I asked.

"I never met her," he replied. "Don't look so sad. I was never without. It's alright."

His smile was warm, but a little hollow.

"So, you know everything about this place, don't you?" I asked.

"I do. More than I should ever know." His eyes fell to the ground. He smiled. "I also know the best shoes for going for a run in. Maybe I should get you a pair."

I looked down at my feet. I was wearing flip flops.

There was a glimmer in his eyes as he bowed again.

"I'll leave you to your rest, Princess."

11

SHOW ME YOURS

"I can't figure out this closet thing," I said. "Show me yours."

Nikos raised an eyebrow.

If I could use anyone's vanity against him, it was Nikos. I just needed a few minutes in his room. He had to have some handwriting samples somewhere. I wasn't going to risk trying to sneak into his room like I did with Julian. I was still trying to scrub the image of Julian's bare ankles out of my memory.

"I want to see how you organize everything," I added.

"I can send you a picture," he said.

"Ahh …" I mumbled, trying to think of an excuse. "A picture doesn't provide an explanation. Why don't you show me?"

He leaned forward, grinning with his teeth. "Is my room the only thing you want to see, Princess?"

I shoved him away. "Stop being a pervert. Just show me your stupid closet."

He rubbed his temple dramatically. "I've had hundreds of women beg to see my room. I guess it is time to grant one lucky girl her wish."

"Define the word *lucky* for me," I said. "I think it might mean something different in this country."

Putting his hands in his pockets, he led the way, somehow concluding that my hearing about his daily routine would be beneficial to me. Early morning exercises, a shower, skincare routines, dressing routines, breakfast, then media reviews.

"You do all of that before noon?" I asked.

"It's all I do here," he replied. "I'm the face of Aujina. This face and body always have to look their best. I think I've done pretty well, don't you?"

He leaned in again. I shoved him away. He laughed.

He stepped in front of his door, turning to face me with one hand behind him on the handle.

"Are you ready to see something only a handful of women have had the pleasure of seeing in their lives?"

"How many of that handful were paid?" I asked.

He pursed his lips and opened the door.

It was pretty much what I expected it to be. A bright, sleek bedroom, with a modern Western design. It looked nothing like the rest of the castle. Instead of red and gold like Julian's bedroom, Nikos's color scheme was purple and silver. He had ivory furniture instead of wood, and his entire floor was like polished marble. That would explain why it was so chilly.

"What do you think?" he asked. "Only the best fabrics and wares from the best places."

"Are you warm enough in here?" I asked without thinking.

A strange look crossed his face, a mix of confusion and surprise. He shook it off. "Of all the stupid questions ... Let's go see the closet, hmm?"

He took me to his closet and started showing me around. It was massive — the size of my entire house back in California. He went into detail about his organizing techniques until my mind went numb and I almost forgot why I'd come here in the first place.

I tried to look interested while looking around the room for something with his handwriting on it. After half-listening to him going on about skincare and fabric combinations for God knows how long, I still hadn't found anything.

Someone knocked on the door. Nikos checked his watch, then opened the door.

"Juniper," he said casually. "On time as always. Come in, please."

She shuffled in, eyebrows rising when she saw me. I waved.

"I was giving Marina a tour of my room," Nikos explained. "It seems the girl is lost without me."

Girl. As if I wasn't almost five years older than him.

"I can tell she's been taking your advice," he continued, still talking to Juniper. "Her fashion sense has improved a bit. Has she been doing her regular skin-care routine?"

Before I could answer for myself, his hand came to my face, the back of his fingers stroking my cheek. His fingers were warm and soft, and his touch was the same.

He looked over my face for a moment, then paused to look into my eyes.

I clenched my teeth.

I knew what he was doing … but the look in his eyes was throwing off my equilibrium.

"As far as I know, she's been doing everything you suggested," Juniper replied.

He cleared his throat, pulling his hand away. "Yes, it seems so. It's nice to be a positive influence on someone."

"I'm not doing it for you," I said. "Juniper's more helpful than you are."

Juniper smiled and bowed. "I'm honored."

"Do you have to take care of Nikos every day?" I asked her.

"I assist with all the royal family," she said.

The neurotic Cyrus, the egotistical Julian, and the narcissistic Nikos? God, whatever this girl was getting paid, she needed a raise.

Nikos cleared his throat again and grabbed my hand.

"I won't be needing your assistance today, Juniper. I already have other plans." He turned to me and smiled. "I have a date with Marina."

12

SPEED DATE

"You own a lake?"

The castle grounds were large, but I didn't realize how large until I saw the private lake.

"We own a few things around here," Nikos said, shrugging.

Sure. A forest. A vineyard. A lake. Area 51 and Disneyland were probably around here somewhere too.

"Why are we here again?" I asked.

"So you can tell me what you found out about Juniper."

I raised an eyebrow. "Who said I found out anything?"

"I think you know more than you say you know," he replied. "Just humor me. Also, you need training."

"Training for what?"

"You'll see."

He held out his hand. I looked down at it, then back up to him.

"Let's take the boat out," he said.

I looked at the lake. There was a speed boat docked on the water. I shuddered.

"Umm …"

"Come on. Let's go. It'll be fun."

Before I could speak, Nikos grabbed my hand and dragged me to the boat. He hopped down from the dock onto the boat, then turned and held out his hand for me to join him. I swallowed, gripping onto the post.

"Do we have to do this?" I asked. "Can't we do the training on land?"

He frowned. "Get in the boat."

"Not interested."

"Look, you don't have to fight so hard against your feelings."

"Excuse me?"

"I understand my charm. You don't have to be nervous around me."

"I'm not nervous," I said honestly. "I genuinely don't like you."

His eyes darkened for a moment before he jumped up and grabbed my shirt, pulling me down. I screamed, landing on top of him. He caught me but dropped me on the boat floor.

"All this trouble and I haven't even started the boat yet. Stop whining."

He went to the front and turned it on.

"Don't we have life vests?" I asked.

He smiled and shook his head. "We don't need those. Not unless you can't swim or something."

I opened my mouth, but before I could say anything, Nikos hit the gas. I gripped the seat. He sped until he reached the middle of the lake, talking about his latest accomplishments, like talking with the royal family in the UK, a gala for mental health awareness, a movie premiere with VIP treatment.

He asked me about any goals I had, but I wasn't interested in telling him. If I told him I wanted to be a karate instructor, he would have laughed me off the boat.

We reached the middle of the lake, and he shut off the motor. I was still gripping the chair as he stood to go to the back.

"Let's get started with our lesson," he said.

He lifted the seat and pulled out a picnic basket, wine glasses, and a bottle of champagne. He popped the cork and poured me a glass. I stood up, keeping low to the boat, and walked over to the bench next to him.

"Is the lesson on how to get drunk on a boat?"

"Nope. I'm saving that for your final."

He caught my scowl.

"I'm kidding," he said, handing me the glass. "My job is to teach you about social customs. As a princess, you'll have a lot of scenarios where you'll be drinking with someone you don't really know. So …"

He poured himself a glass and raised it to mine. The glasses clinked.

"Are you even old enough to drink?" I asked, half-teasing.

He pursed his lips as he swallowed the champagne. "You know, if you're trying to get on my good side, it's not working."

"I don't want to be on any of your sides."

"I'm not sure how you'll succeed as a princess with this kind of attitude."

"Who said I wanted to succeed?"

I raised my eyebrows at him. He scanned my face.

"So you're tossing away the opportunity? That easily?"

I didn't respond.

"You're going to pout?" he asked. "Because you're not getting your way about things?"

"Not getting my way?" I spat back. "I was lied to for my entire life and now my dad wants me to become a princess in a matter of months? To do what? I can't run a country. I just want to go back home and get a decent job. I don't want all this."

"Idiot," he muttered. "You have something that's solely yours. No one can take it from you. No one can put you in the back of the line. And you whine because you suddenly have too much?"

I glanced at him for a moment but looked away. What did he understand anyways?

"If you think it's so interesting, why don't you take my throne then?"

He laughed. "I suppose I could. I have the charm for it."

"Like the snake in the Garden of Eden," I replied.

He raised his glass as if I had complimented him. "Welcome to nobility. You'll need some kind of edge yourself. For example, I have a knack for knowing what people like. Especially women." He brought his glass to his lips. "That's why I'm so popular."

I scoffed. "Juniper rejected you pretty hard."

His face fell. "I told you not to talk about that."

"No, you told me not to tell anyone. There's no one else here."

He poured himself another glass, pretending not to be affected. The vein in his neck said otherwise.

"She didn't reject me. She just—" He stared hard into his drink. "She just loves someone else."

I tried not to laugh at him. "Someone else? Someone you can't compete with?"

He stared me dead in the eyes. "Right. Someone I can't compete with."

His tone was so grave I thought it would bury me. Even with his young face, I felt intimidated.

"Forget it," he said, knocking back his drink. "Let's go back to shore. I'm tired of talking to such a spoiled and whiny princess."

He jumped from his seat, leaving his glass behind and going to the front. I stood and picked up his glass along with mine, looking at his back as he turned the key.

This kid was so sensitive about things. I didn't mean—

He hit the gas pedal, and I went straight over the side.

13

RESCUED

The cold water rushed into all my senses as I went under.

I tried to stay calm but found myself flailing to get to the surface. As my head broke through, I gasped for air. The boat sped off ahead, right before I went under again.

Why hadn't I told him that I couldn't swim?

I spent a few moments bobbing up and down in the water, trying to kick my feet in the right way to keep my head above the surface. I could do that much.

I wanted to cry.

It wasn't long before the sound of the boat's motor amplified. I realized the boat was turning, that it was coming back towards me. Then I went under for the third time. There was a splash, and next thing I knew, I was in someone's arms.

"You all right?" Nikos asked. "What the hell was that for? You scared me to death!"

His hands wrapped around my waist as he held me above water. He used one hand to wipe the water out of my face. "You wanted to go for a swim that badly?"

I gripped onto his shoulders, the wet fabric of his shirt under my fingers. "I can't swim, Nikos."

"What?" His grip around my waist tightened. "Why didn't you say something? That's something you mention *before* you get on a boat, idiot."

He held me and swam to the boat ladder, letting me up first.

My jeans sloshed as I stepped onto the boat. He pulled a towel out from underneath one of the seats, wrapping me up in it. He wrung out his shirt and shorts, grunting at me. The wet fabric clung to his skin, showing off the shadows of his muscles. He definitely worked out.

He sighed. "All this time and no one taught you how to swim? Sheesh. Didn't you have to swim in your physical education classes?"

He grabbed my hand and pulled me up to the front seat.

"Don't go out of my sight this time," he said.

His hand lingered for a moment on mine before he turned the key over. The drive back was slower this time. I hated that he knew my secret, but he did come back and jump in after me. Maybe he wasn't so bad after all.

Once we reached the dock, he held out his hand and brought me up to dry land.

"Next time," he said, hand on my shoulder, "we use the life jackets."

I couldn't help but smile. He smiled back. Sincerely.

"You really are an idiot," he chuckled.

He stopped, cocking his head to the side.

Cyrus was on the docks and taking careful steps towards us, almost tiptoeing.

"Cyrus?" Nikos called to him. "You came down? To the lake?"

Cyrus looked at the lake, swallowed, then looked at us. "It is my castle, after all." He turned to me. "My dear, I came to officially invite you to — good grief, why are you wet? Was this Nikos's doing? Nikos!"

Nikos threw his hands up. "It wasn't my fault this time!"

"You expect me to believe that?"

Nikos pointed his finger at me. "Tell him that I had nothing to do with this!"

I pursed my lips. "Well, you did hit the gas pretty hard …"

He growled at me.

"Let me escort you back to your room, my dear," Cyrus said, stepping forward and taking my hand. "We can't have the guest of honor looking like a damp swan."

"Guest of honor?" I asked. "Who? Me?"

"Yes," Cyrus said, beaming. "Tonight, I'm throwing you a party."

§

"Don't scratch at the lace," Juniper told me again.

I couldn't help it. It was itchy. You would think with all the money that they poured into royal gowns that they could afford some fabric softener.

At least the dress was nice. Rose-petal pink was a decent color on me, and the white lace was well done.

But Julian had picked it, which made me hate it for obvious reasons. Nikos approved it, which made it worse, so Juniper spent the better part of twenty minutes trying to convince me to put it on.

"I don't feel like myself," I complained, frowning at my reflection in the mirror.

Juniper smiled. "Are you unable to be yourself in this dress? I made sure that you could still do a decent roundhouse kick. I heard that was your condition."

I stepped back and did a roundhouse for good measure.

"Oh! The roundhouse looks cool with the dress layers like this!" I admitted.

Juniper smiled.

"You're a good person," I said.

I was starting to get why Nikos liked her so much. I already understood why she didn't like him at all.

Although … I had to admit, he was pretty quick to come to my rescue when I fell off the boat. Deep, deep, *deep* down, he might be an attentive sort of guy.

"Clothes don't make you," Juniper said. "Clothes express who you already are. Many people confuse that. Just like makeup doesn't make you beautiful. It enhances the beauty you already have."

She pulled out a hair curler as I sat in front of the mirror.

"You have a deep philosophy when it comes to style," I commented.

"I've had a passion for it for a long time," she admitted. "What are you passionate about, Marina?"

I tried to smile as she tapped the curler against her hand. "My students."

"Students? Are you a teacher?"

"Assistant," I replied. "Just an assistant. I was training to become an official instructor, but … plans changed a bit."

"You have plenty of time to still become a teacher, right?"

I sighed. "I don't know. I'm starting to think I'll never see my students again."

She draped my hair between her fingers, curling my normally straight locks into long, soft curls.

"I used to teach beauty and makeup in a little studio downtown," she said, continuing her work. "My teacher got me this job, and I didn't want to leave my students, same as you. My professor looked me in the eyes — as kindly as he always did — and said, 'Your students are thriving because of you, but there are new students that need you now.' Maybe it's the same for you, too."

The weight of my heart sank slowly into my stomach with each new curl.

After my hair and makeup were finished, Evann came to fetch me. He knocked on the door. His eyes widened as he saw me, and he paused to look around the room.

"I think I have the wrong room," he said.

I laughed. "Is it that bad?"

He brought his eyes back to mine. "No. It's that *good*."

"Are you saying you like me in a dress more than jeans?" I teased, putting my hands on my hips.

"Can't I like both?" he asked. "Come. Their highnesses are waiting for you in the courtyard."

Thanking Juniper again, I allowed Evann to escort me down to the courtyard. There were various potted plants scattered against the walls, and a shallow pool in the middle. At one end was a long table with cushions on the ground. The three brothers were sitting together, talking and laughing as the castle staff brought wine and bread to the table.

They looked so peaceful, with none of the conflicted lines I was used to seeing in their faces. Maybe if I had caused less trouble for them, I could laugh with them.

Whatever. I wasn't going to stay long anyways.

"You're here!" Cyrus said, jumping up from his seat. He trotted over to us, taking both my hands in his. "You look lovely, my dear," he said, drawing in a breath. "Like a real princess."

"What was I before?"

"A real pain in the ass," Nikos muttered.

"I heard that!"

Cyrus cleared his throat. "Come join us."

Cyrus led me to the cushions and sat me between him and Nikos. Julian looked me over, not mentioning anything about the dress. All he gave was a simple nod. Considering it was his fault I was wearing it, and all the work Juniper had put into me, you would think he would at least say something out loud. Nikos played with his phone, as usual. Probably texting his thousands of girlfriends.

"What is this party for again?" I asked.

"For you," Cyrus said.

"No, seriously."

He chuckled. "It's a traditional celebration for our country. You'll see these quite often. I'd like you to feel more comfortable with them."

He gave a warm smile. Julian tutted.

"I doubt she'll ever be truly accustomed to our ways," he replied.

I stuck my tongue out at him. He rolled his eyes.

"So childish."

Nikos tapped away at his phone. I leaned over his shoulder to see what he was typing. He pulled it away before I could see it.

"Mind your own," he said, putting the phone in his pocket.

"Since when do you refuse to show off?"

"You're not worth showing off to," he threw back.

I snorted.

Cyrus sighed next to me. "If we get through this dinner, it'll be a miracle."

First was a large set of hors d'oeuvres, breads, cheeses, and fruit, all famous to the country. Nothing could beat the farmers' markets down in California, but I had to admit that the strawberries here had a great tart flavor and the bright-red grapes were crisp and sweet.

There were musicians as we ate. The first group played a jazzy tune as Cyrus explained the agriculture of the country to me. I wasn't the type of person to talk about farming all day, but Cyrus had a passionate interest in it that was entertaining enough for me to want to.

"The grapes are my favorite," he said. "That's why we have so many vineyards. I actually don't drink that much wine. The flavor is too processed for me. But ripe grapes on the vine are the purest form of nature. Sweet, exciting, and satisfying."

He popped one in his mouth for emphasis, chewing like a happy chipmunk.

"Are we talking about grapes or women?" Nikos asked.

Cyrus picked up a grape and chucked it at his brother's head. "Don't twist my words."

Nikos opened his mouth to say something but stopped. His playful demeanor darkened. "Just when I was getting comfortable."

Tai came to the center of the entertainment floor, a violin over his shoulder like it was an umbrella. He was wearing black dress pants with a white long-sleeved shirt. I loved that kind of style. Simple, but elegant. Most men looked good in it, and Tai was no exception.

"Tai," Julian said. "It's good that you could make it. On time."

"I never miss a party," Tai replied, smirking.

"You never miss a paycheck," Nikos muttered.

Tai bowed to each one of the princes, then to me. He winked at me as he straightened.

"Your Majesty, Your Royal Highnesses, ladies and gentlemen, boys and girls, and the stray cat that roams around here late at night," he said, bowing once more. "I'm honored to play for you this evening."

Cyrus nodded to him. "You always have wonderful music, Tai. Please."

Tai pulled his lips back to a half-smirk, swinging the bow up to his violin. "It's a little short notice, but at His Highness's, Prince Julian's request, I will play some of your classics."

There was a moment of awkward tuning, then a dramatic pause as Tai swung his bow over and around his head. It reminded me of some katas my uncle taught me with a bo staff.

The bow slid against the violin, and the most delicate notes poured out of it. Two other musicians sat next to him, one on a flute, the other on a type of guitar. Between the three of them, I fell harder and harder into the notes.

Tai's eyes closed tight, loosening at the high notes, and crashing tighter together with the low notes. His fingers vibrated against the strings, as if he had forgotten all about us.

I could have watched him play like that forever.

Nikos cleared his throat. "You want a napkin for your drool?"

I frowned at him. "I'm not drooling."

"At least she has some taste in music," Julian said, not looking at us.

Nikos held his glass up to the server as she came to fill his glass with wine. "You don't stare that hard at music notes."

Cyrus shifted in his chair, reaching for his drink.

I lifted my glass to the server as well. "How would you know? The only thing you stare into is your front-view camera."

Cyrus snorted into his glass.

Another line of servers came out, each one with a bowl.

"Our famous fisheye soup," Cyrus commented, dabbing at his mouth with a napkin. "It's a little different from what you're used to, I suppose, but I hope you like it."

They placed the dish in front of me.

There was definitely a fish's eye. It was looking right at me.

The song ended and everyone clapped. I did the same, tearing my eyes away from my eye soup to look up at Tai. He smiled and bowed. Something about his smile was glowing as he stood on stage.

"He plays very well," I said to Cyrus.

"Yes, he's excellent," Cyrus agreed. "He certainly fits in here."

"You're welcome," Julian said with a self-satisfied smile.

Cyrus chuckled at his brother, then leaned back over to me. "Julian was the one who recommended him."

"I found him playing on the street and knew immediately that he had an ear for traditional music," Julian said. "We've lost a lot of our traditional sound over the years. I think if anyone can put the spotlight back on our tradition, it's Tai."

Nikos slurped his soup. "Since when do thieves put things back?"

Cyrus and Julian snapped their heads at him. He casually slurped down more of his soup.

"No one is defined by his past, Nikos," Cyrus said gently. "Remember that."

Nikos popped the fisheye in his mouth. I gagged a little. "It's not the past I'm worried about," he replied.

"Are you enjoying yourself?" Cyrus asked me.

I nodded. "Yes. Everything is nice, thank you."

"You haven't touched your soup," he observed.

I scratched my neck. "I'm having a hard time eating it."

"Why?"

"It's staring at me."

He laughed. "It's just appreciating how pretty you are."

I frowned at him. He only laughed harder.

He took the bowl from me and switched it with his. Nothing was floating in this one.

"Thank you," I whispered.

"No problem," he replied.

I expected the soup to have a strong fish flavor, but it was primarily flavored with pureed squash. It was pretty decent, to be honest.

I wondered if I could get it back home.

… Wherever that was now.

We finished the soup, and then Tai approached the table.

"I have one more song to play for you all," he announced. "Then I'm all out of classics."

"Can you play Ed Sheeran?" I teased.

"Is there a good musician who can't play Ed Sheeran?" he replied.

"Don't make me answer that," Julian warned.

"Let me grace you with the last song of the evening," Tai said. "It has been my pleasure."

He gave me a lingering glance before turning on his heel and playing once more. This tune was a lot happier, more like a folk song.

"A traditional dancing tune," Cyrus said, taking off his jacket. "Would you like to try?"

"Try what?"

He stood, reaching out for both my hands. "Dancing."

Julian raised an eyebrow. "Good luck with that."

"It's my subtle way of making sure you're doing your job, Julian," Cyrus said over his shoulder.

Cyrus pulled me out onto the dance floor, taking me into a dancing stance. His stance was a little weaker than Julian's, but his grip was strong. His shoulders were pulled back, as were his lips.

"Don't be nervous," he said. "It's only a small group this time."

"What do you mean *this* time?"

He coughed over his shoulder, half-laughing. "The crowd grows with time."

"I'm not sure I want that."

"You have plenty of time to decide. Don't worry about that now. Just dance with me."

He led and I did my best to follow. Despite my breaking the flow a few times and feeling obliged to apologize, Cyrus never looked remotely annoyed with me. He just smiled warmly and took my hands back up, teaching me to sway with the music.

At one point, he grabbed my waist. I jumped.

"Easy," he said. "Follow me. You can do this."

I felt my shoulders drop. "Thank you, Cyrus."

"For what?" he asked, coughing over his shoulder again. "I can do more than play chess, you know."

"Not for the dancing," I replied. "I actually don't appreciate that whatsoever. But I do appreciate your helping me. You've been kind to me, despite the circumstances."

"The circumstances weren't up to you," he replied. "I know this. You know, my brothers and I always talked about what it would be like if we had grown up as regular citizens instead of princes. The fantasy always seemed so impossible to us."

"Most people have it the other way around," I said. "They fantasize about being royalty."

"Yes, I realize that now," he said. "I guess we all want to grow up with another life."

I hadn't thought of it that way. He made it sound terrible. To be honest, it wasn't that bad. I enjoyed my time in high school and college, and I had no real complaints about my childhood, other than some terrible teachers in middle school.

But I hated that Dad had lied to me. If I had to choose one or the other, it would have been any life where I could trust my parents completely.

But now …

Cyrus came to a standstill and grabbed my shoulders. "I think we've been spinning for too long. I'm getting dizzy."

"We were spinning?" I asked.

I noticed his forehead was sticky with sweat. Unless he was grossly out of shape, that couldn't be from a single dance.

"Cyrus, are you alright?" I asked, grabbing his elbows.

He nodded but leaned harder against me. "I'm fine. I think I only need to si—"

He started coughing again, this time violently. He grabbed his chest right before collapsing to the floor.

14

POISONED

"What do you mean *poisoned?*"

"They found poison in his bloodstream," Tai said.

I was sitting outside Cyrus's room with Tai and Evann. Tai sat next to me on the bench while Evann stood next to us, staring at the door. Julian and Nikos were inside with Cyrus, speaking with the doctors and nurses.

"But who would … why would they …?"

Tai patted my hand. "He'll be alright."

I shook a little. "Will he?"

Julian came out first. He opened his mouth to speak but paused, his eyes dropping to Tai and my hands. I broke my hand from his.

"Is he all right?" Evann asked.

Julian nodded. "They gave him the antidote. He'll recover, but he's pretty loopy." He turned to me. "He's asking for you."

"Me?"

Julian nodded, gesturing to the door. I stood and went in, passing Nikos on the way. He was biting down hard on his lip and vigorously rubbing the nape of his neck. The playboy prince had disappeared, replaced with a gloomy youngest brother.

He didn't even look at me as he walked out the door.

The door shut behind me. Cyrus's bedroom was rather plain for being the bedroom of a king. It was still lavish — gold, green, and white tapestries; a massive walk-in closet; a collection of books — but it was oddly empty.

I approached the large bed on the side of the room. There were some books and a line of medications on the bedside table. Cyrus lay in bed, his eyes closed and face pale. I couldn't help but put a hand to his forehead. He stirred, looking at me through half-open eyelids.

"It's the pretty lady," he murmured.

His words were all slurred together. He grabbed my hand and held it to his face.

"Keep it there," he said. "It feels nice."

All the blood rushed to my face. "Uh … Cyrus …? Julian said you wanted to see me?"

He drew in a sharp breath like he'd just remembered something. "Yes! Yes, I did. I had something important to say to you."

"What is it?"

He looked at me with his big eyes and smiled. He then burst into a fit of high-pitched giggles. "It's a secret."

"So … you have to tell me something important, but it's a secret?"

He nodded.

"Can you give me a hint?"

He motioned to me to lean closer. He brought his lips up to my ear.

"It has to do with … elephants."

I raised an eyebrow. "Elephants?"

"Yes," he said, nodding enthusiastically. "I never learned how to wash one properly."

"O… k… Cyrus, I think I should probably let you rest …"

I took a small step back, but he grabbed my hand and pulled me to him. His hand held mine, warm and soft.

"Stay for a minute," he said, almost whispering. "Just one."

When he looked me in the eyes, I couldn't resist. I sat next to him on the bed, aware of the way his hand was caressing mine.

"It's nice having a woman here," he said. "It feels warmer, somehow."

I smiled. Even though he was drugged out of his mind, his compliment felt genuine.

"Do you miss your family?" he asked.

I rolled my eyes. "Why would I miss them? They lied to me. I'm furious."

He snorted. "Yes. You probably should be. They kept a lot from you."

I hummed in agreement.

"But I'm glad you came," he said. "I'm glad we met. There's new life in the castle. We've been breathing the same stale air for so many years. You're changing the quality of it."

His eyes were shining as they looked at me. I blushed, smiling.

I patted his hand. "I'm glad we met too."

He shut his eyes, leaning back against his pillows, taking a deep breath. What was it like for him? To run a country alone?

I would have the same fate, wouldn't I?

If I chose to be a princess, I would have to run my parents' kingdom, right? I wasn't even sure where it was. What would my life look like? Could I even run a country?

But then again, if I went back to my old life, I wouldn't see Cyrus again. I wouldn't see Evann, Tai, or even Nikos and Julian again, would I?

It wasn't long before Cyrus fell asleep. I stayed with him for a little while, watching him inhale and exhale. I wondered if he would be mad that his REM cycles would be messed up for a while. Poison didn't care about schedules.

But poison though? Something so drastic? Who would poison him? Who in the castle could even possibly dislike Cyrus, or threaten—

Oh God.

I jumped from the bed and ran to the door to open it. Evann's eyebrows crashed together.

"Princess, what's wrong?"

I tried not to cry as I spoke. "Evann … what had poison in it? We all had the appetizers. We're all fine."

"The soup is our guess," Evann said. "It must have been added to Cyrus's bowl specifically."

I felt the blood drain from my face.

"Evann… I-I need to tell you something."

§

Back in my room, I showed Evann the letters.

"When did you start getting these?" Evann asked.

"The day I got here."

Evann sat on my bed, reading them over and over. "And you didn't say anything?"

"I thought it was a prank! I thought it was a prank and if I couldn't handle it myself, Cyrus would tell my father, and … Evann, it's all my fault."

I covered my face, trying not to shake. His hands caressed mine, then pulled my hands away from my face.

"It's not your fault, Princess. Stop torturing yourself."

"Cyrus …" I said, heart pounding in my throat. "Cyrus switched bowls with me at the beginning of dinner."

Evann jerked his head back. "That means—"

"—the poison was for me."

Evann grabbed me. I didn't even know I was falling over. He sat me down as my head spun.

Someone had tried to poison me. Someone had *actually* tried to poison me. This wasn't a game. Someone wasn't messing around. Someone was trying to harm me.

Who hated me that much?

He wrapped his arms around me, pulling me into a strong hug. I tried not to cry, but I felt so guilty that I didn't know what else to do.

"Why didn't you tell me sooner?" he whispered. "It's my job to protect you, you know."

"Maybe I thought if I ignored it, it would go away," I said in a small voice.

"When you're royalty, you won't be able to avoid things like this. When it happens again, you need to come to me immediately. Understand?"

I nodded against his chest. He sighed. He broke the hug, looking back over the notes.

"Just when I thought these kinds of things were over with," he muttered. "It looks like you don't have the option to go back now."

"What do you mean?" I asked.

"Someone knows you're royalty and isn't happy about it. Which means you may not have the option to go back to your old life or accept a new one. They want you gone, Princess. For good."

15

FALLING

"Do we have to do this?" Nikos asked.

He leaned his face against his hand while his legs swung over the garden bench.

Evann's face was pure stone. "You know that if we cancel, it will raise suspicion."

Nikos sighed.

The castle staff hurried to decorate the castle gardens as if Cyrus's poisoning hadn't happened. Nikos didn't act the same. He was incredibly mopey, even while planning his own birthday celebration.

"We can't allow the media in this year," Evann continued. "They'll snoop around. But that won't affect the rest of the guest list."

Nikos shrugged with one shoulder. "Whatever."

He stood and left us, hands in his pockets.

"He's taking this hard," Evann commented.

"Aren't you?"

His lips pulled back a little. "I'm not allowed to lose my head. As a guard, my job is to protect them. I can't get emotionally involved."

I cocked my head to the side. I knew he was older than Cyrus, but he was starting to look it now.

"I think you're emotionally involved," I said. "Or else you wouldn't have watched them for so long. How's Cyrus?"

"He's getting better." He raised an eyebrow. "You ask me that at least four or five times a day. He won't get better any faster, no matter how many times you ask."

He smiled. I tried to smile as well.

"You are worried about him," he observed.

I watched as Nikos became nothing but a small dot in the distance.

"I'm starting to worry about all of them," I replied.

§

Evann was pulled away to help with security for the evening, and I opted to stay in the gardens. I walked around, through the vineyards, the rose gardens, and back to the main courtyard.

"You do it," a voice said.

"No, you."

"I don't like ladders."

"I hate heights too."

A boy and girl argued while holding a paper lantern, shoving it back and forth between the two of them.

"Let's go find Gerald then. He'll do it."

They dropped the lantern and walked off.

I wondered if they were siblings like Nikos and Julian.

I felt bad for Nikos. Seeing him so broken and defeated was depressing. He was supposed to be obnoxiously confident and charming. Not sulking. Not on his birthday.

Lanterns wouldn't be hard to put up, right?

I picked up the lantern in one hand and made my way up the ladder. The hook wasn't high, but the ladder creaked under me. I should have had a spotter. Oh well. I was halfway there. Might as well finish what I set out to do.

I hooked the lantern on the post.

"What do you think you're doing?"

I grabbed onto the ladder, startled, and looked down to Julian's impeccable frown.

"Do you mind not scaring the girl on the ladder?" I asked.

"Do you mind not being so reckless?" he returned. "A princess shouldn't be climbing ladders. Come down before you hurt yourself."

"Are you concerned?" I teased.

"Yes," he returned. "I don't want anyone blaming me for your clumsiness."

I snorted and started to make my way down the ladder. "I'm not cl—"

Before I could finish, my foot slipped. I felt weightless for a moment, then I hit the ground.

It was softer than I thought it would be.

Then I heard Julian groan.

"If anything is broken," he said, "I'm suing you."

I rolled off him. "Julian! Are you okay?"

"What did I say about being clumsy?"

I stood and tried to offer him a hand to stand up, but he didn't see it. He grabbed onto the ladder to hoist himself up, holding onto his leg at the same time. His face was twisted in pain.

"What's wrong?" I asked.

He rubbed his knee. "Nothing."

He put his leg on the ground and began to walk, only to hiss through his teeth and grab his leg again.

"Are you hurt?" I asked, stepping forward.

He waved me away. "I'm fine."

"No, you're not," I replied, watching him limp.

Before he could protest, I flung his arm over my shoulder and helped him walk to a nearby chair.

"I'll get some ice," I said.

He held an arm out in front of me. "You don't need to be concerned about me."

"I can be concerned about you if I want to be. So, sit down and shut up."

I ran full speed to the kitchen to make a bag of ice.

One brother poisoned. One injured. One depressed. One big happy royal family.

How was I even helping?

I made a bag of ice and sprinted back to where Julian was still sitting. I was surprised he hadn't hobbled off in defiance.

He raised an eyebrow at the bag of ice in my hand. "That's highly unnecessary."

"I'll decide what's unnecessary."

I leaned over and placed the ice pack on his knee.

"Maybe we can tie it to your leg?" I mumbled to myself.

Julian didn't say anything as I grabbed one of the long silk napkins off the table and started to tie it around his leg. It kept slipping.

My hair fell into my face, so I tried to flip it out of my line of sight. I didn't want to break the momentum. But no matter how I tried to maneuver my head, my hair kept getting in the way.

"Being stubborn again?" Julian asked.

Two hands ran through my hair and pulled it back, moving it over to the side of my neck. I froze, stunned. Julian leaned back, crossing his arms and looking off to the side as if nothing had happened.

The ghost of his fingertips still lingered in my hair. His touch was so soft. Who was he, really?

His knee hit my chin, the ice crunching against it. "Finish what you started."

He pressed his lips together, holding back a smile.

A real smile.

He had a real smile somewhere.

"Are you alright, Prince Julian?"

Juniper approached us, holding bouquets of flowers in her arms. Her hair was braided back, showing her soft face, full of concerned creases.

Julian straightened in his chair. "Y-yes, I'm quite alright. Thank you."

There was a pause. She glanced at me, then at my hands on his knee.

"Please let me know if I can assist in any way," she said, bowing before she walked off.

Julian watched her leave, his mouth open as if to say something. He didn't.

I looked at Julian. "What was—"

"There you are."

Evann approached us. He stopped when he saw the ice pack around Julian's knee. He raised an eyebrow at me.

"Did you kick him again?"

"This time she fell on me," Julian said flatly. "Evann, prepare some padding I can wear when I'm around this girl."

"Oh, now you find your voice. Ten seconds ago, you couldn't even speak."

Julian's hand clamped over my mouth. His eyes flared open. He jerked his hand back, then stood, unwrapping the makeshift ice pack I had spent so much time putting together and shoving it into Evann's chest.

"Make sure she comes to her lesson on time," he said.

He limped away.

I stood to go after him, but Evann put his hands on my shoulders. "Let him be."

"He really hates me, doesn't he?" I asked. "Nikos hates me too."

"Nikos hates sharing the spotlight, and Julian hates everything," Evann said. "There are people that will dislike you no matter what, Princess. That doesn't mean you're not likable."

I dropped my head. "I don't know if I can handle it."

He nodded. "Keep doing your best and see where it takes you."

"You sound like my dad."

"He has said some wise things."

"What part of his wisdom is the part that told him to lie to me?"

Evann gave me a hollow smile. "All I can tell you is that there's no way to change the circumstances. What you do in these circumstances is up to you."

I rubbed my face. "Why do you always sound like a fortune cookie?"

"I'll take that as a compliment." There was a long pause. "Have you received any more threats?"

I shook my head. "Only the ones I showed you. Did you find anything?'

"Not yet. I'm waiting for a response from a contact."

"You have a contact?"

"Everyone has a contact. Don't worry. I'll find out what's happening."

I looked up at the castle, towards Cyrus's bedroom window. I had threats. He was poisoned. How could I even speak to him after everything?

"Have you told Cyrus?" I asked.

He shook his head. "He's not well enough yet, but the rest of the guards are aware and investigating. We'll tell him as soon as he recovers."

I nodded, stomach sinking. I didn't want to burden Cyrus anymore. I wished I could keep this to myself.

I needed to solve this problem. At the very least, to show Cyrus that I could.

16

A Book by its Cover

J ulian was waiting for me in the library. So I walked slowly.

It had been a couple of days since the ladder incident. I wasn't sure how to start a conversation with him after that, and he was never around for me to have the opportunity.

Not that I cared. I was leaving anyways.

This library was incredible though. Three stories high, with glass mezzanines and marble staircases. There was even an elevator on the side of the room. In the middle of the library were couches and two fireplaces.

When I walked in, Julian was sitting at one of the tables, nose buried in the book in front of him. He looked up over the rim of his glasses.

I had to admit, he made glasses look *really* good. Kind of reminded me of a chemistry teacher I had a crush on in high school. The only difference was my chemistry teacher had a personality.

"You're here," he said, closing his book. "Have a seat."

I sat in the chair closest to me. Which was near the door. Across the room.

Julian scowled.

"Have a seat *over here*," he corrected.

I came over and sat across from him. He stared at me, like I had something to say. Did I? I wasn't sure.

"How's your leg?" I blurted out.

He smirked, then dropped his face again. "I'm fine. Thank you."

There was a moment of awkward silence.

"I'm supposed to teach you about international policies," he said.

"Dancing prince and networker extraordinaire?" I teased.

He pursed his lips. "I don't network, but I do have three PhDs. One in politics, one in literature, and one in psychology."

"Have you figured out why you're an antisocial mess then?"

"It's not *anti*social. It's *a*social. And that's the pot calling the kettle black."

"Me? How am I antisocial?"

"You've been nothing but trouble since you came here."

"You've treated me like a criminal since I came here."

He huffed, rubbing his face with his hands. "Let's just start the lesson, shall we?"

Boring didn't begin to describe how the afternoon went. I almost wished he was teaching me dancing instead of politics. Even though he barked while teaching dancing, at least he had a softness around the edges. In the world of politics, he was flat. Like a soggy crepe in the world of pancakes.

"Are you listening?" he asked.

I stared up at the ceiling shaking my head.

"Do you really expect to be a princess with this attitude? Is this the kind of disappointment you want to bring to your family?"

I shot a look at him. "Hey, now. I'm not the disappointment here. I never asked for any of this."

"Neither did I," he returned, "but I'm still holding up my side of the bargain."

"It doesn't matter anyways," I said. "I'm not taking the stupid job."

"Your final decision doesn't interest me," he said as if my news wasn't shock-worthy like it should have been. "It's my job to teach you, and I'll carry out my responsibilities regardless of whether or not you stick around, or whether we like each other."

Suddenly it felt like there were stones in my chest.

"I knew you'd be trouble the minute I saw your picture," he muttered.

"How did you get the picture anyw— oh! Wait!"

I opened my bag and pulled out a book. I held it out to him.

"What is it?" he asked.

"Your book. You left it in the vineyard when we first met."

"And you had it all this time?" he complained, snatching it out of my hand. "Do you hold books hostage?"

He brushed off the cover, carefully inspecting it. His concerned muttering made me laugh.

"I didn't hurt it," I said.

"I don't trust your grubby fingers."

"I read it."

He stopped, raising an eyebrow. "You read it?"

I nodded. "My dad had a copy at home. I always wanted to read it … and honestly, I couldn't stomach any more history books. It was pretty good."

He put the book down and folded his hands on top of it.

"Do tell," he said.

He asked me one question after the other, about the themes and symbolism within the book. It was much more interesting than talking about politics, so I obliged.

"I've read it six times," he admitted. "I never had anyone to talk about it with before."

"Six? It wasn't bad, but damn …"

He chuckled. "I suppose in some ways, I relate to the main character. I know why he spent so much time searching for some kind of escape."

I rested my chin on my hands. "Is that why you have ten PhDs?"

"Three," he corrected. "And … perhaps."

Someday we'll be free from this torture.

I watched him trace his fingers over the corners of the book like men did with the rims of their wine glasses or the wax job on their hot rods. Most of the time he was so rigid and closed off … but there were some moments that made me wonder who he really was.

He looked up at the clock and took a deep breath. "Come on. I'll put these books away and then I'll escort you to dinner."

"You don't want to do that," I said, surprised.

"I never said I wanted to," he replied, smirking.

Was he ... teasing me?

He picked the political textbooks up off the table and started to shelve them. I picked up the remaining few, one of them slipping from my grasp. A photograph flew out.

It was a photo of a woman. She had a bright face underneath a red sun umbrella, dressed in jeans and a light, flowy shirt. She was very pretty. I couldn't help but notice how nice her hair was—

No way.

It was Juniper.

The picture was plucked from my fingers. Julian looked down at me, his face suddenly cold.

"This," he said, holding the picture up, "is off-limits."

He dropped his book on the table next to me. The sound of it hitting the table made me jump. He put the picture in his coat pocket.

"She didn't reject me. She just ... she just loves someone else."

"Someone else? Someone you can't compete with?"

"Right. Someone I can't compete with."

Holy hell.

"Are you two together?" I asked.

He looked down at his hands for a minute, then turned away to put away another book.

"You're dating the stylist?" I asked, jumping up after him. "Does Cyrus know?"

"No, and you better keep it that way."

I couldn't tell if his tone was a plea or a threat.

"Why wouldn't you say anything? You should be honest if you really care about her."

"This is not up for discussion."

I blocked his path. "Why don't you want to talk about her? Does she embarrass you?"

His face twisted. "Of course she doesn't embarrass me, but there are certain customs—"

"I get that there are customs," I interrupted, giving a rough sigh. "There are secrets and unanswered questions everywhere around here. Would it kill anyone to be straightforward? Is honesty so freaking hard?"

His eyes fixed on me.

"Is she really that bad?" I asked. "Is she really not good enough? Do you think she can't handle being a royal like the rest of you jerks?"

"Marina …"

"Does she even have to be a royal? Can't she just be herself?"

"Shhh. That's enough," Julian commanded, closing the distance between us.

"Why does she have to accept your standards to be acknowledged?" I continued, my eyes starting to sting.

He hovered close, looking down at me. I didn't want to look at him, but for some reason, I couldn't look away. He searched my face for a long, breathless moment.

"We're not talking about *her* anymore, are we?" he asked.

My face burned and my eyes started to well up with tears. I looked down.

He put a finger under my chin and brought my face back up to meet his. "Listen, I think you should know—"

"Am I interrupting?"

Of all people, Nikos lurked in the doorway. His eyes drifted between Julian and me. Julian released my chin.

"Lesson's going well, then?" Nikos asked, walking towards us.

Julian put his hands in his pockets. "It's fine. Why are you here?"

"I live here," he snapped back. "And I've come with some good news and some even better news."

"What's the good news?" Julian asked.

"Cyrus is coherent," Nikos replied. "The poison is finally out of his system and he should fully recover soon."

I clapped in relief.

"And the better news?" Julian asked.

He looked at me. "Your dresses have come in."

I raised an eyebrow. "Dresses?"

"For my party tomorrow night," he said.

"Wait ..." I said, curling my nose. "I have to wear a dress? Like, a royal ball gown?"

He chuckled darkly. "Of course, Your Highness. My date for the evening needs to look her part."

I blinked. "Say again?"

He draped an arm across my shoulder. "I forgot the best news of all ... Tomorrow night, you're my date."

17

ORDERS

I shrugged his arm off me. "Date?"

Julian didn't say anything, despite my best pleading look.

"Of course!" Nikos said cheerfully. "It's my birthday. I get my pick of dates. And you're the lucky winner."

"Hold on, we still haven't defined *lucky*."

"We can talk about that later. The reason I came to find you was to send you up to Cyrus. He wants to see you. He doesn't sound happy, though."

My stomach sank. Cyrus was mad at me? Cyrus was never mad at me. Cyrus was never mad at anyone.

What did I do?

When I arrived, Evann was already there, hands folded behind his back. He gave me a small smile before turning back to Cyrus, who was in bed with a massive tray of food in front of him.

"Good. You're here," Cyrus said. "I'm upset."

He looked too happy munching on his sandwich to mean it.

Evann lowered his head in shame. "Forgive us, Your Majesty."

Cyrus sighed, reaching over and picking up a stack of papers and throwing them on his bed.

I cringed. The threats.

"I understand why you didn't tell me, Marina," Cyrus said, "but you're not allowed to do this again. Dismissing threats as pranks? Not coming to me when you needed help? If anyone in this castle is in danger, I should be the first to know. Understand?"

I nodded.

"I thought you'd tell my father that I couldn't handle it," I admitted. "I thought you wouldn't give me your approval."

"Since when did you truly want my approval?" His shoulders softened, his eyes falling onto the bed. "I apologize. I shouldn't have snapped at you. To be honest, I feel like I should have been the one you came to and I'm disappointed that I wasn't. Besides, Marina, I wasn't going to give you approval based on whether you could handle everything on your own. I was going to base it on only how you handled it."

I dropped my head.

"So, now," Cyrus said, sucking the mustard off his thumb. "Start from the beginning."

I explained everything. Cyrus's disappointed look was more painful than his upset one.

"I wished this hadn't happened to you so early," he said.

"What do you mean?" I asked.

"It's typical for royals to be in danger. I'm sad to say that this probably won't be the only time you're faced with this kind of situation. We'll do everything we can to keep you safe. But I need you two to be honest with me. Understand?"

We both nodded.

"Good," he said. "Now, let's talk about something a bit lighter. How is Nikos's birthday celebration coming along?"

"Almost finished," Evann said.

"Are you coming?" I asked Cyrus. I didn't want to go as Nikos's date.

He shook his head. "I'm sentenced to bed rest for another couple of days. This cure is worse than the poison."

"I'm glad there was a cure," I said. "Cyrus, it's all my fault ... Why are you smiling at me like that?"

He tried to tame the smile. "Sorry," he said. "I didn't mean to show you how happy I was."

"Happy about what? That it's my fault? That you were poisoned? That I'm losing my mind?"

He chuckled. "No, my dear. That you say my name now without stumbling over the title."

He put his dinner tray aside and propped his arm on his leg. With a long sigh, he reached his hand for mine and looked me in the eye.

"As a royal, you won't be able to take care of everything yourself," he said. "When you feel over-whelmed, come to me... I want you to come to me."

The way he dragged out his last sentence made my heart stop.

Evann cleared his throat. "Orders, Your Majesty?"

Cyrus pursed his lips, dropping my hand. "Continue on as normal. Don't let the enemy suspect that you suspect him."

Cyrus's eyes went a shade darker.

"Then …" he said, "we find the bastard and make him regret being born in my country."

18

DRESS UP

Nikos kept his word. I wished he hadn't.

Knock, knock, knock.

"Marina?"

I debated keeping the door locked. I knew as soon as I opened it that it was going to be a nightmare.

"Marina?" Juniper called again.

I hated all of this, but I couldn't leave Juniper out in the cold like that.

I cracked the door open. Juniper smiled at me.

"I hear you have a date tonight?" she teased.

I rolled my eyes. "Don't remind me."

"I'll need you to open the door wider," she said. "These clothes won't fit through this small of a slit in the door."

"What clothes?"

I opened the door wider, and Juniper charged through my door with an army of people and their coat racks. I stepped aside as they poured in. There were at least six racks filled with dresses, each one more colorful and puffier than the last.

Was this a dance or a fashion show?

"Prince Nikos requested quite a collection for you," Juniper said. "He must find you quite charming."

She nudged me. I tried not to laugh and spill the truth.

Actually, he likes you, but you're dating his brother.

God, why would Juniper date Julian of all people?

Julian and Juniper. Their names sounded good together, anyways. Not the easiest ship name though … Juliper? Junian? JuJu? Team JuJu. That would definitely make Julian annoyed. I decided to keep that one.

"Which one would you like to start with?" she asked.

None of them. I didn't want to start with any of them. I didn't like where this was leading.

But this place was full of situations without choices.

I had never tried on so many dresses. They were itchy and heavy, and I couldn't roundhouse anyone effectively in half of them.

"Can I go in jeans and a leather jacket?" I asked.

"I don't think that would have the effect you want," she replied. "That would annoy Prince Nikos."

"Who said that wasn't the effect I wanted?"

She laughed. "One moment. I think I saw the perfect dress for you."

"Was it on Rack 42?" I teased.

She shook her head and smirked. "Rack 45."

After a few minutes, a blue dress was brought into my room. It was simple — with one shoulder and a pearl cinch at the waist.

"It's silk, so it won't itch," she whispered.

I put it on. It was pretty comfortable, and it seemed to fit my body shape well. I rarely wore dresses, and I had never worn a real gown. Julian's rose-and-white dress had been flattering and classy, but this dress was elegant and mature. The other dresses on the rack had made me feel like a princess at a costume party. This one made me feel … like a real princess.

"You like it," Juniper said.

I gave a single nod. She lit up.

"Good. Now we can do your makeup and hair. Are you ready?"

I looked at my new royal self in the mirror.

"Not really," I said to myself.

She showed me a few different styles and we finally settled on a braided updo. As she braided my hair, I wanted to ask her a thousand questions about Julian. I bit my tongue. It wasn't my place. I don't know why I cared anyways.

"You look stressed," Juniper said. "Relax your face so I can put on moisturizer."

There were layers of lotions and creams, some mascara and eye shadow, and about three layers of lipstick.

"This is a lot," I said.

Juniper giggled. "Yes, but it doesn't look like a lot. That's the trick. Prince Nikos doesn't like women with a lot of makeup, but he likes red lips. I hope you don't mind."

"How do you know all that?" I asked.

"I do Prince Nikos's makeup and hair for media events. He's always talking about how men love red lipstick. He talks about it so much that I think he wants to wear it himself."

I snorted at the thought.

Thinking of him reminded me of the task he had set for me. I wanted my phone, but now, my curiosity was killing me more than anything.

"I want a guy who loves me without makeup," I said. "I go for the outdoorsy type that I can spar with."

Juniper laughed. "I wouldn't imagine it any other way."

"What about you? What kind of guys are you into?"

She shrugged. "I don't have a preference."

Well, at least I knew why she was dating Julian. The girl had no standards.

"Finished," she said, stepping back. She looked at her watch. "Just in time, too. Take a look. What do you think?"

She pointed to the mirror.

Wow. I *did* look good. I didn't even recognize the person in the mirror, but I had to admit … it wasn't a bad look at all.

You will be yourself. Just a different side of you. Or are you completely one-dimensional?

I replayed Nikos's words in my mind as I stared at myself.

"Wait," Juniper said. "I have an idea."

Carefully she put the final touch to my hair — small baby's breath flowers added into the braid. She smiled sweetly.

"Prince Nikos will look handsome, but you'll look breathtaking. Let's see how he likes the competition."

I couldn't understand why Juniper liked Julian, but I could see why Julian had a thing for Juniper. She was kind, wise, and fun.

Maybe she should have been a royal instead of me.

"Are you ready for tonight?" she asked.

"I don't know what's worse — having to schmooze with a bunch of people I don't know or being Nikos's date."

"Prince Nikos is young, but he won't cause any real trouble. He's always been kind to me."

"I may be young, but I'm not a child. Remember that."

No wonder he hated being treated like his age. The woman he was crushing on didn't see him as an adult.

What would their ship name be? ... Niniper? Junikos? JuNi? NiJu? Wow, those were terrible. By ship names alone, Julian made more sense.

"I think you're ready," she said. "Let me escort you out."

I missed Evann a little. I'd rather he escorted me, but he was with Cyrus, trying to track down the person that had poisoned him. Me. Us.

I hoped they found the culprit quickly. And I hoped they brought them around so I could beat the hell out of them.

As we left the room to head towards the party, we crossed paths with a guy wearing a gray patterned silk shirt with a black coat and pants. A single earring glistened from each ear. I almost didn't recognize him.

"Tai?"

He gave his usual charming smirk. "Good evening, ladies."

"Are you playing at tonight's party?" Juniper asked. He nodded.

"The staff always love your playing," she replied.

He cracked a smile. "It's my pleasure to play for such a wonderful audience."

He looked at me, his eyes roaming up and down my dress. He pursed his lips and raised his eyebrows, nodding at me in approval.

"And my audience just gets better and better," he added.

His eyes flickered.

Juniper nodded at him one more time and walked away. I went to follow, but Tai grabbed me by the arm and pulled me close to his side.

"When you get tired of Nikos," he whispered, "come find me."

He winked as he walked away.

Nikos stood at the entrance of the garden, fixing his sleeves. His velvet jacket complemented his white ruffled shirt with a red collar in a way that was so antiquated that it felt modern. It had much more personality than the regular suits back home. More than that, he didn't look like the angsty, conflicted eighteen-year-old he always seemed to be. He looked like a grownup.

I looked at Juniper. She didn't seem affected. I supposed if she loved Julian, it wouldn't make much difference to her, but I felt bad for Nikos.

The gardens were as extravagant as the guest of honor. Blossoming roses, glowing paper lanterns, tables full of food and drink. The stage had at least fifty people on it already, and a few dozen more were at the tables.

"I present your date, Prince Nikos," Juniper announced.

I turned my attention back to him. He glanced at me briefly, his eyebrow lifting and his lips breaking apart. He then turned back to her. "You did a great job, Juniper. I'm always amazed by your skills, despite the obvious challenge."

I rolled my eyes. To think I had gone soft on him for a minute.

"You look beautiful as well," he said to her. "You'll be attending, won't you? Your instructor has already arrived."

She smiled. "Yes, I'm excited to see him."

"Will you save a dance for me?"

Her hand went to her collarbone. "I think your date will want your attention, Your Highness."

No, I wouldn't.

"Besides," she continued, "you'll be busy with your other guests."

"I can always make time for you," he offered.

She gave a small smile, folding her hands. "I appreciate that, Your Highness."

"Please call me Nikos."

"I should meet my teacher. Please excuse me, Your Highness."

She gave a polite bow to both of us before walking into the gardens. Nikos sighed as she left.

I flicked his ear. "Take a hint, dude."

He rubbed his ear, hissing at me. "What's it to you?"

"As I said before, I can't handle the second-hand embarrassment."

He crooked his elbow, which was more like a strike to my torso than a friendly gesture, and said, "Let's just go inside, eh?"

I put my hand on top of his arm. He rolled his eyes and grunted, plucking my hand off and wrapping it around his strong bicep.

"Behave yourself," he said.

"Same goes for you," I replied.

Nikos stopped next to a man in a white suit, nodding to him.

The man turned sharply on his heel towards the guests. "Announcing the guest of honor, his royal highness, Prince Nikos, and his guest, Miss Marina."

Guest. I felt more like a side dish than a date.

There was a wave of golf claps as everyone turned to stare at us. I pulled my stomach in.

Nikos nodded to everyone. I froze. He nudged me forward, stepping down towards the gardens. Many people came up to him to congratulate him on his birthday, and he was polite and thoughtful to each one.

If only they knew what he was really like.

"You know how to put on a show," I whispered as we walked along the gardens.

"Take notes," he replied. "A fake persona will be your future too."

Something stirred in his eyes when he said it, but he looked away before I could grasp his entire meaning.

My attention was taken by a group of people laughing beside us. Julian was in a crowd of people, sipping champagne and having a good time. Laughter *and* smiling? What was that about? But to be honest, he didn't look bad either. He was wearing a white satin V-neck, teamed with slacks and a black vest. The plain black choker around his neck was a bit bold, but it was attractive for reasons I couldn't explain.

Still laughing, he turned his eyes away from the crowd and towards me. I'd never seen him actually smile at me, and even though I wasn't the reason he was smiling now, for a moment I wished I had been.

I turned away, remembering the incident in the library. It was too hard to face him after that.

It was a long night, and somewhat overwhelming, but it wasn't awful. Nikos introduced me to other royal members, CEOs, international celebrities, and world travelers. The entire time, he was oddly sweet, attentive, and light-hearted. I knew it was a game, but in pockets it seemed real.

Nikos introduced me to an older gentleman in a decorated Navy uniform and a woman in an off-shoulder gold gown worthy of the runway. They were like a couple out of the movies.

"She's our guest for the summer," Nikos explained to the couple while introducing me.

They nodded to me politely. I copied, hoping I did it right.

"How did you meet?" the older man asked.

"Not well, really," Nikos replied, laughing. "I've been torturing her ever since she got here."

They gave a quick look of shock, then chuckled.

"How can you torture such a beautiful young lady?" the man said. "Prince Nikos, I'm surprised at you."

"I'm not surprised at all," the woman said. "A boy can be incredibly obnoxious when he likes a girl. Heaven knows you were."

She patted her date lovingly on the shoulder. His cheeks puffed as he smiled.

"I hope she's as forgiving as you are," Nikos said to the woman, patting my hand that was still resting on his arm. He looked down at me. "I think she's beginning to grow on me."

I smiled, quickly turning my head away.

It was all an act.

Wasn't it?

19

Hot N Cold

"Who are all these people?" I asked, exhausted by an hour of introductions. "And why do I need to meet all of them?"

"Get used to it," Nikos muttered, walking towards the buffet. "This is going to be your job too in a few months."

I hobbled behind him. Only an hour in and my feet were killing me.

At the buffet he handed me a plate of strawberry cheesecake. His eyes lingered on me for a long moment, making it hard for me to focus on the cheesecake.

"What's with the look?" I asked.

"What look?"

"Why are you staring at me?"

His eyes shifted back to the table as he reached for the bowl of large strawberries lying next to the cheesecake, bringing one to his lips. "I like that dress on you."

I looked behind me. "Me?"

"Yes, you. Whom did you think I meant?"

"Sorry. You've got to warn me before giving me compliments outside of the public eye. They throw me off. I never know if they're sincere or not."

"It doesn't matter if they're sincere," he replied, chewing. "Your job isn't to sift through real and fake compliments. That would take too long, and there isn't any benefit to be gained."

"You've had too much practice at this."

"I've been around enough fakes to know what I'm talking about."

He kept eating strawberries, looking out at the crowd with narrowed eyes. It must have been difficult to grow up in such a place, not knowing who your real friends were, or not being able to make close connections with anyone.

"So, let's be honest then," I said, finally taking a bite of my cheesecake. "First, this cheesecake is spectacular and makes me hate life less. Second, why did you choose me as your date?"

He swallowed, then licked his lips thoughtfully. "Because Cyrus couldn't make it. He was supposed to be your escort. That left Julian or me. I thought you and Julian hated each other, so I was the obvious choice. But after seeing you two in the library yesterday …"

He raised an eyebrow at me. I rolled my eyes.

"There's nothing between us," I said.

"Good to hear. Especially since—"

Biting his lip, he picked up another massive strawberry and shoved the whole thing in his mouth.

"Especially since what?" I asked.

"Nothing," he mumbled through a mouthful of strawberry.

"What were you going to say?"

"How's the cheesecake?" a second voice said behind me.

I jumped.

Julian.

"Uh … It's good," I said, disoriented from the sudden change in subject.

"Specialty of the castle," he replied. "I was wanting your opinion of it."

I tried to form an opinion, aware of Nikos's glare behind me.

"T-the strawberries are much sweeter here than back home," I replied. "But they have a kind of sour bite at the end."

He nodded and dismissed the topic of strawberries. "I noticed that you met the guests. Now that you've addressed the formalities, would you like to dance?"

It was just as well I hadn't taken another bite of cheesecake because I would definitely have choked. "Right now?"

"It's not exactly something I would schedule for later."

"There are a ton of people here you could dance with," I pointed out. I looked over my shoulder at Nikos. "Also—"

"I've put a lot of work into you the past couple of weeks," Julian said firmly. "I won't take no for an answer."

He held his hand out to me. Dazed, I put my hand in his.

What was I doing?

Julian brought me to the dance floor, then stepped in close, taking me in his arms. His stance was softer than usual.

I couldn't help but look over my shoulder at Nikos. It was his birthday. Like it or not, I was his date and here I was dancing the first dance with his brother. Did that bother him? Maybe not. He didn't like me anyways, right?

"Is Nikos treating you well?" Julian asked as he started to lead.

I nodded. "Yes. And it's weird."

He frowned. "Yeah, that is kind of strange for him. Well, if that changes, let me know."

Awkwardness lingered between us. I still felt embarrassed about the library situation, and the tension from it was killing me.

"I'm sorry ... about what I said."

Julian turned his head to me, eyes widening. His face softened after a moment. "Don't worry about it ... Your Highness."

He smirked playfully, his eyes glittering a little from the lanterns. Anyone else calling me *Your Highness* felt silly. But Julian? It felt a little different.

And this was the closest thing to a smile he had ever given me.

During the dance he was confident enough to spin me, and I actually heard him laugh once. He had never laughed with me before. It was a nice surprise. I hoped to hear it again.

The song ended, and so did our dance. He took a bow and I did the same, only to come up and see his smile. A real smile. One that met his eyes and puffed up his cheeks.

"Not bad for the first dance in front of an audience," he said.

He looked over my shoulder, his smile quickly dropping. I turned back to see Juniper. She glanced between us for a moment, then turned back to the tables.

"I-I should go," he stuttered. He bowed again. "Thank you for the dance. We still have a lot of work to do, but you're at least showing promise now."

He started to walk away.

"You could have left it at the first part!" I called after him.

As he left the dance floor, my eye caught Nikos coming up to meet me. His shoulders were tense, eyes cold. He stepped into my space but didn't acknowledge me. His eyes continued over my shoulder. I didn't have to turn around to know what he was looking at.

I tapped his arm. "Forget her, Nikos. She's not worth it."

He turned back to me, not blinking. I had never noticed how dark his eyes were until now.

"Should I have let Julian be your escort after all?" he asked. He reached out, gripping my hand and waist. "He seems to be everybody's favorite these days."

"Don't take it that way," I said. "Stop comparing—"

"Shut up and dance with me for a moment."

He pulled me in closer, his body pressed up against mine. His hand clasped my fingers, pinching them together.

"What are you doing?" I asked. "You're hurting me."

He loosened his grip. "Sorry."

"You don't sound sorry."

"I'm not, really."

I growled. "You flip between being sickeningly sweet to me and being a complete terror. Are you schizophrenic? Do you have multiple personality disorder?"

"Multiple personality … what kind of TV shows do you watch? Honestly."

"Then what's with you? You can't be this worked up over—"

Before I could finish, he pulled me in close, his face inching towards mine. He cocked his head to the side to whisper in my ear.

"Stay like this for a moment," he said, his breath tickling my ear.

As we continued to dance, I looked around for an escape route. While glancing, I realized something — Julian and Juniper were both watching. I looked back to Nikos, who was smiling at me.

"That smile …" I said. "It's fake."

He laughed. "You can tell now, can you? You're getting better."

I suddenly felt nauseous. Was his smile fake the whole night?

He glanced over to the side, then pulled me closer. Why was he acting like this? He hated me. He didn't like spending time with me. Suddenly I'm his date and he's dancing close to me in front of …

That was it.

"You want to make her jealous, don't you? You asked me to be your date to make her jealous."

His eyes flickered. He didn't say anything, still holding me in his grip. His silence cut through me.

"I'm a joke to you, aren't I? Someone you play pranks on, and mess with when it's beneficial for you."

His jaw locked.

"Let me go, Nikos," I said, squirming in his arms. "Let me go now!"

"Wait—"

I kneed him in the groin before he could finish. He hit the ground on one knee, moaning in pain.

"Don't come near me again," I said, storming off the floor, and running past the crowd.

20

SEEING STARS

I didn't know where I was going. I just wanted to get away. Away from Nikos, Julian, and their weird little love triangle with Juniper.

I went through the first door I found. It led to a tower, with stairs curling up to the top. I climbed the steps, wiping my tears away as they fell. Nikos was a jerk. What did I do to get caught in their little feud? They were adults. Why didn't they act like it? This wasn't my problem.

And ... something about Nikos using me really hurt.

Maybe if he had said something in the beginning, it wouldn't have been so bad. I might have even agreed to play along. At least I would've known the reason he hung on me all night — teasing me and trying to make me laugh. I would have known it was for show.

But I didn't know. I was stupid enough to be touched by it.

How dumb was I?

I stopped climbing the stairs. I leaned my head against the wall and gave way to serious sniffling.

I didn't want to be sad about it. I wanted to be angry. I should've kicked him harder.

"Princess? What's wrong?"

I looked up the stairs. Evann trotted down, skipping some of the steps to reach me. He rushed over, cupping my face with his hands.

"What's wrong?" he asked again. "Was there another threat?"

I shook my head. "No, no. No threats. Just a rough night. Don't worry about it."

He wiped my tears away with his thumbs. "Want to talk about it?"

I shook my head. I was embarrassed enough.

His hands went from my face to my shoulders. There was a long silent pause as he stared at me.

"All right," he finally said. "You don't have to tell me." He looked up the steps, then back to me. "Let me show you something. It might cheer you up."

He took my hand and motioned to follow him up the stairs.

After a few minutes of climbing until my legs burned, Evann opened a door at the top that led out onto the roof.

The view was amazing.

It seemed like I could see the lights of the entire kingdom. Everything shimmered and glowed against the navy sky. Bright stars glistened next to the full moon.

"You like it?" he asked.

I nodded enthusiastically. "I could stay here for hours."

"Go ahead. The castle is yours, Princess."

"Evann," I scolded. "You're off the clock. You don't have to keep calling me *princess*."

He grinned. "But I like calling you that."

The wind caught in his hair as he held a playful smile.

I cleared my throat. "What are you doing up here, anyways?"

"I come up here a lot to stargaze."

He sat on the ground and lay back, his hands behind his head. He looked so happy that I couldn't help but do the same.

"You'll get your dress dirty," he warned as I lay down next to him.

I shrugged. "There are worse things. Like getting kicked in the head." I paused. "Actually, I take that back. That's really not that bad."

Evann laughed. "Not bad?"

"Nah. You get stunned for a bit, but it doesn't hurt as much as you'd think it would."

"You really are full of surprises, you know that?"

He smiled warmly at me and something flickered in his eyes as though he was seeing me in a different light.

"Won't Nikos be upset that you ditched him?" he finally asked, after a short silence.

I curled up at the sound of his name. "No. He only cares about himself, anyways."

His tone went serious. "What happened?"

I didn't answer.

Evann practically growled through his nose. "This little—"

"It's okay," I said. "He didn't do anything serious. I just feel stupid. Let's not talk about it now."

I felt his fingers gently stroke my hair. "You're having a hard time here … aren't you?"

His fingers went from my hair to the back of my head, and he brought me in for a hug as I started to shudder. I wasn't going to cry. Not like this. It wasn't worth it. I could hold it in.

His warm hands came to my back. "It's okay," he whispered. "You're safe with me."

I relaxed in his embrace, letting him hold me. I don't know how long we lay there, but we didn't say anything. I was afraid to open my mouth in case all my emotions fell out.

All I could think about was home. My friends. My family. My hopes and dreams. This castle full of strangers.

And this overwhelming, crushing feeling of loneliness.

If Evann wasn't here … I wouldn't know what to do.

I shut my eyes, wishing I could open them up again to my past.

I felt a nudge. "Princess?"

I opened my eyes, Evann looking down at me.

"Hmm?" I asked, unusually groggy for only shutting my eyes for a minute.

He chuckled softly. "You fell asleep."

"What?"

I sat up, making myself dizzy.

He shook his head. "You looked peaceful. I couldn't wake you up. Do you feel better?"

I fixed my hair, nodding. "Thank you."

He brought his hand back up to my face … then on top of my head, messing my hair up again.

I smacked his hand away as he laughed.

"Well, you two look cozy."

We turned to see Nikos coming through the tower door. I went to stand up, but Evann held his hand out to signal me to stop.

"What do you want?" I grumbled.

"I came up to ask Ev if he knew where you were." He glared at us both. "I guess he does."

"There's nothing to worry about, Nikos," Evann said, his voice with an unusual edge. "She's with me."

Nikos's eyes shifted between the two of us. It took me a minute to realize Evann had dropped the *Prince* in front of Nikos's name.

"I'll be sure to take her back to her room," Evann added.

"I can take her," Nikos said.

"No thank you," I replied, hugging my knees.

I couldn't see him, but I could feel his eyes burning into the back of my head.

"I'll take care of it," Evann said. "Enjoy your evening."

There was a pause.

"If that's what you want," Nikos said.

I heard his footsteps retreat, then a door slam.

21

MIDNIGHT SNACK

Thoughts raced around in my head until they made me dizzy, keeping me from falling asleep. The nap I took on the roof of the castle probably hadn't helped any, either. Defeated, I sighed and got out of bed, making my way down to the kitchen to rummage for something sweet to take my mind off things.

The guards had doubled since Cyrus was poisoned, and if anyone was lurking around, they would have caught them.

At least, that's what I kept telling myself as I went down the stairs.

As I tiptoed against the cool tile floors, I saw that the light in the kitchen was already on. There were a few clinking noises. Probably Tai, raiding the refrigerator again.

"When you get tired of Nikos, come find me."

I should have gone with him then. I could have avoided the whole mess. Tai was much better company than Nikos.

I stretched my neck around the side of the door frame to see not Tai, but Cyrus, wearing a white cotton shirt and purple silk robe, stuffing his face with what looked like hot wings. Sauce covered his fingers and lips. With small gerbil-like noises, he nibbled around the hot wing, humming in satisfaction. I smirked, stepping into the doorway to watch him.

It took him a second to realize I was there. He stopped mid-bite.

"Am I interrupting an intimate moment?" I asked.

He lowered the wing and reached for a paper towel to wipe his hands and face. "I didn't realize I was being watched. That's embarrassing."

I chuckled, glancing at his adorable bed hair and blushing cheeks. "Don't be. Your secret is safe with me … But only if you share."

"It's pretty spicy," he warned.

"I can handle a little spice."

"I don't know …" he teased. "You might regret it."

"My dad always makes spicy food. I can handle whatever you throw at me."

His eyebrows flew up. "Is that so?"

He handed me a wing. I bit in, letting the sauce play on my tongue, the flavor bursting with a good amount of kick and spices. It wasn't that spicy. I shrugged at him.

"Wait for it," he said, before I could say anything.

I swallowed. It still wasn't that bad. What was he—

Oh, Good God.

Everything burned. From my chest, to my throat, to my tongue, and up into my eyes. Every second that passed only brought on more agonizing pain. With tears in my eyes, I started to jump around.

"Oh my God, what is this!"

Without thinking, I reached up to wipe the tears out of my eyes.

"No, don't touch your face!" he cried, grabbing my wrists before I could make contact.

"It hurts!"

"Hold on."

It hurt too much to open my eyes and do anything, so I bounced up and down. After a few moments, Cyrus's hand came to my cheek.

"Sip this," he ordered.

He brought a glass to my lips. Realizing it was milk, I swished it around in my mouth until the burning turned into a dull ache. I opened my eyes to Cyrus's matted face.

"Better?" he asked.

I blinked some of the tears out of my eyes. He caught them in his fingers with a squeaky laugh.

"It's not funny," I muttered.

"Oh, but it is."

I shifted, aware of Cyrus holding my face in his hands. I took a step back. He dropped his hands back to his sides, but that didn't stop his glowing smile.

"I thought the spicy wings would clear my head and help me fall asleep," he said. "But I think you've done that for me instead."

I cocked my head to the side. "What do you mean?"

He reached over and grabbed a paper towel, dabbing the side of my lips. "Why are you up so late?"

"I don't know," I shrugged. "I couldn't sleep."

"How did the party go?"

He stuck out his bottom lip a little, looking at me sideways like a kitten.

"You already know, don't you?" I asked.

He gave a sheepish smile. "I know about everything in my castle. Also, I was watching from my balcony."

I sighed, slumping against the counter.

"Nikos always puts on a show," Cyrus said. "Our parents taught us all to do it, and we complied. Nikos was the best at it. That's why he has all the television spots. But I'm afraid my little brother is breaking under the pressure of being someone always on show, and that hurts people. Especially people who have never had the burden of being someone else."

I picked up a paper towel and started rubbing the sauce off my fingers.

He sniffed, taking another bite of the hot wing. "When my father died, I was angry at him. I was angry he died and left me to rule an entire kingdom alone. He hadn't taught me what I needed to know, and there were so many questions I never got answered."

I threw the paper towel in the trash can, not answering.

"But ..." he continued, "I came to realize that my father did everything he could to the best of his ability, for reasons I couldn't understand. It was better to accept the situation than to focus on the circumstances."

"I have plenty of questions to ask when my dad shows up," I muttered. "I at least deserve some answers."

"What if there aren't any answers? What will you do?"

We stared at each other for a moment, not saying anything.

He rubbed the sauce from his hands with another paper towel. "I'll go ahead and clean up here. That is, unless, you want another one?"

I shook my head. "I'm good."

His eyes glittered as he looked at me.

"Me too."

I left the kitchen, shuffling across the castle floor. No answers? What if there were no answers? Of course there were answers. There were always answers. There had to be.

My thoughts were interrupted when I ran into someone else.

"Couldn't sleep, Princess?" Evann asked, his mouth turning down at the corners adorably.

"Not tonight," I said. "But I guess it's an epidemic. I just ran into Cyrus in the kitchen."

"Ah, yes," Evann said, nodding. "That's not unusual."

"Doesn't he sleep?"

"Occasionally he doesn't stick to schedule. He suffers from persistent nightmares."

"Nightmares?" I asked. "From what?"

"He's a king who rules alone. It's not hard to guess why he would be stressed."

I looked back to the kitchen; a light still glowed.

"I didn't realize he suffered so much," I said.

"Don't worry. He'll be okay. Would you like me to make you some tea and bring it to your room?"

I smiled but shook my head. "No thanks. Maybe I'll read my history of engineering textbook and put myself back to sleep."

He nodded. I walked back towards my room, trying to shake a nagging feeling out of my head.

Cyrus, Julian, Nikos … All of them seemed troubled by something. I couldn't put my finger on what.

I shook my head.

I wasn't going to start caring. I wasn't.

§

"We have a problem."

Nikos frowned as he handed Cyrus his phone. Cyrus narrowed his eyes at the screen, sighing.

"I should have anticipated something like this," he said. "I suppose it was ignorant to think that we could hide her identity so easily."

I stopped eating my breakfast. "What's happened?"

Cyrus passed the phone to Julian, who paused to look at the phone before showing it to me. His eyebrow bounced, but he didn't say anything.

Mysterious Guest Attacks World Prince

"*Attack* is a strong word," I said.

"Are vocabulary choices an issue right now?" Nikos asked.

Julian scrolled through the article. "Look, there's even a video."

Nikos put his hand over his face as Julian played it. All we could hear was the music being played in the background. After a moment, Julian snorted.

"Turn it off," Nikos pleaded.

"If the press starts to investigate Marina's identity, we'll have some trouble," Cyrus said.

"I knew she'd be a pain," Nikos replied.

I narrowed my eyes at him. "The only reason you got kicked in the first place —"

"Regardless of the reason, you've created a problem for yourself," Julian said. "If they find out who you are, it'll set up a whole set of questions we're not prepared for."

"What do you mean?" I asked. "The secret princess thing? Can't we just tell them the truth?"

Nikos tapped his knife against the table. "Sure — if you want you and your family to be harassed with paparazzi and news reporters every waking moment of your life."

"There's an important piece of information that may be worth mentioning at this moment," Cyrus said. "Marina, have you ever heard of the country, Paijeana?"

I sifted through the thoughts in my brain. "Sounds like something from history class."

"Officially, Aujina and Paijeana are two separate countries," Cyrus explained. "But after the war 26 years ago, they joined together to form Aujina as it is today. Currently, I rule over both, but in the future, that might not be the case."

"Why not?" I asked.

"Because Paijeana is your country, Marina."

I dropped my fork.

"Technically, your father and mother still have sovereignty over the country," Cyrus said. "Our countries were in alliance during the war, and our combined legions destroyed the country responsible for terrorist attacks against yours. But the staff within your castle had become contaminated. There were multiple — what do you call it in your country — moles? Double agents were working for and against your family. Our fathers decided it would be safest for your family to go into hiding, and my father would rule over both kingdoms until the double agents could be found and dealt with."

"So, were they?"

"They were eventually found and executed, yes," Cyrus said nonchalantly, "but by then you were born in America, and it complicated the matter. There was also a fear of a second attack if your father retook the throne, and I believe your parents didn't want to put you in a life of constant war."

I looked down at my plate.

"But now," Cyrus continued, "you're old enough to choose between taking the throne yourself or forfeiting it to Aujina."

"If I take the throne, will there be wars?" I asked. "Won't there be another attack?"

"Possibly," Cyrus said, "however, that's a risk for every leader in every country. That hasn't changed since government was invented. I have to fend off wars at least every three months."

He took a bite of his biscuit as if it wasn't a big deal.

"If the press identifies you before we're ready, it will cause havoc politically," Julian added. "It will be a mess to clean up."

"It'll be my responsibility to do so if that happens," Cyrus explained. "Our family has been blocking the media from exposing your family until this point. We can continue to protect you. So don't look so fearful about it, my dear."

He smiled at me as he took another bite of his food. I wanted to sink under my chair. Cyrus's responsibilities were much more than I expected. He was blocking the media from finding my parents? So, it was because of Cyrus and his family that my family had a normal life.

Cyrus's pocket buzzed. He pulled his phone out of his coat pocket.

"If you have any further questions, my dear, I think you'll be able to get them answered today," he said. "It looks like your father wishes to speak with you."

22

THE TALK II

"I kind of figured you'd attack someone while you were there. I'm surprised it took this long, to be honest."

My father's warm smile flooded the video conference screen. I couldn't understand why he would be smiling, considering everything Cyrus had told me.

"Sorry, Dad," I said, almost whispering.

"Don't worry, princess," he said. "I can handle the reporters if they start snooping. I knew something would raise suspicions sooner or later. It's a miracle it's taken them this long to look for me. But I apologize to you and your family, Cyrus. It seems you're always cleaning up after my messes."

Cyrus smiled in his seat next to me. "You've cleaned up quite a few of ours. I owe you just as much."

My dad shook his head. "I'm only sorry I didn't do more for you."

"Dad," I said, "why didn't you tell me any of this? I could have prepared, at least."

He chuckled. "You wouldn't have listened to me. Honestly, I couldn't trust you with it. You were too young to wrap your head around it anyway."

"But you didn't even try!" I threw back. "If I had known that there were so many problems—"

"You couldn't have done anything," he finished. "More than that, I wanted you to have a childhood. A real one. Not like mine and your mother's. Always full of responsibilities, crowd control, fear of wars, and death threats …"

My chest seized up at the last part.

"You were too free-spirited for that, and I was afraid if I told you everything, it would crush you," he said. "But I'm afraid my fears left you too unprepared. Maybe it's time you learn everything."

"I've already made the arrangements, Tylier," Cyrus said. "I can take her tomorrow."

"Take me?" I asked, unsure of the meaning.

"Thank you, Cyrus," Dad said. "You didn't have to do that much, but I'm in your debt for it."

"Take me where?" I asked again.

"To your kingdom, my dear," Cyrus said. "To your castle in Paijeana."

§

If being a princess meant having a private jet, I could get used to it.

Cyrus was my only escort, apart from half a dozen armed guards. I was starting to get used to them, even though they only stared forward. At least Evann talked to me. I wished he was with us to break the silence, but he was fronting the investigation at the castle, and he couldn't leave.

"How big is this kingdom, exactly?" I asked.

"It's about a hundred-thousand square kilometers."

"I don't know square kilometers."

He smiled briefly. "Rounding up, forty-thousand square miles. About ten million people live there."

I leaned back in my seat. Ten million people? Left in my family's charge? Could that many people really depend on us?

"How many people do you have in your country?" I asked.

"Double yours," he replied coolly.

"It must be hard on you to take care of so many people."

His lips pulled back, but he didn't say anything.

"You said my parents helped your family — what kind of problems did you run into?"

He paused for so long I thought he wasn't going to answer. Then he simply said, "We had some problems within our castle, but they were a lifetime ago."

"Like what? Moles?"

He shook his head. "More like demons."

He turned to look out the window. With the way the sunlight hit the deep lines in his face, I decided not to press it further.

After an hour-long flight, we landed. I paused before getting off the plane.

"Is something wrong?" Cyrus asked.

I shook my head. "No. Why?"

He smiled. "You're hesitating."

"I'm—"

I couldn't reply.

He came back to me, wrapping his hands around my shoulders. "It's only yours if you want it. You don't have to rule it. If you should decide to rule, I will be right beside you. Don't worry."

His dark eyes caught the light, and all the fear drained out of my body. His confidence was enough to soothe me.

We stepped out, and the humid air hit my face. It felt like Aujina, yet different.

It was *my* air.

No, wait. I couldn't own air. That was stupid.

But still … knowing that this country belonged to my family somehow made it feel different.

Cyrus and I were escorted to a decorated car and driven around the capital towards the castle.

In many ways, it was like Cyrus's kingdom. The same traditional wooden buildings and outdoor markets, the same stone streets. The difference was that it wasn't as modern. There weren't any skyscrapers anywhere, the streets were narrow, and, although everything was clean, it looked many years older than Aujina.

"I'm afraid I haven't been able to develop the country as much as I wanted," Cyrus admitted when I pointed that out. "That's the trouble when you're looking over a kingdom that isn't yours. The paperwork gets messy."

"What are the major struggles of this country?" I asked.

"There's a struggle to bring in international tourists since this is considered 'Aujina's countryside.' But I think there's more charm to it because of that. It's a vacation spot for most of the people in my kingdom, so the revenue balances itself. At the same time, because there's not a lot of modernization, entertainment is low. The citizens probably get bored easily. There are not a lot of young people, and those that stay here usually become farmers or artists."

"You know your people well."

"No, I know *your* people well. This is your kingdom. Your parents are the most decent people I have ever met. If their country fell apart in my hands, I would never forgive myself."

He chewed his bottom lip, looking out the window with genuine concern. He was a much better ruler than I could ever hope to be.

"Cyrus ... if I don't take the throne, will you continue to look after them?"

He smiled patting my hands. "The plan is to separate the kingdoms once again. If you don't take the throne, then one of my brothers will take it, most likely."

"Julian or Nikos? How would you decide that?"

"I was thinking about a good game of rock, paper, scissors."

I pursed my lips. He laughed.

"Julian would most likely take your place. He's the wisest of all of us, and he has a background in politics. Nikos, however, is planning to pursue economics and engineering, so he would be suitable as well." He chewed his lip again before continuing. "But if you don't take the throne, that means that I would have to separate from my brothers. I don't think I could handle that. I don't like them being in a place where I can't protect them. Also … I wouldn't …"

He stopped. I leaned over. "You wouldn't what?"

It took a moment for him to look at me.

"I wouldn't see you," he said softly.

I held his gaze for a heartbeat before he turned away to look out the window.

"We're here," he said.

§

The palace, *my palace*, was much smaller than Cyrus's, but no less impressive. It stood five stories tall, glowing a brilliant white in the sunlight and surrounded by an outstretched lake that glittered as much as the palace did. The bright blue roof almost blended into the sky, the sides rippling up like waves.

My family … owned this?

As the car crossed over the bridge, Cyrus shifted in his seat and cleared his throat. "What do you think?"

"I think I've stopped thinking," I replied.

He chuckled. "Does it suit you?"

"Not thinking?"

"The castle."

"Depends. Is there a dojo inside?"

He leaned his head back on his seat, laughing. "It can be arranged."

We pulled into the front of the castle, and Cyrus held out his hand to lead me up the marble steps. The doors opened to a large hall, much darker than Cyrus's main hall. There were floor-to-ceiling windows on each side and large gold chandeliers hung from the ceiling.

The walls were accented with deep-cherry wood and rose-gold patterns. I could practically see my entire reflection in the polished floor.

"It's open to the public most days as a museum," Cyrus explained. "But it's closed on Sundays, so there won't be any problems if we do a tour today." He leaned in close to my ear, his subtle musk tingling my nose. "Also, the staff doesn't know who you are. It might be best to keep it that way until you make your decision."

I nodded. I wasn't emotionally prepared for possibly a hundred new people calling me "Princess" and "Your Highness" and all those other titles.

Cyrus held his arm out for me to take. I took it, and he gave me a full tour of the castle. In most ways, the architecture was the same as his castle, but on a smaller scale. There were only half as many rooms (none of which were dojos or movie theaters), but they were charming and breathtaking at the same time, like a cottage built inside Aladdin's cave. Inside, there was a large fountain in the ballroom, a quaint library filled to the ceiling with antique books, a few parlors for meetings and relaxing, and maybe eight or nine bedrooms. Each one was roped off, so we could look inside but not touch anything. It was my castle, though, right? Couldn't I jump over the rope? I fought the temptation.

We stopped at one large bedroom, painted light rose and accented with white furniture. The headboard of the bed was almost as tall as the wall, making it look like lace against the paint.

"This was your grandparents' room," Cyrus said. "Your father's parents."

"My grandparents," I murmured. A thought suddenly hit me. "My entire family lived here … didn't they? For generations?"

He nodded. "What did your father say of his parents?"

I shrugged. "He only said that they were from Aujina, and that they passed a couple of years before he and Mom got married."

Cyrus nodded. "That's technically true."

"My parents said after they got married, they moved to America." I sighed. "You know, I never asked questions about where we came from. I figured where we were was enough."

"Nothing unwise in that statement."

"I was always set on where I was going. Not where I came from. I didn't think it was that important."

"It's not always useful knowing where you're from," Cyrus said, his voice softening. "Sometimes it's better not knowing your family's past."

He looked at the ground before raising his head to meet my eyes with a smile.

"Your grandparents were lovely people, from what I hear," he said. "Your father told me some stories. Your uncle told me better ones."

"You know my uncle, too?" I asked, not knowing why that hadn't occurred to me.

He nodded. "Your uncle was a royal before he met your aunt. He fell in love with her and decided to give up his throne for her. He was the younger of the two brothers, so forfeiting the throne was no real loss in his eyes. Your parents' future was already arranged, and he preferred the civilian life. It worked out well, I think. You wouldn't have known him otherwise."

So, if my uncle hadn't married Aunt Tina, my family wouldn't have moved to California to be close to them, I would have never learned karate. I wouldn't have anything that I have now.

The possibilities of a completely different life made my head spin.

"Wait a minute," I said. "You said my parents' future was already *arranged*? What does that mean?"

He cocked his head to the side. "Your parents had an arranged marriage. Did they not mention that?"

My mouth went dry. "Have they actually mentioned anything to me?"

Cyrus winced and rubbed the back of his neck. "I'm not good with sensitive information, am I?"

I shook my head.

"Don't worry, my dear," he said. "They were always happy. Love at first sight, your father said."

I rolled my eyes. "He would believe in something that cheesy."

"I think I understand why he does."

He looked away as soon as I looked at him, swallowing and stepping forward to continue the tour, only to run into the ropes. With a grunt, he untangled himself, a slight pink tint in his cheeks as he straightened the ropes and then continued forward.

The outside of the castle was as beautiful as the inside, with gardens and an extravagant courtyard I could sit around in all day. It had a perfect view of the mountains behind the lake. I convinced Cyrus to sit with me to take in the view for a moment. A moment turned into minutes, and we chatted about the mountains back home, how I loved hiking, and some of my adventures while in the forests.

After some time, a woman in a long apron and yellow dress brought us a tray of strawberry lemonade and assorted scones and cookies.

"King Cyrus!" she said, bowing. "It's been far too long since your last visit. A gift from the kitchen."

Cyrus nodded in return. "Thank you, Iris. We might need a second pitcher of lemonade. I might drink all of this by myself."

"Are either of the princes with you today?"

He shook his head. "Just our special family guest for the summer."

He introduced us to one another, Iris's eyes lighting up like the walls of the castle.

Once she was sure we had everything we wanted, she wished us a pleasant afternoon and then added with a knowing look that sent Cyrus's cheeks a decided shade of pink, "I'll leave you to your date, Your Majesty."

He opened his mouth as she walked away, but didn't say anything, instead rubbing the back of his neck again.

"Iris is the assuming type," he finally said.

There was silence for a moment. Cyrus cleared his throat.

"Out of curiosity …" he asked, "what is a date like in your country?"

I laughed. "Not very exciting. Usually dinner and a movie, or a walk in the park, a concert, or sitting in a cafe and talking. What is a date like here?"

"I don't know," he said. "I've never been on one."

He gave a small smile. I picked up a scone from the tray.

"I guess … I guess this could count as a date, too," I said, shoving half the scone in my mouth.

He turned his head. "Could it?"

"I mean, it would be better without the dozen guards watching us drink lemonade and scarf down scones."

Cyrus laughed, looking over his shoulder. "Yes, well, that's the price of being royalty."

"Are they getting some cookies and lemonade, too? They've been working hard today."

His eyes lingered on me for a long moment. "Great question. Let's see that they do."

We stayed and talked for most of the evening, the sun beginning to set by the time we finished off two rounds of scones, a million cookies, and three pitchers of lemonade. The last sent me off looking for a royal bathroom. The irrepressible Iris pointed me in the right direction and then said, "I've never seen the king with a woman before. You must be a charming guest indeed for him to escape his palace and bring you here."

"I don't know if *charming* is the word everyone would use," I said lightly and she laughed, clearly thinking I was joking.

Thanking the kitchen staff, we piled back into the car and headed to the airport, climbing back into the jet. The sugar crash from the scones and lemonade meant it wasn't long before I was struggling to stay awake.

"Cyrus …" I said, my eyes shutting against my will.

He hummed in acknowledgment.

"If I become queen, can you come to my castle and drink lemonade with me in the courtyard? I think I'd like it if you did."

I was too tired to look at him when he answered. I could only feel his hand on mine.

"I'd like that too, Marina."

23

A SHADOW

"I won't be here this evening," Juniper informed me. "I'll be attending a festival in town."

I sank in my chair a little as she swept up the locks she had just trimmed from my shoulder-length hair. "Ah, I'm jealous. I wish I could go."

"Why don't you?" she asked.

I broke eye contact. "I … I have other plans."

Staying in my room and reading textbooks. Ugh …

"Anything I need to dress you up for?"

"Uh, well …"

"She's having dinner with me," a voice said behind us. "I can take care of her style for the evening."

We both turned to Nikos, who was adjusting the cuffs of his jacket.

"How the heck did you get in my room?" I asked. "Isn't knocking a thing anymore?"

"I can take care of her, Juniper," he said coldly. "You are free to go."

Juniper looked between us. I closed the conversation as pleasantly as I could, saying that I would see her tomorrow. Nikos leaned up against the vanity next to me, looking through the makeup. When Juniper left, I stood and punched Nikos in the shoulder. He jumped, dropping the blush he was holding.

"Stop attacking me!" he said. "Do you want to be all over the news?"

"Do you want to be in the obituaries? What's your deal?"

"You don't get anything, do you?" he replied, picking up the blush again. "Also, this color is terrible for your skin tone."

"We're having dinner tonight?" I asked.

He chuckled. "Of course not. I wouldn't be able to stand you that long."

I clenched my fist. I went out of my way to avoid him after his birthday celebration, and here he was in my personal space getting on my nerves again.

"Then why did you say we were having dinner?" I asked.

"A woman wants a man more when she thinks he's wanted by other women."

"You're the World's Prince. You're wanted by a lot of women. She knows that. She's not into you, dude."

Nikos rolled his eyes. "That's only because she doesn't know me."

"She doesn't want to know you. Why are you so hung up on her anyways?"

He looked in the mirror, fixing his clothes. He didn't answer.

"Would Julian treat her badly?" I asked honestly. I couldn't tell if Julian could treat a puppy well, let alone a person.

He hesitated, but then shook his head. "He would treat her well … Do you think I wouldn't?"

"Honestly, I think out of all of you, Cyrus would be the best choice. Both you and Julian are nuts."

Nikos stepped forward, clicking his tongue. "What's this? Have you moved on from the musician, then?"

"The musician?"

He raised an eyebrow.

"I was never stuck on the musician," I said. "Don't twist our relationship."

"I disagree. The way you look at him says otherwise."

"How do I look at him?"

Nikos leaned in towards me, putting one hand on each side of the vanity table and trapping me inside his arms.

"The way that my fans look at me," he said. "As if all I have to do is say the word, and they'd do anything I ask them to."

I tried not to shiver as his voice hit my ear. "Yeah, well, I'm not your fan, and if you don't back it up right now, I'm going to punch you in the throat."

He shook his head and pulled back. "Never mind, I shouldn't have to worry about you. With your attitude, you're most likely to die alone anyway."

"I could say the same about you."

He shook his head again before walking out the door.

I got why Julian liked Juniper — she seemed intelligent and wise, which suited his personality well. But Nikos? Why on earth would he like her? They had practically nothing in common. On top of that, he acted so weird around her. He switched from the World's Prince to an awkward teenage boy, making me dizzy trying to keep up with who he was.

"I appreciate that, Your Highness."

"Please call me Nikos."

Juniper kept friend-zoning him, but he wasn't giving up. What was with his obsession?

I threw my arm over my eyes as I lay in bed, trying to find answers for my questions. Even after an hour of going over everything in my mind, I couldn't find even a sliver of an answer.

But I was starting to get used to having more questions than answers.

Click.

I moved my arm away from my eyes and looked around the room.

Click. Pop. Click.

The noise was coming from the balcony. My heart hit my throat. I stood and rushed to the open doors, slamming them shut and locking them.

Thunk.

There was a shadow on my balcony.

24

SECRETS

The shadow walked closer to the balcony door. I was about to scream—

Until the figure's full face came into view.

I grabbed my knees in relief and groaned.

Tai knocked on the glass of the door, smiling. Heart pounding from adrenaline, I opened it for him.

"Sorry," he said, shrugging. "Did I scare you?"

He let himself in. I punched him in the shoulder as he passed.

"You jerk! Did you scale the castle wall just to scare me?"

He flopped on the bed, chuckling. "I didn't do it for that reason, but it was a definite bonus."

"Why didn't you come to the door like a normal person?"

"Not as exciting."

"Why are you here?"

"I'm bored."

"So, what do you want me to do about it?"

He sat up, his eyes sparkling. "Play with me."

I froze.

"Let's sneak out and go to the festival," he continued.

"The festival?"

"I heard Nikos muttering about it. It sounded like something you'd be interested in. Don't you want to get out of this castle?"

More than anything. But …

"I don't think that's a good idea," I said.

"I didn't ask if it was a good idea. I asked if you wanted to do it."

I stared at him. It wasn't like I didn't want to get out. I did. I'd been stuck in the castle for weeks, dealing with dramas all over the place. A night out? Just having fun? That sounded great.

"I shouldn't," I said.

He stood up and walked over. "Which is exactly why it'll be fun. Come on. It'll be our secret."

Secret?

Secrets seemed to be everyone's favorite pastime at the castle. Everyone had one. Except me. I was jerked around every which way, constantly trying to keep up with everyone else. I was so … powerless.

But my own secret …?

"You interested?" Tai asked.

It would probably be the only chance I got.

"Say that I was," I said, "how do you expect to get me out of the castle without Cyrus finding out?"

"Easy," he said, shrugging with one shoulder.

He waved for me to watch him. Stepping over to my fireplace mantle, he pressed a few bricks hard into the wall, and then tugged at the wall itself. It quietly slid out, revealing a staircase.

"What the hell!" I cried. "Is that a secret passageway?"

"One of many," he replied.

"Who knows about these?"

"Everyone," he said. "Naturally, anyone who works here needs to know it in case of emergencies. Come on, let's go before festival ends."

I looked back at my pillow, thinking of the first note I got.

Whoever was threatening me knew about this secret passage too. It wasn't a random threat. It was made by someone who lived here.

§

"When you asked how I felt about riding in the trunk, I thought you were joking."

Tai held up the car trunk door, smirking. "Afraid not. They're not just going to let me walk out with you, you know. You're under tight surveillance as special guest."

Tai could get around the guards, he knew secret passageways, and now he wanted me to ride in the trunk of his car. I didn't like this. But Tai would have no reason to hurt me, would he? He didn't even know who I was.

I hesitated.

"Come on," he said, clapping, "inside!"

I couldn't believe I was doing this. But I had to admit — it was kind of exciting. Better than all those stupid princess lessons. And if Tai was the one threatening me, I could catch him myself.

I climbed inside. Tai closed the trunk, and everything went dark.

"You all right?" he called.

I called back that I was fine. In seconds, the car door slammed and the engine started. We drove slowly for a while, then stopped. Tai gave a casual greeting to the gatekeeper, and the gate creaked open.

The car sped up. Was he going to keep me in the trunk the entire time?

Maybe this was a bad idea. I looked for the child safety latch in the trunk ceiling.

But I didn't need to. The car pulled over and the trunk opened. Tai's smiling face hovered over me.

"It worked!" he said. "Come on out."

I jumped out and bounced into the front passenger seat. He started the car and took off again, leaning his free arm out the window. The wind blew through his hair as we drove.

He laughed. "You excited?"

"It's been a long time since I've done anything — you know — fun."

"You didn't have fun at Nikos's party?"

I frowned. "I don't want to talk about it."

"Oh ho ho. I told you to come to me when you got tired of him, remember? Tsk. I'm insulted now."

Was he teasing me or being serious?

"Sorry, Tai. I'll come to you next time."

"No, you won't," he said, reaching over and interlacing his fingers in mine. "You'll come to me right now."

I started to pull away, but he squeezed my hand, a playful smile decorating his face. His hand was as warm as his smile, and I didn't feel like pulling away.

It wasn't long before we pulled into the parking lot for the festival. The air was heavy with the smell of popcorn and cotton candy; screams of delight heard not long after the rush of the roller coasters nearby. Game booths with blinking lights flooded my vision.

"What do you want to do first?" he asked.

I looked around. "Everything."

He laughed and grabbed my hand again. "Let's get started then."

I smiled, lacing my fingers in his.

I quickly learned two things: Tai was good at eating and bad at games.

"Are you letting me win or are you actually *this* bad?" I asked, shooting my water gun at the puppets dashing across the cardboard mountain top.

"Less talking, more shooting," he said.

"If you're that anxious to lose!"

Naturally I was declared the winner. Again.

"You know, I would think as a pianist you'd be good with your hands."

He grinned and leaned forward. "I *am* good with my hands," he said in a low voice. "Just at a different kind of game."

All my blood rushed to my face.

He shoved his hands into his pockets and walked away. "So, do you prefer pink or blue cotton candy?"

After buying cotton candy, we started to stroll around the festival. It was so strange to think that in a few weeks all these people would know me as a princess.

No, wait. No, they wouldn't. I wasn't taking the job. I'd already made my decision.

"A cent for your thoughts?" Tai asked.

I picked at my cotton candy. "I think you mean a penny. And trust me, my thoughts are worth their weight in gold."

"That explains why you walk around like they're so heavy."

I stopped. He turned to face me, shoving a piece of cotton candy in his mouth.

"Say you've been offered an amazing job, but you don't know if you should do it or not. What would you do?"

"Depends on how much it pays."

"I'm serious."

"So am I." He put another piece of cotton candy in his mouth. "If the reward is worth the work, then I'd do it."

"What if you're not sure the payout is worth it?"

He scratched his head. "I don't have a lot of goals in life, to be honest. Eat well, sleep well, stay out of jail. I'm simple man. I ask myself, what are consequences if I do it? Or, as important, what are consequences if I don't?"

He had a point. If I took over my parents' kingdom, the consequences would be that I would have to give up my dreams. If I didn't, the consequences would be that my parents would have to give up their kingdom to Cyrus.

Cyrus had enough work as it was. Something in me felt guilty doing that to him.

"Aish," Tai cursed, patting his pockets. "I think I left my wallet at the cotton candy stand."

"Go check," I said. "I'm heading to the restroom to get this cotton candy off my fingers."

"Come with me. I don't want to leave you by yourself."

I rolled my eyes. "I'm fine. I don't need a bodyguard all the time. What are you going to do? Follow me into the restroom? Go!"

"You sure?"

I nodded. He eyed me for a moment.

"I'm not a damsel," I said, annoyed. "Would you just go?"

"Don't you dare wander," he said. "Wait for me right next to the restroom."

He finally agreed and I turned to go to the restroom. That's what I liked about Tai. He didn't hover. It was so nice to have a little freedom.

As I turned the corner, there was a man standing outside the restrooms. He was wearing a plaid long-sleeved shirt and a baseball cap. When he lifted his head, it took me a moment to realize that I knew him.

Julian.

His jaw dropped. I'm pretty sure mine did too.

"You!" he said.

I bolted back around the corner, Julian's voice calling behind me. I weaved through the crowd, hoping to lose him. I didn't think he was the athletic type, so he'd give up quickly.

After a few minutes of running, I turned back. He wasn't in the crowd. Did he turn back?

A rough hand grabbed my arm from behind.

"Good to see you again, Princess," a low voice said. "Only this time, you're not getting away."

"Ju—"

No. That wasn't Julian's voice.

I knew that voice.

"Who are you?" I demanded, hoping I didn't sound scared.

"A messenger."

It was the voice that had threatened me at the castle.

25

MEET THE MESSENGER

I couldn't run this time.

That left one other option.

I elbowed him in the gut. When he doubled over, I spiked another elbow in his face. I didn't turn back to look at him. I ran, weaving through the crowds of people.

"Tai!" I cried, not sure which way I was going. "Tai!"

I turned the corner, slamming into a high school girl and spilling her soda. Both of us hit the ground. There wasn't time for an apology. Ignoring her angry protests, I bounced back up and kept running.

Another sharp turn led me to the back of a closed ride. Nothing was there but a wooden fence. I turned to take another way out, but three guys blocked my path. They spread out to keep me from getting past. I didn't recognize any of them, but then the middle one spoke. His voice, I knew.

"Stubborn little thing," he said, crossing his arms. It was the same voice I had heard twice already, a thicker accent coming through. His bleached blond hair was a contrast to his dark eyes, his high cheekbones sharp above his thick biceps.

"Who *are* you?" I demanded, hoping I didn't sound scared.

He smiled. "A messenger."

"You said that before," I retorted. "Who sent you? What the hell do you want?"

He clicked his tongue. "Such bad language for little princess. Right, guys?"

The three men started to circle me. I stepped back to keep them in my sights as much as possible.

"Go back to being a nice little nobody, hmmm?" he continued. "Or else me and my boys will keep coming for you. Over and over again."

I looked from one to the other. Was he behind the notes? Was he the one who'd poisoned Cyrus?

He was going to wish he'd never met me.

"Come at me and see what happens," I goaded.

He laughed, taunting me back. "If you want it that way, princess, okay."

He waved his hand forward.

The one on the left leapt towards me first. I grabbed him by the neck and shoved him into the one on the right. The blond charged. I kicked him in the chest, sending him flying backwards. I tried to escape, only to be yanked back by my wrists. He pulled me into a bear hug. I panicked for a moment, squirming. Then, taking a breath, I jammed my heel into his foot and elbowed him in the face when he loosened up.

When I stepped back, pain hit my shoulder and neck, and the impact sent me sprawling onto the gravel. A boot hit hard into my shoulder. Yelping in pain, I turned and looked up to see the messenger. His bleached hair glowed in the festival lights, a ragged plank of wood in his hand.

"You going to regret this," he said, coming towards me.

A figure jumped in and punched him across the face.

Tai.

The two behind us came forward, trying to come at Tai from both sides. He took a punch to the gut but came up to counter with a jab. He followed with a cross powerful enough to knock his attacker out. The other guy came up from behind.

"Look out!" I cried.

I jumped to my feet and slammed into the guy coming at Tai. He stumbled back but grabbed me in the process. He slapped me hard across the face. I lost my balance. He grunted as Tai grabbed him and kneed him in the gut. The guy grabbed Tai around the waist and sent him to the ground.

I reached down to help him, but someone grabbed both my arms and yanked me back. The pain in my shoulder blasted through my arm.

"Nuh-uh, princess. You leave your boyfriend here and come with me. I have work to finish."

The bone of his arm struck my throat as he choked me, pulling me back. I reached back and scratched his face. He dropped his hands for a moment, and I turned to kick him in the groin. With one last punch to the face, I tore away and went back for Tai.

Tai threw his assailant off and kicked out his knee. The guy stumbled over, giving Tai enough time to flip him over and punch him repeatedly in the face. When his assailant curled up in pain, Tai jumped up and grabbed my hand.

"Run!" he yelled.

We ran out of the festival and towards the parking lot. Tai held my hand tight, rushing to the car and shoving me inside. He turned over his key, then tore out of the exit, almost hitting pedestrians in the process.

I couldn't catch my breath. Terror ripped through my chest, throat, and head.

"They knew who I was," I cried, trying not to full-out sob. "They knew."

"It's okay now," he said, holding my hand tight. "I have you. It's all right."

Blood was trickling out of his lip and nose. His shirt was ripped up and covered in dirt and gravel.

"You're bleeding," I said, leaning forward and wiping away the blood from his face with my shaking hand.

He smiled. "It's okay. As long as you're okay, I can bleed a little."

I held tight to his hand, leaning my forehead against his shoulder as I tried to steady my breath.

Julian.

"Tai, call Julian. He was at the festival."

"Come again?"

I quickly explained. "Whoever came after me might go after him, too."

Now I was really shaking. With one hand on the steering wheel, Tai dialed the number, but I took the phone from him before Julian answered.

"Tai?"

"Julian! Get back to the castle. Now!"

"Marina?" he asked. "Where are you? Why did you—"

"You need to leave," I said. "Get out! Please get out now."

"Stop babbling. What are you saying?"

Tai took the phone from me. "Julian, Tai here. Yeah, I know. Let's talk about that later. Listen, Marina and I were attacked at the festival. If whoever attacked her knows who you are, it might not go well. Get yourself out of there."

With a pause and grunt, he hung up and threw the phone on the seat. His face was stone. Not at all like the relaxed Tai I was used to seeing.

Now I knew who was out to get me, but who were they? Why were they after me?

"Cyrus is going to kill me," he muttered to himself. "He already doesn't like me much and now I've gotten the princess …"

He stopped and bit his lip as I lifted my head.

"What did you say?" I asked.

He sighed. "It can't be avoided, I suppose. The truth is, I know who you are, too, Princess."

26

Unsettled

With another trip into the castle by way of the trunk, Tai snuck me back into my room. I was still confused at how he knew who I was, yet never said anything.

"Julian let it slip," he had said in the car. "He was muttering to himself, but I heard it. He wasn't supposed to tell me, so I pretended not to know. I didn't want to lose my job. Also, it was fun watching everyone act like you weren't a big deal." He huffed. "I shouldn't have taken you out tonight, but … I got sick of watching them lock you up, jailbird. You looked so miserable … and now look where we are."

When we reached my room, I ran to the bathroom and wet down a washcloth in the sink. Tai looked in the mirror and straightened out his shirt. He frowned at the tears in his clothes.

"I kind of liked this shirt," he muttered.

I put the cloth to his face, cleaning his wounds. He winced and hissed a little, but I didn't stop.

"I'm okay, you know," he said. "A hot shower will fix it."

"You saved me. It's the least I can do."

He softly wrapped his hand around my wrist and pulled it down. "Don't worry about me. I'm okay. Honest."

I tried to fight back the tears that were starting to creep up into my eyes. "I was so scared …"

His arms enclosed around me. I stood there for a moment, breathing in his dusty musk — a mix of sweat and dirt from the fight, and his natural woodsy scent.

After a few minutes passed, he broke away and looked me in the eye. "It's going to be all right."

"How?" I asked. "He's here somewhere."

His eyebrows crashed together. "What?"

I told Tai about the threats. Being chased down in the trees on the castle grounds. The letters. The poison.

"So, you've been …" he stopped. He grabbed my shoulders firmly. "You stay here."

I held onto his arm. He looked down at my hand, then smiled and patted it.

"Get yourself cleaned up," he said, nodding towards the shower. His finger traced along my neck, causing it to sting. I didn't even know there was a cut there. "I'll bring you an ice pack, okay? Lock the door until I come back."

With a nod, I let him go. He sped out of the room.

It was eerie and empty without him there. I didn't want to be alone.

Should I call Evann?

No. What was he going to do? Watch me take a shower? Awkward.

I finally gathered the courage to look at my injuries in the mirror. There were scratches up my neck and bruises forming on the side of my face. I got bruises all the time from karate, but this was different. These were wounds from someone who was trying to hurt me.

And they would come back for me.

My mind was swarming, but I was also covered in dirt, sweat, and blood. The only thing I could do was wash it off.

I turned on the shower, hoping to heat up the hot water before getting undressed.

Blood poured from the showerhead.

My scream echoed against the bathroom walls.

I dove into my room, tripping against an ottoman and crashing to the floor. The pain shooting through my leg broke me. All my fears hit my ribs, transforming into sobs.

A knock came to the door. "Hey? Are you alright?"

I couldn't tell who it was. I couldn't even answer. The door swung open and two hands reached down, grabbing me by the arms.

Nikos.

"Why are you crying?" he asked. "Don't tell me the shower freaked you out. It was only Kool-Aid powder."

I threw his hands off and glared at him. "It was you!"

"I didn't think it would scare you that much!"

"Don't – you – ever – stop?" I said, slapping him in the arm between each word. "I've had enough of you! Do you want me gone? Is that it? Is all of this your doing?"

He put a hand on my shoulder. "I didn't think—"

I winced. He stopped. I lifted my sleeve to reveal a gash on my arm. I didn't even remember that one.

"What happened?" he asked.

I pulled down my sleeve and sniffled. "Nothing."

"You don't get a cut like that from nothing. What …"

His eyes wandered around my face and neck. I brought my shoulders up to my ears, hoping it would hide whatever he was looking at.

His eyes darkened.

"Tell me what the hell happened to you. Now."

I opened my mouth to say something but ended up choking and crying again. He wrapped his arms around me, bringing me into his chest. I didn't have the strength to fight against him, so I cried into his shirt.

"How did this happen?" he asked, his voice now softer as his fingers rubbed my back. "Tell me."

He brought my eyes to meet his, his face tight.

"I …"

"She was attacked."

We both turned to Tai in the doorway. He shoved Nikos out of the way and crouched in front of me, applying an ice pack to my face. I held it, trying not to cry.

"Why are you here anyway?" Tai asked Nikos.

"Attacked?" Nikos replied, ignoring the question. "By whom?"

"Not sure. But it's someone in this castle."

Tai gave Nikos a brief account of what I'd told him. Nikos's eyes went three shades darker.

"And Cyrus knows about this?" he asked.

I nodded.

"Why didn't he tell me?" His eyes widened. "Did you think it was me?"

I sighed. "We didn't know who it was."

Silence floated between the three of us. I couldn't look anyone in the eye. I stared at the floor, holding the cold pack to my aching face.

"Who else knows about this?"

"Evann," I whispered. "And now Julian knows too."

Nikos pulled out his phone and dialed it.

"Evann, come to Marina's room, now." His eyes met mine as he spoke into the phone. "Yes, immediately. I need to have a meeting with my brothers."

27

TRACKING

I t had been two weeks.

I hadn't spoken to Tai. Cyrus hadn't mentioned throwing him out of the castle, but I was too scared to ask what had happened. I avoided Cyrus as well, locking myself in my room and refusing all meetings.

Wherever Tai was, I hoped he was okay. It was my fault he was in trouble in the first place. I shouldn't have agreed to sneaking out.

Now I didn't know if I would ever see him again.

"Are you going to leave your room, or should I order in a refrigerator?" Evann asked.

I sighed. "I don't want to go out."

"I don't like watching you mope around," Evann said, grabbing my hands. "Come on. I want to show you something. You'll like it."

When we left the room, the four new guards at my door stepped forward to go with us, but Evann waved his hand to tell them to stay. They bowed and went back to their spot, allowing Evann to escort me down the halls to the other side of the castle.

He muttered on about different facts about the castle, but I wasn't really interested in any of it. All I could think about was the guy from the festival, Tai, and the look on Cyrus's face when he saw the bruises and cuts on my neck.

Cyrus cared. Tai cared. Even that brat, Nikos, cared.

And what was I doing? Causing them grief and trouble at every turn.

I couldn't look any of them in the eye now.

"Here we are," Evann said, pointing to two golden double doors.

I cocked my head to the side. "What is it?"

He smirked. "Something to cheer you up."

He opened the doors. Instantly I was overwhelmed with flashing lights and electric noises.

"Is this … an arcade?" I asked.

He nodded. "Do you want to shoot something?"

I almost cried. "That would be so nice."

He chuckled and put his arm around my shoulder, pulling me into the room. He led me to the shooter games where we played a few rounds. He was a surprisingly good shot. Much better than Tai. A pang of shame flicked my chest, but I tried to ignore it.

"I don't know why I'm surprised that you want to do something violent."

I turned around to follow the voice.

Julian?

Or Julian's alarmingly normal twin.

He was wearing a navy plaid shirt and jeans, his hair messed up and leaning towards the left. He didn't look like a prince at all. He looked like a regular guy at the arcade. It wasn't a bad look on him.

"Didn't expect to see you two here," he said.

"I was trying to get the princess out of her room," Evann replied.

Julian nodded at me. "Yes, you have been there awhile, haven't you? You haven't even joined us for any meals in the last week."

I nodded. *Because I can't face any of you.*

Julian clicked his tongue. "Well, come on then. Since you're finally out, you should at least enjoy the afternoon."

Giving me a small smile, he raised his hand and summoned me to follow him. Evann shrugged. We followed him to the table hockey area.

"You any good?" he asked.

"Of course," I replied.

He nodded, turning on the machine and putting the puck on the table. "Show me your skills, then."

He tapped the puck. I smacked it back. It flew off the table. Evann retrieved it, while Julian eyed me.

"Sorry," I said.

His eyes softened. "I know."

I tried not to cry again.

Evann put the puck back on the table, and Julian tapped it again. I tapped it back.

Tap. Clink clink. Tap. Clink. Tap. Tap. Clink clink clink. Tap.

I was getting tired of the back and forth. No progress. No end in sight. I wanted this to be over. I wanted to win.

I smacked it again, and it flew off the table, right into Julian's chest. He grabbed his chest and bent over, coughing.

"Even when I don't do anything to you, I get injured."

I ran over to the side of the table. "I'm sorry! I'm so sorry! Are you alright?"

He grunted, standing back up. "I'll be fine. Let's try something a little less dangerous."

It was an afternoon of basketball hoops, shooting games, and dancing games. Evann and — surprisingly — Julian did their best to make me laugh and entertain me as the day went on.

For the first time we were laughing together.

After a few hours, Evann's phone buzzed. He picked up. He frowned, nodding. "Yes, Your Highness." He hung up and looked at us. "Prince Nikos needs my assistance."

"I'll stay with Marina," Julian said. "You go ahead."

Evann looked between us, then nodded. "Thank you. I'll return soon, Princess."

I waved at him as he left. An awkward pause sat between Julian and me.

"So … how are you at racing games?" he finally asked, smiling.

§

"Are you a professional race-car driver?" I asked. "How did you beat me like that when you never leave the castle?"

He leaned back in his bucket seat as the game declared him the winner for the sixth time in a row.

He snorted. "Who says I don't leave?"

I thought back to the night of the festival. "Are you allowed to leave?"

"Yes, I'm allowed to leave. I'm not a prisoner."

"Then why did you sneak out to the festival?"

"Because …" He stopped. "Because I didn't want people to know *why* I was going to the festival."

Juniper. Come to think of it, I hadn't seen her in a while either.

"I'm not going to tell anyone, you know," I said.

He paused, looking at me for a long moment.

"About Juniper," I added.

He nodded. "There's no reason to worry anymore. She dumped me."

I nearly jumped out of my chair to face him. "Wait, wait, wait. *She* dumped *you*? What for?"

He didn't answer. He just stared at the racing screen as the demo played.

"Didn't she want to—"

I stopped. Uncle Lloyd and Aunt Tina.

My heart sank. "You were going to give up being a prince for her … weren't you?"

He straightened but didn't look at me.

"You loved her that much?" I continued.

He laughed bitterly. "I don't know. I thought I might. But she didn't want me to."

"If you love her, you should go after her."

His eyes met mine with a stare so strong that I couldn't breathe for a minute.

He broke the stare. "Maybe."

"Julian …"

"I can't focus on that right now," he said, waving it away. "You're more important at the moment."

"What? Me?"

"Yes, you. You're our guest, and your life is being threatened. All this time, and you couldn't tell me?"

I slumped back in the chair. "I didn't think you'd care, honestly."

"I know we got off to a really bad start," he said, his eyes on his hands. "In the beginning, I thought you'd abuse your new status and power. It took me awhile to realize you weren't that type of woman. When I heard that you were attacked … Do you know how worried I was?"

His eyes rose to meet mine.

"You can hate me if you want," he said, "I don't blame you. But even after how I've acted, I don't want anything to happen to you. I mean that."

His last sentence came out as a whisper. I reached out and patted his hand.

"I don't hate you." It was true. I didn't. How could I?

He put his hand on top of mine. "Good. Now, a bet's a bet. You owe me a really large ice-cream sundae for losing."

I groaned.

"Come on," he said, grabbing my hand and leading me towards the door.

Julian led me to the kitchen and sat on the counter as I fixed him a three-scoop sundae.

"Don't go easy on the whipped cream or chocolate syrup," he commanded.

I rolled my eyes. "Yes, *Your Highness.*"

"Interesting that you only call me that when you're being sarcastic."

"Get used to it."

I handed him his ice cream. He glowed like a schoolboy as he shoved large spoonfuls in his mouth. I made myself a bowl and sat next to him.

After a few minutes of silently eating ice cream, he turned to me. "Have you talked to your father lately?"

My shoulders dropped. "No. He hasn't called. Or written. I would settle for smoke signals at this point. I can't call him either."

"Have you decided on what you want?"

I put down the bowl, swinging my legs off the side of the counter. "Not really. I don't know if I'm cut out to be a princess. It's a lot of responsibility I'm not qualified for."

"We'll help you."

"I know. I appreciate that, but I don't want you to have to carry me. Also, I have to think about the people I'm responsible for. I want them to be in capable hands." I turned to him. "But I'm afraid if I don't take it, I'll regret it. I don't want to let my family down, and I don't want to waste all the time that was spent on me. Also … I wouldn't see you guys again if I rejected my station."

He put down his bowl. "I guess that's true. Not to mention, Cyrus—"

He stopped.

"What about him?" I asked.

"Uhh … nothing."

His face twisted.

"It's obviously something," I said. "Spill! What's wrong with Cyrus?"

"Listen," he said, "there's something you don't know yet. There's a reason you're here specifically."

"Of course. Because my father sent me."

"Yes, that. But you … ugh … I can't tell you."

I jumped down from the counter and scowled at him.

"Why are there so many things that people can't tell me?" I asked, blocking his path. "What is it? Why was I brought here?"

He hesitated, opening his mouth to say something. Before he could, someone else cut into the conversation.

"I think I should be the one to tell you that, my dear."

We both turned to Cyrus in the doorway.

He eyed us both. "I'll tell her, Julian. Thank you."

Julian's head dipped. "Cyrus, I apologize. I didn't mean—"

Cyrus held his hand up. "It's okay. I shouldn't have waited so long in the first place."

Julian gave one last sideways glance at me, then nodded. He left Cyrus and me alone in the kitchen.

"Cyrus? Tell me what?"

He walked past me and went straight to the ice cream. "You didn't eat all of it, did you?"

He helped himself to a bowl.

"So, what is it?" I asked. "Why am I here?"

Cyrus finished off a spoonful, stepping in close to me. His eyes met mine as he licked the spoon clean. "You were sent here … for me."

"What?"

He ate another spoonful. "Your father sent you here because of me. Our families arranged us together."

My smile faded. "What …?"

He took a third spoonful, then dropped the bowl and spoon on the counter. His arms came on each side of me, trapping me between him and the counter. He looked directly into my eyes, capturing my attention.

"I should have said this earlier, but I couldn't find the right opportunity. My dear, you and I have an arranged marriage."

28

In-Laws

I laughed. "Stop it, Cyrus. I thought you were serious for a minute."

He didn't smile. He didn't even blink.

"… You're serious?"

He dropped his hands. "I told you that our parents were close friends. I suppose they wanted it to stay that way."

"Then my father … he … he knew? I mean he was the one to …"

I couldn't stop stuttering. How could he do that? Why didn't he say anything? First the princess thing, and now this? Was this some kind of joke to him?

Cyrus's warm hands rubbed my shoulders. "Look at me. Nothing is set in stone."

"It seems pretty solid to me!" I said, my voice rising higher than I expected. "My parents shipped me off to some castle to become a princess I didn't want to become — and marry me to someone I hadn't even met!"

"I know this is a shock for you — it was to me too at first — but ..." His eyes dropped to the floor along with his voice. "I won't make you marry me."

The weight in the room was heavy, along with his eyes. He took my hands, his fingers closing over mine.

"I mean, you don't have to marry me," he said. "It's still common for royals to have arranged marriages, but I won't force you to marry me. No one can force you. But that's the reason you were sent here. For me. I'm sorry for not telling you sooner. I didn't know how to."

"Does everyone know?"

He nodded.

So, Julian and Nikos knew that I was going to be their sister-in-law? Did Evann know? Did Tai?

"You don't really want to marry me ..." I said. "Do you?"

He gave a half-smile. "At first, I was against the idea. I didn't know you. I always admired your parents, but I couldn't imagine being married to a stranger. Now?" His fingers trickled over my knuckles. "It would feel empty here without you. That's not a reason to get married, but it's the way I feel. Having you here turned out to be better than I anticipated."

He dropped my hands with a shaky breath and went back to the bowl of ice cream, shoving another spoonful of it into his mouth. I wrapped my arms around myself, suddenly chilled.

"Take your time making your decision," Cyrus continued. "There's no rush, and I don't want you to feel pressured. You can become a princess or not. You can marry me or ..."

He trailed off as his eyes fell to the side.

I shook my head. "I can't. I can't make decisions like that."

Cyrus stepped in towards me. "Hey, it's okay …"

"Which part is okay?" I yelled back. "The part where everyone has been lying to me? The part where I'm supposed to make decisions that no one ever prepared me for? The part where my entire life has been given to other people?"

Cyrus opened his mouth to say something, but I turned and ran before he could say anything. I didn't want to hear it. No matter what he had to say, it wasn't going to fix anything.

I ran out of the castle completely and into the gardens. I didn't know where I was going, but it had to be better than standing around with people that didn't care about me enough to be honest with me.

I ran until my legs and lungs burned, through the gardens and towards the lake. I sat on the edge, holding my arms and shuddering, trying not to cry. It didn't work.

I cried until I was too exhausted to cry anymore.

Footsteps came up behind me.

"Princess, what are you doing all the way out here? It's not sa—"

"Evann," I said, cutting him off. "I'm engaged."

I looked back to see his face. His eyes widened for a moment, then his shoulders dropped.

"Yes. I know," he said, coming over to crouch next to me.

I shook my head. "I didn't. I didn't know any-thing. I never realized any of this. My entire life … with so many lies … I'm so stupid."

He wrapped his arms around me.

"Nothing makes sense," I said.

His hand combed through my hair. "Sometimes it doesn't."

I held onto his arms. "What do I do?"

"You don't have to make any decisions right now. You can just process the information. That's enough for now."

"Will you stay with me?" I asked, sounding like a child.

He laughed through his nose and pulled me in. "Of course, Princess. Of course."

<h1 style="text-align:center">29</h1>

<h2 style="text-align:center">PONIES AND PROBLEMS</h2>

"So, they're playing golf while riding a horse?" I asked. "Is there a version where you play mini-golf on a poodle?"

Evann hid a smile behind his hand. Nikos rolled his eyes.

"Polo is a popular sport among royals. You'll find yourself at a lot of these matches."

"Watching a bunch of rich guys gallop around on horses with golf clubs doesn't really excite me. Can we at least put them on donkeys instead? It would be more entertaining."

"Tell you what," Nikos replied. "I'll give you a donkey and you can take it around the castle grounds all you want when we get back. Would that make you happy?"

"Why get a donkey when I have you? After all, you're a big enough a—"

"I'll be happy to keep you company and explain the game to you, Princess." Evann cut in. "I won't let you get bored."

211

Nikos gave him a sideways glance. He folded his arms and looked out the window of the limo as we rode to the event.

I wasn't sure why I was being dragged along on this outing. Something about it being a good introduction to royal image. I didn't want an image. And I wasn't in the mood to hang out with Nikos and his attitude.

As I stepped out of the car, I was greeted by a half-dozen bodyguards and the stench of wet grass and manure. My eyes watered.

"What's with the face?" Nikos asked.

I scowled at him. "I was thinking about sitting next to you for the next four hours."

I walked ahead. Why did it have to be Nikos of all people? He still hadn't apologized for the night he used me. Or the prank with the shower. Wasn't he sorry? Probably not. He probably didn't even realize he'd done anything wrong.

I was escorted to a balcony where we could watch the game apart from the rest of the crowd. Once seated, I was offered champagne, fruit and cheese, a platter of seafood appetizers, and tea sandwiches. I would have killed for a hot dog and a bucket of popcorn. After two months of nothing but fancy finger foods (that, sadly, weren't chicken strips), something greasy and fattening sounded amazing.

After the national anthem and player introductions, the teams took the field. The ball was dropped, and each rider swung his golf club — or whatever it was — in the air and at the ball.

Gallop. Putt. Gallop. Putt. Gallop. Putt.

A half an hour of this and I was ready to punch someone. It would have been so much faster if they all jumped off the horses and ran.

"How do you like it so far, Princess?" Evann asked.

"I'd like it more if they fell off their horses once in a while to make it interesting. Even when they make a goal, they don't celebrate."

Someone started a cheer below us for their team. I bobbed to their rhythm.

"At least someone is having fun," I muttered.

"Being a royal doesn't mean you have fun all the time," Nikos replied, stuffing a finger sandwich in his mouth.

"Right. You only have fun when you're playing dirty tricks and using people for your own agenda."

I crossed my arms and stared forward. His arm draped over the back of my chair as he turned to me.

"Not letting that go, are you?"

"Forget it. I don't have any interest in you or your nonsense."

"Oh?" he said, chuckling close to my ear. "Are you sure about that? Because if that night really didn't bother you, then you wouldn't keep acting like this."

I turned to face him, realizing how close he was sitting next to me. I could headbutt him if I wanted. Instead, I glared.

"You should probably turn back in your seat," I said. "I can only imagine what the tabloids would write about us now if I choose to marry Cyrus."

He slumped back. "You know about that?"

I gave a sharp nod.

"And you're going to go through with it?" he asked.

I shrugged. "You just might be stuck with me as your sister-in-law for a lifetime."

He went silent. After a breath, he stood from his chair and left the box.

Evann dropped his head. "Have you accepted the offer then?"

"No. I'm not accepting any offers. I only wanted Nikos to back off a bit."

"It sounds like you want him to be jealous."

"Ew. Don't be gross."

Evann leaned back in his seat, draping an arm over. "It would be easy to be jealous of Cyrus."

"What do you mean?"

He chuckled to himself, not answering.

"Nikos isn't jealous," I assured him. "We're not even friends."

"Is that what he thinks? Because the only time I see him act like this is with his brothers or the people he's most comfortable with. Friends look like different things to different people. You could be his friend and not even know it, Princess."

I looked over my shoulder, Nikos nowhere to be seen. We weren't friends. We didn't like each other. He was mad at the idea of my marrying Cyrus. He clearly didn't want me in the family.

Maybe he hated me even more than I thought.

30

KIDNAPPED

Nikos eventually returned, only to give me the silent treatment for the rest of the game. As if the game wasn't boring enough.

I stood up.

"Where are you going?" Nikos asked, breaking his silence.

"To the ladies' room. Is that okay with you?"

"You can't go by yourself."

"I'm not inviting you."

"Not me. Gross." He rolled his eyes. "Evann, escort Her Royal Annoying Highness to the restroom and then bring her right back."

I stuck my tongue out at him as we walked away.

With Evann outside the restroom, I rinsed my hands in a sink that cost more than my house while thinking about my future. What would it be like if Julian and Nikos really were my brothers-in-law? What would it be like to be Cyrus's wife? He had always been kind to me. I liked spending time with him. Regardless, marriage was too much.

What did *I* want?

A hand wrapped around my waist and face and yanked me back.

I thrashed back, swinging my arms and legs to fend off the attacker. The attacker loosened, and I turned around, slamming his body into the sink. A deep grunt followed. He let go only for a moment, then pain shot through the back of my head. I fell to the ground, my stomach knotting.

I looked up.

It was the messenger.

"You're so feisty," he said, panting and holding his side. "It would be cute if it wasn't so annoying."

"Evann!" I yelled.

The guy reached down to grab me, laughing. "Baby, he's not coming for you."

When he grabbed my arm, I kicked his leg out and jumped up. He was faster, though, and grabbed me before I could escape. He slammed me against the wall. My head hit the tiles; my knees slacked. He slammed my head against the wall again, and I started to black out.

"Not this time, sweetie. Not this time."

He socked me in the stomach before putting a piece of duct tape over my mouth. I tried to fight back as best I could, but the room was spinning. Everything was going dark. His mouth came close to my ear.

"You're coming home with me."

Everything went black.

§

My head throbbed.

When my eyes cleared, I found myself in someone's living room. There were broken black-and-white chairs, a ripped couch, and a scratched coffee table covered in beer cans and travel magazines.

I sat up. There was a chair in front of me, a man sitting in it, sipping on a beer.

The messenger.

How long had he been watching me?

"Good morning, Princess," he sang. "Welcome to our home."

I jumped up to run but fell to the floor. I tried to move my feet and hands, but they wouldn't move. They were tied.

His clothes ruffled as he came closer.

"Sorry, Your Royalness, but you can't leave that easy."

With a chuckle, he pulled me up and put me back on the couch. Leaning in, he fixed my hair behind my ears with mock tenderness. I jerked away.

"Hands off, jackass!" I said.

He smiled, running his hand against the back of my head. It stung. I hissed.

"Awww, are you hurt?" he asked, pouting. "That's shame. I guess it is karma for the things you did to us. But if you'd like ..." His hand ran down my neck. "I can help with pain."

His accent was different from the one I remembered, but his voice was the same. His English was nearly perfect, but his articles kept dropping. Was he Aujinian?

"Keep the hell away from me!"

He laughed but tightened his grip. "You don't have manners, do you, Princess? Maybe if you were nicer, I let you go."

"What do you want?"

He shrugged. "What everyone else does. Money. Success. Power. Free movies."

"Why am I involved?"

"To get what I want, I get rid of you."

"Not sure what your goals have to do with me. Unless *you* want to be a princess?"

He frowned. "You have sharp tongue. I wonder if I could get more money if I cut it?"

He pulled a knife from his pocket. I could only watch it as he waved it in front of me.

"Who do you think would buy you, hmm?" he continued. "I'm sure there is good market for forgotten princesses."

A door slammed. Footsteps pounded across the floor. The man in front of me stood.

"Zhixin!" a familiar voice yelled. "What the hell!"

The figure stepped forward and punched my captor in the face. He went down, hitting the coffee table.

I kept blinking, but what I saw didn't change.

… Tai?

31

TRAITOR

"Have you lost your mind?" Tai yelled.

Zhixin replied in another language, his voice low and a little desperate. Tai cut his hand through the air, responding in the same language. I couldn't understand any of it, no matter how I strained my ears.

Tai then stepped into Zhixin's space and got into his face.

"I won't tell you again," Tai growled.

Zhixin glanced between us, pulling his mouth to the side. Tai yelled at him again in the same language as before.

The messenger glanced at me one more time, clenching his jaw. He narrowed his eyes but didn't say another word as he turned to leave the room.

Tai ripped the ties off my hands and feet, pausing only to graze his fingers gently against my face. The pain made me wince. He cursed under his breath with words I understood but could never repeat, then scooped me up into his arms and carried me out the door to the car.

I couldn't even respond as he buckled my seatbelt and started the car. All I could do was look out the window.

It wasn't until we were driving through the downtown that I could finally speak.

"Tai ...?"

"I'm sorry. I'm so sorry," he replied before I could ask a full question. "It wasn't supposed to go this far. He wasn't supposed to touch you at the festival. As for kidnapping—"

"It was you the whole time?" My voice cracked. "*You* were the one trying to get rid of me?"

"He was just supposed to scare you off. Make you go back to your old life—"

"So, you sent me threats and had those people chase me, and—"

Tried to poison me?

I stopped before saying it.

Tai had *actually* tried to hurt me.

He stopped at a red light and turned to me. "That's not the—"

I hit my seatbelt buckle and bolted out the door before he could finish. I dodged the cars as they screeched to a stop and honked. I heard my name behind me, but it faded as I ran further into the city.

I wasn't sure how long I was running for, but I was in pain. My ankles hurt from being tied. My ribs hurt from being punched.

And none of it would have happened if it weren't for Tai.

I curled up against the back wall of a night club that hadn't opened yet and started to cry into my knees. Why was it Tai? Why would he hurt me like that?

Why did I ignore the signs? How stupid was I?

I couldn't hold back my sobs, as embarrassing as it was, and as much as it hurt my bruised ribs. The sun had set by the time I had begun to calm down. I watched the pedestrians as they passed by the alleyway, wondering if I could get back to the castle on my own without any money or directions.

Who was I kidding? I couldn't do it. I couldn't do anything.

A limo pulled up. Before it even came to a stop, the door swung open and a figure bounded out towards me.

I had never been happier to see Evann in my entire life.

"Marina! Are you alright? What—"

He stopped and his eyes widened. The damage must have been bad.

"Come here," he encouraged, leaning down and taking me into his arms. "Let's get you out of here."

I gripped onto him, unable to speak or walk. I just shuddered. His arms wrapped around me as I tried not to cry. He calmly shushed me.

"You're safe now," he said. "I've got you."

He led me back to the limo, where Nikos was waiting for us. Nikos dropped forward on one knee to look at me. Looking at my face, he cussed.

"Good to see you too," I said.

"What the hell did they do to you?" he asked. "Was it the same people as before?"

Yes ... But ...

Evann jumped into the seat next to me and held my face in his hands. I took a good look at him, realizing there was now a huge gash in the side of his face.

"Evann, what—"

"He got me from behind," Evann finished. "I take full responsibility and punishment for not protecting you."

I held onto his shirt. "I thought you were ..."

I didn't finish.

Evann shook his head. "No. I'm still here. Are you okay?"

I shook my head. Evann brought me in to lean on his shoulder as the limo took off. I wrapped my arms around his waist, his winter-mint scent calming me.

Nikos sat across from us, leaning forward with his elbows on his knees. "Did you see who did this?"

I met his eyes and nodded. "Tai."

"What?" Evann and Nikos cried at the same time.

"It was Tai," I repeated.

I buried my head in Evann's chest, trying not to cry. He held me tight, running his hand against my back.

"What do we do?" he said to Nikos.

"I'm going to kill him," Nikos growled.

"I'm serious."

"So am I."

There was a pause, then the muted sound of a phone ringing.

"Cyrus," Nikos said. "We have a huge problem."

32

SEARCHING

They couldn't find him.

A week had passed. My bruises were fading, but when I shut my eyes, I could still smell beer and old leather. I lied every time Cyrus asked me if I had slept well and lied again every time Evann asked if I wanted him to stay with me.

I couldn't be weak. I had to forget it ever happened.

Cyrus made that difficult, constantly calling me to the castle infirmary.

"This might leave a scar," he muttered, tracing the cut in my neck. He looked at the nurse. "Do you have any anti-scarring cream?"

She nodded and left. Cyrus turned back to me, his eyes almost narrowed shut.

"I'm fine," I assured him. "I can handle a few battle scars."

"You never should have been hurt in the first place," Cyrus returned. "Your father put you in my care, yet I didn't protect …"

I patted his hand. "Don't worry about it. I'm okay."

Our hands trembled together for a moment. I wasn't sure if it was his or mine.

Julian sighed on the other side of the room. "This was my fault. I insisted that we hire him …"

Cyrus waved his hand. "You're not at fault."

Nikos had been unusually quiet, rubbing his bottom lip with his finger and staring into the distance. Evann held his post and, although he was silent, I could see the concern in his eyes when he looked at me.

"Any news on his whereabouts?" Julian asked.

Cyrus shrugged, frowning. "I have people looking for him all over the city. I suppose it's time to start looking outside of the capital."

I tapped my fingers against my thigh. "What will you do with him once you find him?"

There was a long pause as the three of them looked at me.

Julian cleared his throat. "According to law, he'll be tried for treason. He was an accessory to assaulting and kidnapping a member of the royal family."

Treason? Did that mean they would …

"He saved me. There has to be another reason why—"

"He's the one who put you in danger," Nikos said, breaking his silence. "It was probably all an act from the beginning. Don't let your crush blind you."

"It's not a crush. He's my friend." I clenched my jaw. "But you wouldn't know what it's like to have those."

He stood up from his seat, knocking it over. "If you're stupid enough to be friends with someone who tried to get you killed, then maybe you got what you deserved."

"Nikos!" Cyrus scolded.

Nikos slammed the door behind him.

I clamped my jaw, trying to hold in the ridiculous tears crawling up my throat. I wasn't going to cry because of him. I wasn't.

"He didn't mean that, my dear," Cyrus started.

I shook my head at him. He sighed.

"I'll go talk to him," Julian said. He pressed his lips together. "Thoughtless words are the worst kind."

He raised his eyebrow at me as he said it, then left after Nikos. Cyrus sighed again.

The nurse returned, rubbing some cool gel all over my neck. Cyrus watched intently, his lips flattening. He turned to Evann.

"I've commanded extra guards at her post. I want you to take a couple of weeks off, Evann. Wait until—"

"I'm fine," Evann replied. "It's my responsibility to protect her."

"It's my job to protect you."

"The hell it is." Evann's eyes flashed, his hands balling. "I'll keep my responsibilities, *Your Majesty*."

The title dripped in disdain. Cyrus bit his lip, turning to the nurse.

"Treat his wounds as well," Cyrus said.

Evann didn't take his eyes off Cyrus as the nurse applied cream to his face.

Our joined hands started to shake again. I knew for certain that it wasn't mine.

"Cyrus, are you alright?" I asked.

He jerked his head to one side. "No. No, I'm not alright. There's a threat in my kingdom, and I can't …"

He trailed off, gripping his head with a trembling hand.

Evann stepped forward. "King Cyrus …"

"Don't worry about me," he said.

"Do I need to get—"

"No."

Cyrus cleared his throat, pulling on the collar of his suit. I touched his arm, but he didn't respond to it.

"Evann," he said, "bring me all the files we have on the Double Eights."

"Double Eights?" I asked. "What's that?"

Cyrus hesitated. "Double Eights is the name of a criminal gang in our kingdom. They're Tai's old family."

I blinked. "What?"

"Tai's father was the leader of the Double Eights," Cyrus replied. "He was the king of criminal activities until he was put to death six years ago."

Evann sighed through his nose. "It seems that the Prince of the Double Eights has made you his number one target."

§

I liked Evann, but I was tired of him following me everywhere.

I wasn't allowed to be alone. There were guards when I slept, guards when I ate, guards when I had lessons with Nikos and Julian. I was exhausted with all the attention. Couldn't they leave me alone for an hour? I needed time to myself. I couldn't even sleep knowing there were six men outside my room; forget how long it took me to convince them to let me sleep without guards *in* my room.

I looked out to the balcony. Tai had snuck up so easily. He scaled a wall just to meet me and take me to the festival. He was so relaxed about the entire thing, as if he was weightless and invincible.

That's how Tai was. It's what I missed most about him.

"Tai was high in command in the Double Eights," Evann had said. "He was sent to prison after being charged with murder by arson."

It still made my stomach clench every time I thought about it.

Tai wasn't a murderer. There had to be a misunderstanding. I couldn't accept that the man who had made me feel alive was the same one who was trying to kill me.

But after the poison, I wasn't sure what to believe anymore.

Something felt off about the entire thing.

The question was, who were the Double Eights and why were they targeting me?

Knock, knock, knock.

I asked who it was. Julian answered.

"Are you still being defensive?" he asked, opening the door. "I don't want to spend a night going in conversational circles."

"Always the charmer," I grumbled back.

"I could say the same to you." He shut the door. "You're making enemies out of the few allies you have."

"Since when did you decide we were allies, Julian?"

"Since I decided that we were no longer enemies."

I turned my head away from him. "Did you know about Tai?"

He sighed, taking a seat in the chair next to the window. "I learned about him after I hired him."

"And you kept him employed?"

"I had no reason not to. He served his time in the system. He had no way to find work when he got out. If I didn't hire him, he would have ended back on the str—" He sighed. "Well, I guess that's how it turned out anyway."

His eyes narrowed as he looked out the window, head resting on his chin.

"If he murdered someone, why wasn't he imprisoned for life?" I asked. "Or given the death penalty?"

"No proof of the charges against him," he replied. "Just enough evidence to ruin his life. And we couldn't put him to death because his father was a gang lord."

"I don't believe the charges against him. I don't think he would hurt me."

Julian chuckled.

"You think I'm joking?" I asked.

"No, I didn't think that at all. I'm amused. For once we agree on something."

His hand rested against his cheek as he smiled genuinely at me. He stood, meeting me at my bed. He reached out, his fingers grazing my shoulder as he looked at my neck.

"Whoever did this will come for you again," he said. "You know this, don't you?"

I nodded.

He smiled. "It's a shame that they don't know who they're up against."

33

THE ATTACK

Cyrus was missing.

Evann wasn't as alarmed as I was.

"I can't call for the entire castle to search for him simply because he's late for a chess game," he said.

I shook my head. "This is Cyrus, remember? Prince Punctual. King of Exact Minutes. How could he be late for his own schedule? It's like the sun being late for its own rising."

"I'm sure he's fine. Give him a few minutes."

I gave him seven. He still hadn't arrived. I tapped my queen against the chessboard.

"Evann, call for a search party."

He frowned, pressing his lips together. "Stay calm, Princess."

I stood. "I'm going to go look for him."

Evann jumped in front of me and grabbed my shoulders. "Trust me on this. Stay here for a little while longer. He'll come."

I tried to shrug off his hands, but he held firm. "Why are you acting like this suddenly? You should know him better than this."

"I do. Which is why I'm asking you to stay where you are."

I sighed, slowly dropping my shoulders in surrender.

When Evann let go of me, I bolted to the door.

He called for me, but I didn't look back. I ran down the hall towards Cyrus's private rooms, Evann close behind. I was able to hold him off until I reached Cyrus's hallway. Before I could reach the door of his bedroom, Evann's arm wrapped around me and pulled me back. He lifted me off my feet, wedging me between himself and the wall of the hallway.

"You have a lot of trouble following orders," he said, panting.

"I don't take orders from you."

"Yes, you might chemically combust if you took an order from anybody."

The shuffle of feet distracted me from my reply. Beside us, a trio of nurses knocked on Cyrus's bedroom door. They were let in. The door shut.

I turned back to Evann. "Is Cyrus sick?"

He sighed, breaking eye contact. I gritted my teeth, pinching his nose between my fingers and twisting it.

"Stop keeping things from me!" I yelled. "What's wrong with Cyrus?"

"What the hell is this?" a third voice broke in.

We both turned toward Nikos, who was standing in the open doorway of Cyrus's bedroom with an eyebrow raised.

Evann, his nose still twisted in my hand, tried to adopt a military bearing. "I apologize, Your Highness. I'll take the princess—"

Nikos raised his hand for silence and listened for a moment back through the open door. He sighed.

"Forget it," Nikos said. "You can both come in."

Evann released me. I rushed into Cyrus's room.

Cyrus didn't look sick. His color was good. He was sitting straight. He didn't seem like he needed the water and pills one of the nurses was handing him.

"Cyrus …?" I asked.

He swallowed a pill. "Welcome. Sorry I'm late for our match."

I grunted. "Do you know how worried I was?"

"No." He smiled. "Tell me."

"Why are there nurses in your room? Why didn't you show up for our game?"

Nikos, who had plonked himself down at Cyrus's desk, sighed as he rested his elbow on the desk and his cheek against his hand. "Always demanding something, aren't you?"

"I was a bit ill," Cyrus explained. "I didn't want you to see me like this. Yet, here we are."

I approached him. "Are you sick? Is it bad?"

He hesitated.

"You know if you tell her, she'll never leave you alone about it," Nikos warned.

Cyrus reached his hand for mine. He clasped it. I didn't pull away. "Maybe I like the attention."

I sat next to him, holding his hand. "What's wrong?"

He shook his head. "They're just panic attacks."

"Panic attacks? Why?"

"Because he's a king," Nikos said.

"A king that can't control his own mind," Cyrus added. "Is there anything more pathetic?"

He rubbed his face in his hand, until the nurse came to take his blood pressure.

"How often do you have them?" I asked.

"Every day," he admitted.

Every day? How could he go through this every day without my ever noticing?

"Don't give her too much information, Cyrus," Nikos said. "She might use it against you."

"Could you stop being salty for two minutes?" I barked.

"It's nothing the castle doesn't know already," Cyrus said, his voice heavy. He shut his eyes and rested his head on his hand.

I touched his shoulder. "Are you alright?"

Without opening his eyes, he reached up and rubbed my hand with his. "I'm at the exhaustion phase. It's the last phase of my attacks. Don't worry. It'll pass. It always does."

The lines in his face were deep. How could he suffer like this for so long? Why didn't he tell me?

Ding.

Nikos reached in his pocket and pulled out his phone. He hissed as he opened it.

"Dammit," he groaned.

"What is it?" Cyrus asked.

Nikos put his phone back in his pocket. "Nothing. Some bad press about my outfit a few days ago."

He stood.

"Aren't there more important things to worry about?" I asked.

"Yes," he said, glaring. "There are."

He widened his eyes at me and nodded towards the door.

"Get some rest," Nikos said to Cyrus. "I'll entertain the princess while you recuperate."

Cyrus raised an eyebrow at Nikos. He only stared. I clasped onto Cyrus's shoulder.

"I don't want to leave Cyrus like this," I said.

Nikos tsked, rolling his eyes.

"I'm alright," Cyrus said. "I'll be very boring for the next hour, though. We can meet after that. Go ahead."

He patted my hand and shut his eyes again.

Nikos nodded his head at the door once again. I assured Cyrus I would be back, and then followed Nikos into the hallway. Evann followed us out. Nikos cocked his head to the side at him.

"She's my responsibility," Evann said, as if someone had asked a question.

Nikos sighed. "Very well. But don't breathe a word to Cyrus."

Evann nodded.

"What's the problem?" I asked.

"It seems your prediction was correct." He handed me his phone.

There was a picture of him and me at the polo game, our faces close. I scrolled down to the headline.

WHO IS PRINCE NIKOS'S MYSTERY GIRLFRIEND?

34

TABLOIDS

"What the hell?" I cried.

"Tabloids," Evann muttered.

"This is a problem," Nikos said.

"Of course it is!" I replied. "I'd never be your girlfriend."

Nikos cleared his throat. "*That's* not the problem. The problem is the press snooping around your identity after my birthday party. This is going to bring up more suspicions and theories. They're going to figure out who you really are."

I sighed. "They'll figure it out sooner or later."

"Then, have you made a decision?" Nikos asked. "You'll need a statement immediately once the press figures it out. We can't do anything for you at that point."

I didn't answer.

Nikos took the phone from my hand, scrolling back through it. He brought his hand to his face and stroked his jaw.

"I wish they had gotten my right side instead of my left."

"Oh my God, you're so stupid," I said.

"*I'm* stupid?" he countered. "This wouldn't be a problem if you hadn't kicked me at my own party."

"I wouldn't have kicked you if you hadn't been such a prick."

"Hey, I came to apologize, but you were with—" His eyes shot over to Evann. He stopped. "Forget it. You really are a pain. I don't know why I bother trying to help you. It's not like you've ever done anything for me."

I opened my mouth to say something, but nothing came out. I tried to think of something I had done for him to throw back in his face, but … there was nothing.

"Well, look at that," he said, "you're finally speechless."

His eyes went cold as his lips thinned. He put his phone back in his pocket, looking off to the side.

"Nikos …" I started.

"Take this as my last act of kindness," Nikos said, cutting me off. "The press is after you now. Watch your back."

He turned, but my hand reached out and grabbed his shirt sleeve before he walked away completely. He turned back, as surprised as I was at the gesture.

I swallowed. "She likes deep conversations and long books. She said that he can talk to her about anything from the reason for human existence to the themes of *War and Peace.*"

His jaw ticked and his eyes softened. For a moment, he went from the World's Prince to nineteen-year-old

Nikos. He forced a smile that I could tell was empty despite his practice at making them seem genuine.

"It doesn't matter anymore," he said.

He removed my hand from his sleeve and left Evann and me by ourselves.

"Evann? I've been a pain ever since I arrived, haven't I?"

He coughed. "What makes you think that?"

He was smiling when I turned towards him.

"You're too honest when you lie," I said.

"Nikos is known for causing trouble," he replied. "I'm sure he's not the most innocent in this."

"Maybe not …"

But at the same time, he was the one who jumped into the lake to save me when I fell overboard. He was the one who taught me to be confident in myself. He was the one who was the most honest with me.

And I … had done nothing for him.

I hadn't done anything for anyone.

I turned towards Evann.

"Evann … how do we get in touch with the newspapers?"

35

DEALS

Julian rubbed his temple. "Why am I doing this?"

"Because I should apply what I've learned," I replied.

He sighed, leaning against the car window. "If anything goes wrong—"

"I'm not going to do anything."

He narrowed his eyes.

"I'm not! Besides, Evann will be with me. What do you have to worry about?"

"Cyrus finding out," Evann replied, leaning back in the car seat.

"He won't know," I replied.

At least, I hoped he wouldn't find out. I could only imagine what he'd say if he found out that Julian, Evann, and I were meeting a somewhat shady newspaper contact downtown in a closed office building.

That wouldn't go over well.

Really, it was Julian's fault. He shouldn't have mentioned that he had a contact at the newspaper company in the first place.

I knew he was going to stop the rumors about Nikos and me. It affected his family as much as it did mine.

Also, I may or may not have used my knowledge of Julian's personal life as leverage to get him to take me with him ... although I would never breathe a word about it. I couldn't do that to him. Not after everything.

But I could make him *think* that I would do that to him.

"I want to know what I should do in these situations," I said.

"Well, I can tell you that impersonating a guard and standing on the side of the room is completely the wrong choice," Julian muttered.

"Yet you agreed."

The car started to slow. We pulled into the underground parking lot. Julian turned to me.

"Listen to me," Julian said. "If anyone figures out who you are, there's only so much I can do to help you. At some point, you'll need to take care of the press yourself. They'll ask you questions until your soul bleeds. I want you to be aware of this. Do you understand how much they can come after you, Marina?"

I smiled, patting his hand. "Thank you for worrying about me. I'm happy you care."

He looked down at my hand on his and sighed. He patted it with his other free hand.

"I can teach you, but I can't fight for you," he said.

"I know. I tell my students the exact same thing."

He squeezed my hand before letting go. The driver opened the door, and we stepped out of the car.

Besides Evann, Julian's usual bodyguards came with us. The four of us walked with Julian in a square formation around him. Evann's eyes slid to the side every once in a while to look at me. I nodded my head to let him know I was fine. I could handle this.

My heart was pounding, but I could handle it.

We took the elevator to the tenth floor, a long hallway leading us to a conference room. A man in a gray suit sat at the table, alone. He looked up as we walked in, straightening out his beard before standing and greeting Julian.

"It's an honor to see you again, Prince Julian," he said, bowing.

Julian nodded his head and thanked him. Evann and I stood off to the side; Julian and the man sat back down at the table.

"You wanted some information on the Double Eights, yes?" The man pulled a USB out of his pocket and handed it to Julian. "A collection of news-related articles and police reports. Also ... some less than governmentally approved sources. See if there's anything useful in there."

Julian nodded, taking it and putting it in his coat pocket.

"But I have a feeling you have something else to discuss," the man continued. "You rarely come to visit me."

"The tabloids," Julian said. "The ones involving my brother and the girl. Do you know a good way to solve the problem?"

The girl? Thanks, Julian.

The man stroked his beard again. "Celebrity gossip? You've never asked me to bail out your brother before. Why the sudden interest?"

"It has a bigger impact this time."

The man cocked his head to the side. "Are you in love with the girl?"

I had never heard Julian laugh so hard.

"It has to do with some international relations," Julian continued, after composing himself. "Should this get out of hand, it'll be a problem for everyone."

"That only makes me more curious."

"I don't pay you to be curious."

I tried to keep a straight face. Julian's straight-forward manners suited him in business dealings. I couldn't tell if he was playing it cool, or if he was really that apathetic about the way he looked to others.

"So, what should I tell the papers?" the man asked.

His eyes glanced at me for a moment. "Imply that she's a distant cousin or another type of non-interesting family member. If they stay curious, give them this story instead."

Julian pulled a different USB out of his coat pocket.

The man took it, lifting an eyebrow. "You sure?"

Julian nodded. "I've been holding it for a special occasion."

Wait. We didn't talk about this. What was he doing?

The man tapped the USB against his hand and shrugged. "Must be important. You really have me curious, Your Highness."

I was curious too.

The meeting only lingered for a few minutes after that. It seemed so simple and to the point, but my head was spinning and my palms were sweating. The contact left the room first. Julian rubbed his forehead, his eyebrows matting together as he stood from the table.

"What was on that USB?" I asked.

Julian looked forward, not answering.

We walked down the hallway again, towards the elevator. As the elevator climbed towards us, I looked over my shoulder to the large glass window, at the hot and sticky day outside.

A man walked in front of the window, heading towards the stairwell. He didn't look like a business-man. He was wearing ripped jeans and a white shirt, with a ringed cap.

I stopped breathing.

I knew that ringed cap.

When he looked over his shoulder at us, he stopped. Tai.

36

WE MEET AGAIN

He ran as soon as he saw us.

I ran after him.

He threw open the stairwell door, bolting down the stairs. My voice echoed down the stairwell as I called out his name, but the only response I got was the echo of his feet. I skipped stairs, trying to catch up with him.

The door swung open on the bottom floor. I was only a few moments behind, but when I got out onto the street, he was gone. There was a crowd of pedestrians, some honking cars, and a ringed cap in the middle of the street.

It was definitely him.

Footsteps pounded behind me.

"I should have known you'd do something you weren't supposed to," Evann huffed. "How could you —"

I handed him the cap, not saying anything. He looked at it for a moment. His eyes widened, and he took it from me.

"He was here?" he asked.

I nodded, catching my breath.

Evann grabbed my arm. "We need to get back. Now. If he was here, then—"

He stopped in his tracks and stared at the door we had just came out of. I followed his eyes. There was a man leaning up against it, smoking a cigarette. Staring at us.

Evann's hand gripped my arm. "They're here."

"Who?"

Evann looked up, then shoved me out of the way.

Two people jumped down from the escape stairwell.

"Run!" Evann yelled, grabbing my arm and taking off with me down the alley.

We rounded the building, heading towards the front entrance. Evann stopped as we reached it. There were two more men in the front, wearing white shirts and black pants, tattoos running from the ends of their sleeves to their wrists.

They sure as hell weren't businessmen.

"Stay close to me," Evann said. "Don't you dare leave my sight."

I nodded even though he wasn't looking at me.

He looked over his shoulder, grabbing my hand and running towards the street. The two men in white shirts followed, weaving through the crowd and traffic, same as us.

Evann gripped my hand, pulling me towards a bus that was starting to close its doors. He flashed his castle ID and the doors reopened. The bus was full, standing room only, but the bus driver nodded at us. Evann pulled me towards the exit door, grabbing the hanging handle and bringing me close to him. One of his arms wrapped around my back as we both tried to catch our breath.

"How the hell did they know we were here?" Evann muttered to himself.

"Who?" I asked.

"The Double Eights. They knew you were going to be there. But how?"

I gripped onto his uniform as we stood on the bus. Was it aiming for all the potholes?

"We'll get off as soon as I'm sure they're not following us," Evann said. "Are you alright?"

I nodded. "I can handle it."

"My job is to make sure you never have to."

I held his gaze for a moment, but he looked away. He looked over his shoulder. Twice.

Another man in a white shirt and black pants boarded the bus. He smirked at us.

What stupid dress code was this?

The exit doors closed. Evann kicked them back open, and the bus stuttered as he pulled me off. We started running again, down the main street into a narrow street lined with market stalls. He gripped my hand as we cut through the crowd. The marketers yelled on the sides while pedestrians stared at us. Some, recognizing the castle uniform, saluted.

Evann let go of my hand and started unbuttoning his jacket. He nodded at me, and I did the same. He pulled off his jacket and took mine, throwing them to the side of the street. The black sleeveless shirt under his uniform was the least I'd ever seen him wear. There were scars up and down his thin but toned arms. I didn't have time or the breath to ask about them.

"Keep moving," he said. "We need …"

Before he could finish, there was the sound of engines and people screaming. A car swerved in front of the street, blocking it. Another came to the side, but Evann pulled me to the other side before it could get close to us.

There was a flash of light and the sound of firecrackers. People scattered. There was screaming again. Another car engine.

"Come on!" Evann yelled.

We raced down a side street, heading back towards the main street. A car blocked the exit in front of us. Another car blocked the entrance we had come in. A third car blocked the side road next to us.

Evann squeezed my hand.

The passenger doors of the cars opened, two men getting out of one car, and one each getting out of the second and third.

"I think I have to handle it now," I told Evann.

I dropped his hand and raised both of mine to my face.

The man in front of me pulled a knife and charged. I kicked him in the chest, the force knocking both of us back in opposite directions. Another attacker came from the side, kicking towards my face. I backed up, feeling the tip of his shoe graze my lip. Evann jumped in and pulled him back, breaking his arm.

He then reached back for his baton, slamming it across the third attacker's face. I watched for the fourth attacker, who had also pulled a knife. The first attacker with the knife stood next to him, both fidgeting with the knives in their hands.

"Let's go, Princess," one of them said. "Come with us and nothing will happen to your friend."

A hand pulled me back. Evann stepped between us.

"You come through me if you want her," he said.

The man shrugged. "Easy enough."

He charged, blade forward. Evann blocked him, throwing a punch to his face to send him back. The second one with a knife charged for me, and I went to kick him in the chest again. He paused, my kick hitting nothing but air. He stepped in, putting the knife to my throat and pulling me back by my waist.

I turned … only to see the first attacker plunge his knife into Evann's chest.

37

CASUALTIES

Evann stumbled back, pulling the man's arm away and elbowing him in the face. He winced as he pulled the knife out, cutting the man across the throat with it.

He turned towards me and the man with a knife to my throat.

"You're next," he growled to the man behind me.

I was tugged back, jerking me back into reality. I elbowed the man in the stomach, and when he dropped pressure against my throat, I elbowed him again in the chin. I ran to Evann, who was now bleeding down his shirt and arm. He chased the second man with a knife. I turned towards the body of the first.

Did Evann really …

Intense pain burst through my knee. I hit the ground.

The man with a broken arm was standing over me, breathing heavily. He reached down to grab me, but I kicked him in the groin before he could get too close. He hit the ground and I got to my feet, my leg folding under me. I couldn't put weight on my leg, the pain surging through my body.

Evann came into my blurred sight. He kicked the man in the face to send him back to the ground, urging me to follow him. I tried to keep up, but it was no use. I was slowing us down.

"Get on my back," he said, leaning down.

"You've been stab—"

He grabbed me and pulled me on before I could finish the sentence. I wrapped my legs around his waist, holding onto his neck. He ran down the alley, past the car blocking the road and towards the docks.

I could feel Evann slowing as we ran. He was bleeding and he was carrying the weight of two. He couldn't last like this much longer.

We reached a warehouse next to the docks. He was about to go to the door, until someone came through it. He stopped, turning back over his shoulder to see another man behind us.

"Marina," Evann said, voice low. "First chance you get, get out any way you can."

He lowered me off his back.

I shook my head. "I'm staying with you."

One of the men charged, going straight for Evann. Evann stepped in and blocked his punch, only to be taken out by the second. He hit the ground, groaning and curling. His attacker kicked him in the head. I jumped in and roundhoused him in the side with my weak leg, the pain vibrating through me a second time. He went backwards, and Evann responded by pulling him down to the ground and punching him in the face.

The second attacker came at me, a baton in his hand. He swung it at me, and I hobbled back. I got as far as I could from him, but my body was giving out. I couldn't run anymore.

His foot slammed into my back and I hit the ground. I turned over, blindly kicking out. He grabbed my foot, dragging me towards him.

I twisted out, stumbling back towards my feet. I ran as far as I could, but it wasn't long before my knee gave out again, sending me back to the ground. I looked over my shoulder.

He was about fifteen feet away from me.

He only made it three steps closer before a car hit him.

The man flew forward, slamming into the ground. The doors of the car swung open, and two familiar uniforms jumped out.

Julian's bodyguards.

One ran straight for me, while the other ran to the other side of the car. The guard picked me up and ran me back to the car, putting me in the back.

Julian was at the wheel.

"I knew I shouldn't have agreed to this," he muttered.

The other guard brought Evann into the backseat with me, and Julian slammed on the gas before the door had even closed. Evann grabbed his chest, blood covering his arms and pants. He reached out for me, and I clasped his hand tightly, shaking.

"Evann, we have to get you to a hospital," I said.

He shook his head. I could barely sit up straight as Julian swerved the car in and out of traffic, heading towards the freeway.

"Julian, he's going to bleed to death!" I shouted.

"I'm fine," Evann forced out through his teeth. "Don't take me to the hospital. Take me back to the castle."

"As much as I don't want to say this, Marina is right," Julian said. "If we don't get you to the hospital—"

"I can't go to a public hospital!" Evann yelled. "Do you understand, Julian?"

Julian glanced in the rearview mirror. He was silent for a long moment.

"Yes," he said. "Yes, I understand."

He pulled onto the freeway, heading back to the castle.

§

"Of all the stupid — are you out of your damn mind?"

Cyrus's hands shook as he yelled at us. Julian dropped his head.

"It's my fault," he said.

"Of course it is!" Cyrus threw back. "With your IQ, you should have known the dangers in what you did! And for what? A field trip?"

The veins in his neck were popping out of his skin. I didn't even know he could get this angry.

"Cyrus, it was my idea," I said. "Please don't get angry with Julian."

"I'm just as angry with you!" he said. "Why do you insist on doing things your own way? You could have been killed! Evann could have been—"

"I know that! It's my fault! But I couldn't stand being so damn useless! There's a threat on all of us and you expect me to lock myself up in my room? What would you have done?"

"I would have said something! You take reckless actions without consulting anyone with experience. You want me to deliver your dead body to your father?"

I bit my lip. Cyrus shook his head.

"I think it's time you went home," he said.

My mouth went dry as my stomach dropped.

"I'll tell your father what happened," he continued. "He'll understand the situation, so you still have a chance to be his successor—"

"You want me to give up?" I asked. "That easily? I won't run, Cyrus."

"I'm not giving you a choice in this, Marina," he said. "I'm calling your parents to come and get you. You'll be safer with them."

"Or we'll all be in danger. If this group really wants me gone, they'll follow me."

"Maybe not if they think you're giving up."

"Do you want me to give up?"

Cyrus shook his head. "I don't want you to give up … but I don't want you dead. Do you understand that?"

I clenched my teeth. I didn't know how to answer.

"I'll call them immediately," he continued. "I can't protect you here. No matter what I do … it's not good enough."

With that, he walked out of the room.

Julian was still standing with his head down.

"Do you agree with him?" I asked.

He wet his lips and sighed. "Not entirely. Yet I don't disagree either. It's too dangerous here."

"And if they follow me?"

"Cyrus is right. We can't protect you. If they're on the outside and the inside, it's best to send you somewhere safe. You should do as he says for now."

"Why do you submit to him so easily?"

"Because I owe him," he said. "We all do."

I couldn't say anything. I could only clench and unclench my fists.

"Come on," he said. "Let's get you packed."

After an hour, my bags were packed, but I had no intention of going back home. I couldn't leave Cyrus, Julian, and Nikos in the mess I had created. I couldn't leave Evann after he got stabbed to protect me.

Even though it was getting late, I needed to check on him. I kept imagining the blood all over his uniform, all thanks to me.

His room wasn't far, and the lights were on. The door was cracked, so I lifted my hand to knock.

"It's only a matter of time."

Cyrus?

"Don't be so dramatic," Evann replied.

I looked through the crack in the door. Evann was sitting up in his bed, an IV drip hanging beside him.

"I don't like them snooping around," Cyrus muttered. "It didn't take them long to figure out who Marina is. If they figure out who you—"

"That's easy," Evann said, cutting him off. "I'm nobody. Leave it that way."

"You know I can't. It's not that easy."

"Yes, it is. I'm a guard. I will always be a guard, just like my …"

He didn't finish the sentence.

Cyrus sighed through his nose. "If you want to be anything else—"

"I don't! Quit acting like I was made for something else! I've made my path."

Cyrus broke into a smile. "You sound like Marina."

Evann didn't return Cyrus's smile. He looked away, shaking his head.

"Is it good luck or bad luck to be a full-blooded royal, I wonder? I wish I could drain your family's blood out of me. Then I wouldn't have to deal with you or this constant mess."

No. No way.

"You think I'm going to go to the other side of the grave and look our father in the eye and tell him I let you get yourself killed?"

"Don't you dare use the phrase *our father*. You've made it clear where I stand with your brothers — behind them."

Cyrus bit his lip, looking at the ground. There was a long, silent pause.

"She would have killed you," Cyrus whispered, barely loud enough for me to hear. "Mother would have killed your family in an instant. You know it better than anyone. It was the only way I could protect you."

"And yet she's dead, and Julian and Nikos still don't know who I am." Evann rolled his eyes. "Are you still trying to protect me? Or are you afraid I'll try to keep the throne to myself like she did?"

Cyrus didn't answer.

"Get out, Cyrus. Get out before I tell the press exactly what kind of family we came from."

I stepped back into the hall as soon as Cyrus turned towards the door. It opened and shut. I leaned forward.

Cyrus leaned up against the wall, pressing the back of his trembling hand against his lips. He squeezed his eyes tight, as if he was trying to force control back into his body.

He never says his true feelings, not even to us. I think Evann is the only one who knows what's inside his head these days. I don't know why Cyrus talks to Evann and not us.

Now I understood Julian's journal entry. Now I understood why Evann was trying to get out of the castle, and why Cyrus had held Evann back.

Evann was Cyrus's half-brother. A half-prince.

38

PASSAGEWAYS

I went back to my room and shut the door.

Now I knew what Tai meant about having information you weren't supposed to have.

How could Evann be a half-prince? Why didn't Julian or Nikos know? Why was Evann keeping it a secret? Why did Cyrus want to keep it a secret?

But, most importantly, why did Evann hate it so much?

"She would have killed you. Mother would have killed your family in an instant."

I took two steps forward. A hand wrapped around my mouth and pulled me back.

"Miss me?" a voice whispered in my ear.

Zhixin.

I shuddered as his breath fanned my neck and his other arm wrapped around my waist. I was about to elbow him, but he jerked me close to him to prevent it.

"Not so fast, warrior princess," he teased. "We have unfinished business."

I struggled, but there was no escape. The air shifted from warm to cold as we walked backwards. Suddenly there were two doors in front of me, shutting.

The secret passageway.

He pulled me down the narrow hallway, the wall scraping against my shoulder. At the bottom of the stairs, Zhixin pushed me against the wall as he shut the door, tying my hands behind my back. I tried to kick behind me, but he only moved in closer, his body trapping me between him and the wall as his fingers scraped against my wrist with a rope.

Once his hand left my mouth, I screamed, but he only laughed.

"Scream all you want, baby. They can't hear you from here."

"Didn't we get rid of you?" I snapped.

He pushed me to the ground, slamming my ankles together. The pain burst through my injured leg as his fingers dug into my skin.

"You *tried*," he replied. "Thanks to Tai, everyone is on the run."

I tried to kick him, but he gripped onto me and wrapped another strap around my ankles with amazing speed. I didn't want to know how he could tie someone up so quickly.

He reached into his back pocket and pulled out duct tape. I screamed again. He put his knees on either side of me, grabbing his face in his hand. He put a strip of duct tape across my mouth.

"If Tai didn't like you so much, I wouldn't have to do this," he said. "I finish my job."

He lifted me up and flung me over his shoulder. I kicked both my legs into his stomach. He crumpled, dropping me. Even though he had let go, I couldn't get away with my arms and hands tied. He turned me over and slapped me across the face.

"You keep making everything so difficult," he muttered.

He picked me up again and carried me bridal style, avoiding my attacks. The passageway led outside into the darkness, no lights to be seen. I couldn't tell which part of the castle we were at. Everything was distorted in the moonlight, and my eyes refused to adjust.

I squirmed as he carried me out to the gardens and past the vineyards. He constantly looked over his shoulder, digging his fingers into my side while he walked. I tried to make my weight as dead as possible, but he was good at what he was doing.

When I turned my neck to see where we were, I saw the moonlight reflecting off the lake.

Was he really going to …?

The wood of the dock echoed below us. He carried me to the boat, dropping me inside. The back of my head and tailbone hit the bottom of the boat hard, and I curled up as the pain vibrated through my body. He started the boat, tearing out from the dock and into the lake.

I looked around, seeing nothing but black as the lights of the castle got further away from us. The lake was terrifying as it stretched out below us.

The motor vibrated through my head and body. After a few moments, I heard Zhixin cuss, turning the boat sharply. Water rushed over the side, crashing against my face. I shook it off, looking up.

"I knew your twisted ass was here somewhere," a voice called out from the darkness.

I knew that raspy voice too well.

Tai stood on a motorboat next to us, with a look set to kill.

39

THE LAKE

"You're never going to make it out, Zhixin," Tai yelled from his boat.

"Are you going to stop me, then?" Zhixin threw back. "With what?"

"I'm giving you a chance. If you let her go—"

"—I still get arrested. I might as well get something out of it."

His hand reached around my throat and pulled me back to look up at Tai.

"How much do you think I can get for her?" Zhixin called.

"You son of a—"

Tai gunned his boat forward, slamming it into the side of ours. He jumped over the side onto our boat. He grabbed Zhixin by the throat and threw him down, slamming a fist into his face. Zhixin threw him off and forced him halfway over the side.

I couldn't stand, but I could roll. I rolled on my side and kicked both feet into Zhixin's side. He fell. Tai grabbed him and tried to force his hands behind his back, but Zhixin spun out and slammed Tai's head into the side of the boat. As Tai grabbed his head and grunted in pain, Zhixin jumped from our boat to the one Tai had arrived in. He turned over the key and took off.

I sat up, trying to call for Tai through the duct tape over my mouth. He struggled to sit up, grabbing the front of his head. He stumbled over to me, ripping the tape off my mouth.

"You idiot!" I yelled. "You're showing up now just to lose the fight?"

He laughed. "I missed you too, jailbird."

He reached behind me and ripped the ties off my hands and feet.

"Do you want to catch a criminal?" he asked, eyes glittering.

I huffed. "Let's get the bastard."

Tai jumped in the front seat, reaching back and grabbing my hand to help me to the passenger side. He turned over the key and chased after Zhixin. We couldn't see anything in the moonlight, relying on the sound of the motorboat to point us in the right direction.

Soon the sound of the motorboat got stronger and started to meld with the sound of our boat. Two separate motors blended into one.

Wait … three motors?

And a helicopter?

There was a crash. A scream. And the lake flooded with lights from the sides. A helicopter from above swept a spotlight over the lake, landing right on the sound of the crash.

On the third boat was a crew of guards with their guns drawn.

Cyrus.

"Grab him!" Cyrus commanded.

A few guards jumped in the water, pulling Zhixin out. Cyrus came to the side of the boat, reaching out a hand to me.

"Are you alright?"

I put my hand in his and gripped it. "I am. Thanks to Tai."

Cyrus looked over my shoulder at Tai.

"He saved my life," I said. "Please Cyrus …"

He squeezed my hand. "Don't worry, my dear. I'll handle it."

I turned back to Tai. I knew Cyrus would handle it.

How Cyrus would handle it was what worried me.

§

I paced in my room.

I was supposed to change clothes and wait for Cyrus, but I couldn't hold still. I couldn't even sit down.

Both Tai and Zhixin were in Cyrus's custody. What was he going to do with them? Was he going to execute Tai? After Tai had saved me? What about Zhixin? What would happen to him? Not that I cared about Zhixin.

I opened my door, but six guards greeted me. I knew if I tried to get past them, they'd all follow me, keeping me away from Cyrus.

I nodded politely at them and shut the door.

How could I get to Cyrus?

I looked around my room, eyes catching on the fireplace.

That was it.

I ran to the wall and pushed it sideways. It opened.

Once more I walked down the cold, narrow passageway and towards the entrance. I tried to remember each path Tai had showed me so long ago.

I tried a few doors I hadn't recognized until I found one that led to a place I knew — the parlor where I often played chess with Cyrus.

I kept imagining Tai's head on a block, waiting to be cut off. Did they do that here? How did they execute someone? They could do whatever they wanted with Zhixin. But Tai …

Where were they?

I left the parlor, looking over the mezzanine to listen for voices. It was silent. I kept wandering, mentally mapping the entire castle in my head.

Then there were voices.

I jogged down the hallway, following them. It sounded like it was coming from the armor room — the room where I had first met Cyrus on the day of the tour, a lifetime ago.

I followed the mezzanine to the room, peering over the side of the staircase. Cyrus was in the middle of the room, a half-dozen guards circled behind him. In front of him, a figure was held on his knees by two guards, another four guards on each side.

Zhixin. Even from the stairs I could see his crooked smile. I couldn't see Tai anywhere.

Cyrus lurched forward and punched Zhixin in the face. Twice. There were no courteous smiles. No diplomatic speeches.

Just a really, *really* pissed off Cyrus.

"You'll pay for these crimes," he said, his breath jagged. "Assault, kidnapping, attempted murder. This is treason of the worst kind. Did you really expect to get away with this?"

Zhixin laughed. His eyes scanned the room and moved upwards to settle on where I stood. I shifted uneasily, holding my breath as he stared at me, grinning, with blood on his teeth. He looked back at Cyrus.

"Then what about you, Your Majesty?" he said. "Will you be charged with treason? After all, you're the one that hired us."

40

TRUTH

Cyrus struck him across the face again. Zhixin smiled, keeping his eyes on me.

"I didn't hire you for any of this, you bastard. You weren't supposed to lay a hand on her. Had I known you were like this, I wouldn't have asked Tai to—"

He trailed off, then looked over his shoulder at where Zhixin was looking, seeing me for the first time.

"Marina …" he breathed.

I held his gaze as I slid down every single step.

It wasn't true. It couldn't be true. Cyrus would never … he wouldn't …

Cyrus turned back to his guards. "Take him. Tell him his fate when you put him in his cell."

Zhixin shrugged and winked at me as the guards dragged him off. Cyrus rushed to me.

"How long were you—"

"It's not true," I said, my voice and body suddenly shaking. "It's not, right?"

His eyes dropped to his feet. He looked around the room, then grabbed my hand and pulled me into a side room. He shut the door.

"Tell me it's not true, Cyrus," I said again.

He stepped forward, his hands wringing together. "I want to. I want to say I had nothing to do with this. I want to say this isn't my fault. I want to, but …"

He didn't finish his sentence.

"You hired Tai to get rid of me?"

He exhaled. "Yes."

He might as well have stabbed me. It would have hurt less.

"Why?"

His hands ran through his hair. "I panicked when your father said you were coming to us. He mentioned the betrothal — lightly, as he tends to do — and all I could think about was how miserable my parents were, how hideous their marriage was. I never wanted to be married."

"So, you hired someone to kill me?"

"No! It was only supposed to be a few threats to keep you on your previous path. And nothing more serious than the sort of threats we royals get routinely. You would have had to face up to that sooner or later, but I thought I could scare you upfront and get you to leave. But … after meeting you … and everything that happened … And when I found out that bastard touched you …"

"Everything was an act?" I asked, almost yelling. "The letters, being chased, arresting Tai? What about the poison? Was that an act too?"

He nodded. "Yes. I faked the poison. I faked it so well that my nurse thought I was really poisoned and gave me a real antidote." He stepped forward, shaking again. "It wasn't supposed to go this far. I'm begging you …"

His arm reached out for me, but I stepped back. "Everything you've said has been a lie. Everything."

"No, not everything. Please …"

I ran out of the room before he could finish.

I threw open the door, rushing towards the castle entrance. Cyrus's voice rang out behind me, and before I could reach the entrance, a guard stepped out and wrapped his arm around my waist, pulling me back.

"Let me go!" I screamed. "Let go!"

"What are you doing?" a second voice said. "Unhand her now!"

I turned to see Evann, nostrils flaring. The guard let go, just as Cyrus was approaching us.

"Evann!" I yelled, hiding behind him and gripping his coat.

"What the— Your Majesty, why is she acting like this?"

I could hear Cyrus trying to catch his breath, but he didn't say anything.

The air shifted.

"What did you do?" Evann growled.

"Evann," Cyrus said. "Step aside so I can speak with her."

My fingers gripped harder onto Evann's coat.

"I'm sorry, Your Majesty, but my job is to protect her," Evann replied. "Regardless of whom she wants protecting from."

There was a tense moment before Cyrus spoke again.

"Please ... I don't want to leave this here. Please let me talk to you ... if nothing else but to beg your forgiveness."

I didn't reply. I shuddered while holding onto Evann. I heard footsteps move away from us both and peered over Evann's shoulder.

Cyrus was gone.

Evann turned to me. "What happened?"

Still gripping his uniform for dear life, I said, "Get me out of here."

His hands cupped my face. After a long moment, he nodded.

"If that's what you want, I'll do it. Let's go."

41

SAFE PLACES

"Stay here as long as you like," the man in the sweat suit said as he unlocked the back room. "There's some frozen dinners and a couple of cartons of ice cream in the freezer. Help yourself."

There was a small room behind the door. A little kitchen with nothing but a mini-fridge and a couple of cupboards, a TV, a chair, and a large couch.

"It's not much," the man added, "But you're always welcome to use it, Evann."

Evann nodded and thanked him. When the man left, I sank into the couch.

"Want me to order delivery?" Evann asked.

I shook my head.

He was quiet for a moment.

"Are you going to tell me what happened?"

I looked at my hands.

"Must be serious then."

He sat next to me on the couch. It was quiet for a long time. I couldn't speak, but with Evann I knew I didn't have to. He could sit in the silence with me and it would be okay.

The problem was, I didn't know if it would really be okay or not.

I fell asleep on the couch, waking up the next morning to the sound of grunting and yelling. I looked around. Evann was in the chair next to me, sound asleep.

I followed the sound, opening the door a crack to peak out. There were maybe twenty men and women in the training room, working out with the instructor. He was a completely different person from the shy man who had let us stay in his back room last night.

Were there always two people inside one?

"Don't tell me you want to train."

I spun around. Evann was still in the chair, but he was awake and smiling at me.

I shook my head. "I was looking at the instructor. He was so kind last night. Now he's … brutal. I'm starting to think everyone is like that. Maybe Nikos was right about false appearances."

"I wouldn't call it false," he replied. "There are always two sides to a person. One is the person you really are. The other is the person you need to be to survive. You're the same way."

I straightened. "Come again?"

"You spent the last three months telling everyone to back off, but in the end, you care about every single one of them. I've seen the way you care for Julian, Nikos, Cyrus, and myself. You bark to keep yourself at a distance, but you whine because you're not close enough."

I stepped away from the door, shutting it softly and slumping back on the couch.

"At first, I didn't want anything to do with any of you."

He snorted. "I know."

"I wanted to follow my own life path. I spent my life training to be something. I had that picture so strongly in my mind. And then it was taken from me in a day. I wanted to go back to the way things were. I wanted to be a teacher. Not a student."

Evann stayed silent.

"But I think you've changed my mind, Evann."

He raised an eyebrow. "*I* have?"

I nodded. "I think, after watching you, I've realized this is not what I chose, but it doesn't change who I can become. I can still be me, no matter where I came from. I always thought I was meant to be a teacher and a fighter. I never expected to be a princess. But maybe I was meant to be all three."

He leaned forward in his chair, cocking his head to the side. "And what about me inspired you to think all that?"

I chose my words carefully.

I wasn't supposed to know … so I acted like I didn't.

"Because even though you're a fighter, you've always been a friend and a prince to me. If you're all three, then maybe I can be too."

He laughed as he dropped his head, leaning back in his chair. "You're really something different, Princess."

Knock, knock, knock.

"Evann!" the training center owner said as he opened the door. "I have a guest here to see you."

The man opened the door to let in a face I hadn't seen close-up in what seemed like a lifetime.

Tai.

42

BAD NEWS

"It's been awhile," Tai said, putting his hands in his pockets. "What's new?"

Evann stood from his chair. I thought he would jump to his feet and knock Tai out — or even murder him — but he only nodded.

"Thanks for showing up," Evann said.

"What?" I asked.

The training center owner shut the door, leaving the three of us to ourselves.

"When you wouldn't tell me what happened, I decided to roll the dice and call Tai." Evann nodded at him. "I didn't expect him to pick up, but he did. I know everything, Marina. I think you should too."

I folded my arms across my chest. "I know what I need to know."

"You don't know enough to understand what you know, though." Tai stopped, slowly repeating what he said. "Yeah, I said that right."

"I know Cyrus hired you," I said. "I know your job was to get rid of me."

Tai shook his head. "That wasn't the job. That wasn't the job at all. Cyrus made it very clear that if you were harmed, I was dead."

I pulled my collar down to show my scars. "Well, I was harmed. I'm not sure why Evann hasn't ended you yet. I'm not even sure why I haven't done it."

Tai dropped to one knee in front of me. "Listen to me one last time, jailbird. Let it be my last request."

He was teasing, but there was an edge of sincerity in his voice that I couldn't fight against.

"Cyrus came to me a week before you were supposed to arrive," he continued. "He was going out of his mind. I've worked in the castle for three years. I've never seen him that paranoid. His nurses came in twice a day. No one could figure out why he was losing it.

"One day, with a ton of medication in his system, he unloaded a ton of childhood memories on me, most of which I don't care to repeat. Long story short: Cyrus had a screwed-up mom. I come from a gang family, but even I think his family is screwed up."

I looked at Evann. He only dropped his eyes.

"Cyrus wanted me to show you what being royal was really like," Tai continued. "Sure, there are a lot of people on Twitter looking to destroy you, but this country and your country have had a long line of criminals and inside gophers."

"Moles," I corrected.

"Okay, moles. Anyway, Cyrus wanted to know who you really were. Fast. He knew an arranged marriage was a major possibility and he couldn't risk putting his family through hell again. So he asked me to scare you off. Replicate some of the things that he experienced, but on a smaller scale. I wasn't allowed to hurt you."

"Then why do I have scars on my neck?"

Tai sighed through his nose. "That was my fault. Zhixin was part of my group long time ago. He never liked that I went straight to castle living after I got out of jail. The reason I went to jail is another story. We'll talk about that later. Anyway, there were a few events … and … well, he figured out who you were. To keep him close to me, I let him in on the job. It was easier than trying to guess his next moves."

"Better to control your enemy than to let him out of your sight," Evann added.

Tai nodded. "I never expected him to get into the castle. I never gave him that option. He found his own way. I should have known better. *I* was the reason you weren't protected. Cyrus did everything he could to protect you."

"How can you say he did everything he could to protect me?" I yelled. "He was the one who set everything up!"

"In his head, it was self-defense," Evann pointed out. "He and his brothers were tortured daily by their mother. I imagine in his mental state, he was trying to keep history from repeating itself. An arranged marriage like his parents probably set him off. He was so paranoid that you would be like her. But now that idiot has caused a bigger mess. Now he's doomed his own country by his own hands."

"Doomed his country? What do you mean?" I asked.

"You think your father is going to let him off the hook when he finds out what happened?" Evann asked. "I wouldn't be surprised if it started a war between your countries."

I exhaled. Cyrus being punished was one thing. Innocent people getting punished because of it was another. Evann was right. Once Dad found out about this, he was going to kill Cyrus himself.

"Cyrus might welcome the blow," Tai said, pulling out a newspaper. "Take a look at this."

Evann unfolded the newspaper and stared at the front page. His eyes widened.

"Dammit, Julian," he whispered.

I stood up to look at the paper over his shoulder. The headline said it all.

LATE KING'S DEATH MAY HAVE BEEN MURDER

<h1 style="text-align:center">43</h1>

<h2 style="text-align:center">RETURN</h2>

"Are you sure about this?" Evann asked. I held my breath as the car pulled up to the castle.

"I can't disappear now," I said. "It's my fault these rumors about Cyrus's father started. Julian would have never handed over that USB drive if it wasn't for me."

"That was his choice. You don't have to answer for it."

"No," I agreed, "but I can't ignore it either. Besides, you need a doctor to look after you."

Evann huffed. "I can find another doctor. I'm not bound to this castle, you know."

"I know. But I also think that if you really wanted to leave this place, you would have already. I think you're worried about their suffering even more than I am."

He looked away before I could say anything else. He stepped out of the car, reaching out a hand to help me. We walked through the same castle doors I had stepped through three months ago. It was strange how the unfamiliar had now become the familiar. It was like

I had stayed at a hotel for a night, and now I was returning home.

"There you are."

Nikos was chewing on an apple as we came through the front door.

"We've been looking for you," he continued. "Your parents are here."

My throat seized up. "*What?*"

"They're with Cyrus in the parlor."

I looked at Evann.

What was I supposed to do now?

We stepped up to the parlor and opened the door. Mom and Dad were both on the couch, while Cyrus sat in one of the armchairs. They all turned to look at us.

"There's our girl!" Dad said as Mom jumped up to give me a hug.

Cyrus stood from his chair but folded his hands behind his back and dropped his eyes to the floor. Mom squeezed me, and I couldn't stop myself from hugging her back.

"I'm still mad at you," I muttered at my dad through Mom's hug.

Dad stood and came over to hug me too. "That's nothing new."

As he wrapped his arms around me, his bitter old man cologne hit my nose. It felt like ages since I had smelled it. The tension in my shoulders disappeared. I wrapped my arms around him, deciding to yell at him later.

Mom petted my hair. "Did you have fun? Who did you meet? Did they feed you well enough? You haven't eaten enough, have you? And look at how gray your skin looks!"

I smiled. "I'm good, Mom."

"Evann!" Dad said. "Good to see you're still in one piece. Did my daughter behave herself?"

Evann bowed. "Yes, Your Majesty."

"Ha! At least now I know he's a liar. Look at all these bruises. It's worse than when I leave you with your uncle. I can't teach you to stop fighting, can I?"

I exchanged a glance with Cyrus.

"No," I said. "I'll always keep fighting."

Cyrus's lips pressed together.

"But why are you here?" I asked. "I thought you weren't coming until the fall?"

Dad huffed. "We were planning on that. But Cyrus called, concerned about your safety. When we saw the papers, we understood why."

Murder rumors were why they'd showed up? Not the fact that someone was actually trying to murder me?

I guess Cyrus had left out that part.

"Just tell us what to do, Cyrus, and we'll do it," Dad said. "The press is a bloodthirsty lot. I don't want to see your entire family destroyed over your parents' sins."

Cyrus shook his head. "I have my own to pay for. It seems only fair."

Mom frowned as Cyrus sat back down in his chair.

"Is it true then?" I asked.

Everyone looked at me. I regretted asking.

Cyrus shook his head. "I never looked into it. I … I couldn't."

"The important thing is protecting your family now," Dad said. "If any harm comes to them, the regret will be stronger than any truth."

I tapped my foot.

"The information is already released," Cyrus replied. "I'm not sure there's anything that can be done."

"I still have plenty of connections with the press," Mom said. "I didn't stay a fashion designer for nothing. We're going to find a way to keep you and your brothers safe, sweetie."

Cyrus swallowed. "I don't deserve your protection, Leona. I … I need to excuse myself for a moment. I apologize."

He stood and left the room. He didn't even look at me once. It kind of pissed me off, to be honest. He hired an ex-gang member to threaten me, the gang nearly killed me, and I came back because his family was in trouble and he couldn't even acknowledge me?

I hated his guilt. I hated that he wanted to be ruined.

If anyone was going to ruin him, it was going to be me. I wasn't going to let a bunch of nosy reporters steal my glory.

But I couldn't punch anyone in the face this time. I had to learn another way of fighting back.

I turned towards my parents.

"I have a few questions for you."

44

PAYBACK

It was hard to work with someone you were mad at. But what could I do? Dad knew more about reporters than I did.

The problem was that we couldn't do what Julian did. We couldn't find bigger news to cover up small rumors. What could outshine Cyrus's father being possibly murdered? Nothing.

The reports were vague, but more than enough to incriminate Cyrus's family. There were reports on the rocky marriage of Cyrus's parents, the queen's mental disorders, and anonymous accounts by former employees of the castle.

"Was it really as bad as it sounds?" I asked my dad.

He sighed through his nose, eyes glazing over as he looked at the wall. "We heard stories, but there wasn't a lot we could do about it while in hiding. In the beginning, I was able to come and visit the boys and hopefully give them some relief from their parents. Their father was a stern man, but he had a gentle side when no one was looking. Their mother was the opposite. Gentle in public, batshit insane when no one was around."

Usually Mom would scold his language, but she didn't bother this time.

"When he died before she did," he continued, "it crossed my mind that she could have killed him. Hell, she tried with Cyrus. Getting that kid near a bathtub was a nightmare."

I asked what he was talking about.

"His mother left him to drown once," my mom said. "At the lake on the property. He was such a small boy ..." She started to tear up, fist clenching. "That woman is lucky she died before I found that out. I would have killed her myself had I known sooner."

She shook her head and rustled back through her newspapers.

Cyrus's mother really *was* batshit crazy.

No wonder Cyrus was so scared of me. They all were. It didn't excuse Cyrus's actions, but I could understand them better now. I was angry at my parents for keeping so many large secrets from me, but I had never in my life been afraid that they would try to hurt me. How were you supposed to cope with that?

I guess the same way the brothers did. Adhering to rigid schedules. Getting a PhD in psychology. Putting on a show. And scaring off anyone who might try to hurt you.

This is my fault, Princess, Tai had said at the gym. *If we ever meet again, you can give me the death penalty. But I don't plan on dying before I've made sure that you're protected.*

He left right after he said it, and neither Evann nor I stopped him. If anyone could bring down the Double Eights, it was their prince.

I don't know why I cared about helping Cyrus, really. It was Cyrus's fault that I got beaten up, and I could hardly call Julian and Nikos friends. But despite that, each of them had done a lot for me. For once, I wanted to do something for them.

Then maybe we could call ourselves even. After that, I could walk out of their lives forever.

§

"What do you mean she's gone?" I asked.

The strange, skinny man with a lop-sided haircut wasn't allowed to be my new stylist. I wanted Juniper. I'd had enough of new faces for a while.

"She put in her resignation a few days ago," the man replied, speaking through his nose. "I was told to take her place."

"Is it so easy to take someone's place? Sorry, I didn't mean to snap at you. It's not your fault."

He nodded sympathetically. How could Juniper leave like that? Without telling me? Was she mad at me for something?

Come to think of it, I hadn't seen her since the day of the festival.

Nikos had been moody ever since. And with everything happening now, I decided I should talk to him, even if he didn't like me.

I expected him to be half-drunk in the wine cellar, but to my surprise, he was in the arcade, casually playing a game of pool. He looked like he had finished a day at the office. His silk shirt was unbuttoned at the top, his sleeves rolled up past his elbows. All he was missing was a cigar smoldering in the corner and jazz playing in the background.

"What?" he asked, not looking up from his shot. He hit one of the solids into the pocket.

"I'm sorry," I replied.

He looked up. "For what?"

"For everything going on around you."

He sighed, hitting another ball into the pocket. He shrugged with one shoulder as he lined up another shot. "It's all part of the game."

I stepped in closer, leaning against the table. "How do you do it?"

"What?"

"If I were your age, I would be losing my mind. Throwing things. Yelling at people. Crying my eyes out."

"What do you mean *at my age*? You do stuff like that all the time *now*."

"I don't throw things."

"Only your fists and your knees."

Another ball went into the pocket. I smiled. He wasn't wrong.

"You're right. I also throw around words I regret, too."

The white ball bounced around the edges. Nikos didn't say anything.

"I shouldn't have said those things to you," I continued. "You've been a pain in the ass, but at the same time, you've done a lot for me. I think anyone would be lucky to have you as a friend."

He stuck his cue in the ground and leaned against it. His face was young, but his eyes weren't.

"I don't have any friends, Princess."

"I can be your friend," I offered.

"No."

He leaned back down and went for another shot. He missed.

I frowned, holding up the bottle of champagne I had in my hand. "Who am I supposed to drink this with, then?"

He looked at me, then took the bottle from my hand, looking at the label. He laughed to himself. I hoped he noticed that it was the same champagne we drank together that day on the boat.

"I suppose it doesn't hurt to keep your enemies close," he said.

"Or drunk," I added.

After three glasses of champagne, Nikos gave up on pool and propped himself up beside the dance game. I sat with him, sucking down the last of my second glass.

"I found her," he said, whispering.

"Who?"

"Juniper."

"Where is she? Tell her to come back."

He shook his head. "Not now. Then."

Was he drunk, or was I? I asked him to explain.

"Julian brought in Tai. I brought in Juniper," he said. "I was at an event for our war veterans, and she was giving a workshop on hair and beauty to the men's wives. She was so happy. I wanted to see her happy like that for a long time. So I contacted her studio and had her sent to us."

I stayed silent, putting the pieces together.

"Funny how I was the person who never made her smile after that. Julian did. I lost to my brother. I lose to him even when I have the upper hand."

"Stop making it a competition," I said. "You'll go insane."

"I want to win for once."

"You win at being Nikos."

He looked down into his drink, taking a long sip. He swallowed. "That's the dumbest thing you've ever said."

I took the glass from his hand, making him look at me.

"Julian did a lot for me," I said, "but so did you. For the one who puts on the biggest show, you were the one to be the most forward and honest. Not everyone deserves to know the real you. I'm not glad I met the World's Prince. I'm glad I met Nikos."

He held my gaze for a long moment. The lights from the games around us flashed in his eyes, crowding the hint of appreciation I could see in them.

"Maybe you're not so awful either," he replied.

§

I knocked on Julian's door. He opened it, raising an eyebrow.

"Can I help you?" he muttered.

I tried not to smirk at his ruffled long hair and rumpled nightshirt. He obviously wasn't expecting company at midnight.

"I need to talk to you," I said, letting myself in.

I flopped in a large chair by his bed.

"Talk to me during regular business hours," he said. "I don't do pajama parties."

"Why not? I know you're not sleeping well either."

His jaw clamped shut as he walked over. He looked down at the ground before lying back down on the bed.

"Are you alright?" I asked.

"About?"

I adjusted my legs in his chair. "I heard Juniper left."

He sighed. "You know, a woman shouldn't come to a man's room late at night to ask if he's doing alright after he recently got dumped. Your lack of common sense is quite incredible."

I frowned at him. Honestly, it was a miracle he ever had a girlfriend in the first place.

"I know you won't do anything," I said.

He rolled over on his side, resting his head on his hand. His hair fell over the side of his face as he gazed at me.

"Won't I?" he asked, his voice low.

I swallowed my heart back down my throat.

He chuckled, lying on his back again. "I've never seen your eyes get that wide."

I cleared my throat. "Actually, I also wanted to thank you for what you did for me. The reporters … I didn't realize what you were giving up."

He shut his eyes. "Who said it was for you?"

That was the first time I heard his voice so ... broken.

"I wanted answers," Julian continued, opening his eyes to stare at the ceiling. "I was saving the questions for the most opportune time."

"And what if there aren't any answers? What if it was for nothing?"

He turned to look at me. "I can accept that there aren't any answers. I can't accept that there aren't any questions."

There was silence.

"Evann told me," I said, barely above a whisper, "little pieces of your family's past."

He half-frowned, half-smiled. "Cyrus took the brunt of it. Even if our mother's wrath was aimed at us, he took it on himself." He held up his pinky finger. "That's why Cyrus's little finger is crooked. Did you ever notice that?"

I shook my head.

"I broke a vase. Cyrus took the blame. Mother broke his finger."

He dropped his hand on the bed with a thump, biting his lip.

I sighed, frustrated. First, because someone I cared about had grown up that way. Second, because I was realizing how protective Cyrus was. The more protective he was, the more I couldn't stay mad at him.

I wanted to. I wanted to hate him so much.

"Cyrus has done a lot for all of us," I said, half-bitter about it, "but you've done a lot for others, too."

He scoffed. "Like what?"

"Like protecting Cyrus from an annoying princess who could hurt him. Or sacrificing family secrets for said annoying princess. Or hiding a relationship with a woman your younger brother is in love with, just so he didn't feel inadequate around you."

Julian shut his eyes again, rubbing his forehead.

"Also," I continued, "let's not overlook the fact that you hit a gangster with your car to protect me."

He laughed. "Not my finest moment."

"I disagree."

He opened his eyes and turned to me again, staring at me for a long moment. The harshness I had first encountered months ago was now completely gone, replaced by edges that were as soft as the silk sheets around him.

I cleared my throat again. "I have a gift for you."

His eyes followed me as I stood up.

"Hand me your phone," I said.

"I thought this was a gift for me? Why am I handing things over?"

I wiggled my fingers. He reluctantly handed it over, and I logged into a music website. I handed it back to him. He pursed his lips.

"What is this?"

"When I had my first breakup in middle school, my best friend gave me a heartbreak playlist. It has songs on it written by people going through the same pain as you. In a weird way, it makes you feel like you're not alone." I shoved my hands back in my pockets. "Thanks to you and the others, I don't feel alone here. Not anymore."

He scrolled the list, his face scrunching in disgust.

"There are a lot of pop songs," he said.

"Ugh, so picky. Even with gifts. Does everything have to meet your standards?"

He lowered his phone, resting his arms on his knees and smiling up at me. "Not always. Sometimes the things I think won't reach my expectations surprise me in the most intriguing ways possible."

His glance lingered. Blood rushed to my face.

"I have a gift for you, too," he said.

"Really? What is it?"

"Hold out your hand."

I inched it forward. When I had fully extended it, he grabbed my hand and yanked me down on the bed. In a moment, I was looking at the ceiling, Julian's face hovering over mine. He pinned my arms to my chest.

Damn, he was stronger than I thought.

"A lesson," he said. "Never come to a man's bedroom at night. The thoughts he has during the day are much harder to control once night falls."

I swallowed.

He chuckled, then stood from the bed. He grabbed my wrist and yanked me forward, stepping out of the way as I projected towards him.

"Leave," he commanded.

I turned around as he sat back down on the bed, leaning back on his hands. The sparkle in his eyes was teasing and playful, yet still with that arrogant air of intelligence.

So, this … this was the real Julian.

I left before my curiosity got the better of me.

45

THE LAST BRUNCH

American breakfast again. The first time was to welcome me. This time, it felt like an apology. Only because of how quiet Cyrus was during the whole thing.

Nikos and Julian were happy to spend time with my parents, asking them questions about our humble little lives in California. The more they talked about it, the more I missed it. But something felt different as they pulled up old memories. I found myself not as anxious to go back. Things could never return to the way they were, but I could appreciate them existing in the first place.

"Tell us, Cyrus," my dad said, chomping on his toast like a teenage boy instead of a king, "how did Marina fair in her training? Does my daughter have your approval as a princess? I want your formal recommendation."

Leave it to my dad to bring up a life-changing topic over a mouthful of toast.

Cyrus rested his elbows on his chair and rubbed his fingertips together. He looked me over, dropping his eyes and then raising them again. Instead of answering my father, he stared at me.

"I think she's capable of handling any task in front of her," he finally said. "Her strength and her spirit will bring her success, no matter her decision."

He gave me a weak smile, then dropped it.

"She has my approval," he continued. "She had it from the very beginning."

Dad applauded. "I can rest easy in my grave, then."

I frowned. "Did you think I couldn't handle myself?"

"Of course not, princess," he said, "but a father's job is to make sure his daughter is ready for the challenges in front of her. Had I not done my job, I couldn't rest in the afterlife."

His rough fingers rubbed my chin, then he pulled me in to kiss my forehead.

I tried to ignore the weight in my chest. I was mad at him. I had to remember that.

His eyes slid over to Cyrus. "And what do you think about your host? Cyrus is a handsome young man, isn't he?"

Mom elbowed him. I knew where this was going. I looked over at Cyrus, but when our eyes met, his head dropped.

"He is," I agreed.

Cyrus shut his eyes, his shoulders tensing up.

"You agree?" Dad asked. "Well then! How would you feel about—"

"Marrying him?" I finished.

Everyone looked at me.

"Cyrus told me what you did, Dad," I said. "How could you set up an arranged marriage and not tell me? Are you out of your mind!"

He leaned back in his chair and laughed. "Ah, yes. That. Cyrus's father and I made that pact when we were very young. I don't think Cyrus was more than a couple of years old. It seems a little stuffy for the modern day and age, doesn't it?"

I narrowed my eyes at him. "Stuffy isn't the word I'd use for it. More like f—"

"Language," Mom warned.

"I had no intention of forcing you to go through with an arranged marriage," Dad said. "If it were up to me, you'd stay single until you're forty."

Mom rolled her eyes at him.

"But still, Cyrus grew up to be very smart, strong, and a man of good character. Honestly, Marina, is there any reason *not* to marry Cyrus?"

Cyrus's eyes met mine again.

"Yes," I replied. "There's a very good reason."

Everyone waited. Cyrus remained still.

"I've only been here a few months," I finally said. "I can't decide to marry someone that quickly. Are you crazy?"

Cyrus slouched in his chair. My parents laughed.

"My daughter's nothing if she isn't wise," Mom said. "A good marriage is better than a rushed one."

"Sorry, Cyrus," Dad said. "It looks like you're going to have to work a little harder."

Cyrus gave a nervous laugh, his voice squeaking. He cleared his throat.

Brunch lasted until mid-afternoon, until all of us were too full to finish what was left on the table.

"Now, the only matter of business is for Marina to decide what she wants," my dad said. "What do you think, princess?"

Looking around at everyone at the table, I wrestled with my feelings. I had become so used to these faces. I couldn't imagine not seeing them again.

Could I really go back to my old life?

"I … don't know," I said honestly. "I need more time."

"Royalty works on deadlines," Dad replied. "But fair is fair. I said that you could decide at our welcoming celebration. I'll hold to my promise. But you must make the announcement by the end of the night. Old life or new. It's in your hands now."

"Speaking of which," my mom said, "I think we should go see our old home. Together."

Dad nodded. "Great idea. Maybe that will help Marina decide. What do you say, Cyrus?"

Cyrus nodded. "I'll have the jet prepared immediately."

He waved to Evann, who nodded and left. Cyrus then went back to fiddling with his fingers, annoying me even more.

I was sick of watching him mope.

As everyone stood from the table, I walked over and grabbed his arm. "Let's talk."

§

The parlor felt like the safest place to talk. I wasn't in the mood for a chess game but sitting at the table with him made me feel more at ease.

"Why did you do that for me?" he asked, looking at the chess pieces on the table.

"It wasn't really for you," I replied. "Evann made me realize that if my parents ever found out what happened, our political relations would be strained. It would hurt your people and mine."

"Does that mean—"

"I haven't decided on what I'll do about the princess thing," I said, "but I do know that I don't want to have to coax a country out of war as my first act. Our countries would end up paying for this. I don't want that."

He nodded. "You certainly have the makings of a leader. I'm in your debt for a lifetime."

"I'm counting on that," I said. "In fact, I'm going to collect on it. So the next time something comes up, remember that you owe me *big*."

He gave a weak smile. "Spoken like a true diplomat."

"Thank you."

His eyes glossed over a little. "I'm afraid my brothers won't be so forgiving of my sins as you. I'll have to tell them sooner or later what I've done."

"Hey, I wouldn't say that I'm forgiving you. I plan on using this to my advantage for a *long* time."

He laughed through his nose. "Whatever you ask, I'm willing to give it to you. It's the least I can do for my mistakes. Marina, I'm truly—"

I waved my hand at him. "I know."

There was an awkward pause.

"About Tai …" I started.

Cyrus tensed up. "Yes?"

"What will you do with him? Will you execute him?"

Cyrus cocked his head to the side. "Execute? Whatever gave you that idea?"

"You don't execute traitors?" I asked, my heart fluttering in relief.

He chuckled. "We don't. We imprison people for a long time. Which is what's happened to Zhixin. Where he is now … well, trust me, he'll wish for execution."

I swallowed. "And Tai?"

"I couldn't imprison him. Not for my own poor decisions and judgment. After all, I am king. I gave a command. Tai had no choice but to follow. This was all my doing. If I could take all of it back, Marina—"

"I know. But it can't be undone. Punish the ones that deserve punishment."

Cyrus's eyes drifted to my neck. I knew he was looking at the cuts.

"I will," Cyrus said. "You have my word."

I smiled. "Then I guess we can celebrate."

46

THE CHOICE

The party to mark my parents' arrival was triple the size of Nikos's party, with more people to meet and more finger foods to stuff in my face. Some of the older guests recognized my parents, and excited chaos burst through the room when everyone realized who they were. There were a few cheers and a strange moment involving everyone tossing champagne at them, but a flood of smiles filled the room for the royal family back from the dead.

The orchestra played, led by an older man in a gray suit. His suit wasn't half as stylish as Tai's, and the way he led the orchestra seemed mechanical in comparison.

King Cyrus opened the dancing but didn't approach me, turning after a moment's hesitation to my mother instead. I could see his hesitation. So could Julian. With a courteous nod to Cyrus, Julian stepped towards me, holding out his hand.

"I believe with all the work I've put into you, I should be allowed the first dance."

I smiled and took Julian's hand. His black-and-white suit was modern and Western, with the top two buttons popped off.

"You want to be my first?" I teased as he led me to the dance floor.

He coughed, still frowning. I was starting to get attached to that frown. Regardless of his face, his embrace was warm as he took me into a dance stance.

"Someday I'm going to crack that shell of yours," I said.

"Are you going to be around long enough to try?"

I pursed my lips together. "I'm still deciding."

He faced me, as we began to dance.

"Well, in that case, this may be my only chance to say something." He took a deep breath. "Whatever you decide, I want you to know that I'm happy that you came to us. You're so much more than I expected."

In a moment, his scowl morphed into his small, sincere smile. I couldn't help but smile back.

"You don't suck that much either," I replied.

His eyes rolled to the top of his head. "That's a compliment, correct?"

I shrugged. "Sure."

He pursed his lips, leading me gracefully around the dance floor. He laughed with me more than once, and only scolded me for bad form twice.

Only Julian could be both the coldest mind and the warmest heart I'd ever met.

Nikos was the next one to ask me to dance.

Well, maybe not so much *ask*.

He pulled me into his arms unannounced. I stepped on his foot.

"Ow!" he yelped.

"Sorry,"

"You don't seem sorry."

"I'm not, really."

He laughed, pulling me back into his arms again. "Fair enough, Princess. Fair enough."

There was a long pause as we danced.

"I'm sorry," he finally said.

I looked up at him. His young face wrinkled into frown lines.

"I'm sorry for all the ways I hurt you," he said.

I smiled. He was kind of cute when he was being sincere.

"I'm sorry for all the things I didn't do for you," I returned. "And thank you … for all the things you've done for me. I won't forget it."

He smirked. "I know. I won't let you."

"You're a pain in the ass, Nikos. But you're a good friend."

He cocked his head to the side and smiled.

This time, his smile was genuine.

When the song ended, he bowed out gracefully, a small hop in his step as he found a new dance partner.

"Nikos didn't try anything, did he?"

I laughed as Evann approached me. "What are you worried about?"

"I guess you would have kicked his ass if he had." He nodded, satisfied with his own answer. "Can I have this next dance, Your Highness?"

"You dance?"

He straightened and took my hand. "Of course. Dancing isn't just for the rich and famous. And I am off duty — as well as an old family friend."

"But you're hurt …"

"I'll be more hurt if you reject me."

He spun me around the room to the fast tempo, making me laugh. I was relieved that he wasn't in serious pain. I wasn't sure if he and Cyrus had made amends, but Evann hadn't mentioned leaving the castle in recent days.

"Thank you, Evann," I said.

He looked surprised. "For what?"

"For being there for me through this entire thing."

"It was my pleasure, Princess," he said, squeezing my hand. "Truly."

After some time, Cyrus, who had been standing on the sidelines since his dance with my mother, shuffled his way up to me, bowing without a single word. I wasn't sure which of us felt more awkward. He held out his hand in a silent request. I took it, letting him pull me into his embrace.

Putting my hand on his broad shoulders, I couldn't help but think about when we first met. We knew so little about each other then, and both of us weren't the best at making decisions because of it. Regardless, he had been sweet and encouraging through it all. Maybe it wasn't all fake. The way he held my hand in his didn't feel fake. The way he had punched Zhixin after saving me wasn't fake. Something about him had been real.

In this moment — after everything had been said and done — this dance was real.

I didn't trust him right now, but that was okay. Trust could always be built again.

I held onto that hope as the music played.

The only prince I didn't dance with that night was Tai. What was he doing now? What was going to happen to him? Seeing another person at the piano bench didn't feel the same.

"How are you doing, sweetie?"

I looked up at my dad, who had spent most of the night standing on the side of the room drinking champagne and chatting with guests. It was still weird to see him in a full suit. He hadn't worn anything this expensive since Mom made him a model for her men's collection in Paris. Of course, he wore a fake mustache the entire time, so it didn't feel serious.

I shrugged. "Good."

"Do you like the party?"

"It's fun. I don't know if I could ever get used to the extravagance, though."

He paused for a moment. "You know that today is the day you announce what you want to do."

I nodded.

Dad threw his arm around me. "Whatever you decide, I understand. I only want you to be happy. I wouldn't want anything in this world except for my baby girl to be happy."

"Really?" I grumbled. "Is that why you lied to me for my entire life?"

He chuckled, kissed my forehead, muttered something about finding Mom, and left.

In only a couple hours I'd have to announce what I wanted — who I wanted to be. I could walk away from everything and become the ruler of an entire country. I wouldn't have to look for a job, I wouldn't have to worry about physical security, and I could have the power to help a lot of people. Or, I could go back to my old life. I could take over my uncle's dojo and go back to all my old friends and hobbies.

But if I went back to my old life, I'd never see this castle again, would I? I would never see …

I touched the scab on my neck. The one Zhixin had cut into me. The day he broke into my room and kidnapped me a second time, I knew who I wanted to save me. I knew who I wanted to see every day.

There was one person I knew I'd miss too much.

There was someone I couldn't give up.

47

THE END — FATE I

The one who hurt me the most.

But I knew he was hurting as much as I was.

I searched the ballroom for him but didn't see him anywhere. Where would the king go?

I climbed up the stairs leading to the parlor where we had met almost every day. As I slid the door open, memories of chess games, bad jokes, and sweet smiles flooded my memory.

Does this even make sense? After everything? Should I feel this way about him?

Cyrus was at his usual spot in front of the chessboard, his head in his hands. The room was dark except for a single yellow lamp off in the corner. He didn't stir. I watched him for a moment, imagining in his place a small boy growing up in constant fear and agony. Now he had grown into a man, still as scared and anxious.

Perhaps it was pity that drew me to him. Maybe it was forgiveness. Whatever it was, I couldn't leave him.

"Cyrus?"

He looked up. He jumped to his feet, knocking over the chessboard and sending the pieces flying all over the floor.

"What are you doing here?" he asked, reaching down for the chess pieces.

I shut the door and met him at the table. "Evann told me everything. About your childhood. About your mother."

He stopped collecting the chess pieces, sighing as he scattered what he had back on the board. He leaned on the table with one arm.

"I suppose the papers will expose it soon enough," he said. "It was only a matter of time."

He tapped his fingers on the chessboard.

"I wanted to protect my brothers," he said after a moment. "That's how I justified what I did. Looking back, I don't know why I thought you'd tear us apart like she did. From the moment I saw you ... I began to change my mind about everything."

He looked up at me, his dark eyes catching the light. I turned away, not knowing what to say.

"You're nothing like her," he continued. "But I am. Somewhere in my pursuit to be nothing like my mother, I succeeded in doing the opposite. I want — again — to ask for your forgiveness, but I don't think I can do anything to deserve it."

"No one earns forgiveness, Cyrus."

"I don't expect it for free."

"When I'm ready to give it to you, it will be. I just need a little bit of time."

He nodded. "Of course."

"But …" I continued. "I would like for us to start over."

"Start over?"

There was a hopefulness in his eyes that I didn't want to encourage into something else, but I also didn't want to crush him either. I couldn't. I cared about him too much.

"I'm not saying that I want to marry you," I continued. "But … I don't want to leave you either."

Cyrus stood tall to face me. I was struck again by how broad his shoulders were. Maybe they had to be, for all the weight he carried.

I wanted to be angry with him. I wanted to hate him and never speak to him again. There was no reason to trust him, no reason to make amends. But somewhere deep down I knew that Cyrus had never aimed to hurt me, and after spending the last three months here, I was more than aware of how easy it was for small things to spiral out of control.

Forgiving Cyrus was a risk … but I liked risks.

"Spend some time with me, King Cyrus," I said. "So you never doubt who I am ever again."

His hand inched up to my face. He took the end of my hair in his fingertips, twirling it. "I'm in your debt until the day I die, Marina."

"I'm okay with that."

I smiled at him. There was no reaction for a moment, then he burst into laughter, pulling me in and pressing his lips on mine.

I froze.

He did too.

He pulled back. The color drained out of his face.

"I apologize," he said. "I didn't mean — I shouldn't have — I keep making horrible decisions, don't I?"

I licked my lips, my mouth going dry. The taste of him saturated the tip of my tongue for a moment.

"It's okay," I said. "I didn't hate it."

He lingered for a moment. I could tell he wanted to ask, but he wasn't going to. He started to pull back.

"You can do it again, if you want."

I wasn't sure why I said it, but I meant it. Despite everything that had happened, despite his poor decisions, I wanted to be closer to him. I wanted to be so close that neither one of us could be afraid anymore.

He stepped back. "I …"

"You don't want to?"

He shook his head, making my heart dip in my stomach.

"Of course I do," he said. "I always have."

I grinned. "Do you need to pencil it into your schedule?"

He brought my hand up to his face, resting against it. "I don't need to schedule you in, Marina. Even when you're not with me, my time is devoted to you."

After a deep breath, he brought me into his arms. He swept down and met my lips with a long, deep kiss. We pulled apart for a moment, but no longer than that. There was a second kiss, just as long as the first. His hands traced down my sides, then around my waist. My hands rested on his chest, as his jaw pushed hard against mine. His heart raced under my palm as he brought me in for a third and final kiss, slower and deeper than the first two kisses combined.

Damn. He was a good kisser for someone who had never been on a date.

His lips left mine, and I was pulled into his embrace. I'd never been captured in a hug so tight before.

"I'll dedicate the rest of my life to making everything up to you," he murmured into my ear. "I promise. Believe me when I say that I care for you."

I smiled. "I know. I can tell."

It would take some time for us to trust one another, I supposed, but it would be worth it. For both of us.

§

That night I declared that I was taking my rightful place as the Crown Princess of Paijeana. My parents were ecstatic, naturally. Cyrus stayed by my side the entire party, causing mass rumors to spread by the end of the night. I didn't mind.

Julian eventually took my advice and went after Juniper. A few weeks later, he announced that he was giving up his royal station. Cyrus was against it at first, but eventually he caved, seeing how much Julian and Juniper cared for one another. He couldn't ask for more for his brother. Team JuJu came to the castle almost every weekend as honored guests.

Nikos worried me the most at first, but he bounced back the quickest. Maybe it was the gift of youth. The more time I spent at the castle, the stronger our friendship became. Despite his aggravating pranks and immature antics, he was genuinely encouraging to me as I transitioned from commoner to royalty, and for that, I would be forever grateful.

Tai stayed low for a few months, but then there was a huge surge in arrests involving the Double Eights. They weren't gone for good, but, with Tai's help, enough were put behind bars for them to cease to be a threat and for him to come out of hiding. Cyrus pardoned him, and Tai was able to go back to making music.

Cyrus finally approved Evann's leave. There was an academy in the west where he could teach. Even if he couldn't fight on the frontlines himself, he was pleased he could help those that did. He came to the castle periodically to teach the guards there, which put Cyrus in good spirits. Evann and I agreed not to speak of Cyrus's crimes. Evann had his own secrets to keep, and I needed something to hold over Cyrus's head in case of a political emergency.

Whether or not Julian and Nikos figured out who Evann really was … that's another story.

Cyrus meant every word he said to me. He spent all his time trying to make up for his mistakes, to the point that I couldn't stand him doing it anymore. Once he had my full forgiveness, I couldn't keep milking it for all it was worth. It would be too exhausting to do that. Instead, I enjoyed my time with him. As I stumbled through my new responsibilities, Cyrus encouraged me and helped me through. He was valuable to me, even if he had made mistakes that seemed unforgivable.

But in truth, nothing was unforgivable. Life was too short for that.

In time, I saw that Cyrus truly had more light in him than darkness, even if the darkness held onto him in pieces. If I had been in the same place, I couldn't say whether I'd have acted any differently than he had.

Now that nothing was hidden, I could explore both his darkness and his light. And, truth be told, I was in love with them both.

48

The End — Fate II

The one who had always stood beside me.

But now … where was he?

If he wasn't in the ballroom, where would he be?

I ran up the steps of the tower, my legs and lungs burning from the exercise. Reaching the top, I found Evann leaning over the side of the castle wall, rubbing his hands together as he looked at the lights of the kingdom. The soft glow below highlighted the strong curve of his jaw and the soft curls in his hair.

I wanted to know what he was thinking. What he was feeling. What he thought about me. I thought of a thousand questions, but none of them got past my chest. I could only slide up behind him and wrap my arms around his waist. I leaned against his back.

He shifted a little. "Princess? Is everything alright?"

I broke my grip as he turned to look at me. Those same puppy-dog eyes that greeted me the first day I arrived felt warm and safe. I was always safe with Evann.

"Evann, will you leave the castle?"

He smiled, but it didn't meet his eyes. "I want to, but it doesn't look like it's in the cards for me."

"Do you really want to leave? Do you want to leave Cyrus, Nikos, and Julian? After all, they're your …"

I stopped. He raised an eyebrow at me.

"… friends," I finished.

He snickered. "I doubt they all recognize me as their … friend."

"Why don't you stick around until they do? They'll be disappointed if they realize after it's too late."

He sucked in his cheeks and looked over the wall. "Perhaps. And you? Are you taking your place as princess? Or are you returning to your freedom?"

I leaned over the wall with him. Truth was, I still hadn't decided, even though I needed to make my decision in less than a few hours.

There was something I needed to know first.

"Say I became a princess," I said. "Would it be possible to hire you as my guard?"

"Didn't you just say to stay with *this* royal family?"

"You wouldn't be that far from them." A heartbeat passed. "And most importantly, you'd be close … to me."

He turned around, leaning his back against the wall. "Is that what you want?"

"You've always been there for me, Evann. I can't imagine you not being there."

With a deep breath, he shook his head. "I'm afraid I can't take up that offer, Princess."

"Why not?"

"I can't accept being a guard for you for a lifetime," he said. "I think that would annoy me too much."

"Yeah?" I asked, frowning. "And why is that?"

He leaned his chin against his shoulder. "Because I don't think I could handle being that close to you every day."

Before I could ask him what he meant, he reached out and moved a strand of my hair out of my face, his fingers caressing my cheek softer than a breeze.

"This is your one chance at freedom, Your Highness," he said. "You should take it before it slips through your fingers."

He pulled his hand away, leaning back down on the wall and staring at his fingers. I chewed my lip, trying to gather up courage.

"No matter my job, I'll always be free to make my own choices," I said. "And there are certain places ... certain people ... I can't imagine being without. It's not freedom if I can't have those people beside me."

I stepped in and laid my head on his shoulder.

"Wherever you are, Evann ... That's where I want to be."

He didn't move. I wanted him to wrap his arms around me and say that's what he wanted too. But he didn't.

"I'm a guard, Marina," he replied, my name sounding so sweet on his lips. "I have no intention of ever being anything other than that."

I looked up at him, still resting against his shoulder. "I don't want you to be anything else but yourself. You don't have to be anyone else than who you are now. I want you beside me. Guard ... or otherwise."

He turned his head to look down into my eyes.

"Do you want to stay beside me?" I asked.

He exhaled. His eyes swept down my face, then he turned away. He gently shrugged me off, then turned to face me. His hands wrapped around my shoulders, thumbs pressing into my skin.

Hold me, you idiot.

"You don't know what you're asking," he said.

I brought my hands up to rest on his. "I do know. And I'll ask again. Do you want to stay beside me?"

He stared at my lips for a moment, then raised his eyes to mine. I stopped breathing.

"Answer," I commanded playfully. "As a member of the royal family, I demand you answer honestly."

A glimmer of a smile danced behind his lips, quickly erased by a swallow.

"Yes," he whispered.

I wasn't sure if I was relieved or more nervous. My heart was pounding out of my chest. I looked up at his lips and leaned in.

He stopped me.

"Princess," he said, the word sounding more like a pet name than a formality. "You can't. We can't."

"Why not?"

He dipped his head down, brushing his nose against my cheek. "I'm afraid if we start ... I won't be able to stop."

I inched in closer, feeling his breath on my lips. "Then don't."

His lips brushed mine and he paused, maybe waiting to see if I would pull back. I didn't. His arms snaked around my shoulders, bringing me into his embrace. He gently kissed my lips. Once. Twice. His kisses suddenly doubled in intensity, throwing me off balance. Holding me tight to his chest, he continued to kiss me, each kiss more intense than the last.

When he said he wasn't going to stop, he wasn't kidding.

After a while, I put my hands on his chest, signaling that I needed a moment to breathe. Because, damn.

He pulled back, giving a breathy laugh.

"I'm sorry," he said in a low voice. "But I did warn you."

He leaned in and placed a single kiss under my ear, his warm arms still around me. I laid my head against his chest. His heart was pounding as hard as mine.

"You're sure about this?" he asked.

"More than anything."

"As the Crown Princess, you would have your choice of prince …"

"There are many types of princes, Evann." I wrapped my arms around him and squeezed tight. "And you … you're my favorite kind."

§

That night I declared that I was taking my rightful place as the Crown Princess of Paijeana. My parents were ecstatic, obviously. Evann kept his post as I gave my announcement, smiling even though we weren't completely sure what it would mean for us in the long run. All I knew was that if I wasn't a princess, I might never see him again, and I couldn't take that risk.

I forgave Cyrus eventually and the bad blood between us dissolved. He ended up going to therapy for paranoia issues, and that made it easier to rebuild our friendship. It wasn't long before he could start opening his heart more, and after a few years, he found a woman he could really do that with. We were all relieved that he wasn't going to spend his entire life alone.

Julian eventually took my advice and went after Juniper. A few weeks later, he announced that he was giving up his royal station. Cyrus was against it at first, but eventually he caved, seeing how much Julian and Juniper cared for one another. He couldn't ask for more for his brother. Team JuJu came to the castle almost every weekend as honored guests.

Nikos worried me the most at first, but he bounced back the quickest. Maybe it was the gift of youth. The more time I spent at the castle, the stronger our friendship became. Despite his aggravating pranks and immature antics, he was genuinely encouraging to me as I transitioned from commoner to royalty, and for that, I would be forever grateful.

Tai stayed low for a few months, but then there was a huge surge in arrests involving the Double Eights. They weren't gone for good, but, with Tai's help, enough were put behind bars for them to cease to be a threat and for him to come out of hiding. Cyrus pardoned him, and Tai went back to making music.

Evann and I agreed not to speak of Cyrus's crimes. Evann had his own secrets to keep, and I needed something to hold over Cyrus's head in case of a political emergency.

Whether or not Julian and Nikos figured out who Evann really was ... that's another story.

My parents and I moved back into our family's castle. I called Evann to come see me often, and the more he visited, the more my parents caught onto how we felt about each other. They adored him as much as I did, and though I never breathed a word about his situation, I think my dad knew something was different about Evann. That would be the only explanation for why my dad suddenly felt the need to hire lawyers to find loopholes in the royalty-can't-marry-a-commoner clause.

But whether or not Evann ever decided to become a king or a prince, a guard or a beggar, it didn't matter to me. Who he could have been and who he was were different. I loved who he was. It didn't matter who he could have been. And since he felt the same about me, we never felt the need to be or become something we weren't.

And in the end, that was all either of us wanted.

49

THE END — FATE III

The one I couldn't stand in the beginning.

But now, I couldn't stand to be without him.

I couldn't find his face among the ballroom dancers. I looked for a scowl or a smile, since both sides of him seemed so different that they could be different people. But now I understood why he had two such distinct sides. What walls did he have to build to live through such a childhood?

I wanted to ask him, face to face. Then I wanted to break down those walls, little by little.

I snuck out of the ballroom and went to the only place I could imagine he'd be on a cool evening.

Creaking the library door open, I peeked in. Julian was lounging on the couch next to the fireplace and reading with those dark glasses of his.

"Leaving early?" he asked, not looking up from his book as I shut the door.

"I could ask you the same."

"I'm not the guest of honor."

"Since when have you considered me a guest of honor?"

I flopped on the couch next to him, leaning over his shoulder to see what he was reading. He turned towards me, scanning my neck.

"I'm alright, Julian," I assured him.

"I know," he said, still staring. "But you almost weren't."

"Does that bother you?"

"Of course it does." He cleared his throat and looked back at his book. "You're going to be part of our family. I should care, right?"

I leaned closer to his shoulder, brushing my chin against the fabric. "Is that the only reason?"

He didn't move. "Do I need another?"

I pulled back. Maybe he wasn't interested. He was in love with Juniper, wasn't he? He would go after her. At least, I thought he would. I wanted to ask, but I wasn't ready to hear the answer.

"I suppose not," I returned, standing up from the couch. "Do you think you can handle me as your sister for a lifetime?"

I threw my hands up dramatically, hoping it would make him smile. Maybe if he smiled, my soul wouldn't feel so crushed.

He slammed the book shut.

"You're really going through with the engagement then? After all the trouble you caused about it?"

I lowered my hands. "What's with the attitude all of a sudden? It's not like you'll be here to see it."

He raised an eyebrow. "Am I going somewhere?"

"Aren't you going to the love of your life?"

"The love of my ... you mean ...?"

"Yeah, her."

He put the book on the side table, folding his glasses on top. "I have no intention of going after Juniper. She's a lovely woman, but our lives were not meant to mix."

"Why?" I asked. "Because she wasn't bred like you?"

"I have no interest in breeds. Only in things that are sustainable."

"Why aren't you going after her?" I asked. "Don't you want to be with her?"

He put his elbow on the arm of the couch and his chin on his hand, not answering.

"Don't you love her?" I continued. "If she loves you, she's waiting for you. She's waiting to hear that you care about her. She's waiting for you to go after her. She wants you to come after her."

He stood to face me, his eyes unusually soft. Somewhere in the corners of his lips was a faint smile.

"You should tell her how you feel," I continued, losing the strength in my voice. "Or she'll always wonder."

He cocked his head to the side. "We're not talking about *her* anymore, are we?"

I stepped back, breaking eye contact. He gave a short laugh before curling his finger under my chin and bringing it up.

"Should I tell her my feelings, then?" he asked. "Despite the obvious consequences?"

I looked to the side. "Well ..."

"If I kiss her, will that tell her my feelings?" he asked.

I opened my mouth, but it went dry before I could say anything. Not knowing how to answer, I nodded.

He smiled. "Then … I should apologize in advance."

"For what?"

His lips crashed onto mine, his arms wrapping around my back. He didn't waste any time being shy. His kisses were slow, but rough. His fingers reached forward and forced their way between mine as he clasped one of my hands to his chest, holding all of me against him tight as he continued to kiss me. One rough kiss after another, I lost myself in a haze of pleasant confusion.

Julian wasn't kissing Juniper. He was kissing me.

He broke away.

"My apologies," he said, exhaling with a smile.

I gaped at him. "Holy hell. Where did that come from?"

His hands ran up and down my back. The smile behind his lips made me want to kiss him all over again.

"I wanted to touch you like this so badly," he said, "but I knew you belonged to my brother. I couldn't come near you. Seeing anyone close to you drove me insane. Yet, I couldn't ask for you. Even though I wanted to, I couldn't."

It never occurred to me that Julian would hold himself back from something he wanted. But that's how he was, wasn't he? Behind his scowl and his smile was a man who wanted the best for his family. Caring didn't always mean obvious kindness.

"Why me?" he asked. "Didn't you hate me?"

"Yes," I said flatly. "But ... I think there's a lot more to you than meets the eye. I want to be the person that knows every side of you."

"Then be glad I'm not schizophrenic."

I slapped his arm at the terrible joke. "If you were, it would make more sense."

He chuckled and pulled me into his arms. "Then let's learn about each other. Every side, every strength, and every weakness."

I leaned back and smiled at him. "You'd be willing to share?"

He nodded. "Life isn't worth living until you find someone you can be every side of yourself with."

§

That night I declared that I was taking my rightful place as the Crown Princess of Paijeana. My parents were ecstatic, obviously. I caught Julian on the side of the room, glowing in his rare smile. He stayed with me the entire night, and it started mass rumors around the castle by the time the night ended.

I forgave Cyrus eventually and the bad blood between us dissolved. He ended up going to therapy for paranoia issues, and that made it easier to rebuild our friendship. It wasn't long before he could start opening his heart more, and after a few years, he found a woman he could really do that with. We were all relieved that he wasn't going to spend his entire life alone.

Nikos worried me the most at first, but he bounced back the quickest. Maybe it was the gift of youth. The more time I spent at the castle, the stronger our friendship became. Despite his aggravating pranks and immature antics, he was genuinely encouraging to me as I transitioned from commoner to royalty, and for that, I would be forever grateful.

Cyrus finally approved Evann's leave. There was an academy in the west where he could teach. Even if he couldn't fight on the frontlines himself, he was pleased he could help those that did. He came to the castle periodically to teach the guards there, which put Cyrus in good spirits. Evann and I agreed not to speak of Cyrus's crimes. Evann had his own secrets to keep, and I needed something to hold over Cyrus's head in case of a political emergency.

Whether or not Julian and Nikos figured out who Evann really was … that's another story.

Tai stayed low for a few months, but then there was a huge surge in arrests involving the Double Eights. They weren't gone for good, but, with Tai's help, enough were put behind bars for them to cease to be a threat and for him to come out of hiding. Cyrus pardoned him, and Tai was able to go back to making music.

Julian, not surprisingly, spent a lot of time with me at my parents' castle. He spent most of his time helping us rebuild our library and the garden, the two places that meant so much to us in his home. Dad let him do it and started to treat him like a son.

As my family invited him into our home, his walls started to fall. He smiled more and more, in ways I never imagined he could. And there was nothing more irresistible than a poetic heart with a smile.

He was the one to see all sides of me. Even though he teased and reprimanded me for some of them, he still stuck around despite them. Maybe that's what true love was: staying despite the things you didn't like about each other.

And no matter what side he showed me, I was happy to stick around.

50

THE END — FATE IV

The one who gave me the hardest time. But there was no one else I'd rather fight with for the rest of my life.

He was on the balcony alone. From the glaze in his eyes I could tell he was lost in thought, but from what, I couldn't be sure.

I hadn't even intended on becoming friends with Nikos. When I met him, he was a kid that pulled pranks and threw temper tantrums. The more I got to know him, however, the less of a child he became. He was someone who held the attention of the world, someone who could never truly be himself for fear that it would disappoint someone. In some ways, he was more mature than I was.

Not that I was going to admit that to him.

"Planning another prank?" I teased, standing next to him.

He snapped out of his daze and smirked. "I could be."

"Who's the target?"

"Wouldn't you like to know?"

"I would. It seems like I'm your favorite to torture."

"That's because you are my favorite."

My heart jumped.

"Am I?" I asked. "Am I your favorite, Nikos?"

A heartbeat passed. I couldn't ask the questions I wanted to ask. I wanted him to say that I was his favorite out of everyone, but not for pranks. I wanted to know that I was his favorite in general — that he cared for me more than he showed. That all his teasing was simply his way of getting my attention.

He looked away, not answering. He bit his lip and patted the balcony rail, looking up into the stars. With such a solemn response, my questions faded, already answered. His head fell, then he turned to look at me, his head cocked to the side. With a long glance he backed up and turned to leave.

I couldn't turn around to watch him go. It was the nicest rejection I'd ever gotten, anyways. Maybe it was for the best, after everything. He was too young for me, right? Maybe he still liked Juniper. Maybe there was nothing for him to love about me. There were plenty of other women he could love. Younger women with higher breeding—

Then I felt his hands on my shoulders, his cologne surrounding me from behind. His hands slid down my arms, his chest leaning in and pressing against my back.

"Nik—"

His head dipped to my shoulder, his breath against my neck. I shivered as his lips brushed against my nape, while his fingers intertwined with mine. He brought his head up and leaned his forehead against the side of my face, breathing into my ear.

"Be mine," he whispered.

My knees went weak.

"I don't care if you were meant for Cyrus," he said. "I can't watch you with anyone else, and I won't allow you to be my sister. Not with the way I feel about you."

I wiggled out of his embrace and turned around. "The way you feel …?"

He shrugged, the persona of the World's Prince dropping away with his shoulders. "I like you more than I care to admit, Princess."

"Me? Why?"

He paused, reaching his hand up to tuck my hair behind my ear. "You cry so damn much."

"I'm sorry, you lost me."

"I'm surrounded daily by people with fake emotions. But you … it's impossible for you to be fake."

He stepped in closer.

"I know I messed up a lot," he continued. "I'm going to make it up to you. I promise you that."

"What about Cyrus?" I said.

He frowned. "I won't let him have you. I won't accept that you belong to him."

I had to giggle at his tantrum. "Such a greedy child."

One of his arms wrapped around my waist, while the other ran through my hair. I couldn't form a complete thought in my head.

"How many times do I have to tell you?" he asked, his mouth against my ear. "I'm not a child."

He pressed his lips against mine. I jumped at the sudden kiss, but he held onto me tighter. He kissed me gently a few times, then broke the kiss to take in a sharp breath. He pressed against my lips again, this time more eager. I melted into him, unable to resist such a hungry kiss.

He broke away. "Are you going to call me a child again?"

I put my hands on his shoulders, still light-headed.

"Well?" he asked again.

He leaned in again, but I pulled back.

"I got the message," I said.

"Good."

He smiled, leaning his head against mine.

"But ..." I said, breaking the moment. "When did all this happen? I thought you hated me."

He shook his head. "I never hated you. I hated how stuck I felt. Julian had Juniper. Cyrus had you. I had nothing. I had no friends, no crown, no real purpose."

I leaned my head on his shoulder. He hid so much under the surface.

"You bothered me," he continued. "I thought you only bothered me because I didn't have anyone. Then I realized ... it was you. It bothered me that you didn't belong to me."

His arms wrapped around me.

"Don't go to Cyrus," he whispered. "Don't go."

I reached up and kissed his cheek. "I'm not going anywhere, Nikos. I plan to torture you for a lifetime."

He smiled as he looked down at me. "Same here."

§

That night I declared that I was taking my rightful place as the Crown Princess of Paijeana. My parents were ecstatic. So was Nikos. He stood on the side proudly nodding at my speech like all of this was his doing. Rumors about us started by the end of the night … mainly because he kissed me on the balcony, in plain sight of just about everyone. Oops.

I forgave Cyrus eventually and the bad blood between us dissolved. He ended up going to therapy for paranoia issues, and that made it easier to rebuild our friendship. It wasn't long before he could start opening his heart more, and after a few years, he found a woman he could really do that with. We were all relieved that he wasn't going to spend his entire life alone.

Julian eventually took my advice and went after Juniper. A few weeks later, he announced that he was giving up his royal station. Cyrus was against it at first, but eventually he caved, seeing how much Julian and Juniper cared for one another. He couldn't ask for more for his brother. Team JuJu came to the castle almost every weekend as honored guests.

Cyrus finally approved Evann's leave. There was an academy in the west where he could teach. Even if he couldn't fight on the frontlines himself, he was pleased he could help those that did. He came to the castle periodically to teach the guards there, which put Cyrus in good spirits.

Evann and I agreed not to speak of Cyrus's crimes. Evann had his own secrets to keep, and I needed something to hold over Cyrus's head in case of a political emergency.

Whether or not Julian and Nikos figured out who Evann really was … that's another story.

Tai stayed low for a few months, but then there was a huge surge in arrests involving the Double Eights.

They weren't gone for good, but, with Tai's help, enough were put behind bars for them to cease to be a threat and for him to come out of hiding. Cyrus pardoned him, and Tai was able to go back to making music.

Eventually my parents and I moved into our own castle, and Nikos was quick to follow. With no purpose in his own kingdom, he took it upon himself to become my personal tutor for everything and anything in mine, whether I asked for it or not. But I couldn't turn him away for it. I knew it was the first time he felt like a real prince — not like a child or like the youngest of the brothers.

He could be his annoying self with me; and, in turn, I could be my annoying self with him. That was the basis of our friendship and our romance. We could be ourselves no matter the rough edges. We shared real pain and real emotions. Whatever the world saw or demanded of us, we could be our real selves with each other.

The world didn't have to know both sides of us. Only we had that honor.

51

THE END — FATE V

T he one who had always come to my rescue. Maybe now it was my turn to go to his.

I grabbed Evann and pulled him to the side of the ballroom.

"I need you to make a phone call for me," I said.

§

Evann waited in the car as I walked up the apartment stairs. He had offered to go with me, but I wanted to talk to Tai alone. Tai had disappeared after that night he came to the training center to speak on Cyrus's behalf. There wasn't a word spoken about him since. It was like he was someone I had made up in my head, and now I had to see for myself that he had been real. My heart pounded with each step, wondering if he was missing me as much as I was missing him.

Room 301. This was it.

I knocked on the door. There was scuffling on the other side. Each step I heard made it harder to breathe.

The door cracked open. "Marina? What are you—"

The sound of his voice was too much. I pushed the door open and threw my arms around his neck. He stumbled back, his hands raised in surprise.

"Tai …" I said. "I missed you."

After a moment, his arms wrapped around me. "What are you doing here? How did you get here?"

I leaned back to gaze into his eyes. "I missed you."

His hands traced my shoulders as he exhaled. He nodded. "I missed you too, jailbird."

He broke away from the embrace and sat on a tall stool next to the bar in the kitchen. I shut the door and walked over to him.

"How much of it was real?" I asked.

"How much of what?"

"Everything you said to me. Saving me. Our relationship in general."

He sucked in his breath, laughing quietly to himself. "I don't think any of it was fake. I'm not as good as carrying out a job as I used to be."

I paused, waiting for him to continue.

"Cyrus knew who I was when I came to work for Julian," he said. "He knew who my father was, but decided not to punish me for my father's crimes. Maybe because of his own parents. He never brought up my connections … until you came to us. Cyrus asked me to scare you off. He made it clear I was not to hurt you in any way. He only wanted out of the arranged marriage."

I rolled my eyes. "He could have just told me that he didn't want to get married. I don't understand why that was so difficult. Anyways, what made him think that I'd want to marry him?"

Tai rolled his eyes back at me. "A young woman not want to be a princess … a queen? Sure, they exist, but it was too big a risk. And he was afraid of retaliation if he backed off. He didn't know what you would do to him or his family." He tapped his fingers on the chair under him. "I should have known Zhixin would take it further than it needed to go. He was supposed to scare you at the festival, but … once he hit you … I snapped. Thinking of you in danger … I couldn't stand it."

I stepped in closer to him. "You're the reason I was in danger in the first place."

Tai shut his eyes and dropped his head. "I know it."

"But you also saved me."

He looked up at me, silent. I stepped in even closer, standing between his knees and putting my hands on his shoulders.

"I want you to always be there to save me," I continued. "Promise you won't leave me again."

"What are you trying to say?"

I hesitated. When he didn't move, I leaned down and kissed his forehead, letting my lips linger for a moment. His hands came up to my waist, gripping hard and bringing me in even closer.

"This isn't a good idea," he warned.

"I didn't ask if it was a good idea."

I smirked as he looked into my eyes. In a swift motion, his hand came to the back of my head and slammed my lips against his. I gripped his shirt — more out of surprise than anything — as he wildly kissed me. His other hand wrapped around my waist and pulled me in tighter to him, and he slowed down the kiss, deepening it.

Everything was real. I could tell from the way he was kissing me that everything had been real.

He pulled his lips from mine, then stood and enveloped me in his arms. His jagged breath tickled my ear as he held me close.

"You don't know how badly I missed you, jailbird."

I hooked my hands over his shoulders. "Don't disappear again."

He paused. "Can you love me knowing who I used to be?"

I nodded and leaned against his chest. "Yes. Because it made you who you are now. The man you are now doesn't have to be punished for the man you once were."

His warm hands stroked my arms as he pecked my forehead. "Then I'll stay right here. I'll rescue you anytime you need it. You can bet on it."

§

Eventually Evann came up to take me back to the party. I complied, but only so I could go back and announce my decision. I was taking my rightful place as the Crown Princess of Paijeana. My parents were ecstatic. I wondered how they would feel when they found out that I was only taking the job to hunt down members of the Double Eights. I also wondered how they would feel about hiring a castle musician.

I forgave Cyrus eventually and the bad blood between us dissolved. He ended up going to therapy for paranoia issues, and that made it easier to rebuild our friendship. It wasn't long before he could start opening his heart more, and after a few years, he found a woman he could really do that with. We were all relieved that he wasn't going to spend his entire life alone.

Julian eventually took my advice and went after Juniper. A few weeks later, he announced that he was giving up his royal station. Cyrus was against it at first, but eventually he caved, seeing how much Julian and Juniper cared for one another. He couldn't ask for more for his brother. Team JuJu came to the castle almost every weekend as honored guests.

Nikos worried me the most at first, but he bounced back the quickest. Maybe it was the gift of youth. The more time I spent at the castle, the stronger our friendship became. Despite his aggravating pranks and immature antics, he was genuinely encouraging to me as I transitioned from commoner to royalty, and for that, I would be forever grateful.

Cyrus finally approved Evann's leave. There was an academy in the west where he could teach. Even if he couldn't fight on the frontline himself, he was pleased he could help those that did. He came to the castle periodically to teach the guards there, which put Cyrus in good spirits.

Evann and I agreed not to speak of Cyrus's crimes. Evann had his own secrets to keep, and I needed something to hold over Cyrus's head in case of a political emergency.

Whether or not Julian and Nikos figured out who Evann really was … that's another story.

Tai eventually came to work for us in our castle, and Mom picked up on our relationship long before Dad did. Or Dad was living in denial. It was hard to tell. I don't know if Dad ever found out that he was an ex-gangster, but I wasn't going to say anything about it. Regardless of his past, I was always safe with Tai. He protected me in the castle, and constantly protected me outside of it.

There was a high chance that eventually I would have to give up my new throne for Tai ... but I didn't mind the trade.

Even though there were dark patches in Tai's past, his future was getting brighter. He poured himself into his art more each day, to the point that I got jealous of all the attention his sheet music got. I couldn't scold him for it, though. I knew he was trying to move forward from his family's past, and his own. He may have been a product of his past, but he refused to be trapped by it.

Who he was and who he wanted to become were two different people.

That's what made me love him even more.

APPENDIX

SCENES FROM HIS
POINT OF VIEW

Don't like any of the endings? Well then, write your own! At the end of the book there are blank pages for you to create whatever ending you want.

For further inspiration, or to spend more time with your favorite prince, here are some scenes from the points of view of the five princes: Cyrus, Julian, Nikos, Evann, and Tai. Get to know them better by seeing the story through their eyes.

CYRUS

WELCOME, YOUR MAJESTY

S he seemed harmless. But then again, they always
did.

Evann assured me that if Marina crossed any lines,
we could escort her out of the castle. Perhaps we could.
Then again, her father wouldn't take that news well. I
didn't want to create any more enemies.

I trusted her father. He had done so much for my
brothers and me when our parents were alive. He never
asked for anything in return.

Until now.

I hoped all my suspicions were unfounded. After
all, Marina was the daughter of two people of strong
character … but that character had been built over years
of royal conditioning.

Marina had gone from powerless commoner to
future queen overnight. There was no telling what she
would do with her new power.

I grabbed my head, getting light-headed. I was
breathing incorrectly again. Why was it so difficult to
breathe like a normal human being?

I tried to think of anything calming. Babbling
brooks. Orange sunsets. Fluffy kittens.

But all I kept seeing was her face.

I walked in a circle around my room. I didn't want to risk going outside the door and running into her. She had probably found the letter I placed under her pillow, right? It seemed like an obvious enough place. Easy to find. Not easy to determine who sent it. She wouldn't suspect me, would she?

After all, kings didn't normally threaten princesses.

Tai would take care of the rest. There was no reason for him to betray me, given the conditions of the agreement. He wouldn't harm her, but I would see how she acted under pressure. See who she really was.

I started walking counterclockwise.

I had to watch her carefully. If I messed this up, Julian and Nikos would pay for it. Again. They had paid too much already. Their childhoods were terrifying wrecks. I couldn't protect them effectively back then. I tried my best, but there was only so much I could do. As king, I had the power to protect them now. I had to. They were my brothers. I had to.

When my knees weakened and my hands started tingling, I sat on the bed. It was time for breathing techniques.

Inhale, 1, 2, 3.

Hold breath, 1, 2, 3.

Exhale, 1, 2 …

RIIIIING

I jumped, grabbing my chest. Coughing, I picked up my handphone.

"Tai! You scared the hell out of me."

"Nice to hear your voice too, Your Majesty," he replied, always with that hint of mockery. "Just wanted to let you know that everything is set."

"You won't touch her, understand?"

"Yea, I understood the first twelve times you told me. She'll be safe. Stressed, but safe. That's what you want, right?"

I rolled my tongue over my lips.

There was a pause at the other end. "You sure you want to do this?"

I tapped my fingers on the bed. Marina could be an innocent young woman, or she could be power-hungry and ruthless. It was hard to tell. She had only known she was a princess for a matter of hours. Who knew how that was affecting her mind right now? Who knew how it would affect her later?

If it was anything like my mother, I didn't want to see the ending.

"Yes," I said. "It's nothing that wouldn't come up for her later anyhow."

"Hmmm. Threats from strangers are a little bit different, though. Threats from other royal members … eh … could be more problematic."

"Then make sure it doesn't come back to us."

It felt dark as I said it.

"Understood," he replied. "Shouldn't be a problem."

I hung up.

He didn't think it was a problem … but I wasn't so sure.

DRESS UP

There was a knock at my door. Before I could even ask the question, I got the answer.

"It's Tai."

I told him to enter. He was dressed in the suit Julian had given him for special in-house events. Ah, that's right. Tonight was Nikos's party. I had been too lost in my thoughts to remember.

"Any news?" I asked.

"They lost my pants at the dry cleaners. I stole Julian's."

"I meant about Marina."

"Ah, right. Nothing to report, really." He walked further into the room, taking some cheese from the tray on the table next to me. "She's uncomfortable, overwhelmed, and awkward. Power-hungry and crazy aren't words I'd use for her. I've seen enough crazy to know what I'm talking about."

Some tension left my shoulders.

"Also," he continued, "you didn't see the look on her face when she thought you were poisoned."

I tapped my foot. "Was she concerned?"

"Incredibly."

I took in a long breath. She barely knew me. She had no reason to be concerned. Her hand was so gentle against my face when she had come in and checked me for fever. I wished I didn't remember that day, but I did.

And it made me question everything I was doing.

"Earth to King Cyrus," Tai sung. "Do you still want to keep going with this? You seem on the gate."

"On the fence," I replied automatically as I rubbed my neck to ease the tension building again. "You'll keep your word that you won't touch her, right?"

He gave a sharp nod.

"I-I'm not—" Words were failing me. "Let's keep an eye on her a little longer. Nothing else."

Tai shrugged. "As you wish."

He bowed and started to walk towards the door. He stopped when his hand reached the doorknob.

"She's wearing a blue dress," he said over his shoulder.

I wasn't sure why he was telling me that. "What?"

He nodded over towards the balcony. "Just in case you get curious."

With that, he left.

I stared at the balcony door for a moment. Could I see her from here?

The cool summer air hit my face as I swung the doors open. I wasn't cold, but I wrapped my silk robes around me anyhow.

Nikos's party had turned out wonderfully. The soft lights, the music, the crowd. If I didn't have so much anxiety during large events …

My eyes caught something blue. Focusing, I could see it was Marina, like Tai had said. For a second, I stopped breathing. She looked lovely. Her skin in the lamplight, the way her hair was brushing her neck — I could have stared at her for the rest of the night.

Wait, what was I saying?

Still … a couple minutes couldn't hurt anything, right?

I sat in the chair next to the railing and leaned my arm against it, watching her. Who was she dancing with? Julian? I smiled. They were a little clunky at the waltz, weren't they? But they seemed to be having fun.

Watching them both, I realized the smile on Marina's face held no threat for Julian. He wasn't in danger. He was at ease. I hadn't seen my brother that relaxed in years.

Marina really wasn't going to hurt him, was she?

I looked down at the pinky finger on my right hand. The one that Mother broke when Julian accidentally broke the Qing-dynasty vase. I knew she'd lose it, so I told him to keep quiet.

A broken finger for a broken vase. Eye for an eye. Tooth for a tooth.

That was just her way of thinking.

But Marina ... she didn't seem to think that way at all.

What was I doing?

Hot N Cold

"Get Nikos. Now!"

The guard bowed and left. I wrung my hands. Why had Marina attacked him? Was he really hurt? Was he suffering?

Maybe she *was* as bad as I thought.

I couldn't sit still in my room. I couldn't handle the waiting. I went down the stairs and into the hall. Just as I was walking down, Nikos came to meet me, slightly limping.

I took his face in my hands to look at him. "I saw what happened. Are you hurt? Why did she kick you? Do I—"

He wiggled out of my grasp. "Stop coddling. I'm fine."

"What happened?"

His eyes rolled to the side. "Well ..."

"He was an idiot and earned it," a voice chimed in from the entrance.

Julian stepped in to meet the both of us.

"I thought you might have been watching," Julian said to me.

"What happened?" I asked again.

Nikos put his tongue in his cheek.

"I don't think Nikos has been the best of hosts," Julian explained. "I'm guessing Marina didn't want to put up with your nonsense anymore?"

Nikos dropped his head.

"Is that true?" I asked.

He laughed. "Maybe. I don't know."

"How do most women respond when you dance with them so aggressively?" Julian asked. "I thought you'd break her spine in half."

I sighed. I wasn't sure if I was frustrated or relieved. I thought Marina hurt him for no reason. Why hadn't I even considered the possibility that Nikos had started the trouble? He started trouble all the time.

"She looked pretty upset, Cyrus," Julian added.

I nodded. "Understood. Go back to the party."

Nikos's eyebrows rose. "Go back? But shouldn't we—"

"Go back, Nikos. And for the sake of my sanity, behave yourself."

He frowned but nodded. They left together, Julian muttering a few wise words to Nikos himself as they walked.

Where was Marina now? Was she upset? Did she run away?

Still in my robe, I searched the castle for her. I don't know why I didn't get someone else to go after her. After all, I had men to do this for me.

For some reason, I wanted to find her myself.

She wasn't in the dining hall, kitchen, her room, or any of the upper floors. I went back to the bottom floor, opening any door I ran across. I even went so far as the towers. Why would she be there? The doorways were so far out of the way.

Then I heard sniffling.

I turned my head up the stairwell, catching sight of that blue dress again.

Even when she cried, she still looked lovely.

I took the first step when a voice rang out.

"Marina?"

Evann.

I stepped back so they couldn't see me.

"What's wrong?" he asked, wrapping his hands around her face and wiping her tears. "Were you threatened again?"

She shook her head. "No, no. No threats. Just a rough night. Don't worry about it."

My heart sunk. Why didn't she come to me instead of Evann?

Idiot. You're the one sending the threats. Why would you want her to come to you?

"Let me show you something," Evann said, taking her hand. "It might cheer you up."

She gave a weak smile and followed him up the stairs.

When they disappeared, I turned around and walked back towards my room.

She didn't need me.

And for some reason, that bothered me.

TRACKING

I gripped the sides of my chair. "You said she wouldn't be harmed."

Tai chewed his bottom lip in a thoughtful way, instead of the nervous way he should have been chewing it.

"She wasn't supposed to be," he growled. "Zhixin lost his damn mind."

"Zhixin? Who's that?"

"Someone I'll be tracking down and taking care of. Trust me."

He took a deep breath, wincing. I didn't know how he would be able to track down anyone with a broken rib, but I wasn't concerned about his logic at the moment.

"I failed to keep her safe," he said. "I'll take responsibility for that. But it's best for all of us if I track down the bastard first. No offense, Majesty, but you won't be able to find him. You don't know him like I do."

"Yet you didn't know he was hiding in my castle?"

"If I don't find him, you can execute me yourself."

He stared me straight in the eye, challenging me. We both knew his power in the realm outside of my castle. He might have been prince of the Double Eights ... but I was king.

"You have one week," I said. "If you don't track him down and reveal his whereabouts to me, then—"

"— then Julian will be disappointed in all the time he wasted. Got it."

He shrugged at the thought, making my fingers dig deeper into the chair.

"Fix it, Tai. That's a command."

He smirked. "I would have done it regardless. But you don't have to trust me, Your Majesty. I wouldn't if I were you."

His eyes fell for a moment. I could see the thoughts running through his mind.

"I'll pay off your debt, as promised," I said.

He raised an eyebrow at me.

"Regardless of the result, I made an agreement," I explained. "I won't deport your mother and uncle, and I'll pardon their debts."

"Thank you," he said, rubbing his shoulder. "Good to know that they'll be taken care of when I go back to prison."

I hadn't decided yet whether to arrest him. I should arrest him. His people attacked a member of the royal family. But I was to blame for this. I had hired him to pressure her, to threaten her; and he had befriended her in a moment, doing everything I had told him to.

How could I not see that it would spin out of control? It was too late to understand that control was an illusion. As much as I tried, I couldn't grab hold of anything … past, present, or future.

And Tai … I had dragged him into my poor attempt at power. He was trying to escape his past — same as me — yet I dragged him back into it. I dragged myself along with him.

"I know you didn't kill that man in the fire," I said.

Tai looked me over for a quick moment, shrugging again with labored breath. "I didn't save him either."

I pinched the bridge of my nose, dizziness returning. This attack was well deserved. I should bare the anxiety for screwing up so badly. I shut my eyes, trying to center myself.

"When you find Zhixin," I said, "bring him to me. Then forget everything I've told you to do."

He chuckled. "You finally calling this off?"

I nodded.

"About time," he replied. "I was wondering when you'd realize your own feelings."

I opened one eye to look at him. "What?"

"You hired me, yet you don't like me to be alone with her. Your anxiety has shifted from protecting yourself to protecting her. You didn't notice? Because I did."

My mind went blank. Tai cleared his throat.

"I'll find him," he said. "No fee required."

He bowed and left before I could say another word.

I looked deep into my glass, rolling the whiskey in it. I thought about Marina … the cuts and bruises on her arms, neck, and face.

I looked at my crooked pinky finger, the same thought pounding against my skull over and over:

I should have taken those bruises.

TABLOIDS

"Actually, I have something for you," Marina said, reaching down into her pocket.

I scratched the back of my neck. "For me?"

She pulled out a necklace, the silver pendant sparkling in the lamplight. When I didn't move, she took my hand in hers and laid it in my palm.

Taking a closer look, the pendant had the face of a lion on it.

"Where did you get this?" I asked.

"I made it."

My head shot up. She … *made* this for me? Why on earth would she do such a thing? I didn't deserve it. I owed her. Not the other way around.

"When did you have time to do this?" was the only thing I could say.

She gave me that bashful, beautiful smile of hers. "I've spent a lot of time in my room the last couple of days, remember?"

Yes. Thanks to me. Thanks to my lies, you've been trapped in your room, scared to death.

Oh, Marina … I don't deserve this.

But that sweet look in her eyes made it impossible to give it back. I hung it around my neck.

"It looks good on you," she said. "I'm glad."

I couldn't help but touch the pendant. It was cool. Soothing. And the lion on it gave me some strange feeling of courage that I couldn't describe. It was ridiculous. It was only a plain little necklace. It wasn't anything special.

But then again, it was incredibly special in every way.

"Why did you do this for me?" I asked. I could feel my voice starting to shake.

She shrugged, dropping her eyes to the side and moving her hair behind her ear. "You've always been nice to me. You let me stay in your home and took time to teach me everything you know. You even took poison for me. The least I can do is a silly necklace."

She didn't even realize what she was saying. If she only knew what this gesture actually meant to me.

I couldn't speak for a moment. I couldn't find any words. All I knew was that I wanted to show her how much it meant to me. I wanted to tell her how my feelings had grown for her in such a short time. But if I told her all that, I would have to tell her what I had done.

And I'd lose her forever.

I stood up from my chair and dropped to one knee, not positive if the next words out of my own mouth would be an apology or a proposal. She shifted in her chair.

"It's not silly," I said, looking into her eyes. "Not to me. I want you to know that I've been honored to have you as my guest, honored to have you as a friend, and if you decide to marry me … I'd be honored to have you as my wife."

I took her hand in mine and brought it to my lips. The taste was sweeter than I deserved.

Consider this my apology, Marina …

I couldn't say anything else. The weight in my chest had begun to suffocate me. I had to leave.

I got twenty feet down the hallway before I had to make a turn and hide myself from sight. Even in this darkness, I could still see the lion glistening.

I grabbed my knees, trying to breathe. Never once had a woman given me such a personal gift. My own mother wouldn't even acknowledge my birthday. Yet the woman I had asked Tai to get rid of had gone to the trouble of giving me a piece of her heart.

I slid down the wall, clutching my knees.

What have I done?

CYRUS'S ENDING

I lost her.

I deserved to.

Alone in the parlor, I dropped my head into my hands. I could still smell her skin on mine, playing our last dance over and over in my head.

That would be the last time I would ever hold her.

How did I get to this? I only wanted to protect us, and I ended up messing up everything. Maybe I was just as bad as Mother. Maybe I deserved to be alone. Maybe I really couldn't love someone right.

"Cyrus?"

At the sound of my name, I jerked my head up.

"Marina?"

I stood up, knocking over the chess set we played with every week together. As if I wasn't awkward enough around her.

"What are you doing here?" I asked, picking up the pieces and trying to collect my thoughts.

She shut the door and came to me. "Evann told me. About your mother."

Damn. I never wanted her to know about that. But after everything I'd done, it wasn't like I could get mad at Evann.

"I suppose the papers will expose it soon enough. It was only a matter of time." I sighed. "I wanted to protect my brothers. That's how I justified what I did. Looking back, I don't know why I thought you'd tear us apart like she did. The moment I saw you … I wanted to change my mind about everything."

She inched forward, like a cat with a stranger.

"You're nothing like her," I added. "But I am. Somewhere in my pursuit to be nothing like my mother, I succeeded in doing the opposite. I want nothing more than to beg your forgiveness, but I don't think I can do anything to deserve it."

"No one earns forgiveness, Cyrus."

"I don't expect it for free."

"When I'm ready to give it to you, it will be. I just need a little bit of time."

I nodded. "Of course."

"But …" she continued. "I would like for us to start over."

Start over …? Did she mean?

"I'm not saying that I want to marry you," she quickly added. "But … I don't want to leave you either."

God, she was beautiful. Inside and out. Even if she couldn't love me, I wanted to know her like this.

She stepped in even closer to me, close enough to reach out and touch her. I wanted to.

"Spend some time with me, King Cyrus," she said, eyes sparkling. "So you never doubt who I am ever again."

Despite my better judgment, I reached up and ran my fingers against the soft tips of her hair. "I'm in your debt until the day I die, Marina."

"And I'm okay with that."

She smiled.

After everything I had done, she was smiling at me.

All my emotions erupted against my chest and I couldn't help but break into laughter.

That smile of hers cured everything.

Then I realized … I was kissing her.

I sensed her surprise and pulled back, my stomach dropping to my feet.

"I apologize," I stuttered out. "I didn't mean — I shouldn't have — I keep making horrible decisions, don't I?"

My heart was going to explode from her lack of response.

"It's okay," she finally said. "I didn't hate it."

I snapped my head to her. Did she say what I think she did?

I couldn't help but drop my eyes to her lips. They felt good on mine. I wanted to feel them again. But I couldn't. I couldn't ask …

I started to pull away, but she grabbed my hand.

"You can do it again if you want," she said.

Now my heart had stopped completely. I swallowed. "I …"

"You don't want to?"

Panicked, I shook my head. Her smile dropped a little, and I realized my mistake.

"Of course I do," I said, finding my thoughts. "I always have."

She smiled. "Do you need to pencil it into your schedule?"

I brought my hand up to her face, the feeling of her skin melting the tension in my shoulders in an instant. "I don't need to schedule you in, Marina. Even when you're not with me, my time is devoted to you."

I leaned forward and kissed her again, bringing her in close to me. With slow, deep kisses I tried to tell her how I felt about her. I wanted to take my time with her … but I wanted to keep her.

I'd do anything to keep her.

I pulled away, smiling at the trust of her closed eyes. With a tight embrace, I gave her my deepest apology.

"I'll dedicate the rest of my life to making everything up to you," I said. "I promise. Believe me when I say that I care for you."

I could feel her smile next to me.

"I know," she said. "I can tell."

JULIAN

RUNNING

It seemed that I had Cyrus's disease. Now I was wandering the castle aimlessly, unable to sleep.

My legs ached from running around the grounds, looking for our wayward guest. If this was her idea of being a princess, then she would need more lessons than I had anticipated. It was hard enough keeping Tai in line, never mind trying to keep track of two rebels. I didn't have enough energy for that.

Why did she run off with him earlier today, anyway? Wouldn't the future princess of a country with her newfound power and status want to hang around those with a higher status than a court musician? A woman who found out she was royalty should want to revel in her newfound wealth and luxury, shouldn't she? This girl, however, seemed to be more interested in disappearing, causing trouble, and being as un-royal as humanly possible.

Maybe it was a ruse. Maybe it was sincere. Whatever it was, it was going to give Cyrus a heart attack.

Noticing that my feet were scuffing against the floor again, I picked them up while I looked around the main hall, half-looking for my older brother. He hadn't been sleeping well for at least a month, and we all knew why. It was the damn elephant in the room. Cyrus pretended that he wasn't bothered, paranoid, or apprehensive, but everyone knew how much guests unnerved him. Losing control in his own castle ... that's what he feared the most.

But Cyrus wasn't up. Everything was quiet and still, unlike the thoughts in my head that were making me pace.

Maybe some fresh air would take care of it.

I stepped outside, letting the summer breeze hit my skin and relax my muscles. The air here was damp this time of year, but I enjoyed it. I loved my home, despite the childhood experiences. I had replaced most of the negative memories with positive ones, doing my best not to suppress them into something that would cause a mental disorder as I grew older.

After all, mental disorders were genetic in my family. I couldn't be too careful.

Marina knew nothing of our past, I assumed. If she had, she probably wouldn't stop asking questions about it. That would be incredibly annoying if she agreed to marry Cyrus.

I grimaced at the thought. That woman. My sister-in-law.

Of course she would accept the proposal. Being the wife of a king was the dream of the average girl. I had seen the large amount of American romance books and movies based on that exact scenario. And wasn't it every woman's primal instinct to find security and stability? Who could offer more than a king?

Even as a prince, I couldn't offer as much.

I swatted a bug from my ear, looking up to realize how far I had walked. How long had I been thinking about this?

How annoying. She wasn't even here and yet she was taking up my time.

I turned to walk back to my room, momentarily hesitating at the sight of a creature barreling towards me.

Marina.

The look on her face was sheer panic. I could see it even in the dark. There was another shadow behind her, running after her.

What on earth?

She flew past me and I stepped forward behind her.

Then I was hit by the universe. I assumed that's what it was, because in a second I was on the ground, seeing stars.

Then I heard a grunting sound. I blindly reached out, grabbing the creature's leg. He kicked me, and then ran towards the gate.

"Wait!" I yelled. "Guards! Guards!"

By the time I had risen to my feet, two guards met me.

"What happened, Your Highness?"

I rubbed my aching ribs and arms. "Find whoever that was just now. He's headed towards the gate."

They left me to go find him. I pulled out my phone, limping my way back towards the door.

"Evann!" I yelled into the phone when he picked up. "Check on Marina. Now!"

I hung up before he could ask any questions. I looked up towards her window, wondering if I should check on her myself.

What would I say to her? She would only berate me for getting into her business. Forget it. I didn't need her ungratefulness.

I turned back to the gate, squinting to try to see into the distance. There was nothing but shadows.

Who was chasing her? And why?

BOOK BY ITS COVER

"You're dating the stylist?" Marina asked. "Does Cyrus know?"

I folded my arms. Tell my paranoid brother that I had feelings for a woman in the castle? Not likely. He'd lose his mind, and she'd lose her job.

"No, and you'd better keep it that way."

"Why wouldn't you tell Cyrus? You should be honest if you really cared about her."

I tried not to outwardly laugh. Affections were well and good, but the life of a royal wasn't that simple. She should have caught onto that by now.

"This is not up for discussion," I replied.

She stepped in front of me, her nose crinkled in anger. "Why don't you want to talk about her? Does she embarrass you?"

"Of course she doesn't embarrass me, but there are certain customs—"

"I get that there are customs. There are secrets and unanswered questions everywhere around here."

She wasn't wrong. We had a lot of those. It was simply safer for everyone that way.

"Would it kill anyone to be straightforward?" she continued. "Is honesty so freaking hard?"

Her eyes settled on me in a way I hadn't seen before. It was like Cyrus before he had an attack. A clouded, painful expression, full of questions that couldn't be answered.

"Is she really that bad?" she asked. "Is she really not good enough? Do you think she can't handle being a royal like the rest of you jerks?"

Wait. This …

"Marina …"

"Does she even have to be a royal? Can't she just be herself?"

"Shhh. That's enough."

"Why does she have to accept your standards to be acknowledged?" she asked, her eyes glossing over.

I closed the distance between us. She went silent, waiting for me to answer.

When Cyrus had shown me her picture and told me that Marina would become a princess overnight, I was positive that the power would go to her head. She would be like a viral Hollywood star who was famous enough to be arrogant about it, but not famous enough to handle it properly.

But as a scholar, I knew movies were poor representations of reality. Even my own assumptions were weak predictions.

I thought she would take advantage of us. Instead, she was terrified.

"We're not talking about *her* anymore, are we?" I asked.

Her head dropped down in defeat. I tried not to smile at the weight on her shoulders, the irony obvious only to myself. She was a bird who demanded to fly, yet for some reason, didn't realize she could.

I put my finger under her chin and made her look at me. She bit down on her lip, trying not to let her feelings escape from her eyes.

But I could already see everything.

"Listen," I said. "You should know—"

"Am I interrupting?"

I looked over to the library entrance.

Nikos?

Well, this was awkward.

I dropped my hands.

"Lesson's going well, then?" he asked, coming towards us.

There was an edge to his voice.

"It's fine," I replied. "Why are you here?"

"I live here," he snapped. "And I've come with some good news and even better news."

I braced myself. "What's the good news?"

"Cyrus is coherent," Nikos replied. "The poison is finally out of his system and he should fully recover soon."

Marina clapped.

"And the better news?" I asked.

He looked at Marina, his eyebrow twitching. "Your dresses have come in."

Marina looked as confused as I was. "Dresses?"

"For my party tomorrow night," he explained.

She crinkled her nose again. "Wait. I have to wear a dress? Like, a royal ball gown?"

"Of course, Your Highness," he replied, the title not holding any weight. "My date for the evening needs to look her part."

I hoped I hadn't heard that correctly.

"Say again?" she asked before I could.

"I forgot the best news of all," he said, throwing his arm over her shoulder. "You're my date."

Her mouth dropped open, but she didn't say anything. I tried to instead.

"Um, Cyrus might—"

"Ah, right, Cyrus," Nikos interrupted, turning to Marina. "You'd better go see him while he's still awake."

Marina looked between us, then nodded. I didn't say anything as she left. Nikos started to follow, but I pulled him back by the collar of his shirt.

"What are you doing?" I asked.

"What?"

"Drop the act. Why is Marina your date?"

He shrugged. "Cyrus won't be able to make it. She needs an escort."

I didn't like the glimmer in his eye. He was up to something.

"She belongs to Cyrus, Nikos. Remember that."

His eyes wandered around the room before coming back to meet mine again. "I could say the same to you."

With a sarcastic grin, he left the room.

What was he implying?

I grabbed the books from the table and started to put them away. The last of the books went on the shelf right next to *Dr. Jekyll and Mr. Hyde.*

I sighed.

The last few hours with her weren't terrible. I hadn't expected her to be so well-versed in literature. There was hope for her yet as a royal. She might be a decent partner for Cyrus, with a little bit of time.

… But why did Nikos's smirk bother me so much?

DRESS UP

"Anything?"

The guard bowed. "Nothing yet, Your Highness."

I nodded and signaled his dismissal. There had been no news on the person who'd chased Marina that night I stepped out in the gardens, and Evann hadn't confirmed any information either. Whoever this was, she was keeping tight-lipped about it.

Was it Tai? No, Tai and Marina were friends, even out in the open. She wouldn't have run from him with such fear in her eyes.

And Tai wouldn't do that to me. Not with everything I had done for him.

I tried to rest my brain for the evening. I couldn't get myself so wrapped up in this business on my brother's birthday. Nikos had enough attention, sure, but he had been worn out recently. I couldn't offer him any comfort in our current situation. I was part of the reason he was so depressed. I was part of the reason he had been so agitated these days. I didn't know how to fix the problem, but I was dreading the outcome.

A rivalry of hearts between brothers was bound to bring destruction sooner or later.

I knew why he distanced himself from me. But even with my best attempts to reach out, he still barely spoke to me, except for a few pranks every once in a while to let me know that he was still alive. He wasn't cruel, but he wasn't kind either.

Nikos had swarms of women following him and begging to be his future bride. I didn't have the luxury. It was difficult to have any woman drool over me in the way he was worshiped. He was young and popular. He would move on.

But tonight was his birthday, so I would put that aside and be a gracious brother.

Where was the idiot, anyway?

Juniper mentioned assisting Marina prepare for the festivities, and I was worried that she could have been injured by Marina's strange overreactions to anything royal.

Still, Marina had agreed to wear the dress I had chosen for her for our private function, and I had to admit she looked rather refined in it. If I thought she would have accepted my honest compliment with grace, I would have given it.

Then Cyrus was poisoned and it didn't seem proper to say anything at all.

"Your hands seem rather empty," a rosy voice bellowed next to my ear. "Here, my boy. Let me fill it with a drink."

A man with full rosy cheeks to match his voice smiled as he handed me sweet champagne. I took it, raising my glass to him.

"Duke Richardson," I said. "Quite an honor to see you again."

"It's boring without me around, isn't it?"

I smiled. "Of course. Tell me, have your travels gone well?"

He stroked his salt-and-pepper beard before taking another drink. "I've seen most of the world now. I have to admit, it gets boring after a time."

"The world too small?"

He chuckled. "The world I live in, yes. I'm looking for something that challenges my expectations."

I cheered with him. "I can drink to that."

"Announcing the guest of honor!" the front guard called. "His royal highness, Prince Nikos, and his guest, Miss Marina."

I spit my champagne out.

The woman standing next to Nikos ... that couldn't be ...

But it was. Her blue gown cascaded against her body like a waterfall, her hair up with flowers and small curls around her neck.

How did the awkward beast of the castle turn into the swan of the lake?

"Who is the charming young woman with Nikos?" the duke asked me.

I dabbed my mouth with my handkerchief. "That's our guest for the summer."

"Dignitary?"

"Troublemaker."

He chuckled. "Fond of her, then, are you?"

I laughed with real amusement. "Did you catch some sort of disease while abroad? The girl is nothing but a pain. Unpredictable, unaccountable, irresponsible ..."

He patted me on the shoulder. "And yet you haven't taken your eyes off her since she arrived."

I turned to look at him, realizing I had been talking to him the entire time without facing him.

He patted my shoulder again, raising his glass. "Don't be so bashful about it, Prince Julian. Many of us have fallen for women who we thought were the wrong type but ended up being the right type for us."

He winked as he drank down the rest of his champagne.

I looked over my shoulder for one last glance at her. When her eyes met mine, I felt my chest tighten.

No. I had no feelings for her.

After all, the right woman for me could never be my brother's betrothed.

UNSETTLED

I rushed to the gardens, heart pounding. Half of me was thrilled to see Juniper again. The other half was wallowing in guilt.

It had been almost a week since the festival. After Tai's call, Juniper and I had come straight home, only for me to be pulled into an impromptu meeting by Nikos. There was no chance to speak with her after that.

And if I was honest, I hadn't been thinking of her as much as I should have, either.

All I could think about for the last few days were the bruises and scars on Marina's face and neck. She assured me constantly that she was fine, but the thought of someone physically hurting her made it impossible to sleep.

Why? Why did I even care? I didn't want to think about her like this. She wasn't mine to think about. She was Cyrus's fiancée. Not that she knew about it yet, but why would she turn him down when she found out? He was king. I had no future throne.

What was I saying? I was in love with Juniper. I couldn't possibly …

No. I didn't. I couldn't.

Whatever these ridiculous emotions were, seeing Juniper's face would clear up everything. I'd hold her in my arms and forget Marina. I would laugh at myself for even acting this way.

When Juniper came around the vineyards into view, I threw my arms around her and pulled her close.

"You don't know how badly I've needed to see you," I told her before a proper greeting. "But you shouldn't have asked to meet like this. The castle isn't safe …"

Her arms wrapped around me as they often did. But something was off. Her embrace didn't feel as warm as it usually had.

I pulled away. "Is something wrong?"

She pouted. "Julian, is it true?"

My heart jumped into my throat.

"No, of course not," I said. "Whatever you've heard, there's nothing going on between us."

Her face scrunched. "What? What are you talking about?"

"Wait … what are *you* talking about?"

"That if you announce our relationship, you have to give up your title."

Oh. That.

I breathed out, relieved. "Ah, my title. Yes. Anyone who wants to marry a non-royal has to give up their status."

"Why didn't you tell me this?"

"Why did I have to?" My heart sank. "You weren't with me because of—"

She quickly grabbed my face in her hands, shaking her head. "I don't care about your status, Julian. That was never part of this. I adore you whether you're a prince or a pauper. But ..." She frowned. "I've realized something."

I swallowed my heartbeat as best I could.

"King Cyrus and Prince Nikos both depend on you," she continued. "They need you. I never thought that our relationship would take you from them, but if it does, I don't know if I can go through with it."

My mouth went dry. "What are you trying to say? You know that I care for you very deeply—"

"Yes, my darling, I know." She smiled, cupping my cheek. "And I adore you. I also know how much your family means to you. I know how much your people mean to you. I can't ask you to give that up."

"I want to be with you."

"Do you want to marry me?"

My jaw clamped shut. I loved Juniper. I loved everything about her. I spent every day imagining living out the rest of my life with her. Well, perhaps not recently, but usually. And now, for some reason, I couldn't bring myself to say any of those things.

"Don't look so guilty," she said, with a sad laugh. "I don't know if I want to marry you either. We've only been together for a short time, and it's a huge decision. And if that decision leads to you leaving the people you love most, I don't think I can do it."

I shook my head. "Please don't say things like that. I care about you."

"I care about you too. Which is why I can't let you do something I know you'll regret. Leaving your brothers behind would put a hole in you even I couldn't fill."

There was a long pause. I couldn't think of anything else to say to her. In the silence, she leaned in and pressed her lips against mine. I could tell by the light touch of her hand on my face that it would be for the last time.

She pulled away, giving that smile of hers. "It's for the best, Julian. We both know it is."

And with that, she walked away.

And I ... I didn't go after her.

IN-LAWS

"You and I are engaged," Cyrus said. "We have an arranged marriage."

I leaned against the wall outside of the kitchen, hanging on Cyrus and Marina's every word.

This wasn't my business. I shouldn't have been standing there. I shouldn't have been listening to their conversation, clasping my shirt like their marriage affected me.

But it did.

I didn't think I could handle any more guilt. Juniper had not known of my feelings for Marina, but I did. They were clear to me now. How long had I been feeling this way about her? Since the beginning? Since we danced together? When did I start obsessing over her?

Juniper was a beautiful woman. Kind, intelligent, funny. Even without telling her, she knew how much I was struggling with the idea of leaving my family and our people. The guilt of thinking of someone else while being with her made me feel like slime. Grade A slime. And worse ... my feelings were for my brother's fiancée.

I was the biggest jackass in the history of the universe.

"It seems pretty solid to me!" Marina said, panicked. "My parents shipped me off to some castle to become a princess I didn't want to become and marry someone I didn't even know!"

His hands were on her shoulders, trying to soothe her. "I know it's a shock for you — it was to me too at first — but I won't make you marry me."

My heart skipped a beat. I leaned over to look at them. His hands held hers with affection ... more than I had seen from him in years.

"I mean you don't have to marry me," he continued. "It's still common for royals to have arranged marriages, but I won't force you to marry me. No one can force you. But that's the reason you were sent here. I'm sorry for not telling you sooner. I didn't know how to."

"Does everyone know?"

He nodded.

I sighed. There was nothing Marina hated more than secrets.

"You don't really want to marry me … do you?" she asked.

He smiled weakly. "At first, I was against the idea. I didn't know you. I always admired your parents, but I couldn't imagine being married to a stranger. Now? It would feel empty here without you. That's not a reason to get married, but it's the way I feel. Having you here turned out to be better than I anticipated."

I swallowed, realizing that I felt the exact same way he did.

I pulled back from looking at them and shook my head. Cyrus cared for Marina. I could see that. Maybe he wasn't in love, but she was the first woman he had let himself relax around. He seemed more at peace. I couldn't take that from him. I couldn't let my brother give that up.

I stepped away from the conversation, unable to keep my feelings from rushing through my body. There were two things I knew were true, and neither of them had a solution.

I couldn't have her. And I couldn't give her up.

Julian's Ending

I couldn't stay in the ballroom any longer. Seeing her dance with Cyrus made my chest ache. Soon she would be in his arms in a white gown …

I couldn't stomach it.

I circled the empty halls. What now? Was I just going to live the rest of my life with Marina as my sister? Could I hold myself back for a lifetime?

Maybe in time I would get over her.

I walked back towards the ballroom, leaning in to watch everyone on the floor.

Marina was now dancing with her father, smiling and laughing.

I smiled. At least she was finally happy here.

"Have your eyes on anyone in particular?"

I turned to see Cyrus's usual smile. I cleared my throat.

"Just watching," I replied, shaking my head.

There was a pause.

"I saw the look on your face," he said.

"What look?"

"That scowl when I was dancing with Marina. I haven't seen that scowl since the Lolita Fisher incident."

"God, Cyrus, I was six years old when that happened," I grumbled. "Can we forget about that, please?"

"But it's the same scowl! The very same one. The frown of a younger brother who likes—"

"My tastes have changed."

"Yes. Yes, they have."

He smiled at me. "You care for her," he said.

I coughed. "Of course. She's going to be my sister-in-law, right?"

"I don't buy that. You didn't care about any of that in the beginning."

I swallowed.

"You have feelings for her, Julian."

I shook my head. "No. No, she belongs to you."

"She belongs to whomever she wants to belong to. And from what I've seen … I think she's warmed up to you too."

I dropped my head. "I won't take her from you. I can't ask you to sacrifice anything else for us."

"I'm not sacrificing anything," he said, laughing. It was a real laugh. Not one of the polite ones he usually gave people. "I've found peace. I want you to now find happiness. And I want this happiness for you. Both of you."

He patted me on the shoulder and left. I leaned into the doorway, watching her dance with her father. Her smile was so addictive.

A pang of guilt hit my chest.

I couldn't keep staring at her like this. I turned and left before I lost myself.

Going to the library was a mistake. As soon as I walked in, all my memories of Marina came flooding back. The way she talked about books with me. The way she laughed at my jokes once she stopped hating me. Even the way she hated me. I had become so attached to these memories.

I grabbed a book off the shelf and sat down in front of the fireplace, hoping it would clear my head.

I didn't expect her to come to me.

When the door creaked open, I didn't look up. I knew it was her. I didn't want it to be. Part of me hoped halfway through the door she would morph into someone else.

Because if she didn't, I wouldn't be able to control myself.

"Leaving early?" I asked.

"I could ask you the same," she replied.

"I'm not the guest of honor."

"Since when have you considered me a guest of honor?"

She sat on the sofa next to me, her scent throwing all my focus out the window. I couldn't stop myself from turning to look at her, the bruises and scratches up and down her neck reminding me of how many times I had almost lost her.

"I'm alright, Julian," she said, reading my thoughts.

She wasn't supposed to be able to do that.

"I know," I replied. "But you almost weren't."

"Does that bother you?"

"Of course it does," I said, a little too firmly. I cleared my throat. "You're going to be part of our family. I should care, right?"

Her chin brushed against my shoulder. "Is that the only reason?"

The drop of her voice to a whisper made me shiver.

"Do I need another?" I asked.

I swallowed. Why was she teasing me? Didn't she know how difficult she was making everything already?

"I suppose not." She stood from the sofa and threw her hands up like a Hollywood actress. "Do you think you can handle me as your sister for a lifetime?"

I slammed the book shut.

"You're really going through with the engagement then? After all the trouble you caused about it?"

Her hands and face both dropped. "What's with the attitude all of a sudden? It's not like you'll be here to see it."

"… Am I going somewhere?"

"Aren't you going to the love of your life?"

"The love of my … you mean …?"

"Yeah, her."

I put down the book and took off my glasses. "I have no intention of going after Juniper. She's a lovely woman, but our lives were not meant to mix."

"Why? Because she wasn't bred like you?"

"I have no interest in breeds. Only in things that are sustainable."

It was true. Juniper had been right about everything. I couldn't leave my family. I couldn't leave behind my people. It wasn't in me.

And somewhere … I knew I couldn't leave Marina either.

"Why aren't you going after her?" she asked, her eyes wide with concern. "Don't you want to be with her?"

I rested my chin on my hand. This conversation felt familiar.

"Don't you love her?" she continued. "If she loves you, she's waiting for you. She's waiting to hear that you care about her. She's waiting for you to go after her." Her voice dropped again. "She wants you to come after her."

I stood, seeing her fight against her own words. Maybe we had more in common than I thought.

"You should tell her how you feel," she said, now whispering. "Or she'll always wonder."

I tried not to smile, but it was hard to suppress it. "We're not talking about her anymore, are we?"

She stepped back and dropped her eyes from mine, showing me everything I needed to know. She cared for me as much as I for her. And now, I didn't have to hold back.

"Should I tell her my feelings then? Despite the obvious consequences?"

She shuddered under my touch as I held her chin to look at me. "Well …"

"If I kiss her, will that tell her my feelings?"

She opened her mouth, but there was silence. Then, she nodded, giving me permission.

"Then … I should apologize in advance."

"For wh—"

I kissed her. The kiss I had been holding back since the beginning. If this was my one chance to show my feelings, I was going to take it. I put all my passion in it, intertwining her fingers in mine and bringing her closer to me. She kissed me back, following my lead.

Pulling away, seeing the dazed look in her eyes, I knew.

She was mine. After everything, she was mine. And I wasn't giving her up to anyone.

NIKOS

Welcome, Your Highness

I wrapped another layer of duct tape around the horn. This would scare the hell out of her.

It was only appropriate that the daughter of a king be greeted by a welcoming trumpet. Except, we didn't have trumpets. Just air horns. That nicely fit behind her door. When she opened the door, it would sound off and she would scream. Her heart would pound. She would be frightened and upset. She would find out I did it, and probably yell at me. She would not feel welcomed.

And that's how I would start my relationship with my future sister-in-law.

The first impression was the best impression, yes?

Was my brother really going to marry a complete stranger? Why did kings have arranged marriages anyway? They didn't derive any pleasure from it. Neither did their wives. It was a lifetime of misery and pain for both sides.

They could have refused. That's all they had to do.

I could make them if I tried.

I put my hands in my pockets, looking over my handiwork. It was good. The perfect amount of tape, the perfect location.

I opened the door to test it.

BWAAAAAAAAAAAAAAAAA

Yep. Perfect. Of course it was. I'd done it.

I left her room and whistled as I walked down the castle stairs.

"What trouble are you making now?" a voice said below.

Julian raised an assuming eyebrow at me. I wasn't sure why he was even hanging around this part of the castle anyway. Didn't he have a thousand books to read, and counsel to give to the masses? He couldn't leave me alone for twenty minutes without giving me a lecture. It wasn't like I could do anything with his useless information. I didn't have a throne.

"Who says I'm making trouble?" I asked. "Can't I walk around in my own home?"

"You can, but you can't do it with a bouncy step and a whistle and expect me not to ask questions."

I came to the bottom of the stairs, putting on my best showcase smile. "Mind to your own."

I stepped away, hoping to get something from the kitchen before the cooks scolded me for snacking before dinner.

"She's coming tomorrow," he said.

I stopped. The slight serious inflection at the end of his words told me that he was worried more than he was showing.

I turned around and shrugged. "I know. So?"

"Have you seen her picture?"

He pulled out his phone and scrolled through his photos, stopping at one of three people in front of the Leaning Tower of Pisa. Tylier and Leona were there, and between them was a lanky girl with black hair cut off haphazardly at the shoulders, a rock band t-shirt, and a pair of naturally muddy and ripped jeans.

She … looked nothing like a princess.

"Cyrus sent me this," Julian explained. "It looks like we'll have a lot of training to do."

"*You* have a lot of training to do," I corrected. "I'm staying out of this."

He shut off his phone and shoved it back in his pocket. "She's our responsibility. Don't leave her to only Cyrus."

I tapped my fingers against my thigh. Why bother trying to train her at all? Cyrus was an obsessive-compulsive basket case and Julian was an arrogant know-it-all. I was sure she was going to hate us anyway.

"Do you really think she'll be that much to handle?" I asked. "She'll be distracted by shiny earrings and silk dresses. She'll probably be so thrilled that she has her own personal staff that she won't even bother taking us seriously at all."

"Yes, I agree."

"Well, I didn't ask for your opini— Wait. What?"

Julian sighed. "She probably won't take any of us seriously. Cyrus, included. I don't know if this … *arrangement* is best suited for him."

At least it was something we could agree on. Not that I would ever tell him that.

"Then what do you want to do?" I asked.

"Nothing," he replied. "If Cyrus was to ever suspect foul play, he'd lecture us to death."

Funny that Julian should be complaining about lectures.

"We should just keep an eye on her for now," he continued. "If we can find anything that points towards unstable behavior, or any type of narcissism ..."

"Leave it to me," I said. "I have enough charm to make any girl reveal *everything*."

He squinted, disgusted. "Do you now?"

I shrugged.

"Don't do anything stupid," he cautioned.

"I won't make any promises."

"I'm not sure if I'm more afraid of the things you do or the things you don't do."

I leaned in and smiled. "Be afraid of both."

I turned away from him, walking towards the kitchen.

In all honesty, it would be better for her to return to her world in the end. Joining ours would only crush her.

HOT N COLD

Just because Marina was wearing a ball gown didn't mean she was a princess. Regardless of how the color suited her skin, or how her hair was curled to complement the deep cut of the neckline, she was still a stubborn little nobody. Even if she pulled her lopsided shoulders back and looked at me with those fearless eyes of hers, I couldn't accept her as the future queen.

My brother would never marry her. I couldn't let that happen.

I introduced Marina to anyone of importance, ending the long training with a stop at the refreshment table. I handed her a plate of strawberry cheesecake. Her face lit up as she eagerly took a piece. When she smiled, the lanterns highlighted the glow of her face and shoulders.

I had to admit … with that dress and that glow … she looked like a royal.

"What's with the look?" she asked.

"What look?"

"Why are you staring at me?"

Was I? I reached for the bowl of strawberries on the table. "I like that dress on you."

It didn't hurt to throw her a bone occasionally. I wasn't lying or anything, for once.

She looked around. "Me?"

"Yes, you. Whom did you think I meant?"

"Sorry. You must warn me before giving me compliments out of the public eye. They throw me off. I never know if they're sincere or not."

"What does it matter if they are?" I replied. "Your job isn't to sift through real and fake compliments. That would take too long, and there'd be no benefit to it."

"You've had too much practice at this."

"I've been around enough fake people to know what I'm talking about."

Half of them were here at the party, actually.

"So, let's be honest then," she said, taking another bite of cheesecake. "First, this cheesecake is spectacular and makes me hate life less. Second, why did you choose me as your date?"

I took another strawberry. "Because Cyrus couldn't make it. He was supposed to be your escort. That left Julian or me. I thought you hated Julian, so I was the obvious choice … but after seeing you two in the library yesterday …"

"Don't let your imagination go anywhere, Nikos."

So, she wasn't interested then? "Good to hear there's nothing there. Especially since—"

I stopped. Damn. I almost told her about her own engagement. Was I crazy?

Keep your mouth shut.

"Especially since what?" she asked.

"Nothing," I muttered.

"What were you going to say?"

"How's the cheesecake?" Julian said, cutting into the conversation.

Marina jumped, spinning around and stuttering in his presence. I chewed the rest of the strawberry as it soured in my mouth.

"Now that you've addressed the formalities," Julian said, "would you like to dance?"

She hesitated. "Right now?"

"It's not exactly something I would schedule for later."

"There are a ton of people here," she replied. She looked over her shoulder, her eyes meeting with mine. "Also—"

"I've put a lot of work into you the past couple of weeks," he replied. "I won't take no for an answer."

He held his hand out for her. I narrowed my eyes as she placed her hand in his.

Of course. No matter where I was, Julian was right there to remind me that he could take anything I had.

He drew her into his arms to dance like he owned her. Hadn't he already taken Juniper from me? Did he have to show off how much power he had?

I wasn't as powerless as he thought. I could take whatever I wanted, too.

As if she could read my thoughts, Juniper walked across from the other side of the dance floor, her eyes glued on the two of them. She didn't see me at all.

But she was going to.

I let them dance once, but when they finished, I stepped out onto the dance floor to meet Marina. I stepped close. Her hands came up to stop me.

"Forget her, Nikos. She's not worth it."

I looked at her, taking her by the hand and waist into a dance position. "Should I have let Julian be your escort after all? He seems to be everybody's favorite these days."

"Don't take it that way," she said. "Stop comparing—"

"Just shut up and dance with me."

I pulled her closer.

"What are you doing?" she protested. "You're hurting me."

I backed off. "Sorry."

"You don't sound sorry."

"I'm not, really."

"You flip between being sickeningly sweet to me and being a complete terror. Are you schizophrenic? Do you have multiple personality disorder?"

"Multiple personality … what kind of TV shows do you watch? Honestly."

She muttered something else, but Juniper turned her head toward me, and everything around me went mute.

Game on.

I leaned in to whisper in Marina's ear.

"Just stay like this for a moment," I said.

Let them watch. Putting on a show was my specialty. I smiled at Marina as she frowned back.

"That smile …" she said. "It's fake."

I laughed. "You can tell now, can you? You're getting better."

After a pause between us, the air shifted.

"You wanted to make her jealous, didn't you?" she asked. "You asked me to be your date to make her jealous."

I tried not to act surprised. No one could see through my acts. Why could she?

"I'm a joke to you, aren't I?" she continued. "Someone you play pranks on, and mess with when it's convenient for you."

Juniper feels something for me. She has to.

I couldn't say that. The way Marina was looking at me now, I couldn't say that.

She pushed away from me. "Let me go, Nikos. Let me go now."

"Wait—"

Suddenly, pain burst through my groin and I hit the ground. The pain kept growing, aching, and making it hard to say anything.

"Don't come near me again," she said above me.

I could only watch her feet as she walked away.

UNSETTLED

"Calm down, Nikos."

Cyrus frowned at me from his armchair, as Julian frowned to himself on the sofa.

"Calm? You want me to be calm? You knew Marina was in trouble this whole time and you didn't tell us because you thought *we* were the issue?"

"And how should I have done differently?" Cyrus replied, calm as always. "Julian, you've been treating her like our enemy since she arrived. And you," he said, pointing at me, "you've been causing trouble all over the place. Under these circumstances, am I really supposed to trust you?"

Julian's eyes dropped to his hands. I narrowed mine.

"I'll arrange for more security immediately," Cyrus continued. "Where is she now?"

"In her room with Evann and Tai," I said.

Julian raised an eyebrow. "Didn't Tai cause all this trouble in the first place?" he grumbled. "Why would you leave her with him?"

"You expect me to take care of her?" I replied.

Cyrus stood from his chair. "Yes, I do. There's a chance she'll be part of this family, Nikos."

I hated that calm stare of his. I looked away, scoffing.

"So you're really going to marry her?" I asked. "You don't know her."

"I'm getting to know her. You should do the same. Both of you. I don't want to hear of any more issues with either one of you. Understand?"

Julian and I looked at each other. We both nodded at Cyrus.

"Good," Cyrus replied. "I'm going to go check on the situation. You two get yourselves together."

He left the room. I turned to Julian.

"Do you really think he'll marry her?" I asked.

He shrugged one shoulder, shaking his head. "I don't know. He's never acted like this before. He's always been very adamant that a woman never set foot in the castle. Now ... I think he's actually starting to change his mind about those sorts of things."

My mind went blank.

Julian stood up from the sofa and walked over towards the door. He patted my shoulder on his way out.

"Maybe it's time to be more hospitable," he said.

"You expect me to accept this?"

"What else are you going to do about it?" he asked, turning around. "Start a protest? Start a war? Threaten to hold your breath until you pass out?"

"I can't accept that my brother will marry someone we don't even know!"

Julian clasped his hands against my face. "And you can't dictate which relationships matter and which ones don't!"

The room went quiet. I could only hear my heart pounding in my head. He stared at me. His forehead shifted.

"Nikos … I didn't mean—"

Grunting, I shook him loose and left the room. Julian called for me, but I didn't turn back. I went straight to my room, slamming the door.

"I'm getting to know her … There's a chance she'll be part of this family …"

She would be my sister-in-law? My sister?
I suddenly felt nauseous.
I didn't know if I could allow that.

THE ATTACK

"I want about half a dozen guards in this wing and half a dozen in the north wing."

I pointed to the blueprint. The head of the guards sucked his bottom lip.

"I'm not sure we have the resources for extra reinforcements," he replied. "I'll have to speak with the king about it."

I gritted my teeth. "My command doesn't count?"

He bowed. "That's not what I meant, Your Highness, but there are certain things that require clearance. Even Prince Julian doesn't have the authority to bring in reinforcements. Only the king can do so."

I rolled up the blueprint. "Then I will just have to go convince him myself."

The guard bowed again as I left the courtyard and went back inside the castle.

Cyrus had reorganized some of the guards, but it wasn't enough. Not to me, anyway. I couldn't even talk to Cyrus about it, since he was holed up in meetings. I was stuck wandering around the castle, being as useless as I always was.

No power. No authority. Just a title and an empty reputation. I couldn't protect anyone, or command anything, or be of any real use.

I stopped and leaned against the wall, sighing. There was nothing I could do to truly protect her, except for maybe following her around. But then she would get irritated, and possibly hit me …

Come to think of it, I probably needed the protection more than she did.

"Are you alright, Prince Nikos?"

I looked up to see a pair of clear eyes I didn't think I'd see.

"Juniper? What are you doing here?"

Then I noticed the luggage in her hand. Something in the corner of her lips told me that it wasn't a simple workshop flight.

"You're leaving?" I asked.

She nodded.

"Why?"

She fumbled with her luggage and her words at the same time. "I appreciate this opportunity, but I think it was more responsibility than I anticipated."

"Should I lessen the workload? I can ask—"

"No, it's okay. Julian offered the same, and Cyrus did as well. I think this is what's best."

I held her gaze. If she had come to me a couple of weeks ago, I would have told her my feelings and asked her to come to me. I would have insisted until she couldn't tell me no. And now as she stood in front of me with that broken look on her face, I knew we couldn't ignore the obvious anymore.

"You love him, don't you?" I asked.

She raised her eyes to mine, breaking eye contact as soon as she made it. "Who?"

"Don't worry," I said. "I know you do. I've seen the way you act around him. Even though I tried—"

I stopped myself. There was no point in confessing anything at this point.

"You've always been so kind to me, Prince Nikos," she said. "That kindness has been invaluable to me. I mean that."

She gave me a weak smile. I gave her an empty one in return.

"I know," I replied. "You've never lied to me. I don't expect you to start now."

There was silence.

"I think you have your heart set on someone too, don't you?" she asked.

I straightened. "What do you mean?"

"You seem focused on … other things these days." Her eyes filled with a little bit of light. "On a lovely foreign girl, perhaps …?"

I rolled my eyes. "I don't care about her."

Juniper analyzed my face. I turned away.

"If that's what you want to believe then," she said softly. She touched my shoulder. "I do hope you find great happiness. And I hope you hold tight to it once you do."

Her hand dropped. I nodded.

I didn't look up as her footsteps became a whisper. I felt my heart sink in my chest.

I always knew that I had only a slim chance of winning her. I knew she had feelings for Julian all this time. Before, it had tortured me. I wanted a connection like he had with her. I wanted a connection with someone. Someone that gave me a purpose.

Juniper was that ideal … but it wasn't meant to be.

And neither was Marina.

Both of my brothers had their own purpose and their own love to share it with. Someone to be their real selves around. I should have been happy for them, but I wasn't. I was even less happy with myself for choosing two women I couldn't have.

I had to say goodbye to both.

CASUALTIES

The wine cellar was the last place I liked going, but it seemed like a good idea tonight.

I didn't even know what I had been drinking, really. Alcohol was all the same anyway —it was all just a way to drown yourself from the inside out.

And I needed to drown everything out tonight.

"You shouldn't be here, Nikos."

I laughed, throwing my head back over the chair and looking at the ceiling. "Yes, yes, I know. I'm not allowed to be anywhere, or to do anything, or to be anybody. Thanks for the reminder."

I could feel Julian staring at me. "You've been drinking."

I looked up from the table and shook my finger at him. "According to the law, I'm allowed to do so. Don't try to treat me like a child."

"Alright then, I won't. But I think I should tell you that you're about to drink out of a vase."

I looked at my hand. There was a porcelain vase in it. Figures.

I threw it across the table as Julian sat next to me.

"You've been acting strange since the polo match," he said. "I've never seen you this torn up about something. Are you still worried about Marina?"

I scoffed. "Why would I be worried about her? She doesn't mean anything to me. I don't mean anything to her, either. I don't mean anything to anybody. That's the way my life is."

He tapped his finger on the table. "Do you want to mean something to her?"

He raised an enquiring eyebrow at me.

"You're asking stupid questions," I growled.

"I never ask stupid questions," he countered.

"Everything is the way it's supposed to be. I can't disrupt those things. Even if I wanted to, I can't do anything."

His eyes bored into mine. "Do you want to do something?"

"Why are you asking me these questions? Why do you keep bothering me about it?"

"Because you're bothered about it. And that bothers me."

His hand came to my shoulder, but I didn't look at him.

"What's with you these days?" he asked. "You're not yourself at all."

I reached for my drink. "What good is it, being myself? I don't have any purpose."

He grabbed the drink from my hand and put it down out of my reach. "Purpose is found in the little things you do daily. It's not some ultimate realization of a grand universal responsibility. Life isn't a superhero movie."

He put my face between his hands and turned me to face him.

"You're my brother," he said. "If you were paralyzed from the neck down and couldn't say your own name, I'd love you as my own flesh and blood. That doesn't change, whether you think you have a purpose or not. Love isn't rooted in purpose. Love is simply rooted in itself."

I shifted in my chair. He let go of my face.

There was silence.

"So, what do you do when love is worthless ...?" I asked.

"Love isn't worthless," he replied, "but sometimes it has bad taste."

He smirked at me. I hated how he knew everything I was thinking. He grabbed my glass, putting it back in front of me.

"I won't treat you like a child," he said, shifting in his seat to stand up. "But I will leave you with this idea in case you haven't thought of it: love isn't worthless, but sometimes it's too late." His eyes wandered around the table for a moment and then landed back on mine. "And sometimes it's too late because we pretend it's not there at all."

He patted me on the shoulder, standing up. As his footsteps went back up the stairs, I grabbed my drink to shoot it down. As the rim touched my lips, it suddenly tasted unbearably bitter. I put it down, staring at the liquor as it swirled in the glass.

It's not like I was pretending. I knew exactly where my feelings were, of how my daydreams were changing. I knew they were breaking away from one hope and attaching to another. I knew who it was I dreamed of holding, of kissing, of spending my time with …

… and it wasn't Juniper.

There was no denying it. There was no pretending.

But there was no future in it, either. There couldn't be. Not with who I was, and not with who I couldn't be.

It was too late.

NIKOS'S ENDING

I rested my elbows on the balcony rail, looking up at the stars. Even if there was a shooting star right now, my wish wouldn't matter.

I had lost.

I never wanted to be a king. I watched my father and Cyrus rule as kings, constantly tormented by publicity, policy, and safety. Father hid his misery better than Cyrus, but as we grew older, Cyrus learned how to fake a peaceful demeanor as well. I knew he was suffering. I knew he didn't sleep. I knew he would have chosen a different path if he could have.

Juniper … she was my slice of different.

The moment I saw her, I knew I could spend the rest of my life with a woman like that. Someone real. Someone who didn't have the curse of playing in front of a camera, but who could understand those of us who did.

I wanted her to be the one to understand me. To see past the charade.

But she only saw Julian.

The more and more I realized this, the more and more I realized that there was one person who saw me for who I was this entire time.

I looked over my shoulder, watching Marina dance with Cyrus. She had come in so easily, breaking down the walls of our traditions as if she was built for it all along. She had no fake appearances — she cried when she wished, she rebelled when it suited her, and she only laughed when she meant it.

"You just might be stuck with me as your sister-in-law for a lifetime."

I spent so many days and nights wondering why those words bothered me. Why I hated the idea of her becoming my sister-in-law. Why I was ripped apart when she was kidnapped.

Seeing her dance with Cyrus … feeling the weight in my chest … I knew why.

But I couldn't say anything now.

I had lost.

The stars were beautiful, anyway. A small reminder that the world was bigger than my intense feelings that couldn't find a home for themselves.

"Planning another prank?" a voice asked next to me.

That voice …

I tried to hide my emotions with a smirk as I turned to Marina. "I could be."

"Who's the target?"

"Wouldn't you like to know?"

"I would. It seems like I'm your favorite to torture."

"That's because you are my favorite." I couldn't believe I had said anything so lame.

"Am I?" she asked. "Am I your favorite, Nikos?"

Her small voice made me turn my head again. She stared into me. Hard. I couldn't catch my breath for a moment as she waited for an answer. But how could I say anything? I didn't have the option. I had already made a fool of myself with Juniper. I couldn't risk it again.

I looked away, trying not to spill my soul to her. She wanted to know if she was my favorite? Did she want to know my feelings about her? How could I say them now?

I bit hard on my lip, looking back up at the sky. But I couldn't speak.

I looked at her one last time, deciding to leave before I lost control. As I took one step from her, her face fell, her eyes dropping towards the floor. It was like seeing her heart drop.

The farther I walked away, the more I couldn't stand the idea of it.

Maybe … just maybe …

I turned back, but she wasn't looking at me. Her shoulders were slumped, her back facing me as she looked up at the stars.

It was my last chance. What did I have to lose anyway?

I stepped back towards her, putting my hands on her shoulders and gliding them down her soft arms. I leaned in, embracing her.

"Nik—" she started.

But I leaned closer, kissing the nape of her neck. I reached for her fingers, capturing them in my own. She responded, holding my hand in return. I couldn't help but lean my face against her hair, smelling the sweet coconut scent.

I wasn't going to hold back this time.

"Be mine," I whispered in her ear.

She didn't speak.

"I don't care if you were meant for Cyrus," I continued. "I can't watch you with anyone else, and I won't allow you to be my sister. Not with the way I feel about you."

She pulled away from me. "The way you feel …?"

I could feel my heart pound in my head. "I like you more than I care to admit, Princess."

Her eyes glittered in front of me like the stars.

"Me?" she asked. "Why?"

The wind caught a strand of her dark hair and I reached up to put it back behind her ear. "You cry so damn much."

She wrinkled her nose. "I'm sorry, you lost me."

"I'm surrounded daily by people with fake emotions. But you … it's impossible for you to be fake." I stepped in closer. "I know I messed up a lot, but I'm going to make it up to you. I promise you that."

"What about Cyrus?" she asked.

"I won't let him have you," I replied. "I won't accept that you belong to him."

To my surprise, she laughed. "Such a greedy child."

That line again? If she didn't take me seriously even now, then so help me …

I wrapped an arm around her waist, running the other through her hair. She stared at me, dazed.

"How many times do I have to tell you?" I whispered, leaning into her ear. "I'm not a child."

I pressed my lips against hers. She stepped back, but I brought her back into my arms. I couldn't lose her now. I kissed her lips gently, wanting to show her my true affection. The taste of her made my chest burn. I pulled back and sucked in my breath, hoping the ache would subside.

It didn't.

I would have to kiss her more.

I returned my lips back to hers, kissing her harder than before. This time, she didn't step away. She relaxed in my arms, kissing me as much as I was kissing her.

After a moment, I pulled back.

"Are you going to call me a child again?" I asked.

She stared at me, not answering.

"Well?" I asked again.

She didn't answer again.

When I leaned in for another kiss, she said, "I got the message."

I couldn't hold back a smile. "Good."

I waited for something to break the spell. For her to push me away. For her to tell me I was crazy. But she didn't say any of those things. When I pulled back to look into her eyes, I couldn't find a trace of irony. She was staring at me the way I had always hoped a woman would. How long had she been looking at me with those eyes?

I held her close, leaning back in to smell her hair. Everything about her smelled so good. Her hair, her skin, her breath. I wanted to absorb all of it. I wanted all of her to be mine. I wanted to protect her. I wanted to stay beside her. I wanted to prove myself to her.

She not only saw behind the act ... she gave me purpose.

She showed me what purpose looked like — natural, unanticipated, and pure. Something small and simple that made a lasting effect.

She didn't even know what she had done for us.

But I could spend the rest of my life telling her.

EVANN

TASKS AND ASSIGNMENTS

She wasn't what I'd expected.

I had patrolled many royal events and meetings with formidable princesses, intimidating queens, and even the aggressive daughters of billionaires, but I'd never seen a woman put a dent in the wall with her foot. There was a strange air of excitement, mystery, and unpredictable behavior around Marina, which was a welcome change compared to the cautious circles I was forced to walk in around the castle, keeping an eye out for imaginary dangers.

Cyrus could keep this place. I wanted freedom. Risk. The unknown.

Speaking of which, I had a bone to pick with Cyrus.

I knocked on his door long after dinner, which might have alarmed him if I hadn't done it so often for so long. When he couldn't sleep, I was the first one he called, which left me in the awkward position of being the king's number one guard, but the last in my station.

He opened the door himself and nodded for me to come in, pressing it shut immediately after. He knotted his hands, straightening the imaginary wrinkles in his robes.

"Is she cared for?" he asked.

I nodded, holding up her cell phone. "She's annoyed that I took this from her, though."

I handed it to him. He played with it in his palm for a moment while seeming to play with a question in his mind. He shook his head and looked up at me. "Thank you. She'll be safer this way. The press might find her out sooner otherwise."

He put the phone in the dresser next to his bedside, then sat in the armchair next to the wall. He picked up a cup of tea, chamomile by the smell of it.

"She's not the reason I'm here," I said.

He swallowed. "You want to ask about the position up north, right? You know, you could have at least told me about it—"

"You would have denied me the application."

"You don't realize the requirements."

"I do. I also realize that you'll never allow me to leave this place."

His lips twitched to the side, a familiar pitiful look rippling across his face. "This is where you belong."

I had let that excuse pass quite a few times. At first it was flattering. But I had grown tired of how he manipulated me to feel guilty for wanting to have a life of my own.

"Is it?" I asked. "Is my place standing behind your family and working below you?"

His lips parted, agitated. "That's not what I meant. You know that. But if you leave here and they find out who you are …"

"Is that so bad?"

A heartbeat passed.

"You've never been in the midst of a media scandal," he said finally. "They'll rip you to shreds."

I huffed. "I don't think the media bothers you. I think the idea of losing control of your secrets does."

He paused, not answering. But the heavy drop of his head told me everything I needed to know.

"You can't decide whether I stay or go, Cyrus," I continued. "And I'm tired of spending a lifetime not using the skills and gifts I was given. I won't walk patrol until the day I die. Not for you. Not for anyone."

After a long moment, he nodded. "I'll remember that."

He gave me a weak smile, turning to drink his tea. He was holding back his real thoughts. The grimace on his face while he looked into his cup showed his apprehension.

I knew he didn't want me to leave because of who we were. But despite who we were, I couldn't continue being held back. I was a brother only in blood. I would never be regarded as the others were.

"I need to return to my patrol," I said. "Call me if you need anything."

I turned and stepped away, closing the door behind me, getting ready for another night of empty circles.

STAR GAZING

I reached the top of the tower, the warm air soothing the thoughts that were bouncing around in my head.

The entire kingdom lay before me in a brilliant display of mountain shadows falling over skyscraper lights that illuminated the harbor. Everything stretched in a mixture of shadows and light, energy and stillness.

All of it could have been mine.

When I was young, I wondered what it would be like to be king. After watching Cyrus, Julian, and Nikos be severely disciplined in order to meet the standards expected of them, I decided it wasn't for me. But even back then, something pulled me to take care of them. I wanted to protect them. I wanted them to see me as a big brother.

I hadn't realized the irony until my early twenties when I discovered who my father was.

It's amazing how long a family can keep a secret, even from each other. I assumed I looked like my mother, whom I had never known, since I didn't look much like my father. I did have a striking resemblance, however, to King Hugo. The castle staff always joked that Cyrus and I could have been brothers, since we had the same nose and the same jaw, but we always assumed it was a coincidence. As boys, the truth had occurred to neither of us.

I looked up to the stars, wondering which one my father was.

Tell me where to go next, Father. Tell me what I should do.

I dropped my head and scoffed, realizing that my prayer could have gone to two different people. What if they both answered? What if they were both silent?

Would they agree on my path?

I scratched my head with both hands, strands of hair coming off on my fingers.

I needed out of this place.

I left and walked back down the stairs, stopping at the sound of sniffling.

When I caught sight of a blue dress and dark hair, my heart sank.

"Princess? What's wrong?"

When her eyes met mine, I practically flew down the stairs. Was she in danger while I was feeling sorry for myself?

"What's wrong?" I asked, putting her face between my hands. "Were you threatened again?"

She shook her head, the strands of her hair falling down her face along with her tears. "No, no. No threats. Just a rough night. Don't worry about it."

"Want to talk about it?" I asked, wiping her tears.

She shook her head again. Why did royals insist on keeping their emotions bottled up until they exploded? Not that Marina had shown much inclination toward bottling her feelings, not until now.

I couldn't be mad at her. Not at Marina.

"All right," I said, "you don't have to tell me. Let me show you something. It might cheer you up."

I took her hand and led her up the stairs, back to the view of the entire kingdom. She stepped forward, her glossy eyes widening.

"You like it?" I asked.

She nodded, the smile returning to her face. "I could stay here for hours."

"Go ahead. The castle is yours, Princess."

She laughed and shook her head at me. "Evann, you're off the clock. You don't have to keep calling me Princess."

"But I like calling you that."

If it kept her smiling, I'd keep calling her that.

"What are you doing up here, anyways?" she asked.

I shrugged. "I come up here a lot to stargaze."

For emphasis, I lay on the ground and put my hands behind my head. I should have been annoyed to share this place with someone, but it was nice to have someone here with me for a change.

I didn't, however, expect her to join me on the ground.

"You'll get your dress dirty," I said as her dress rustled beside me.

She shrugged. "There are worse things. Like getting kicked in the head. Actually, I take that back. That's really not that bad."

I laughed. "Not bad?"

"Nah. You get stunned for a bit, but it doesn't hurt as much as you think it would."

"You really are full of surprises, you know that?"

I gave her my best reassuring smile. Looking at the way she was dressed — her gown, her hair, her makeup — I couldn't help but think about how in a different world where people like me could still inherit, she and I might have been betrothed.

I almost laughed out loud at the thought. Cyrus would lose his mind.

"Won't Nikos be upset that you ditched him?" I asked, refusing to let my mind wander any further.

She didn't answer for a moment, bringing her shoulders up to her ears.

"No," she said weakly. "He only cares about himself, anyways."

Her eyes started to gloss over again. I clenched my teeth.

"What happened?" I asked.

She didn't answer.

Nikos was known for his flirtatious manners. It was always a show, and someone always got hurt.

And it seemed like tonight was no exception.

I grunted. "This little—"

"It's okay," she assured me, tugging on my arm. "He didn't do anything serious. I just feel stupid. Let's not talk about it now."

She sighed as she looked at the stars, and I couldn't stop my hand from reaching out to comfort her. I ran my fingers over her hair, wondering if she felt the same pain I had felt so many times: the pain of being somewhere you don't belong.

"You're having a hard time here ... aren't you?" I asked gently.

I must have struck a nerve because she started to bite down on her lip. I wrapped an arm around her and brought her into a hug, hoping it would give her strength.

"It's okay," I whispered. "You're safe with me."

She held tight to me, relaxing in my hold as I kept her close. She stayed silent, but it didn't matter. I understood exactly how she felt. She didn't need to explain herself.

I would stay with her until she had the strength to face it.

Realizations

Cyrus was pissed. Like I gave a damn.

"You kept this from me?" he asked, tugging at the sides of his blanket as he sat up in bed. "As much as I put my trust in you?"

I folded my arms in front of me. "If you trust me, then you should know I kept silent for a reason."

He straightened the wrinkles in his robe, frowning at the answer. He leaned over from his bed and took a sip of water from his nightstand. I waited for whatever speech he was preparing.

"Your job includes reporting everything to me," he said. "You've been lax with your responsibilities these days."

"I never stopped doing my job. I just started doing it in a way you don't like. If I told you, would you let me do my job? Would you even allow me to protect her?"

His eyes narrowed. "She's not your assignment, but you're awfully protective of her—"

"That's my job, regardless of my assignment. To protect. To risk my life. That's what I was trained to do. Why do you insist on getting in the way of that?"

He glanced at the door, as if to check if anyone was listening. They never were, but he always acted like it was the worst thing in the world if there was someone on the other side of the door.

"I need to protect you—" he started.

"Will you lock her up too?" I asked.

His eyes shot open. "What are you talking about?"

"You know exactly what I'm talking about. Will you lock her up in your attempts to keep her safe? Like you do with the rest of us?"

"I'm trying to protect my family, Evann—"

"So am I!"

The words came out harsher than I anticipated. Silence passed between us.

I tried to unclench my fists. "There's a difference between protecting someone and shutting them away."

When he said nothing, I assumed the conversation was over. I started to walk away.

"She's my fiancée."

The words made me stop dead in my tracks. I turned to look at him.

"What did you say?" I asked.

The lines of his face deepened. "It's an arranged marriage. Father and King Tylier set it up some time ago. There are a few reasons it's beneficial ..."

Marina and Cyrus ...? Was he insane?

I shook my head at him. "She'll never agree."

He winced, and I realized my incorrect assumption. I had assumed that he didn't care for her.

"I have no intentions to make her marry me," he said, "but my responsibility to protect her goes beyond simple hospitality. If she takes the throne, I have to keep the masses from tearing her apart." He took a deep breath. "Do you have that ability?"

I swallowed, trying to find words to throw back at him. I hated it when my younger brother was right.

"I see," I replied, not responding to the question. "I didn't realize."

"Please let me be the one to tell her. I don't want her to think this is something she has to do."

"And what should I do, then?"

"Watch over her," he said. "Tell me of any changes in her behavior, or anything that might be a threat."

I didn't even have the sense to nod. I couldn't imagine Marina accepting this kind of arrangement. Not the glossy-eyed girl who had lain on the rooftop with me to look at the stars. Not the one who trembled in my arms when she was scared. Not the one with dreams beyond this place.

She didn't belong here.

"And Evann," he said, interrupting my thoughts. "I don't cage the people I love. I can't let them go until I know they won't get destroyed the moment they find freedom."

I pressed my lips together as he wrung his hands.

"If you don't set them free," I said, "they might end up destroyed anyway."

ESCORT

"Why did you agree to this?"

Julian frowned over his glasses, which would have been intimidating if he wasn't such a bad fighter. Even if he tried to swing at me, he would have been easy to trap in this tiny stone hallway full of ancient paintings.

Why *did* I agree to let Marina come to this meeting? It wasn't safe, but it wasn't dangerous either. But I knew her. She was in a castle full of people handling her. It was time for her to handle herself.

"She needs to learn eventually," I replied. "Something more than textbooks and dance lessons."

"I agree, but don't you think it would be better to wait until after she's decided whether or not to take her position?"

"Wouldn't this help her decide?"

He eyed me for a minute. As a soldier, I wanted to keep solid eye contact and let him know that I wasn't intimidated. As someone who had grown up with him, I wanted to look away before he could psychoanalyze me.

"You're trying to get fired, aren't you?" he asked.

Dammit. I should have looked away.

"There are more effective ways, I promise," I replied, not meaning it.

"That isn't a no."

"She should know what this life is like."

Truth was, this life would suffocate her. She was a free spirit. Rules and walls as thick as the ones here would close her off from the world completely. She would hate the lies and secrets, the hidden suffering and fake smiles.

She would hate it as much as I did.

Julian gave a frustrated sigh, shaking his head. "I've never understood why you keep trying to leave, and I've never understood why Cyrus keeps refusing it. What is it you both know that the rest of us don't?"

My stomach clenched, but I tried to keep my poker face. I had always looked for an opportunity to tell Julian and Nikos who I was, but the outcome wouldn't have made a difference. If Julian and Nikos knew, then eventually the castle would know. If the castle knew, then the public would know. And if the public knew, then the name of our father would be shamed in the history books.

I could handle the press harassing me about who I was. I couldn't handle them shaming the name of someone who had treated me with care.

I didn't think of King Hugo as my actual father, but he was certainly not my enemy. He protected my father and me for years. I wanted to return the favor.

"There's nothing to know," I said. "I simply want a less safe position — some adventure. Cyrus doesn't want to lose a friend."

His eyebrows furrowed. "I've watched you two for my entire life. There was always some connection you had with each other that I couldn't figure out. At first, I thought it was because you were older. I thought it was because you grew up together. But the older we got, the more and more tense you two became ... and yet nothing else has changed."

I tried to wrap my head around what he said. "As in?"

"He still comes to you before anyone. Even when you're angry with one another. He hides from us, but he goes to you. There's something I'm missing."

"Things to do in your free time, it sounds like," I returned. "Listen, if I'm fired for this, so be it. Cyrus knows who I am and where I stand."

He nodded to himself, leaning back against the wall. The sad look in his eyes made me think of little ten-year-old Julian, the kid that followed me around the castle to talk about military history and tactics, the kid who begged to play checkers on rainy days.

The little brother who could never know me.

"Yes, Cyrus knows you better than anyone," he said. "Someday, will the rest of us know who you are?"

He raised an eyebrow at me, a glint in his eye that I'd never seen before. I couldn't read it.

I swallowed a thousand words I could never say.

"I hope so," I said.

PAYBACK

I couldn't stare at the ceiling anymore.

I knew straining myself while injured would only mess me up in the long run, but this hospital bed was turning more and more into a coffin. A coffin that was giving me back pain.

My chest ached from the knife wound, but I didn't mind that as much. That had been for a good cause. It was proof that all my training had finally paid off.

And … it was proof that she was safe.

What was she doing now? Did she feel safe without me? Was she worried about me?

I smiled, remembering her fight. There was nothing weak about her physically, and she wasn't held back by a few bruises or cuts. She was an amateur compared to the women I had trained with in the Academy, but she had the potential to be as good as the rest of them. Maybe better.

"Evann?"

I sat up, wondering if the medication was making me hallucinate. After blinking a few times, I smiled, seeing the woman I had been thinking about.

"Princess," I said. "Come in."

She tip-toed into the room, as if making a noise would break my monitors.

"How are you feeling?" she asked.

I shrugged, regretting the movement immediately. "I could use a massage. Other than that, I'm not too worse for wear."

She came by my bedside, looking me over. "I can help with that."

"I was kidding. Don't do that."

"I'm not going to bust out massage oils or anything, but I think I can do a good, old-fashioned foot massage."

"I'd rather you didn't."

But I spoke too late. She already had my feet uncovered and, sitting on the edge of the bed, was lifting one of my feet up into her lap.

"I used to do this for my uncle all the time," she said. "At least your toenails aren't black and yellow. I appreciate that."

She pressed her thumbs into the heel and made little circles. Tension released from my body.

"You really don't have to do this," I repeated.

"You sounded less convincing that time," she laughed. "Let me at least do this for my hero."

I snorted. I wasn't her hero. I was just a guard. One that was trying to get as far away from castles as possible.

I had to admit, though, it had felt good to protect her. It was the first real thing I'd done for her since she arrived. Something that had made a difference.

And this foot rub felt good too.

"I bought a stack of books that Julian said you might like," she continued. "I think I'll also get some flowers for your room. It's pretty boring in here, isn't it?"

I smiled and gave a short nod, my thoughts starting to slur together. Her warm hands on my skin and the soft sound of her voice were sending me into a trance.

My heartbeat monitor started beeping.

Her eyes widened. "Are you alright?"

I motioned to her to sit back down. "I'm fine. Don't worry."

I sighed. She was making my heart race and now she would know it.

She went back to rubbing my feet. With empty but comforting small talk, she rubbed down my feet until the tension in my body completely subsided.

I watched her, taking note of the way her hair fell around her neck and the way her lips puckered when she smiled. She was quite the contradiction. A soft heart with a strong fist.

She was perfect in so many ways. I couldn't think of anyone like her.

My stomach dropped.

"Is something wrong?" she asked.

I laughed, far more nervously than I wanted. "Everything's fine. Just some back pain."

I patted my back for emphasis. To my horror, she stood up to help.

"Should I …?"

I grabbed her wrists before she could finish the sentence. "No need to help, Princess. I'll make it."

God, if she touched my back, I wouldn't know what might happen.

Wait … what was I thinking?

"Thank you, Evann," she said.

"For what?"

"What do you mean for what? For saving my life. For protecting me. For taking care of me."

"Of course, Princess. It's my job to look after you."

Her face fell a little. "Is that the only reason?"

Realizing that I was still holding her hands, I released them. She clasped them in front of her, waiting for an answer.

"No matter who you are," she said, "I mean, regardless of your job, I think of you as a mentor. You've taken care of me since the beginning. You comforted me in ways that you didn't have to. I look up to you for it."

I swallowed, digging my fingers into the bedsheet. *Mentor.* Something about that word was so … unsatisfying.

"In a way," she continued, appearing to pick her words, "I feel like you're the closest friend I have here."

Friend. A little better, perhaps, but still unsatisfying.

"Thank you," I replied, giving my brightest smile as I lied through my teeth. "I see you as a great friend too, Princess."

"I'm going to go get some flowers for your room," she said. "Do you want some brownies from the kitchen while I'm at it?"

I laughed. "You're an angel without wings, Princess."

She smiled and left, a new bounce in her step. I leaned against the headboard, looking back at my heart monitor.

I knew the reason my heart was racing. The rush of feelings that hit me once she touched me with affection had sent me over the edge.

I couldn't deny what I felt.

But I could never speak of it either.

It was another secret about myself that I would have to keep.

EVANN'S ENDING

It was too ironic, really.

I looked out over the city, thinking of all the things that could have been.

If I had been recognized as my father's firstborn son, I would now be king instead of Cyrus. If I were king, I would now be betrothed to Marina. If I were betrothed to Marina, then I wouldn't be standing here with this hole in my chest. Literally and figuratively.

But it wasn't meant to be. I wasn't meant to be king — thank the stars — and I wasn't meant to be beside her. Despite my feelings, however, I was grateful for what she had given me: the chance to prove myself. The chance to protect someone. The chance to become stronger.

I could take this with me, if nothing else. The world was about to open for me.

Cyrus had finally approved my leave. There was an academy in the west where I could teach, and even if I couldn't fight on the frontlines myself, I could help those that did. I was promised a few missions, meaning that I could do something for my country other than look at it.

I was free … but it didn't feel as good as I had hoped.

Even freedom came with concerns, anxieties, and the unknown.

Suddenly there were arms around my waist, a familiar scent enveloping me.

"Princess?" I asked. "Is everything alright?"

She looked at me with wild eyes. "Evann, will you leave the castle?"

I bit hard on my tongue and forced a smile. "I want to, but it doesn't look like it's in the cards for me."

"Do you really want to leave? Do you want to leave Cyrus, Nikos, and Julian? After all, they're your friends."

Ha. If she only knew.

"I doubt they all recognize me as their … friend," I said.

"Why don't you stick around until they do? They'll be disappointed if they realize after it's too late."

I looked back over the wall. "What about you? Are you taking your place as princess? Or are you returning to your freedom?"

She stood next to me, taking a moment to answer.

"Say I became a princess," she said. "Would it be possible to hire you as my guard?"

"Didn't you just tell me to stay with *this* royal family?"

"You wouldn't be that far from them," she quickly said. "And most importantly, you'd be close … to me."

I leaned back against the wall, my heartbeat becoming irregular once more. "Is that what you want?"

"You've always been there for me, Evann. I can't imagine you not being there."

Her smile was so genuine when she said it. For a split second I imagined what it would be like at her side, protecting her for the rest of my life.

The problem was that it would be far too tempting to see her as more than my employer.

"I'm afraid I can't take that offer, Princess."

"Why not?"

"I can't accept being your guard for a lifetime," I said honestly. "I think that would annoy me too much."

She scrunched her nose. "Yeah? And why is that?"

"Because I don't think I could handle being that close to you every day."

I tucked a strand of hair away from her face and behind her ear, grazing her cheek as I pulled my hand back.

"This is your one chance at freedom, Your Highness," I said. "You should take it before it slips through your fingers."

She was quiet for a moment.

"No matter my job," she said, "I'll always be free to make my own choices. And there are certain places …

certain people … I can't imagine being without. It's not freedom if I can't have those people beside me."

Before I could ask her what she meant, she leaned against my shoulder.

"Wherever you are, Evann … that's where I want to be."

My heart was pounding against my ribs, taunting me with my feelings. Yes, I loved her. But love wasn't enough. I couldn't provide her with what Cyrus could. I couldn't provide her with even one-hundredth of what her parents could. I had nothing to give her.

"I'm a guard, Marina," I said. "I have no intention to be anything other than that."

"I don't want you to be anything else but yourself," she said without hesitation. "You don't have to be anyone else than who you are now. That's who I want beside me. Guard or otherwise."

I looked down into her eyes as she smiled up at me. She was far too close. I could feel my heart nudging me to make a bad decision.

"Do you want to stay beside me?" she asked.

I steadied myself, nudging her off my shoulder. If she stayed there any longer, I'd lose control.

"You don't know what you're asking," I grumbled.

"I do know. And I'll ask again. Do you want to stay beside me?"

She grabbed my hands and forced me to stand in front of her. I looked at her, my heart still whispering.

Say it.

"Answer!" she said playfully. "As a member of the royal family, I demand you answer honestly."

I held back a smile. She wanted honesty? She didn't know what she was in for.

"Yes," I said.

She glanced down, then leaned in. I pulled back, putting a hand up between us.

"Princess, you can't. We can't."

"Why not?"

"I …" I dipped my head down, the smell of her perfume tempting me to come closer. "I'm afraid if we do … I won't be able to stop."

"… Then don't."

I brushed my lips against hers. She didn't pull away, and I couldn't hold back anymore. I pulled her tight against me, and pecked her lips, giving her one last chance to reject me. When she didn't, I kissed her harder. And harder. Until she understood everything I felt for her.

She put her hands on my chest and pushed me away. Her eyes, usually clear, were now dazed.

I couldn't help but laugh.

"I'm sorry," I whispered. "But I did warn you."

I leaned in and pecked the skin by her ear, before leaning my head against hers again.

"You're sure about this?" I asked.

She nodded against my chest. "More than anything."

I laughed to myself. All this time, I had been asking for a risk, and here I had the greatest risk of all. Great risk meant great disappointment, or it meant great reward. She … she was worth either outcome, because I couldn't think of a reward greater than her love, and I couldn't think of a greater disappointment than not having the chance to love her.

TAI

ESCAPE

She was cute. It was too bad I had to get rid of her. I hadn't seen someone so deliciously awkward in such a long time. The way she folded her arms tight against her chest as Julian barked his orders. He was so hard on her. So was Nikos. I would have to thank them for that later. It made it much easier to do my job.

The crueler they were to her, the sooner she would fly into my arms. Then I'd make her leave.

I wasn't sure why Cyrus of all people wanted her gone — my gut told me there was more to it than dislike of an arranged marriage — but it wasn't my business. I was here for the paycheck.

The guard looked me over, skeptical.

"I have an appointment," I explained.

He pursed his lips then knocked on Cyrus's door. "Yang Tai is here to see you, Your Majesty."

"Let him in," Cyrus commanded.

I threw a peace sign at the guard as I walked past.

Cyrus stood to meet me. I did the respectful thing and saluted.

"King Cyrus," I said. "You called?"

Not waiting for an answer, I walked past him, heading straight for the bar.

"You're late," he said.

"Yeah, punctuality was never my thing," I said, pouring myself some whiskey.

He sighed. "Should I trust you with this task, Tai?"

I swirled the liquor in the glass. "You have someone else you can hire?"

"Don't make me regret this," he said, his eyes dull. "If you break any of our agreements …"

"I won't touch her," I said, throwing back the drink. "Except maybe in fun ways."

I thought about our conversation in the gardens. She was intriguing. I couldn't help but smirk at the way she flushed when I used my charms on her.

"What do you mean by that?" he asked.

"Hey, you wanted out of an arranged marriage," I replied, pouring myself another glass. "Let me work with my own methods."

"I don't want her hurt, physically or emotionally. I just … don't want her here."

He scratched the back of his neck, eyes darting around the room. He was such a bundle of nerves. It was amazing that he was king. It made sense that he had to hire an asshole like me.

"So, what you're saying is, I can't take her to bed with me?" I teased.

It was worth it to see the way Cyrus's eyes shot over at me. I raised my eyebrows at him. The color drained from his face.

"You do that, and I swear to God—"

I laughed. "Don't worry. I don't want her dad coming after me. Calm down."

I threw back my second drink. He reacted more than I thought he would. I should have figured he would have some genuine feelings for the girl after meeting her. She was cute. Why wouldn't he?

"I slipped the note in her pocket, like you asked," I continued. "I have to say that it's a cute idea — these little threats and all — but it's not going to get the job done."

Cyrus sat on the couch across from me. "It's common for royals to get threats. I'm just giving her a taste of what's to come."

"Not much of a sample," I replied. "You get hate mail, sure. But you also get death threats. Throw a little of that at her. She'll leave soon enough."

He shifted uncomfortably, silent. Was he thinking about backing out? I couldn't have that. I had my paycheck to consider. And my conditions.

"I won't hurt her, Cyrus," I promised. I meant it. She was too adorable to harm. "That was part of the bargain. I expect you'll keep your side of the deal?"

He looked at me, but his face softened. "Of course. As long as no harm comes to her, your record will be wiped clean, and I'll take care of your mother and uncle's restaurant and citizenship."

I nodded. "Then let me take care of it, Your Majesty."

I put my glass on the counter before walking out of the room.

Sorry, Marina. Nothing personal.

BAD COMPANY

The bell jingled as I opened the restaurant door. The smell of garlic and sesame oil hit my nose and released the stress from my muscles. I only came here once a month, and every time I came, I wished that my ambition didn't keep me from coming more.

"Tai!" Ma called from the kitchen, her smile lighting up her entire face. "My baby boy! Why did you not tell me you were coming?"

"I—"

"You're just in time. Come help me carry these vegetable boxes."

I should have known I'd be put to work as soon as I walked in. Oh well. If Ma kept smiling like that, it didn't matter how much work I had to do.

I carried in the crates of vegetables and set them down in the kitchen as Ma chattered on about everything that had been happening with the family. It was nostalgic to hear her speak in our native tongue. I had become used to speaking English, thanks to the program in prison for rehabilitation, and Julian forcing me to take formal English classes after hiring me.

When I finished carrying crates, Ma patted me on the back.

"You were always my favorite," she said.

"I'm an only child," I replied, kissing her cheek. "Can I get a table?"

She raised an eyebrow. "For what?"

"I'm meeting someone."

She clapped her hands. "Oh, finally! I've been waiting for little babies to play with."

I grunted. "Not that kind of meeting."

Her eyes narrowed and she raised a finger at me. "If you're getting into trouble again, I swear …"

I grabbed her hand gently and put it back down. "I'm not in trouble, Ma. Don't worry."

Despite my tone, she slapped me in the arm. "Don't you dare think about going back to your old ways. You have a good job now, and you make an honest living. If you get mixed up with that damn gang again …"

"You know I left that life years ago. I don't want to go back."

It was the truth. I didn't. Yet somehow, I had found myself mixed up in this job for Cyrus. I suppose I could have turned him down … but how do you turn down a king?

Ma sighed, patting her heart. "You better not. I'd rather lose this restaurant and our house than visit you behind that wall of glass again."

My stomach knotted. I remembered how broken she was every time she came to see me in jail. The lines on her face, the way she blamed herself for my poor upbringing, how she told the officers that if she hadn't made bad decisions – like marrying my father - that I'd be a better man. None of my prison time was her fault, but she kept blaming herself for it. I didn't want her to do that ever again.

"I'm meeting with a friend," I said. "He's new to town. I want to show him your amazing soup dumplings."

I'm not sure whether she believed me, but a smile came back to her face. She nodded, pointing to a table in the corner of the room.

"Oh, I'm so happy whenever I see your face," she said, putting my face between her hands. "Don't get yourself in trouble. I'm afraid I won't see it again."

I patted her hands, smiling at her. "I wouldn't dream of it."

Ma brought out egg drop soup while I waited.

I didn't even have to look up when he walked in. I could smell his arrogance and bad cologne from across the room.

"Prince!" Zhixin greeted me as he pulled out a chair and sat down in front of me. "What's happening?"

I cringed at the title, pouring some beer for us both. "Glad you could make it."

Sort of.

"Of course. You know I've got your back."

I couldn't argue with him there. Zhixin had always backed me up. If there was a job that needed to be done, he was one of the few people with both the skills and courage to pull it off.

The problem was that he was a wildcard.

Ma looked at me from the corner of the room, frowning. I don't think she recognized Zhixin, but I'm sure she had an idea of what kind of person he was.

I won't go to jail again, Ma. Don't worry.

"How's the girl?" he asked.

"Uncomfortable," I replied. "It will make our job a lot easier. So don't get creative."

He laughed, sucking down a lettuce wrap. "You afraid of having fun?"

"I don't want either one of us behind bars again. Just stick to the script and we'll both make it out okay."

He leaned back, slowly chewing. "Are we still on for the festival?"

I nodded. "She seems to like me well enough. I can convince her to go. I'll leave her alone for a minute. You scare her a bit."

One of the waitresses brought out the dumplings, taking off the lid for us. The steam from the bamboo case highlighted his twisted grin.

"That'll be fun," he said. "You know, she's kind of pretty. We might be able

to—"

"Hey," I said, slamming down my chopsticks. "Remember what I said. Don't touch her."

He held his hands up innocently. "Sorry. Didn't know she was your girl. I thought she was a job. Or maybe she's both?"

I picked the chopsticks back up and gripped them. "What's that supposed to mean?"

He put another wrap in his mouth. "Don't worry about it."

"I mean it, Zhixin. Those are the orders from the king."

He giggled through his full mouth. "A king's servant now, eh? Didn't you want to lead us to tear down the monarchy?"

"That was a long time ago. Now, I want to make an honest living."

"Pfft, honest living? Tons of people make honest livings. They're all miserable for it, too. The reason we all got together back then was to change things. We all knew you were the smart one. You'd change things." He paused. "That's why I took the heat for you back then. Or did you forget the six months I did for you?"

I shook my head, staring at my soup bowl. "I haven't forgotten. But I'm still the lead on this. Remember that."

He eyed me for a moment, then gave a half-shrug. I ordered more beer. It didn't take much for Zhixin to get plastered.

"A toast!" he yelled, holding up his glass as if he hadn't already drunk three bottles of beer. "A toast to our bright, happy futures once that paycheck rolls in. Right, Prince?"

I clicked my glass with his, but I didn't smile. Bright futures?

Marina's innocent, troubled face flashed through my mind.

Did I deserve a bright future after taking away hers?

HOT N COLD

D amn, I looked good.

I'd run away with me.

I straightened my jacket out, trying to look as professional as possible. Well, at least as professional as I could without wanting to set something on fire. I didn't want to fit in with all those royal types. Their style was too stuffy for my liking.

I put my earrings in. Much better.

Honestly, I couldn't afford to mess up this gig. It was just a party for Nikos, but there were a lot of fat cats out there. They might need a pianist, and I needed more jobs.

Speaking of which, I had to think about the girl.

This was her first formal gig. She was probably nervous, hoping not to screw anything up.

It could leave me with some opportunities.

I left my room to join the festivities. On my way through the hallways, I crossed paths with Juniper and Marina. I had to admit, Marina didn't look like a royal when we first met, but she looked the part now. Her ball gown really brought out her smooth skin tone and bright eyes.

If I wasn't planning to get rid of her, I might have thought she would become a decent princess.

"Tai?" Marina asked, sounding surprised.

"Good evening, ladies."

I would have bowed, but it was too bothersome.

"Are you playing at tonight's party?" Juniper asked.

I nodded. *Yes, thanks to Julian.* He was a pain in the ass, but he was also a decent person. Unlike myself.

"The staff always love your playing," she replied.

"It's my pleasure to play for such a wonderful audience," I replied.

I looked at Marina, who was drinking in the way I looked. I couldn't help but tease her for it. I looked her up and down and smiled.

"My audience just gets better and better," I added.

I think I saw her ears blush.

We all said our farewells for the moment, but I couldn't stop myself from teasing her one last time.

As Juniper walked away, I grabbed Marina by the arm and pulled her close to me, leaning my lips to her ear. Her sweet perfume overtook my senses. I stepped closer.

"If you get tired of Nikos," I whispered, "come find me."

She stood, stunned, for a moment. I tried not to laugh as I walked away.

She'd be thinking about me, for sure.

This birthday party was going to be fun to watch.

I went to the gardens, taking my place at the piano. Some people clapped that empty, polite clap that said, *Who's this guy?*

They'd remember me when it was over.

I could hear the guests behind me, cheering and laughing as I played. It was a good feeling, knowing you were making someone happy. To see them smile when I looked over my shoulder was better than gold.

Not that I was knocking gold or anything.

It took a while for Marina to take to the floor. With Julian, no less. She seemed awkward and unsteady. I didn't like the look on his face. He was oddly happy in his demeanor, as was she. What was that about? Didn't she have an arranged marriage to Cyrus?

I tried to ignore it and focus on my music. I needed to build my reputation. Not worry about princesses falling for the wrong princes.

After a few more minutes, I turned to glance over my shoulder, just in time to see Julian leave the dance floor and Nikos step up to it. He grabbed her and yanked her close to him.

My fingers slipped and hit the wrong keys. Damn.

I focused back on my playing, trying not to look over my shoulder again. It was like having an intense itch. What was Nikos doing? Why was he holding her like that? That wasn't like him. He was a pest, but he was usually a reserved pest. And she was an innocent little thing.

I didn't like it. I didn't like Nikos holding her like that.

I heard a yelp. I couldn't help but look over my shoulder this time, and I was glad I did.

Nikos lying on the ground while Marina was walking away.

Well, maybe she wasn't as innocent and as helpless as I thought.

Laughing, I continued to play. This was going to be a good night.

UNSETTLED

My rib was broken. Again.

I tried to ignore the pain as I drove. It wasn't the first time I had broken a rib, and it wouldn't be the last. No matter how much I tried to run from my old life, there would always be something pulling me back to this type of pain.

Marina held onto my arm as we made our way back to the castle. Her shattered breaths were killing me. She was terrified, and it was all my fault. The bruises on her body were because I had agreed to this stupid job.

I snuck her back into the castle and into her room. I didn't want to face Cyrus yet. He would find out soon enough that I had broken our agreement, I knew that. But I wasn't ready to be torn away from her. Not yet.

I pulled her into the bathroom, taking a good look at the damage Zhixin had caused. She was beat up, and I wasn't looking so great either. My shirt was ripped, splattered in blood.

"I kind of liked this shirt," I complained.

She grabbed a washcloth, ran it under the water, and brought it to my face. I winced at the sudden coarse cloth stinging my skin.

"I'm okay, you know," I said. "It's nothing a shower can't fix."

Well, except the broken rib.

She pouted. "You saved me. It's the least I can do."

Her eyes were so innocent. I couldn't bear the guilt. She shouldn't have been taking care of me.

I reached up and pulled her hand down. "Don't worry about me. I'm okay. Honest."

It's you I'm worried about ...

Her eyes watered. "I was so scared ..."

She was going to cry. Man ... I knew scaring her out of the castle would be painful, but I wasn't prepared for watching her break down.

She was so ... vulnerable.

I opened my arms and pulled her into them. I could sense her holding back her tears, but regardless, she held onto me. She was so warm. I could hold her like this for hours.

... No, don't think like that, Tai. You can't get attached to things. Cyrus wouldn't be happy about it.

I pulled back before I could do anything stupid.

"It's going to be alright, Marina. I'll make sure of it."

"How? He's here somewhere."

I stopped. "What?"

"The day I got to the castle, there was a note under my pillow saying I wouldn't be a princess for long."

That was Cyrus.

"Then I found a note in my back pocket."

That was me.

"Also," she said, tearing up again, "I think the poison was meant for me."

That was fake.

"And one night, I was walking in the yards, and a voice came from the trees and told me to run. It was the same voice as the blond guy from the festival."

Wait. That was Zhixin. How the hell did Zhixin get in here? He was supposed to be on the outside, not the inside.

This bastard …

"So they've been …" I stopped myself. I grabbed her shoulders. "You stay here."

I was going to kill him.

She grabbed my arm and pulled me back. Her grip was strong and desperate. Of course she didn't want to be alone after everything that had happened. I didn't want to leave her alone either.

"Get yourself cleaned up," I said, tracing my finger along the scratches on her neck. Even with the scratches, her skin was soft. "There are cuts all over you. Get a hot shower. I'll bring you an ice pack, okay?"

She thought about it for a moment and then nodded. Her grip released.

I left the room and went to the kitchen, grabbing an ice pack from the freezer. What now? I knew Zhixin was a wildcard, but I didn't think he'd go this far. Would he take it further still?

I had to warn Cyrus.

I came back to her room, only to find Nikos holding her as she sobbed into his chest.

My hand gripped the ice pack. Did he have to hold her so close?

"How did this happen?" he asked her. "Tell me."

He pulled her chin up so that she could look him in the eye.

"I …" she started.

They looked at each other for a long moment. I hated how close he was. She was just in my arms. She couldn't go to another's so quickly.

"She was attacked," I said.

They both looked up at me. I shoved Nikos out of the way and crouched in front of her, putting the pack on her face.

"Why are you here anyway?" I asked him.

"Attacked?" Nikos asked, ignoring my question. "By whom?"

"Not sure yet," I lied. "But it's someone in this castle."

I decided to give Nikos some of the details of what was going on. I could control the information a little bit this way.

"And Cyrus knows about this?" Nikos asked.

Cyrus set the whole thing up.

I nodded.

"Why didn't he tell me?"

Good question.

Marina answered instead. "Because we—"

She stopped.

There was silence for a moment.

"You thought it was me?" Nikos asked.

I tried not to laugh. Like he'd be able to pull off something like this. Even I was struggling to pull it off.

"Who else knows about this?" he asked.

"Evann," Marina replied, which was news to me. "And now Julian."

Basically, everyone, huh?

Nikos pulled out his phone. "Evann, come to Marina's room, now. I need to have a meeting with my brothers."

He eyed me as he turned his phone off.

I had a feeling that he wasn't keen on the idea of leaving me alone with her.

And after that meeting, nobody would be.

TRAITOR

I ripped the keys out of the ignition and put them between my knuckles.

Zhixin was going to regret this.

I flung the door open.

"Zhixin! What the hell!"

I threw the hardest punch I'd ever thrown in my life straight into his face. The keys dug into my palm as I did it, but it hurt him more than it hurt me.

"You crossed the line this time!" I yelled. "Do you understand?"

Zhixin didn't even seem affected. He stood up, wiping the gash on his face that was beginning to bleed. "I'm doing my job."

"That wasn't part of your job. The job was to scare her, not kidnap her and commit actual treason. Have you lost your mind?"

"We can get more out of her if we do it this way."

More out of her? *More?*

"I'm not trying to get more out of her," I said, stepping into his space. "I won't tell you again. Just do what I tell you to do. Stop going off script."

No matter what he'd done for me in the past, I couldn't allow this.

He looked at Marina, then at me, smirking like he knew something.

"Get out of my sight!" I yelled. I was literally going to kill him if he kept this up. "I'll deal with you later."

He walked away … but we both knew it wasn't over.

I turned to Marina, who hadn't understood a word of our exchange but whose eyes were full of questions. My lungs burned at the sight of her; both from not seeing her for so long and from seeing her arms and legs bound together.

I leaned over and ripped the bands off, cursing. I wasn't this person anymore. I couldn't — wouldn't — be part of this life anymore.

Ever.

She seemed too shaken up to walk, so I lifted her in my arms and carried her to the car. It stung my ribs a bit, but it didn't matter. I put on her seatbelt and jumped in, driving off.

"Tai …?"

I knew what was coming and rushed into speech. "I'm sorry, Marina, it wasn't supposed to go this far. I didn't think he'd dare touch you. As for kidnapping—"

"It was you the whole time? You were the one trying to get rid of me?"

I hated the sound of her voice breaking.

"We were just supposed to scare you off, so you didn't take your position. Make you go back to your old life—"

"So, you sent me threats and had your men chase me, and—"

I stopped at a red light and turned to her. "Marina—"

She jumped out of the car before I could say anything else.

"Marina! Marina, wait!"

I chased after her. For someone who couldn't walk moments ago, she seemed to find her feet, and she was running faster than I anticipated. I chased her down the streets, but she didn't turn when I called her name. I only saw her back as she disappeared between the cars.

I couldn't lose her.

I ran back to the car, ignoring the angry drivers honking as I jumped inside and took off. I drove around the city looking for her — on every main street, in every alley — but after an hour, I knew it was a lost cause.

She was gone.

Cyrus was legitimately going to kill me this time.

I pulled my phone out and dialed the number, waiting for my sentencing.

"What happened?" Cyrus asked.

"Zhixin," I said. "The bastard went rogue. I smeared his face in his own blood if it makes you feel any better. God willing, I'm not done with him yet, either."

"It makes me feel a bit better, but it's not enough," he replied. "Is she safe?"

"Shaken, but okay," I said. "I got her away from Zhixin, but she's gone. Once she found out who I was, she ran off. I can't find her. I've looked everywhere. I lost her."

"I'll get someone to take care of it. In the meantime—"

"I'm going back to find Zhixin," I said, delaying the inevitable. "As long as he's intercepted, she should be fine. You have to find her, Cyrus."

I hung up before he could say anything else and looked at my phone.

"I lost her ..." I repeated as the screen faded to black. "I lost her."

TAI'S ENDING

God, I missed her.

She was probably dancing with everyone tonight. I wondered what gown she was wearing. I bet the stylists had done her hair nicely, too.

Cyrus had called before the party. He told me Zhixin had been arrested and would be severely punished for his crimes. I couldn't even feel bad for him, regardless of our history.

"I also cleaned your records and paid off the fees on your mother's restaurant," he said.

"Why?" I asked. "I didn't keep my end of the bargain."

"But you did. You didn't touch her. Zhixin is the one that deserves punishment. I'm not a total fool, Tai."

"… Thanks," was all I could say.

I could get any job I wanted now. I had a stash of cash in the bank. I had this studio apartment all to myself.

Why did everything feel so … empty?

I helped myself to a beer. Tonight was a cause for celebration. Even if I didn't feel like celebrating.

Stop thinking about her, Tai …

There was a knock at the door. I looked through the peephole.

It couldn't be …

"Marina …?"

I opened the door.

Before I could ask her why she had come, she threw her arms around me. Her scent crowded me; her touch was even softer than I remembered.

"Tai," she said breathily. "I missed you."

Her scent … *Don't make it so difficult, Marina …*

Hell … just one more time.

I wrapped my arms around her. "What are you doing here? How did you get here?"

She leaned back, looking at me. "I missed you."

She was so honest. And so close … I ran my hands against her shoulders and nodded. "I missed you too, jailbird."

I couldn't hold her like this anymore. It was killing me. I stepped away, sitting on one of the barstools next to the kitchen counter.

"How much of it was real?" she asked.

"How much of what?"

"Everything you said to me. Saving me. Our relationship in general."

It was fake in the beginning, to be honest. It was just a job.

But then again, I never thought of her as a job, did I?

I laughed to myself. "I don't think any of it was fake. I'm not as good as carrying out a job as I used to be."

She didn't say anything.

"Cyrus knew who I was when I came to work for Julian," I said. "He knew who my father was, but he chose not to punish me for my father's record. Maybe because of his own parents. Anyway, Cyrus asked me to scare you off. He made it clear not to hurt you in any way. He just wanted out of the arranged marriage."

"He could have just told me that he didn't want to get married. I don't understand why that was so difficult."

Because Cyrus was difficult.

"Anyways," Marina added, "what made him think that I'd want to marry him?"

"A young woman not want to be a princess … a queen? Sure, they exist, but it was too big a risk. And he was afraid of retaliation if he backed off. He didn't know what you would do to him or his family."

Regardless …

"I should have known Zhixin would take it further than it needed to go," I continued. "He was supposed to scare you at the festival, but … once he hit you … I snapped. And I don't know how he got into the castle. I was supposed to be the only insider. Thinking of you in danger … I couldn't stand it."

She stepped in closer to me. "You're the reason I was in danger in the first place."

I shut my eyes. "I know it."

"But you also saved me."

I opened my eyes, looking back into those innocent eyes of hers. She stepped in closer, wrapping her arms around my shoulders.

If she didn't step back …

"I want you to always be there to save me," she said. "Promise you won't leave me again."

My heart was beating in my ears. "What are you trying to say?"

She stared at me for a long moment, neither of us saying a word. She leaned down, and I felt her lips press against my forehead. She stayed close, breathing on my face. I brought my hands up and gripped her waist.

"This isn't a good idea," I said.

She looked me in the eyes and smirked. "I didn't ask if it was a good idea."

To hell with it.

I grabbed the back of her neck and forced her lips against mine. I had wanted to do it for so long, but finally feeling her against me sent me over the edge. I couldn't go slow. I'd held back for too long already. I rolled her lips between mine, grabbing her waist and pulling her closer. Her hands gripped my shirt, her knuckles digging into my chest. They rose and fell with my breath as I tried to slow down.

I really was a greedy bastard — I wanted everything.

We broke away from each other. Glancing into her eyes, I stood to my feet and wrapped her in my arms, burying my lips in her neck.

"You don't know how badly I missed you, jailbird."

Her hands ran up my shoulders. "Don't disappear again."

I laughed to myself. "Can you love me knowing who I used to be?"

"Yes," she said, leaning against my chest. "Because it made you who you are now. The man you are now doesn't have to be punished for the man you once were."

I pulled her back into my arms, sighing.

I never imagined someone saying that to me. I never imagined someone showing me mercy for the past, or the past of my family. I didn't deserve her mercy, but it was mine. I couldn't take another chance for granted. And I didn't want to.

I kissed her forehead. "Then I'll stay right here. I'll rescue you anytime you need it. You can bet on it."

WRITE YOUR ENDING HERE

Not satisfied with any of the five endings of this book? Have an idea of your own? Write your own ending to *The Five Princes* here!

Write Your Ending Here

WRITE YOUR ENDING HERE

WRITE YOUR ENDING HERE

A CHOOSE THE ENDING NOVEL

THE
FIVE
PRINCES
DEIDREA DEWITT

Turn the page for an excerpt from

THE REBELLION

A CHOOSE THE ENDING NOVEL

Coming Soon

"You can't take him!" I screamed.

The guards grabbed me before I could reach the door. I couldn't even see my brother, the front door blocked by an old, unforgotten shadow.

"It's too late, Jaehwa," the shadow replied.

I narrowed my eyes, the guards' hands gripping hard into my arms. "You expect me to back down that easily? He's all I have left, Saejun! You know that!"

The shadow stepped into back into the house, his dark eyes showing no regrets nor sympathy as the living room candles lit his face. The red robes of the emperor clung to his skin like blood, a testament to his new position of power.

"He's a murderer," he replied, cold. "He brought this upon himself."

"You're wrong!" I tried to twist out of the guards' hold, but they held fast. "Kiwan would never commit treason against the emperor! You know that. How can you take him away to be executed?"

I tried to catch my breath, my eyes beginning to burn. He stepped in closer, but I only stared at his expensive boots, refusing to let him intimidate me. His fingers curled under my chin, lifting my head up to look at him. His features were just as I remembered - sharp and strong - but there was a new darkness in his eyes that wasn't caused by the late hour.

"Stop fighting against me," he replied. "You won't win. You know *that*."

I jerked my face from his hand. "Get out of my house."

"I hate to say this," he said, rubbing his fingertips together and stepping back, "but this house no longer belongs to you."

"What do you mean?"

His jaw clenched before he opened his mouth again. "This house was in your brother's name. Now that he's been arrested, it has defaulted to the emperor."

"Saejun —"

"You can live here for the time being," he continued, cutting me off. "But you can be thrown out at any time. These are the orders of the emperor."

I twisted hard, breaking free from the guards, but only for a moment. They pulled me back again, bringing down to my knees.

"Who the hell do you think you are?" I spat at Saejun.

"Enough," he warned.

"You disappear for five years, become captain of the guards, and then show up at my door to take my brother and my home away from me?" The guards twisted my wrists, attempting to silence me. "Who the hell do you think you are? What right do you have to come back here?"

"Put her under house arrest," he told the other guards, not blinking. "Secure the first floor."

He turned his back on me. It was something he was good at.

"Saejun!" I called.

He stopped. With two heavy footsteps, he turned back.

"That…" he said, "will be the last time I allow you to say my name and live."

COMING SOON

Author's Note

There are a crazy amount of people to thank for the making of this book.

First and foremost, I want to thank God for answering my desperate writing prayers, sending me the right people at the right time to help produce this book, and giving me strength. I can't think of anything I love more than writing, and to have God give me this gift is a great honor.

Next, I have to thank my readers – those I fondly call my Tigers. Your support is the reason this book was created, and I would have never produced this book without your encouragement. You are all my beautiful beasts. I'm thankful to have you as part of my family.

Shout out to my editor, Monica – thank you for all your tips, helps, and feedback. This story is much cleaner and stronger thanks to you.

Thanks to all my family and friends who have supported my writing for so many years. This is the fruit of your encouragement and support. I was able to better my craft because of you. I was able to keep going when it was hard because of you.

Special thanks to Ryan – for being honest enough to tell me that my romance writing was weak. I wrote this entire book as an experiment because you said that… and it became the start of my whole writing career. Thanks for the honesty.

A big shout out to my beta readers, Becky and Denise. Your honest feedback helped make the plot and characters so much stronger. Thanks for your support!

And thanks to anyone who read this entire author's note. That's dedication. You're awesome.

There are many more books to come. I look forward to all the people I get to thank in my next book.

~ Deidrea